PLAYERS NUMBER SIX:

The Ballad of Pork and Mutton FC

PETER WYNARCZYK

To my wife Pooran, who has been by my side
for more than forty years, I salute you.

To our daughters, Natasha and Anoushka, many
thanks for enriching life's journey and always
have humour as a travel companion.

To family and friends, both near and far, I hope
to have captured something we shared.

To those who play or follow 'the beautiful
game', dream big and don't mind the gap.

Finally, to everyone, just pick up the book and
enjoy the read, it may just surprise you and put a
smile on your face - that would be priceless.

Contents

Preface .... *i*

Chapter 1: Time Gentlemen Please 1

Chapter 2: The Money Man 11

Chapter 3: Black Letter Day 16

Chapter 4: The Big O 23

Chapter 5: Finding The Holy Trinity 29

Chapter 6: Training Day 40

Chapter 7: (N)Ever Reddy 47

Chapter 8: Trouble Brewing 56

Chapter 9: Nothing Happens 67

Chapter 10: Tackling the Minotaur 73

Chapter 11: Letting Off Steam 81

Chapter 12: Vlad the Inhaler 88

Chapter 13: Nobbled by Baying Munching 95

Chapter 14: Blitzed Bombed *bei* Bierkeller 99

Chapter 15: Unholy Orders 111

Chapter 16: Greeks Bearing Gifts 117

Chapter 17: Who's In(n)? 124

Chapter 18: The Goldwasser Boys 132

Chapter 19: Playing Neverland 143

Chapter 20: The Fortunate Cookie 152

Chapter 21: Sunday Roast (with all the trimmings) 161

Chapter 22: Trunk Calls 168

Chapter 23: CORE, Blimey! 178

Chapter 24: Crazy Horses 188

Chapter 25: Back in the Doghouse 197

Chapter 26: Grounded, Hounded and Sounded 201

Chapter 27: Breaking Bad 207

Chapter 28: Being Adam's Keen and Able 211

Chapter 29: Feeding Leviathan 221

Chapter 30: O(h) Hec(k) 229

Chapter 31: Germany Calling, Germany Calling 241

Chapter 32: This is the Winter of Our Content 248

Chapter 33: Going for Gold 253

Chapter 34: Drat Ma 261

Chapter 35: Shirley Not 270

Chapter 36: Polish Tango 277

Chapter 37: A Different Class 285

Chapter 38: Ex's Mark His Spot 293

Chapter 39: Norman's Wisdom 300

Chapter 40: More Than Another Miner Setback 311

Chapter 41: Spotted Dick 319

Chapter 42: Better Never Than Late 329

Chapter 43: Scorer, Scorer, Scorer 338

Chapter 44: Being Number 1 346

Preface

Football remains a 'funny old game' especially at its non-elite margins buried deep below an increasingly serious soccer pyramid. This is a comic and fictitious tale, drawn from football's subterranean depths, of the poorest pub team, Pork and Mutton FC playing in the worst league, The Restaurant and Business Houses League (North) Division 2, and their hilarious search for redemption. They had been seen as chumps to be chopped rather than champs to be crowned.

The story unfolds during a full season in real time and place, set during the 1970s (you can follow the clues to discover exactly when), in the the North East of England, which allows for a wistfulness linking what has been truly lost and that which has merely passed. Football fiction has yet to scale the dizzy heights of the classics or the popularity of other genres prevalent today, such as thrillers, magic or fantasy, although it can capture all three without the need for any sense of make-believe. Such writing has tended to focus on either elite levels in the sport or some giant-killing act by a minnow. What follows is no David overcoming Goliath tale so often found in comparable sport fiction. Neither is there murder or bloody mayhem strewing its pages rather a purposeful gentleness hopefully betraying a delicacy of yearning and nostalgia as the main dramatis personae make their entrance to reclaim something lost. For many on this journey there is also a search for identity and belonging whether within the game or without.

It is intended as a humorous romantic ballad of sorts, with whimsy trumping lament, and fun providing clearance over an air of melancholy. When football had some of its grassiest roots but also its barest pitches; the game still innocent, rough and unpolished. The joy of kicking a laced-up globe of stitched leather had yet to be infected by serious money and was played outdoors, often in fading light, rather than indoors on a well illuminated computer or TV screen using hands not feet. Whether on concrete or turf, games set their own boundaries with uneven surfaces often making for a more level playing field. There was still enchantment to be found in engaging directly with 'the beautiful game' and the bonhomie shared by characters, some long passed but still made flesh by memory as enlarged caricatures of myth and legend. This book hopes to recapture such a time, before signwriters were replaced by tattooists, and the high street was invaded by estate agents and bookmakers, with a flavouring of humour to show how we have been diminished by its passing. Professional football has helped mark this transition, being more than a shot in the arm for tattooists, boosting expensive house sales, and adding directly and indirectly to gambling's coffers. It is to be read with pleasure and a tinge of regret. The march of time continues to trick us all by turning lifetimes into seconds and seconds into lifetimes thereby making the past both invitingly close and dishearteningly distant. If 'the past is a foreign country' then grab your passports and let's ride; our journey times may be different, that's all.

It is part mourn and greater part celebration, to praise rather than bury, and give unto Caesar what is rightfully his. It blends together a crazy heady cocktail of the age of Bremner and Keegan, the delicious foibles in Tobias Smollett's comic character sketches, the romance of Sir Walter Scott, a dash or two of Charles Dickens, and the talent recruitment searching of *The Magnificent Seven*. Its leading colourful players are not soccer pin-ups, chivalric heroes, or guns for hire, but rather those simply caught up in the magic, love and poetry of participating in a sport, not of kings, but of the everyman. They were at the margins of the game, but making up its central core, and its heart.

It is within this humble world and its backdrop of West and East Shields, with its crummy league, that humans not only err and stumble but also learn, rise up and continue to dream. The tale that you are about to consume is intentionally served with a fair dollop of exaggerated, ridiculous, absurd and comic storylines because life and its living are always a farce to be reckoned with. I truly hope you tuck in, let this farce be with you, and eat your fill. As Marc Bolan correctly pointed out 'Life's a Gas'.

Peter Wynarczyk
January 2023

CHAPTER 1:
Time Gentlemen Please

F red had called time often enough but this gave him far less pleasure than ever before. Most of the people in his bar had just arrived to sup within the limited time frame that the licensing laws allowed. But this was not just any given Sunday and definitely high noon for the four men he had summoned sat huddled together at a table within earshot. Decisions have consequences and they were now charged with making an irreversible one as the clocks were ticking and their time was running out. All had been guilty of procrastination but this was judgement day and he was finally forcing their hand just as others were forcing his.

Although there was a license above the outside door of the premises with Fred's name on it, it was not to kill, however tempting, the pub team that so embarrassingly carried the establishment's name. Pork and Mutton FC had been flatlining for years and any life support machine would have been switched off long ago. The landlord had emotional and real capital invested in the side - both as an ex-player and ongoing, but increasingly reluctant, benefactor - but was unwilling to take full responsibility for sanctioning the last rites for a club he still loved. They would have to carry out the coup de grâce not him.

Their footballing skill set had been no better than in Fred's day but they also shared his sentiment of feeling for Pork and Mutton FC. While there had never been a best of times this was certainly the worst and no one would blame them for ending it. The game had brought them more humiliation than celebration, so on that score alone their decision looked easy, yet they still wavered over officially declaring it a corpse. Any signs of life were not auspicious. This 'Gang of Four' may have been far removed from their Chinese namesakes or a culture where the number 4 is associated with death but they represented the remaining body count at risk of despatch. The scene around the table was close to matching a funeral in its solemnity. Glum faces all. It was 25 degrees outside and early summer but there was a frozen reality etched across the faces of that small group of pallbearers; with nothing in hand but glasses neither half empty nor half full, currently devoid of any liquid refreshment whatsoever. This was a dismal scene but not one that was a total loss. Another round of drinks would help and Fred duly obliged. They may be the tangible carcass of an almost defunct football team, with the vultures circling outside, but the obituary had yet to be written and only they would be its designated authors.

Fred had made this abundantly clear in yesterday's telephone call demanding that, "You must get your arses into gear, get down to the pub for opening, and commit one way or the other, it was now in your own hands." Fred knew his closing words were something of a simplification, and not strictly true, but that is what he wanted them to think.

The team played in the lowest league possible, a league where the bottom team could not be relegated because there was nowhere left to fall, this was rock bottom, where terra met firma. The football authorities in East Shields would doubtless have a ready replacement lined-up in the wings to make a grander entrance than the sorry exit being considered here.

They were pretty familiar with rock bottom, even before Lynsey De Paul and Mike Moran's Eurovision Contest runner-up entry, albeit a few years hence, would neatly capture the predicament they faced with its words 'Where are we? – Rock bottom, Tragedies? – We got 'em'. They had just experienced the ridicule of finishing there two seasons in a row. Two miserable seasons that had taken its toll on the team. Even before then failing to progress beyond the bottom three. They were widely viewed as the lowest of the low, the local dregs of soccer. Bottom of the 'Salt and Pepper' League Division 2, as it was sometimes sarcastically known. There was promotion, to the division above, but that was still a dream to the four sat around the small formica topped table sticky with spilt alcohol residue long past. They were the rump of a team bottom of the pile, anchored to the floor of Division 2 of The Restaurants and Business Houses League (North), giving rise to an unfortunate but nevertheless appropriate acronym RaBHL, where the only thing connecting the teams was a rather tenuous link to commercial outlets that had hospitality and food as their key uniform, rather than unique, selling point.

They had yet to decide on their course of action although the song's next lines, had they been able to anticipate it's lyrics, would have offered an as yet unuttered prompter, 'Remedy? – Why don't we, Rub it out and start it again?' If the rubbing out bit was hard then the starting again would be even harder. They, somewhat masochistically, liked playing together and would be extremely lucky to find another team willing to sign them up individually, let alone as a package. Should they somehow insanely continue, seek redemption and reclaim their dreams or be logical and simply just give up, surrender to reality and gamely vanish as a team of miserable no-hopers; the lowest of the lowly, with no chance of ever being bottoms up?

Their manager had gone, unbeknownst to them their meagre sponsorship was about to dry up, and most of their players had flown. They were viewed as an embarrassment by the League Administration who would have no regrets over their demise although opponents would be sad to miss these whipping boys whose existence served to improve all others' goal difference and add succour to their soccer. They were at a crossroads, either seek absolution and carry on or pack it all in and only be remembered as little better than a laughing stock. Objective rationality recommended a mercy killing, a time to cut and run, over any further prolonging of the agony. But subjectivity and emotion cannot fail to interpose on the conversation. Minor imagined past glories and present bruised pride would play a part in any future decision they made.

There they sat, the unfab four. They were fortunate in having Simon at this wake as the key member of their group. He was not only the club secretary and captain but willing, should they continue, to also act as interim manager and general dogsbody too. This was taking his position as a utility player rather too far, filling any role both on and off the park, but that was Simon for you. He was joined in deliberations with Stuart, a midfield dynamo with a limited battery and even less running range; Norman, a left wing back with a tendency to wander all over the pitch like an explorer on medication; and Roger, a right winger in politics and football with an inclination to go missing in action following a heavy Saturday night often bailing out anywhere but on the pitch for Sunday morning's fixture. Should they continue to carry the weight of all the teams ahead of them by renewing their league membership and subscription for one more season or simply end it all now; not missed, loved, or cherished except by the few with fond memories of being associated with the team or the many who enjoyed thrashing them. They had certainly done great service to Benthamite calculus and maximising the utility of the n-1 other teams in their league.

There had been dark days before, lots of them, but nothing to match this. They all agreed that while it may be tough at the top it was far tougher at the bottom. To which Roger added, "it's like baldness versus piles, and I know which one I would prefer," which a thinning on top Norman found to be an inconvenient truth.

"The defining moment has now arrived," Simon said, as he tried to call the group to some semblance of order, then calmly and somewhat coldly added, "Fred is right, we have chewed on for long enough and the time has come to make our mind up".

Stuart then chipped in, saying for some unknown reason, "That it was a bit like the title of the recent movie with that new James Bond chap, Roger Moore, called *Live and Let Die*," without explaining further.

Norman at this point asked him to clarify this random remark, supposing Stuart was supporting giving up, but before giving him any right of reply, continued his opposition by stating, "The McCartney lyrics of the theme song had 'live and let live' coming ahead of 'live and let die'. Others could 'give in and cry' but he would not." In this darkness some light had just inadvertently been rekindled a flicker rather than a glow, but a flicker nonetheless. Simon sensed the changing mood to seize the moment and suggest they turn their attention to the beautiful rather than uglier side of the game.

Fred now took the opportunity to add to the emergent upbeat disposition he was witnessing. He expressed his willingness for this team of sorts to continue to use his official pub's name just as it had done in the past, bravely willing to put up with both ridicule and contempt engendered by association with these serial losers. He even thought it advisable for the team to continue getting its dirty kit cleaned in the pub's washing machine and his dryer would restrict the need for any public airing outside. But, and he was most emphatic about this, "There was the need for alternative financial support as he was finding it difficult to justify subsidising this lost cause; throwing real money, hard earned money, that could be used more wisely, down a drain, albeit a very small drain. Some other good samaritan had to be found as this volunteer had run out of financial goodwill but not good cheer." Freddie would not totally give up on his dreamers - it was his pocket rather than his sentiment that was wanting. Only now did he confess, "There was an urgency to find some other sponsor, or mug (my wife's alternative word for it), willing to pick up the tab for league membership and team playing dues". He had purposely kept this decision to himself knowing full well that it would have negatively influenced the deliberations taking place. "That was the bad news", he said, "but there is also better news," before informing those present that he had found an interested and suitable candidate for that position and that had been another reason behind calling them here. Fred would give the mystery man a call and get him to come over and join them if he had their go ahead. He revealed little else apart from confessing that, "He was sad to let go, but this was only partial, anyway the person coming was well acquainted in dealing with other people's loss." The whole enterprise was now reliant on this new backer not only agreeing to the role but also meeting RaBHL (North) approval, never mind finding enough additional recruits to make up a team alongside getting a permanent manager to reduce the club burdens on Simon. Such were the stringent demands placed upon them, made black and white by the forms laying in front of them, awaiting confirmation of their being able to meet all such ongoing league obligations.

As club secretary, let alone captain and potential interim manager, Simon had the authority, to be so used, he made abundantly clear, "Only if they all so wished" to commence completion of the paperwork now partly glued to the table courtesy of the spilt remnants of beer drunk largely without enjoyment.

An execution, especially one's own, concentrates the mind wonderfully, to paraphrase Dr Johnson, and this was even more true for the potential self-harmers considering their own demise. The rays from the early summer sun had yet to pierce through the prevailing localised gloom intensified by recent widespread power cuts and strikes. Simon didn't need to catch Fred's eye to order another round of drinks as the group remained the keen focus of the landlord's attention. Yes, they had roles to fill and challenges ahead, but it was time to look at the positives and more refreshments would surely help. When people drink together it is largely to remember and share the joy while those who sup alone often do so with tears and regret. These four were somewhere between forgetting and laughter as the latest delivery of beers hit the table. The length of their ongoing deliberations suggested that they already knew something valuable would be lost if they just ended things, although often struggling to put into appropriate words or clearly express their feelings on just what that something was, but fulfilment from the game and the opportunity to restore footballing pride ended up taking centre stage.

There they sat, humanly erring in collectively over-calibrating their footballing co-experiences and togetherness, reasoning heads now losing out to passion and hearts, reality trumped by dreams. In this way the game can make fantasy footballers out of all of us. It was less a matter of personal ego and more about slowly realising that their collective sell by date had not yet arrived. This emergent joy of re-connecting, of sharing something that means something, could not so easily be discarded. While this something remained largely undefined it was no less real for that. Billy Bremner may have been in good company when he believed 'you get now't for coming second' but for this band of re-united brothers this was not true. All the striving and shared effort had given them something, something more than just a trophy. Why have silver(ware) when they had gold and these footballing conquistadors now felt a renewed need to search for more of it.

They would go on, they had to. Simon hastily signed the forms, on all their behalves, as a declaration of their collective intent even though the document remained incomplete. In doing so, he and they knew the clock was still ticking. At this point Fred couldn't resist coming over to endorse their decision accompanied with a tray of whiskies.

Stuart, trying to make amends for earlier, then said "What about *You Only Live Twice?*" before trying to explain his latest outburst in terms of their having a second chance to make good.

To which Fred added that "The person now making their way here may have philosophical cause to disagree with you," before mischievously leaving them dangling on this, his latest line. They needed this new financial benefactor to commit in order for the forms to be returned by the impending deadline. They also had a meagre six weeks to find the necessary additional players ready for the start of the new season. There was now less urgency for a manager as Simon had unanimous agreement to add that role to all his others. They still had skin in the game along with Fred, Pork and Mutton, and fingers crossed, the unknown sponsor, but they would need a lot more than just sauce - be it apple or mint. They would need to go prospecting and luckily their first strike was very close at hand.

As Simon looked across at an empty table alongside theirs he pointed to a discarded, seemingly empty and crumpled cigarette packet - Player's No. 6 - and told the others, "A couple of additions to that number would be a good start". The writing was literally on the wall when he turned his head and saw a sign, 'Player's Please', advertising the very same brand hanging opposite and below it sat two young men whom he had never seen before. He called Fred over from behind the bar to ask about the strangers brought to his attention by the sign, viewing it as some sort of omen or even biblical message.

It was Fred, rather than the Almighty, who informed him that the two young lads were looking for bar work to subsidise their attendance at the local Polytechnic. One was called Byron Preston and studying English Literature while the other, Salvator Samba, is studying Economics. Without thinking about their footballing credentials Simon decided to approach them, not only in desperation but largely after deciding it was a truly sacred instruction, sent from way above where the sign was actually placed.

Once Fred had added that "Samba was also Brazilian," Simon inserted his own exclamation mark rather than quiet comma and now imagined the boys with halos above their heads and already duly anointed.

"After all," Simon informed his group, "didn't Byron's surname belong in any historical roll call of English football clubs, being not only a founder member but also first and second time winners of the league championship over eighty years ago," without making any mention of the missing North End component. He then, even more optimistically added, "All Brazilians played football as second nature, much like Pelé, right?" To which they all nodded, somewhat infectiously. Simon did not know that Salvator also meant saviour in Portuguese otherwise he might have been totally overcome in holy rapture. Both lads agreed to join the cause once Fred had promised them a few hours of evening bar work a week. No questions around their footballing credentials were raised given the need to follow holy orders; as far as Simon was concerned these two recruits were somehow unquestionably legitimately touched by the hand of God, looking reasonably fit and with presumed pedigrees to match. For Simon the spiritual and material worlds had been satisfied. Less *Angels With Dirty Faces* more angels with studs and laces.

Our belief systems have been largely sustained by searching for confirmatory rather than falsifying evidence. It would have been interesting to see how Simon would have interpreted the sign falling off the wall, an event he missed, as it happened just at the point when he had disappeared into the Gents. Fred managed to put it back up before his return and told the others to keep quiet about what they had all just witnessed. He may have been none the wiser but Simon knew something was up by all the smirking that greeted him causing him to check his flies in advance of retaking his seat.

CHAPTER 2:
The Money Man

Money usually talks but on this occasion it didn't. Max Mortimer walked stealthily into the bar just as the capture of the two young unknowns had been concluded and Simon bid them adieu until training scheduled three weeks hence. He was the man no one was intended to notice, until it was too late and only when one had lost a loved one or even a relative. Max was the town's only undertaker and had been such for a very long time, now appearing much more at ease with the dead rather than the living. In a sense, and not to put too fine a complexion on it - which he often did but only for those customers passed helping themselves - he had a local monopoly on the celebration of death. Little did the four know it, but by some irony of fate, some parody on existence, Max Mortimer might turn out to be just the lifeline they needed to get their ball rolling again.

Only Fred had been on the lookout for the sneak now heading his way and was familiar with his preferred tipple. As the cold dark guinness slowly entered the glass the landlord also served up fresh information regarding the sad plight of the band of desperadoes sitting nearby. Fred fed his latest news quickly and quietly, carefully directed into the left ear of Max, his good ear, unlike his right ear which had long ceased and now shared much of the silence, rest and peace bestowed upon his principal clients. While Max had known something of the team and its history he knew little directly about those close by, or the full extent of their current predicament, until now. Unlike most, Fred was greatly relieved by Max's arrival. This demonstrated to him the latter's keen interest in picking up the financial tab that he had just relinquished. As Max whispered to Fred, "I'm looking for the opportunity to be seen to be putting something more back into the community than merely dispensing spent locals into the earth." He also had other motives which were soon to be made known.

Fred solemnly guided Max to the table and formally introduced him to the group: "Lads, this is Max Mortimer," then added, "this is the chap who wants a chat with you about possibly covering the costs of your playing next season."

Having successfully received and digested what had been relayed to him Max was better acquainted with those he was now being introduced to than they were of him. This gave him an advantage that he was unlikely to squander. None of the four had ever spoken to, let alone noticed Max before, as they never previously had need to - after all, the grim reaper's calling card had only recently been dispatched for what remained of the team. They were all of an age to know of his existence, as principal handler to another place, but none had yet sufficient cause to engage his services in a professional capacity. Like others before them, however, they now needed his help in addressing their own deadline.

Max tried to set everyone at ease by opening his address with a touch of irony that was lost on some of his audience, "Given that you have remained here and not already departed, you nevertheless appear to be desperately in need of my services!"

With black suit and tie Max stood formally before them spelling out his conditions for patronage. "They only totalled two," he said, "neither of which, I trust, you will find too demanding." The first condition was that as he was paying their running costs, the minimum costs appertaining to any club anywhere on the planet, that they would have to advertise his wares. This would mean running around wearing shirts publicising his business. "I take the view that there is nothing more hospitable than providing a final resting place and that sponsoring a team in The Restaurant and Business Houses League (North), albeit Division 2, was not only appropriate but would justifiably extend the boundary of recognition for my particular brand of customer care," he boldly stated. Not only was it the right vehicle from which his firm could give something back but it would help raise the company's profile and make a refreshing change from the usual ashes, tears, and comforting words said to warm a cold exchange. He was, as they would later discover, a most enterprising undertaker.

Max would supply all the kit, including his specially branded shirts. He stipulated that, "The kit must be all black to reflect my business and its sobriety." At the moment of its uttering it seemed of little consequence for the four. Yes, they had previously played in all white, costly on Fred's laundry bill for sure but rather easy to procure. No thought was given to the consequences of changing from white to black, from moving from purity to darkness, to them it only meant survival, they could have an afterlife with a meaningful future. The team would remain registered as the Pork and Mutton, Fred was fine with that, and it allowed Max communion with the living.

The other condition Max imposed received just as little attention as the first given they were in no position to negotiate. "My second condition is that my son Doug is an integral part of the team." No one appeared to know who Doug was, apart from his father (and he only barely), or dared to seek clarification of Max's definition of integral. Fred had never seen Doug in the pub and he couldn't recall Max ever mentioning him before. His future teammates were clueless and his father wasn't willing to reveal that even he had little more than a passing relationship with his son, only rarely occasioned when Doug left the sanctuary of his bedroom to help his father in the funeral parlour when someone did not turn up for work. He was otherwise held in reserve should a deadly epidemic, major accident, or mass shooting ever happen to take place, which to date they hadn't. Almost all deaths so far had been extremely predictable and far from unusual. So Doug was another unknown entity, almost as much to his father as to the rest sitting there. Max wanted his son to get out more and extend his horizons, basically mirroring what he craved for his business, and his chief motivation for supporting the team. His father had no idea whether Doug could play or not, let alone whether he had a preferred position other than his normal horizontal found on bed or floor. Would Mortimer the Younger, just like the Elder, be part of their deliverance or downfall? They might even dig Doug rather than have him ensure their graves were finally dug.

None of the four, like Steve McQueen in *The Magnificent Seven*, 'had ridden shotgun on a hearse before', but they were willing to try, and readily agreed Max's terms. At least they now totalled seven, albeit hardly magnificent. They would happily settle for a lower level of attainment but were playing the lottery with regard to their three new playing recruits and sponsor. At least they were a committed four and now had financial backing to boot.

This was no Faustian bargain and they were in Pork and Mutton not Auerbachs Keller. The football authorities might view matters somewhat differently and see it as a pact with the devil but Simon and the others were trying to regain their soul not sell it. Their new benefactor would still have to meet the strict qualifying demands of the league administration. A couple of things now needed to be amended on the document before them. The first related to the colour of the team strip. All white was crossed out and all black inserted in its place. To this had to be added Max's details, in place of Fred's, as the new sponsor and chief source of funding alongside making the case for his direct involvement.

They were back in the game but it would mean nothing unless they had more players, especially ones' who knew how to kick a ball. There was some limited cause for optimism and the signs were looking good, or at least better than before.

Just then Norman tapped Simon on his arm pointing to an old dosser sitting at the corner of the bar, who was laughing loudly at something the barmaid said whilst simultaneously pulling out from the inside pocket of his dishevelled jacket a packet of Player's No. 10, before saying, "He's got what we need now, or pretty soon". A fuse had been lit, as was the cigarette. Here was another sign, a pointer to their next challenge. They had a chance, a fighting chance, and they were right not to give in, to capitulate, to ignore the odds stacked against them. Getting up from the table was a lot easier for the four than sitting down had been. Walking out of the pub they all agreed that the sun was a lot brighter and warmer than it had been on their arrival (although the temperature had actually fallen to 18 degrees). The search was on to find and sign some reasonable players and the now duly completed forms, bearing a stamp provided and ceremoniously affixed by Max, were immediately posted off to the footballing authorities. They hoped for a quick and positive response as time was still racing against them.

CHAPTER 3:
Black Letter Day

S imon waited patiently for more than a week to receive at least an acknowledgment from those in power. Ten days after posting, a letter arrived as he was about to finish his breakfast. The clatter of the letter box had announced its coming and he rose and rushed to the front door in anxious welcome. It bore the RaBHL (North) stamp on its reverse having landed backside up. He hoped the team's submission would not share the same fate and also fall flat on its face. He was more than a little apprehensive in picking it up from the floor as he really did not know what to expect and had never really considered how the team's completed paperwork would have been entertained at League HQ. The future of Pork and Mutton FC now lay entombed within the brown envelope he held in his hands and he carefully carried it back to the dining table. He placed the letter, still unopened, against the empty toast rack and just stared at it. Should he open it now or wait until he called a meeting with his fellow stakeholders? He decided to wait and resist what limited temptation, but heightened trepidation, there was to open it. It was getting late and he really needed to leave for work at the Town Hall as the good citizens of the borough would wait for no man, let alone him. He would convene a meeting, that evening at the Pork and Mutton, where he would open the letter in front of his interested party. The still sealed brown envelope was placed gently inside his briefcase and set off with him to work. This wasn't one of his best ideas as the close proximity of the letter cast a shadow over the rest of the day leaving him brooding over its unknown contents rather than attending to the rapidly filling in-tray on his well organised desk.

His working day was completely unproductive and about as useful as the days spent at home during the Government imposed three day weeks that had only recently ended. Finally, after labouring longer than usual but remaining less than gainfully employed, vegetating and stewing his way through his usual contractual obligations, he made his way directly to the Pork and Mutton for the grand letter opening arranged for 6.30pm. On arrival at the bar, a full fifteen minutes ahead of schedule, he found that the others - minus their latest benefactor - were all already there sitting nervously yet eagerly.

Roger, never one to wait or hesitate, wanted the letter to be opened there and then. "Come on Simon, open it, the suspense is killing us," he said like some impatient child.

But Simon continued his resistance saying "This damned letter has been my companion all day and I am not giving in to temptation now just to suit you." He then reminded them of the protocol he had intimated earlier that day.

At one minute before the half hour mark Max somehow appeared as if from nowhere, unnoticed until that very moment. Simon called Fred over to join them given his continued association and support alongside the fact that the team still carried his establishment's name. It was not lost on some of those present that this was a time for propriety and formality.

Simon rose and was about to tear the envelope open when Max stopped him, putting his hand on his arm before saying, "Use this to do the honours," handing him an ornate silver letter opener theatrically pulled from his inside jacket pocket. After which he added, in an unmistakeable funereal tone, "Whatever life - or death - throws at you my boy, face it with style and fortitude."

The following letter was read out by Simon to the eager band united in their desire to finally know its contents:

RaBHL (North) Football Administration Office

66b Lower Lenin Street
(over the Co-op)
East Shields

1st July

Mr Simon Washington
Secretary, Pork and Mutton FC
3 Freedom Square
West Shields

Dear Sir

Thank you for submitting your team registration and accompanying forms by the required due date. After much serious reflection, followed by utter surprise at our conclusion, we have decided to accept your continued membership of The Restaurants and Business Houses League (North), Division 2, for the forthcoming season, and hereby acknowledge such by means of this correspondence.

A number of issues arose when considering your submission, however, which we wish you to note.

Although you still carry the name of the Pork and Mutton FC we duly recognise that you have a new sponsor under the name of Max Mortimer who is the proprietor of a funeral parlour. After much internal office deliberation, head scratching, and effort, we were unable to prevent your involvement in the forthcoming season on the grounds of failing to meet our main criteria. We certainly found Mr Mortimer's novel claim that providing a final resting place for customers alongside wakes for friends, relations, and whoever turns up, to be a rather weak and tenuous association with hospitality and food rather than the grand cherry on the cake he rather inventively describes. That being said, the fact that he demonstrated an active use of a wide array of condiments at such events counted in your flavour, sorry favour, and swayed our final decision.

Selection of your team colours and kit is not something we normally get involved in as the rule book clearly states (under 15.6.82) that it is a matter for the team itself (with or without input from its sponsor). The radical colour change of your kit from all white to all black has led to unforeseen consequences which has serious knock on effects for our administration of all your upcoming matches. As you are doubtless aware, referees and linesmen wear black. Your decision now means that your games will require our match officials to have an extra alternative change of kit so as not to confuse all players on the pitch or lead your opponents to conclude that you have extra men albeit with whistle or flag. This means significant additional clothing expenditure being added to our administration costs which we did not anticipate in advance of the season ahead of us. Given the prevailing kit colour choices of

the teams in Division 2 of the RaBHL (North), the most
cost effective alternative match official kit which will
not require us to have a third change of outfit, and that
we have now been forced to hastily order for purchase,
to be worn only on YOUR match days, is bright pink
to ensure no clash with you or any of your opponents.
Needless to say, a large number of our referees and
linesmen have expressed serious concern with regard to
not only the need to move away from their customary
black to satisfy your choice but also the extra abuse
and ridicule the alternative match official kit is likely to
generate from players and supporters alike. We remain
certain, however, that any remaining hostility regarding
this matter will not impact upon the absolute, resolute
and unshakeable neutrality of our officials in carrying
out their duties on your match days.

We wish you to be aware of these matters and trust
that your participation over the season ahead will not
result in your creating any additional problems in our
administration of an established and well-respected
league or any further unsettling of our staff.

Sincerely yours,

Mr Iam Wright-Pratt
Senior Administrative Official
RaBHL (North)

So the North had spoken; but the letter took some digesting
as well as interpretation. Yes, they were back in the game, and
the League had accepted their registration as Pork and Mutton
FC under the direct sponsorship and association with Max.

None of them had anticipated the unforeseen consequences of their kit colour change resulting in resentful match officials having to run around in bright pink.

"Just like in a game of snooker, to finally sink the black you first of all need to get at the pink," Norman was quick to wittingly remark. This caused them to ponder at what they had just inadvertently done, leaving them all wondering, as Norman continued, "Whether our season may well be over before it's even begun."

"In a way, we have just bet our shirts on the fact it isn't!" Simon replied, recognising that the letter, albeit in rather poor bureaucratic speak, was a bit of a broadside unforgiving of any further deviations from the straight and narrow.

So the football authorities had accepted the amended submission, both Max's direct involvement and his first condition, or so those present thought. The undertaker appeared to be quite cheerful and viewed the contents of the letter as little more than some minor irritation expressed by some jobsworth pen-pusher. Simon had decoded it all rather differently, as a clear warning of sorts from one fellow administrator to another, that not only were they were more than a little narked by all this but had also felt impelled to be less than diplomatic in signalling the need for the team to follow their P's and Q's.

Max, however, took the opportunity to remind the ensemble that his patronage also depended on the team publicising his business. At this he nodded to Fred who went to the back room and then returned with a large box followed by a pale, sallow young man, dressed completely in black and exhibiting what would be only recognised some twenty years hence as Goth-like tendencies, transporting an identical package. Both boxes were laid to rest directly to the side of Max who then ceremoniously used his returned and overly grand letter opener to cut through the tape. The boxes contained their new kit, the first, their shirts, the second, shorts and socks. Max then made quite a show of removing one of the black shirts from its protective covering. Then, to almost everyone's complete surprise emblazoned across the front in stark white capital lettering was the equation 'MORT=MORTIMER' with slightly smaller lower cased lettering below boldly announcing 'Total Afterlife Care'.

"By the way, I would like to introduce my son, Doug, your latest recruit." At that point, Doug, a most unconvincing Milk Tray man, did an embarrassed and less than energetic semi wave in the direction of his new teammates while simultaneously keeping his eyes cast downward on the floor. Almost immediately Simon looked to the heavens and wondered what Pork and Mutton FC had done to deserve all this. Only now were the full implications of getting Max on board starting to be realised by those present. Whilst the son may not have impressed Simon, the father certainly had. Simon recognised that Max must have moved both heaven and earth to get the new kit and its signage ready in such a short space of time. He was also greatly reassured in Mortimer's commitment to their joint enterprise by his willingness to incur such risky expenditure prior to the league administration's agreement. The team's salvation now resided in being both Fred and Buried.

CHAPTER 4:
The Big O

Few men in life are happy with nothing. Owen Bigalow belonged to an even rarer breed of man, he was completely ecstatic about nothing. The growing band of players at Pork and Mutton FC would only fully discover the extent of this obsession when Owen joined them.

It was Roger who first came across Owen on one of his drunken expeditions to several local nightspots in East Shields. He couldn't fully remember the exact where of their paths crossing but perfectly recalled the how. Roger had been in the audience awaiting the next Cabaret act to arrive on stage and the next turn to be announced under his stage name of the Big O was none other than Owen Bigalow. He came on stage looking nothing like Roy Orbison apart from the sun glasses and holding a guitar. He was a big man with hands to match. To most of the audience's surprise, however, his voice faithfully delivered a medley of Orbison hits that were barely distinguishable from the original. Roger, and those around him, were blown away, and demanded more.

After giving his now adoring public, including Roger, what they wanted, the Big O left the stage to the sound of what seemed like thunderous applause for a small venue show. The place was not packed but it wasn't sparse either - Owen must have attracted some extra punters that night and may even have an emergent fan base, as he was the best act by far. Witnessing this performance had been a happy accident for Roger and their paths may have never crossed again had it not been for another random event.

Roger, later that same evening, quite literally bumped into Owen on his return from the Gents, "Sorry mate, my mistake, can I buy you another?" he asked with trepidation in his voice. It wasn't that Roger was running scared but Owen had an even greater towering presence close up and personal. How the hell did he manage to crash into this juggernaut? The offer of a replacement pint was graciously accepted and the two men engaged in polite friendly conversation. Roger was not surprised to find that Bigalow was a builder by day as his hands appeared to resemble shovels and looked able to scoop up anything in their way. He was, however, greatly surprised by the content of much of their, or rather Owen's, subsequent conversation which he only later recalled through the haze of a too regularly raised beer glass.

Owen had been more than a trifle over obsessive regarding both the letter O and the numeral 0 that the two appeared to morph into each other, or so Roger remembered. Anyway, this was not the normal level of discourse between two new buddies having some Saturday night banter and it was its sheer remarkableness that allowed it to somehow remain in Roger's usual semi-consciousness. After all, it's not every day, or every night, that one hears someone express their love of a particular giant vowel or of the number zero.

It would be difficult to pinpoint when Bigalow's fascination and love affair started, it may have been with his being given the name Owen and the way in which the O commences domination of the rest, or how the surname Bigalow gives a curtain call final flourish to his headiest of vowels, this is pure conjecture and even he was not sure. But it was pure unadulterated obsessive love. He recalled the choosing of his first Airfix model aircraft on the basis of its name, the Japanese Zero, with its, "Having a big red sun transfer, like a big O filled in, crying out to him." He delighted in having a toy train set (with an O gauge) that allowed him to make a giant O with the track and his first Scalextric never adopted the customary figure of eight pattern but the more exciting (only for him) figure zero pattern. How he found fascination in studying the German hyperinflation at school and the perverse increase in his attraction to the Mark as it collapsed to a trillionth of its value due to its endless addition of countless zeros. He even confided that, "I subsequently purchased such a note and always carried it in my wallet for inspiration." His school days had also given him an unusual affection for the statistical test of the null hypothesis followed later by his early bizarre keen interest in the Eurovision Song Contest after four countries achieved nul points in 1962.

For some reason Roger had also patiently sat through Owen's ten minute discourse on the invention and discovery of the numeral zero from its first beginnings in Mesopotamia predating the birth of Christ through to its development by the Mohammedans in the eighth century. He recounted a time in hospital when, "I immediately fell in love with a nurse who had written 'nil by mouth' at the end of my bed." Maybe his love of impersonating Roy Orbison arose because of the latter being known as the Big O or because of the O in Orbison rather than the gentle positioning of the o in Roy, who knows? It was anyone's guess, although Roger had given up questioning long ago.

What was clear is that Owen's favourite lines in any movie were those expressed between Cary Grant and Eva Marie Saint in Hitchcock's *North by Northwest* when Saint (playing the part of Eve Kendall) asks Grant (playing Roger Thornhill) what the

O on his monogrammed matchbook ROT, between his first and last name, stands for and he replies 'nothing'. This was pure Bigalow and Owen had told Roger so. His favourite actor, for an obvious reason, was Zero Mostel.

"I was greatly disappointed when Ian Fleming added 7 to his hero's moniker believing the first two digits were more than enough for anyone."

Roger could not recall all the details of their, or mainly Owen's conversation, but it followed an increasingly familiar trend into sport. He loved games where zero or nil played a large part. "Tennis was utterly sublime with its truly ingenious association of zero with love," Owen rejoiced. Whereas cricket was OK because it had the saving grace of being out for a duck. He disliked golf for obvious reasons, and basketball and rugby gave 0 little chance. By digression he mentioned gambling and he liked roulette, especially the American variant with 00. Then he got on to football and Roger suddenly pricked up his ears and became more attentive. This man mountain, this Bigalow, loved football!

"O(h), the joy of the goalless draw, of the 0-0 in print against the team names, now that was something to be adored!" Owen was now in full flow and there was no stopping him. He mentioned that he had kept goal at school and was quite good at preventing the opposition scoring past him. "Keeping a clean sheet had become nothing short of a religious mission for me," he confessed, almost falling to his knees during this deliverance. He had also turned out for a few works teams in the more recent past but nothing serious or involving a sustained commitment to challenge his missionary zeal.

Roger seized this moment to finally cut in and direct the conversation. Although more leathered than a football, he hadn't forgotten that the team were in desperate need of a goalkeeper. Their last one had to pack in due to severe lumbago occasioned by his frequent recourse to bending down and picking up the ball from the back of the net. Maybe, just maybe, Bigalow was the answer? Surely, Roger thought to himself, having a fanatic, a zealot, fixated on zero, as a goalkeeper could do no harm? After all, weren't all goalkeepers deemed to be a little bit crazy? Bigalow might be a little more crazier than others but maybe that made him even better than others.

"How do you fancy playing in goal for my team?" Roger asked, pushing another pint in Owen's direction, and hoping his patience would also finally be rewarded.

"I would be more than happy to turn out for any team that had you playing for it," Owen responded, confirming that a sense of camaraderie had already been quickly established.

True to his word, Owen Bigalow signed up for the team a week later, following his introduction to Simon at the Pork and Mutton. On this occasion he did not repeat his earlier long discourse on the joys of O and 0 he had previously had with Roger, that could wait for another time, and anyway he presumed that Roger would have already relayed much of it. He had come with a test instead. He remembered that Roger, his new best mate, hadn't displayed any discrimination against the letter O or the number 0, indeed, he had listened intensely and enthusiastically. He wanted to be sure that Simon, as club secretary and its only real official at present, would also be zero tolerant.

Before Owen would commit he only wanted one thing, "I would like to be allowed to wear the number 0 on my back," he said, a request that took Simon somewhat aback. This builder by day and impersonator by night knew that asking for nothing was less than he deserved but he would be delighted to get it. Goalkeepers always in those days wore 1 not 0, it was tradition. This was still an age when only one substitute was permitted during a game and players were numbered 1-12 rather than the high squad numbers (such as 66 and 99) used by players decades hence. He wanted to see if Simon would allow his wish, break with custom, and recognise 0 as a number the equal of other numerals.

Roger had mentioned to Simon that "Owen was a little barmy but harmlessly so." This request was a little left field but not viewed as either outrageous or potentially troublesome. Given their desperation for a goalkeeper this seemed a small price to pay.

"Having a goalkeeper with 0 on his back showed both commitment and intent," Simon happily conceded when sealing the deal. They had had been the worst defence by far in the league for the past two seasons and maybe this would send out a message that things would be different this time. It was also very difficult to refuse a man who wanted for nothing.

Owen was about to go down in history as the first, and to date, last man to wear 0 on his back. As Simon shook hands with the delighted Owen he became acquainted with the vice like grip of his last line of defence. Now they were eight, of sorts. They had doubled their roll call and with an untested 'wealth of talent' had only four weeks left to find additional players. The release of Pilot's hit single was only months away otherwise Owen would doubtless have wanted Simon and he to duet its lyrics 'O, O, O, it's magic you know, never believe it's not so'.

CHAPTER 5:
Finding The Holy Trinity

It was another very hot day when Simon decided to leave the office rather than eat his sandwich at his desk as per usual. He rarely left the Town Hall during the hours of 9-5. Indeed, the dash between the hours represented less of a race and more of a fixed location. Hit by the strong rays of the sun he was also hit by how little he really knew about the commercial area surrounding his workplace. Yes, he was familiar with the park nearby, which he cut through on his way to and from work, but not really aware of much else. He would have his sandwich there first and then have a walk around the Town Hall and the shops that bordered it.

He passed a number of shops on his brief sojourn, none of which he had meaningfully observed before, having been merely markers at the beginning or end of his working day. His sandwich had tasted better outside even though it was the usual boring ham and cheese but without the garnish provided by the telephone ringing at his desk and the need to respond to this or that minor issue stirring up the Council Chamber. The fresh air and the wander made him still feel a little peckish. Now that he was outside and the sun was casting its longest shadow he thought it would be nice to treat himself to an ice cream if he could find one. As luck, or perhaps fate, would have it, he was about to pass the answer to his current immediate desire. From the outside the shop did not look that big but once inside it became the tardis. It was the large scale model of an ice cream cornet situated on the pavement outside that had first attracted Simon to the premises. He had not paid any attention to its name 'Tripolini Deli and Ice Cream Parlour' or the giant model of a Parma ham in the right hand window that looked out longingly to the external world enjoyed by its fibreglass partner.

Once inside, Simon could see that the rather cavernous space had seating for around forty. There was a continuous display and serving counter that represented a straight rather than curved letter C from above which partly escorted three walls of the establishment. To the left, as you came in, was the array of ice creams; directly in front was the coffee and sandwich bar; on the right was the deli meats and other Italian specialities.

The central counter was where most of the action was taking place, with a door leading presumably into a back kitchen, Simon thought, as he heard a female voice barking out what appeared to be orders like some modern day il Duce.

"Porchetta di Ariccia, Panino al Prosciutto, tavola sei!", declared Donna Mussolini.

Only now was Simon able to make out that each of the counters was attended to by what appeared to be the same person albeit in triplicate - height, features, demeanour and dress were all the same. For a second or two he tried to make sense of it all before he decided to treat himself to a Knickerbocker Glory. He waited patiently behind two young girls who deliberated over their respective toppings. Upon taking his seat Simon commenced a more careful perusal of the terrain before him. It appeared to him that all three men shared the same fate of the giant displayed ham in longing to be elsewhere, away from the stultifying but well ventilated atmosphere of Tripolini's. The same three pairs of eyes looked somewhat distant, possibly dreaming of other worlds, as they attended to the requests of customers and the commands emanating from the rear.

There were a few pictures of famous Italian destinations randomly located on the walls alongside offerings and price lists. The only thing out of the ordinary, apart from the three male triplets that is, was the two scarves hanging over the doorway to the back - one was black and blue and the other was black and red. They almost formed a canopy to any toings or froings and a blessing to such frequent pilgrimages by the busy tre employees.

Simon did not have to wait too long for the arrival of his summer lunchtime treat. He engaged the left clone in brief conversation after thanking him for the Knickerbocker Glory.

"Excuse my asking, but are those scarves hanging up there not rival Inter Milan and AC Milan colours?"

"Yes, how did you know? My brothers and I came from that City along with our mother - you can hear her at the back - following the death of our father ten years ago. We had an aunt living in West Shields and she was keen for us to start a new life here," before scooping up some vanilla ice cream for the impatient customer standing behind Simon.

As he sat tucking into his rare treat Simon began surmising that their mother, departed father, and still resident aunt, had all supported Inter whereas, perhaps in some uncharacteristic act of youthful minor rebellion or gang peer pressure, all the boys switched their allegiance to AC. The positioning of the scarves could reflect a coming together and mutual respect for the family's footballing choices and their love of 'the beautiful game', or so Simon hoped, possibly over-filling in the blanks, something he was prone to do.

It had been a long time since Simon had enjoyed an ice cream such as this. As he paid up and made his exit he resolved to return the next day, perhaps for a coffee, to find out a little more about the intriguing Tripolini brothers and his romanticising of their apparent family footballing truce. As he walked back towards the Town Hall Simon confided to himself that he had enjoyed his lunchtime liberation and scolded himself for not doing it sooner or more often.

The next day had none of the sunshine of the day before, but the rain did not prevent Simon from being somewhat instinctively and curiously drawn to return to Tripolini's for his intended coffee. He had quickly eaten his sandwich at his desk and hastily answered the latest telephone enquiry in order to give himself a reasonable amount of caffeine time. The wet had brought in a different clientele from the dry of the day before but the three triplets were there, in what appeared to be their rightful positions, answering every demand. Simon added to the workload by requesting a double expresso and was politely given a tray with the said item and a small glass of water along with a smile of recognition from the day before. This served to suggest to Simon that perhaps all the brothers were far more attentive than he had thought and little passed them by. As he walked to an empty table Simon missed the middle brother, who had just served him, winking at the ices brother to show him that he had identified his customer from the day before, a motion that was not missed by deli brother as he was wrapping up some proscuitto crudo.

After finishing off his coffee and taking a small sip of water Simon decided a cake would be in order and returned to the counter from whence he had come earlier. The middle brother made a sweet suggestion and Simon took his advice and watched as this triplet brother cut him a huge slice. The calorie provider introduced himself, "My name is Massimo," he said before continuing, "I am the eldest brother by two minutes, followed by Mario on ices, who you talked to yesterday, then two minutes after that came Marco over on the deli." Those two minutes had probably been the only time that Massimo had been separated from his siblings since, or rather by, birth. He freely admitted that, "For most of our adult lives we have positioned ourselves pretty much as we are now – Mario to my right and Marco to my left – that is also how we sit together at home and walk around on the streets," adding a smile. Their daily positioning had clearly become second nature to them and no one got between them for long.

Simon took his cake and sat back down. It was suddenly becoming quite busy and the Tripolini's were hectically covering all their bases with little time for prolonged conversation. Just then a load of pensioners added to the work burden, bused in from who knows where. Simon wasn't in the know until he turned over the flyer on the table announcing that Thursday, today, was over 60's lunch discount day with 30% off orders between 12.30-1.30pm. He knew the oldies could smell a bargain a mile off and yet still miss the pong of odour much closer to home. As he pondered over whether the triplets had been positioned in the womb as they were now and if Massimo had been squeezed out first by the movement of the other two, his solitude was broken by the arrival at his table of two old guys in need of some lebensraum. The cutlery they dropped either side of him noisily served to declare their intent as did the zimmer frame one of them allowed to crash into his leg.

"Are you OK?" asked his accidental assailant.

"No harm done, I'm sure, just a little knock, I've survived worse," Simon answered politely.

"That's good, we don't want to cause a fuss," said the non combatant.

"Why don't we swap seats and the two of you can sit together?" suggested Simon. He wasn't looking to play at being the Massimo filling in anyone's sandwich today.

Simon was fortunate in getting his kind offer duly accepted as these two codgers ended up speaking very loudly into each others hearing aids throughout their conversation. The one with the zimmer allowed the content of his nose to dribble down onto the flyer Simon had been reading only a few seconds earlier. This was the only running that any part of his body was now capable of achieving. Until a week or so ago Simon, given his degree of desperation, may even have seen this oldie as a possible well-ripened but necessary recruit, but not now. He ate his cake as quickly as he could and checked his watch, it was only 12.50, but it was time to go, as his lunchtime companions made him feel like he was intruding rather than them.

The unfolding of the Tripolini story would have to wait until the invading Darbys and Joans had their hunger satisfied and that still had forty minutes left on the clock. As luck would have it, Massimo approached the table to take this subset's order, affording Simon the opportunity not only to pay his bill but inform this true middle man, "That was a great slice of cake, and the taste was too!" his winking doing little to improve the subtlety of its translation, before continuing, "I will be back tomorrow around the same time to try your sandwiches." The victuals to date had been to his liking and he wanted to know more about this little oasis and those encamped there. On his way back to work he caught the last of the rain, but it did not dampen his spirits, nor would it return for another month.

The sound of a neighbour's car alarm going off dragged Simon from his slumber well before his radio alarm announced "Heah man, it's Friday." His usual morning routine was further disturbed by his burning of the toast and lack of milk for his tea. All of this served to poison his mood for the morning and undermine any joys from the day before. Things were made worse by the constant ringing of his telephone as he tried to finish the remaining paperwork piled up in his plastic red in-tray. It was a hopeless task and his lunch break came and went without any reprieve for sustenance. He was starving and now also sweating as the air conditioning decided to withdraw its labour just as he over-applied his. Simon had no sandwich packed and his pact for a sandwich at Tripolini's looked broken until destiny once again intervened, or so it seemed.

Unlike earlier in the day, he was saved by what turned out to be a benign bell this time. The Town Hall fire alarm went off at 3.55pm and the workforce assembled in the car park to await the arrival of the engines. The excitement was over by 4.20pm when the assembled flesh and metal were finally informed by the Chief Clerk that, "Both the fire alarm and malfunctioning air conditioning system have been caused by dodgy electrics and all staff should leave immediately whilst I await the arrival of emergency maintenance." No one was given cause to return inside and Simon headed straight for his missed rendezvous over four hours later than planned but just ahead of its closing for the day.

His eventual arrival at 'Milan United' was still warmly greeted with a smile from the brothers three, even though they had almost given up any hope of his custom today and were in the early stages of preparing for closing. There were plenty of indications that they had spent another busy day catering to the needs of their clients. As Simon looked around he could see that very little appeared left in the deli from which to adorn the bread of his planned sandwich.

"I must apologise for being late but it has been one of those __"

"Please forgive the barren state of our larder," Massimo interrupted on behalf of himself and his siblings.

But things were not totally as it seemed, after witnessing Simon's contained disappointment, and with a twinkle in his eye, Massimo called to the back. A small and stout elderly woman appeared with an already prepared sandwich the likes of which Simon had never seen before.

"Grazie mille, Mamma," Massimo said lovingly before planting an affectionate kiss on her cheek.

Simon's introduction to the whole of the workforce was now complete and Donna Mussolini displayed a far more gentle and generous side to her actions than that first barking of commands from the rear experienced by Simon earlier in the week. She still looked a formidable and resourceful woman, nevertheless, in typical il Duce like pose with fists on hips imitating a trophy of sorts or two handled cup, albeit one that few would try to pick up.

The sandwich, like Simon's eventual arrival, had gone down well and he felt his day was finally turning itself around. He had been made to feel both welcome and at home despite the degree of busy work activity around him in order to bring the curtain down on another day's trading. Their mother departed from this stage first, along with the takings, leaving the front of shop cleaning chores to the boys; this was done almost silently and religiously and in such a way that it was clearly an established routine that had been well choreographed over the passage of time. True, there had been limited opportunity for conversation and the feeding of Simon's ongoing curiosity. He had thought that his growing fascination with Tripolini's was one way traffic, but unbeknown to him it was reciprocated, and they were just as interested in this unfamiliar character.

"After we finish locking up on a Friday we usually head off for a drink at a nearby wine bar. You are more than welcome to join us," Massimo kindly mentioned to Simon.

"I would be delighted to accept your kind invite," Simon responded in an instant, unable to resist this chance to learn more about his soon to be drinking buddies and waited patiently for the triplets to make good the premises defences.

Simon had never been in this particular wine bar, or any particular wine bar for that matter, before. It was obvious that the triplets knew the place, the custodian Carlo, and their Italian wines, very well. As the Chianti kept flowing, so did the conversation, and Simon got to learn more about the brothers and their past. There had been no teenage rebellion or gangland acquiescence in favour of AC. Whilst Inter and AC had successfully book-ended the previous decade's domestic honours for the city of Milan the boys had only changed their allegiance to AC following their father's death. All of the maternally connected side of the family had supported Inter as religiously as they had supported Rome in matters spiritual.

"It had always been assumed that our father was also a lifelong supporter of Inter as he always took us to home games at the San Siro and shouted just as loudly as we," Massimo said, his eyes lost in reflection on happier times.

As the elder brother bravely held back the tears, Mario chipped in, "What only came to light subsequently, following our father's death bed confession, was his hidden support for AC which he suppressed in order to keep the love of our mother as her family would never accept *I Rossoneri* in the house."

Marco then took up the verbal baton to relay that, "Ground share was one thing and matrimonial bed share was another. Inter presented themselves as a different class, both the club and its supporters deemed themselves superior and more upwardly mobile. Our father never told mother, or her family of this allegiance and knew it would have scuppered any chances he had of advancing their relationship to matrimony."

"One passion had to be traded for another and our father kept his secret until the very end. It is in fond memory and homage to our late father that us boys, mother, aunt, and all the rest of the maternal side of the family, now honour his sacrifice by openly recognising his earlier hidden love," Massimo said, concluding this reveal to Simon, much as if the triplets were speaking with only one voice.

The two scarves above the doorway signified not only Milan now truly united but also two sides of a man made one. Being party to the story almost made Simon feel as if he had been given membership to the group. In a way, the Tripolini's had experienced their own private family *Risorgimento* with their deceased padre as Garibaldi.

It was football that could have kept the parents apart and it was their father's sacrifice that ensured that did not happen. It also came to light, following his funeral and reminisces from an old long-standing, but now long-sitting, formerly estranged rural friend, that their father had been offered a trial by AC but the war and then true love intervened. It was a tale of two Mussolinis': with both Mussolini Oumo (intentionally) and Mussolini Donna (unknowingly) getting in the way of this aspiring football career.

Simon, at this point in the Tripolini narrative, and fortified by his third glass of wine quite openly asked, "Maybe one, or given you are triplets, all of you have inherited some of your father's footballing genes?"

He found out that they did play football, but always together, and in their fixed planetary universe of Mario, Massimo, and Marco running (and orbiting) from the viewer's Left to Right. They enjoyed defence and watching *Catenaccio* at work in their native Italy. They longingly missed the days playing with their ageing father as sweeper alongside them in friendly informal neighbourhood matches up until his unexpected death.

"We have kicked a ball around since coming to England but very occasionally and only between ourselves," Mario confessed.

"If you can lock-up the opposition forwards like you locked-up the Deli that would be something," Simon jokingly replied, selfishly thinking about that how their recruitment could improve his team's chances. He then did a reveal of his own, filling them in about Pork and Mutton FC.

"Strange name for a football team," quipped Marco.

"Strange football team," answered Simon.

"How strange?" asked Mario.

"Come along on Sunday afternoon and find out. We are holding a low key training session, a kick-about really, at the West Park at 3pm. You can check us out and we can see how rusty you are."

"Why not, we have nothing to lose, and can maybe show you a thing or two in the bargain!" replied a wine loosened up Massimo. The brothers now had a Sunday to look forward to rather than just the more usual forced regular march to early mass accompanied by mother superior.

CHAPTER 6:
Training Day

It was a hot and sticky Sunday afternoon when Pork and Mutton FC held their first rather casual training session on a five-a-side pitch at the West Park. Both the Park and the team had seen better days - the former had once basked in the glory of Victorian and Edwardian civic municipal beneficence and the latter had at least sometimes been able to draw on a full roster of players. Today only ten players had showed with there being no sign of Doug.

Simon split the ten into two teams as best he could in the full knowledge that he would have to keep the Tripolini brothers together in order to maintain diplomatic contact and assess their joint defensive attributes.

"Owen, you go join the brothers and take up your position in goal, and Roger, you can complete the side," Simon ordered. Before further instructing Roger (Owen's chief advocate and best new buddy) that, "You'll be playing up front largely on your own mate." He wasn't totally overjoyed at being told that. Not least because he may have to do a proper workout and he hadn't finished digesting his heavy lunch. Anyway, he was a right winger by inclination of foot and brain, not some versatile attacker.

They faced a team composed of what remained; with Simon sacrificing himself, as all good secretaries and utility players do, to a stint in goal. Norman and Stuart were asked to play in defence although more used to playing left wing back and central midfield respectively. That left Byron and Salvator to share midfield and attacking responsibilities as best they could against Pork and Mutton's expected first choice future defence.

Just before they were about to kick-off Doug suddenly appeared from out of nowhere (if VAR had existed it would have shown he had exited from a clump of bushes which had served to screen him from the others while he made up his mind to commit one way or the other). His arrival was hardly auspicious as he was dressed in normal non-sporting attire including inappropriate footwear.

"Where have you been and why aren't you changed!" Simon barked.

"There are times during matches when players don't have their shooting boots on but this was the first time that a player had actually forgot to bring them!" joked Roger, trying to calm things down.

It was clear that Doug had left home with no intention of participating with the team and was probably planning to break the earlier agreement between Mortimer the Elder and Pork and Mutton FC. As in life, he was unsure of what to do. To be fair, at least he finally showed up, in his own fashion, to express whatever decision he had decided to make in person.

But before he could say anything Simon gave him an additional, but more gentle, dressing down saying, "The only role you will be playing today will be referee and consider yourself lucky in getting the whistle."

This was another position not well-suited to Doug who had yet to show any real decisiveness or strong character traits. He consoled himself with the fact that he was given a shinny silver whistle, that he only gradually became familiar with, to make everyone stop when he wanted - for the first time in his life he had some authority over others and he increasingly saw it more as a reward than a punishment as the game progressed. Maybe, after all, there were some benefits from being there and he could always opt out at the time of his own choosing - this was a commitment of sorts, a little flakey, but that was Doug.

The plan was to play for half an hour each way at a gentle pace and for the first fifteen minutes everything seemed to be working reasonably well. The remnants were unable to pierce the Tripolini defensive line or get a shot away at Owen's goal. The only downside had been that Roger had rarely received the ball upfront from any of the triplets given their tendency to sit back, play the ball between themselves, and shoot from distance to no avail. Simon was no goalkeeper but even he could easily handle this. On his side, Norman and Stuart had little to do at the back given Roger's limited threat and they made constant forays in support of Byron and Salvator's attacking endeavours. Simon could see some serious potential in the way Byron played - he was spraying good passes quite literally all over the park - and he would be a very good addition to any team in the league. Salvator was more of a disappointment and played with less fluency than his name or nationality suggested. His movement both on and off the ball was rather restrictive, cumbersome and often badly timed. Simon had rather mistakenly expected more and had been guilty of imagining someone with a flashy agile Copa Cabana skill set whilst Salvator had never made any such claims. It was not that he was terrible rather he was just not Pelé, and that was Simon's fault rather than his.

The next fifteen minutes remained 0-0 but was more eventful than the scoreline suggests. During the early part of his refereeing baptism Doug had remained, as in life, quiet and invisible. For some reason, possibly boredom, he then decided to be more involved and started blowing his whistle and making decisions decidedly lacking any rule based rationale. Many of his pronouncements were less than welcomed by the others whether in their favour or not.

"Why the hell are you blowing now?" shouted a frustrated Roger just as he was about to have his first meaningful strike at goal.

"Because you are offside," said Doug with a misguided air of authority.

"This is five-a-side football, you idiot! There is no offside!" Roger exclaimed as he threw the ball in the fool's direction.

The more he tried to get involved the more he was ignored by those around him.

"I will take the blinking whistle back if you keep blowing it without good reason!" an extremely patient Simon finally snapped. It would not take him long to regret not acting on this.

Doug had gone from initial supposed help to obvious hindrance only to arrive at total liability a minute later. It was he who finally, and inadvertently, broke down the Tripolini defensive line. The course of the afternoon was about to change when he accidentally took out two players. It was a silly collision followed by a ricochet: Doug had somehow placed himself between the ball and Marco such that he banged into the latter and then bounced off him into Byron. He was the white ball in a game of billiards. Three men down, including the referee, strewn across the pitch. Simon had little choice but to call a temporary halt to proceedings, what would later be called a timeout, to assess the damage. Although none of the injuries were presumed serious it was decided that the downed three skittles should sit out the rest of the training. This was a workout that clearly hadn't worked out. Simon thought there would be little merit in continuing a four a side game and suggested that they move over to the full size pitch and play a game of attack and defence.

As they walked across the park towards the larger expanses of turf Simon was stopped by a man with a dog.

"Any chance that I could join in your kickabout?" the dog walker enquired.

"It may look like that but it was supposed to be a little more serious, if truth be told," Simon admitted looking a little embarrassed by what the stranger must have witnessed.

"I live close by and could get my gear and lose the dog. It would only take a few minutes. That's if you don't mind, of course, and I'm not intruding?" The dog answered its master in the affirmative before Simon added his agreement.

This decision was easy to make in the circumstances. No one wants a stranger to suddenly gatecrash their party but Simon wanted to play attack and defence and it would allow Owen to be better tested in a full-size goal with four defenders facing four attackers. During the dog man's absence Simon decided to put himself with the remaining two triplets and Salvator in defence. This left Roger, Stuart and Norman in attack plus the mystery man, of course, should he arrive, which he duly did, within the time interval promised.

"Thanks for letting me join in," the stranger gasped after running all the way there.

"Our pleasure, we are Pork and Mutton FC," Simon answered before introducing each member of his motley crew.

"My name is Jonathan Cruft, but you can call me either Jonah or Jonas, both these nicknames have carried over from school and that's what my friends call me," said the potential inductee.

Simon began to fixate on the new man's name, as he watched him lace up his Stylo Matchmakers, and thought to himself that his participation may not bode well. On the other hand, his name was pretty close to that of the great Johan Cruyff and if he only had a minuscule amount of the silky Dutchman's talent that would more than suit Simon.

Simon outlined his new training plan, "The game will last for thirty minutes. When the defence gain the ball we can pass to each other, but only once, before either booting it out or sending it to the half way line for the attack to regain possession. Jonah you will be part of the attacking team."

Simon took up the position vacated by Marco and asked Salvator to act as defensive cover in front of the new back three. On the attacking side, he asked Roger to play his usual right wing position, with Norman on the left wing, and Stuart playing behind them in midfield being tasked with retrieving any said cleared balls and feeding the front line. This left Jonah in the middle of the attack as centre-forward - a role he and his boots were delighted to play.

To Simon's utter surprise this session went well. Not only did the make-shift defence work well together but Salvator played much better as a central defensive midfielder than his previous role as an attacking one. He had a talent for picking up loose balls and blocking attacking passing lanes. The two triplets were a little confused by having Simon alongside them early on but quickly adjusted to their substitute sibling. Owen was a revelation between the big sticks - he not only commanded his area but the defence around him. The only negative was the one solitary goal conceded throughout the entire half hour by the defence. Of course this negative was also a positive for the team - the attacking component, that is. The attack had worked well together but created few real chances, especially given Owen's considerable presence. The goal when it came, at the very end, could be seen by some as fortunate and by others less so. Jonah had linked up well with his fellow attackers throughout the session and on this occasion had hit a rasping twenty yard shot that had Owen beaten but not the post which rebounded the ball back into the face of Norman and on into the net. This led Owen to intentionally, and somewhat bizarrely, head butt the goal post as punishment for conceding a goal he could do little about. Deadlock was broken, Norman had a bloody nose, and Owen a large bump on his forehead. These were yet more casualties to add to an eventful and revealing day. Still, everyone, bar Doug, walking wounded included, looked reasonably happy.

Even Jonathan Cruft agreed to continue his association and join the team as he jokingly confessed "Like my namesake, I've had a whale of a time!"

As they were about to disperse Simon, somewhat casually, informed them that "We have been given the opportunity to play a friendly match against a Town Hall XI, mostly my work colleagues, next Sunday morning, here, in the Park, if you are up for it rather than having another training session in the afternoon?" Simon knew that preparation time was running out and that only one other formal friendly game had been arranged prior to the league season commencing in three weeks. "We have a friendly match against another Division 2 side, The Tea Pot Cafe, two weeks today," he said, before continuing, "next week would provide us with a much needed additional test, help aid team preparations, and raise our fitness levels for the challenges ahead".

Almost every hand was raised in agreement with Simon's proposal, and one could almost have expected this chorus to sing, "Here we go, here we go, here we go" but for the simple fact that this chant was still a few years removed from vocally adorning the terraces.

The one exception to all this excitement was Doug. He, rather characteristically, had offered neither approval nor dissent, and simply hid his hands in his pockets while muttering quietly to himself, "Maybe."

"Great! By the way, the match with the Council will be an hour earlier than we usually play on a Sunday, it's a 10am kick-off, I trust no one has a problem with that?" Simon said apologetically.

CHAPTER 7:
(N)Ever Reddy

The forthcoming match against the Council was the talk of the Town...Hall. Simon knew his team were in for a tough match even though his work colleagues did not play regularly together in any organised league. He was also fully aware that five of his likely opponents had represented the county, in their earlier days, which for some had not been that long ago, and now played for different teams at a much higher level than Pork and Mutton FC. The rest of their line-up remained a mystery, not only for Simon but also his co-workers. It was clear from lunchtime conversations in the corridors of local power that more than enough volunteers had expressed an interest in taking part so that a considerable number would be disappointed in not making this particular council cut. Not only those playing, but the numerous and soon to be sidelined, would all be after getting one over on Simon and his hapless charges.

One person, among the many, who had expressed a keen interest in representing his employers was Juan Ever Reddy, the interim head of traffic policy and parking enforcement in the borough. With Australian and South American parents, he had arrived from the land down under after marrying an East Shields girl returning from her gap year with him in tow. Ten years later and he was widely viewed as someone who had ended up in his current elevated position more by luck or, as some claimed malevolence, rather than merit. Always effortlessly climbing the next rung in the ladder after the person ahead of him would inevitably fall off and generously cede their place to him. His good fortune was always the result of others misfortune or so it seemed and he was treat with envy by those below him and trepidation by those above. Jealousy and suspicion hung over his perceived unjustified promotions and his always being in the right place at the right time. Many foolishly wondered about, and some feared, the outcome of his next hex. Whatever the truth of the matter, whether he created or merely benefitted from the opportunities coming his way, Ever (as he preferred to be called) always seized and made the most of them.

Envy, spells and curses apart, he was also greatly disliked by the Shields public (or more accurately, all those who owned cars). In his latest new role he had courted notoriety following his implementation of draconian policies resulting in both a significant increase in car parking fees across the borough alongside a plethora of double yellow lines in the town centre. This served to unite shoppers and shopkeepers against him with the local press dubbing him Ned Kelly. This association was a little unfair, however. Whilst Ever did have a tendency to shoot from the hip on occasion he never faced his foes with metal helmet or body armour. The only protection that covered his head was a rather obvious ginger wig which drew attention to any long departed brown hair while also ill-matching the strands that stayed. This total failure of concealment served to reinforce Reddy's being singled out as a marked man in most peoples eyes and was a source of workplace ridicule. Behind his back, especially within the lower council circles, he was known as 'The Rug'. Most of these carried their deep-seated resentment into scoffing at his decision to volunteer his footballing services by claiming he had thrown his hairpiece, rather than his hat, into the ring. His background, professional judgement, and dress sense had all come under attack.

Unbeknown to Ever or his critics, the self-promotion of his middle name over that of his first was pure happenstance but not inappropriate: having ties to a Hebrew name meaning beyond, which he certainly was, being largely held at arms length by others; alongside a Scandinavian name meaning as wild as a boar, which he certainly wasn't, although his hairpiece could be seen as a sort of rusty-brown version of that animal's fur. It would certainly have been another name for Simon to dwell on had he been so inclined at the time.

Given the level of controversy surrounding Reddy, the Town Hall XI selectors knew that his inclusion in the match would most likely stir up trouble.

"What are we going to do about that guy Reddy wanting to take part?" selector one asked his two other junior colleagues composing the meeting held behind closed doors.

"He's a real problem, nobody likes him or wants anything to do with him," selector two said, confirming both his bias and character assassination in a single sentence.

Group think was made unanimous by selector three adding, "We don't want him in our hair, look at the state of his own!" which drew chuckles from all of them.

"He is out," selector one replied.

"Well he was never really in. We can give him some flannel and say how difficult it was given the level of interest and how we discussed his case in more depth than all the others," added selector two along with a smile.

"We are all agreed then, he is not in the starting eleven, nor on the touchline as substitute, or even our backup reserve. I personally wouldn't even have him preparing the half-time oranges!" selector three concluded.

As far as the selectors were concerned they were never for Ever. When the team announcement was finally made, on the

Thursday morning, Reddy was naively surprised by his omission. He was both disappointed and angry, more sinned against than sinning. Others may see him as 'The Rug' but he would not let them walk all over him. For whatever reason he now felt a sense of injustice alongside his hurt pride. This may explain his decision to approach Simon later that same day.

"Sorry to trouble you, but have you got a minute?" said Ever, after forcefully knocking, then immediately opening, the door.

"Of course, please come in and park yourself down – excuse the pun!" replied Simon without thinking, but then instantly regretting, what he had just said.

"I have been excluded from the Town Hall team and would like to ask if you have room for me in your team for the match on Sunday? I would be delighted to switch my allegiance as they have shown me no loyalty whatsoever. I would like to show them what they turned down." Ever stated, before making his case for inclusion.

Simon was sympathetic and had never felt any animosity toward Ever. He was certainly far harder to refuse in this direct face to face discussion. Given the paucity of resources at Simon's disposal and Ever's backstory it would be impossible to not offer him something.

"The best I can do at this stage is to put you down as first reserve," Simon said, without mentioning that he was the only reserve they had.

"No problem, at least I will be somehow involved in the match," a slightly relieved Ever replied.

From that moment on, others in the council, from a variety of corners and for different reasons, commenced putting pressure on Simon to retract his offer to Reddy and bar his entry, however minor, into the game. To his credit, Simon stood his ground and kept his promise. He was most unwilling to surrender his own team selection to others (alongside his carrying no ill will toward Reddy).

"So you don't like him, that's obvious, and I cannot do anything about that. None of you have the bottle to call him 'The Rug' to his face. Well, I won't let the likes of you pull him out from under me!" Simon said defiantly to the last person trying hard to make him change his mind.

Simon had arranged for the team to wear the old kit for the last time. They would be wearing all white and Owen would have to have number 1 on his back for one game only. Owen was less than happy about this but when Jonah invited them all back to his gaff for a barbecue after the game Simon tried to placate his dissenting and rather impetuous goalie with the promise that he would cast this particular jersey into the flames.

"Good. This number 1 top is pure heresy as far as I am concerned", Owen informed Simon and Roger as if they could somehow be unaware of his feelings.

"Never mind, it will be the last time you are anybody's number 1!" Simon assured him.

"We will burn this heretic with the steak rather than at the stake!" joked Roger.

The Town Hall XI turned out in a variety of kits representing teams some of the players either represented or supported, luckily none of those were white. The match officials, given the informality of the fixture, were all council employees experienced in refereeing the laws of the game with the utmost neutrality and Simon had no qualms about the agreed arrangement.

The plan had been for Pork and Mutton FC to play a 3-5-2 formation with Doug as substitute and Ever as reserve to replace anyone who was a no show or unable to play. Simon knew that this set-up was an unfamiliar one and quite unlike previous seasons or the standard 4-4-2 or 4-3-3 found throughout the game. But he was trying to play to the team's identifiable weaknesses just as much as to any strengths. The initial playing XI would line up as follows:

(1) Owen

(2) Mario   (5) Massimo   (3) Marco

(7) Byron   (6) Salvator   (8) Stuart   (4) Simon   (11) Norman

(9) Roger   (10) Jonathan

Given their limited options up front, this meant that Roger would have to play a striker role and Byron would have to cover the right wing as part of his midfield responsibilities. Additionally Salvator and Simon would play a little deeper in midfield to support the triplets back three. This plan slightly unravelled prior to kick–off given a no show by Doug. Ever was delighted by this, as good fortune had once again intervened, to promote him - albeit to substitute. Simon started to share in the belief of the Reddy hex when Roger pulled up in the warm up and had to surrender his position to 'The Rug'. The game was about to commence and Simon was already two men down, now without substitute or reserve, with the 'detested' Aussie on the pitch, and facing a council team including the five talented players he had expected and feared.

For the first twenty minutes or so the all whites and the all sorts appeared evenly matched. A handful of council supporters barracked, booed and gesticulated whenever Ever touched the ball. This was their new active recourse to stop him from playing. To their growing annoyance this didn't work. Rather than fazing him their behaviour just made Ever more determined and he seemed to relish their touchline remonstrations. He had gone close on a couple of occasions and he was clearly more than a reasonable temporary addition. Doug Mortimer turned up just as Jonah somehow smashed in a free kick outside the edge of the box following an aggressive and untimely tackle on Ever. This was virgin territory - the team were 1-0 up with fifteen minutes to go until the half-time break. Doug was once again the outsider and was surprised more by the team actually playing than the goal he had just witnessed. As he was to rather limply explain to Simon and the team during the oranges that he had thought kick-off to be at 11 rather than 10.

"Everyone else turned up on time for the game apart from you. No one here had a problem comprehending last week's instruction. Pay attention and listen in future and stop trying my patience!" Simon balled out at Doug.

Some of his teammates were a little more sympathetic, especially as things hadn't turned out too badly so far. After all, this unfamiliar scoreline for Pork and Mutton FC had carried on through to the interval. Simon had expected to have 13 probables rather than the 11 possibles at the commencement of the referee's whistle. Both he and Doug had got their numbers wrong this morning and he was frustrated by it.

Simon did not really know what to say during the half-time break apart from the brief scolding of Doug. He couldn't remember the last time he had the privilege of leading a team to the sidelines for their requisite breather being ahead in a game.

"Keep it up lads and maintain your effort and commitment," was the best Simon could come up with at the time.

Both he and his players remained largely silent during the break apart from the sucking of citrus and deep intakes of breath. Owen took the opportunity to remind Simon of his promise to burn the monstrous and ill-fitting number 1 jersey that he had already come to loathe. The signalling of the referee to restart the match brought some relief to Simon and he had resolved himself not to use Doug in the game, if it could be anyway avoided, to teach the miscreant an important lesson.

Within ten minutes of the restart the team were 2-0 up following another heavy and illegal tackle on Ever in the penalty area. He had neatly rounded one defender whose only success had been to rob him of his hairpiece before being scythed down by another hapless opponent. Whilst wig disengagement may possibly lead to a controversial penalty decision the second infringement would not and the player committing said violation was lucky to stay on the pitch.

"Keep your hair on!" shouted Roger from the touchline, as Ever retrieved his piece of very personal attire, and placed the ball on the penalty spot. This was a stupid thing to say as it got the hecklers going again, repeating in unison what had just been said.

"Don't you worry, I always keep my head," he calmly replied after neatly slotting the ball home.

No one could really believe it apart from the goalscorer and match officials, who registered his success. Simon tried to block out the thought that they might actually win this game and was fearful of both complacency and fatigue setting in.

Within five minutes Simon's fears were starting to be realised when the Town Hall XI grabbed a goal back following a corner. Most of the midfield were starting to run on empty, including Simon himself. Norman and Byron were especially slow in getting back in time to provide additional defensive cover when the cross from the corner came over. Owen somehow managed to push the ball away to the edge of the penalty area where it was retrieved and returned into the top left hand corner of his empty net. Norman and Byron were supposed to be positioned on the goal line for corners but neither sentry had been at their post. Unfortunately it was Owen who was once again at his post, however. Walking back to collect the ball nestling in the back of the net he decided yet again to reacquaint his forehead with the upstanding squared piece of wood and head-butted it in full temper. This not only served to make him immediately downstanding in his physical demeanour but knocked him out cold. He was escorted off the pitch following his return to consciousness as there was no way he could be allowed to continue, even though he clearly wanted to. Simon had no choice but to bring on his wayward substitute Doug as a poor replacement for his wayward goalie. Simon would, however, have to go in goal and get Ever to switch his position to that vacated by Simon. Doug was asked to play up front wide on the right. During the rest of the game he managed to touch and then lose the ball twice and otherwise failed to make his presence felt.

The last thirty minutes were little more than a blur to Owen. He had his memory refreshed over the charcoal and burgers by the homeowner Jonathan and stand-in goalkeeper Simon. The five regular players in the opposing team had started to make their talent and fitness count. They had scored twice more, in the last ten minutes, to snatch victory away from Pork and Mutton FC. It had been a close run affair, however, and the 2-3 defeat to the council failed to engender the embarrassment usually experienced following match day encounters. Indeed their opponents had demonstrated a renewed respect and regard for not only the the team's efforts but Simon and Ever's contribution. Whatever standing they previously had in the workplace new brownie points had been clearly won and served up when the all sorts applauded the all whites off the pitch. None of this really helped Owen's recovery and merely served to increase the guilt he felt in letting his teammates down by his ill-tempered behaviour and latest lapse in self-control.

"I have been very stupid and cost you the game," said Owen remorsefully as Mrs Cruft handed him a fresh cold compress.

"You don't need me to tell you, a builder, that bone and timber make a poor combination," replied Simon.

This unhealthy episode had also made Owen forget all about the promise to burn the jersey with number one emblazoned on the back. Simon had not forgotten this promise, but deciding that enough had gone up in flames today, he unceremoniously disposed of said garment in the first bin he passed on his way home.

CHAPTER 8:
Trouble Brewing

The barbecue at Jonathan Cruft's house had served to further bond the team and help christen the enhanced possibility of a phoenix rising (or should it be clambering) from the ashes - especially since Ever had committed to the cause. They were all now eagerly looking forward to their next test in a week's time against an old foe - The Tea Pot Cafe. Even Doug showed some enthusiasm for the encounter. Not only would this friendly match pit them in a formal competitive game against another team in the same league but it would be the first time for the new all black kit to get a public airing.

You could not class The Tea Pot Cafe as a rival to Pork and Mutton FC as they had aways hammered them in the past by a margin of at least three or four goals. Rivals should have some sort of parity and this had never really been the case. The Chi finished 10th in the division last season, with Pork and Mutton bottom in 16th position, but a world away in terms of performance statistics. They would provide a telling barometer for Simon and his teammates in terms of not only a measure of any improvement but of likely challenges ahead over a long 30 game league season.

The cafe was a well known eatery on the edge of town, along Chichester Road, with its main lunchtime customer base drawn from the nearby Wright's Biscuit Factory (which lacked its own refectory). Such was the degree of association between these two establishments that the team was now largely composed of players drawn from the factory rather than the cafe. But the cafe remained home in terms of the headquarters for meetings and non-alcoholic refreshment and its premises were hard to miss given the giant tea pot gently angled to pour directly above its entrance. Simon knew that they had never taken the biscuit before but now they had an outside chance.

Sunday duly arrived and so did a full complement of players for both sides. The 11am kick-off had even helped ensure the more punctual appearance of Doug (although Simon believed it was most likely down to his previous berating). Although it was a friendly final pre-season game the match would be refereed by the league's officials and take place on The Links playing fields which Pork and Mutton FC called home along with most other teams in their division, including today's opponents. This led to a sizeable crowd of around twenty or so intent on watching a full game rather than the usual meagre viewing audience of occasional dog walkers with their cursory curiosity lasting a matter of minutes. Pork and Mutton had thirteen available players alongside three very interested spectators - Max, Fred, and rather surprisingly a turnout by the Tripolini mother. Max appeared less interested in the state of the flesh on this occasion and more interested in the cut of their garb. The kit he had provided certainly looked good and had been greeted with envy by the opposing team as the sides exchanged glances on exiting the nearby portacabins serving as permanent changing rooms.

The remaining touchline spectators were all strangers to Simon and his teammates and most likely supporting The Cafe. This was confirmed by the guffaw and loud abuse that greeted the arrival of the match officials from the timber changing facilities. Most of the crowd had expected the green kit of the Chi (although at a time when green tea was largely unknown here) but not the professionally looking all black outfits of their opponents, much less the authoritative bright pink of the referee and linesmen.

"I'd forgotten all about the officials having to wear their alternative kit and how it would be received. It looks even worse than I imagined!" Simon confessed to Roger.

"I wish I'd brought my sunglasses, this won't do my hangover any good," Roger replied, far quieter than usual.

The dreaded ridicule and abuse had materialised and the senior match official would subsequently report to the league administration the public response to their change strip alongside the strenuous effort required to initially coax one of his linesmen out of the changing room to dutifully perform their responsibilities.

Simon had revealed which of his thirteen would be in the first XI by personally handing out the one size fits all numbered new tops. He had made the rather risky decision to drop himself to reserve and put Doug as substitute. Given the full complement at his disposal this meant that he would not be playing unless something happened to Doug, or his other teammates, prior to kick-off. The 'number 13' shirt (which was actually blank) was already on Simon's back hidden beneath his track suit top as he passed out the rest. Doug received his and greeted it with a fair amount of anticipated resignation.

"Owen this is for you. The largest goalkeeping jersey we could find and now especially customised with a zero on the back," Simon said, keeping an earlier promise.

"Much appreciated, it looks the business," replied a beaming Owen.

"Not fully, I'm afraid, we didn't have the time to get Max's signage on the front", answered the giver.

"That's OK, it's what's on the back that counts for me," the receiver retorted with a lump in his throat before heading for the nearest mirror to check out his rear.

The team (and their shirts) lined up as follows:

(0) Owen

(2) Mario **(5) Massimo** **(3) Marco**

(6) Salvator **(4) Norman**

(7) Roger **(8) Stuart** **(11) Byron**

(9) Ever **(10) Jonathan**

Simon asked Norman to play a deeper defensive midfield role alongside Salvator, as Simon had partly done in the previous match. In consequence of this Byron was instructed to play on the the left wing so allowing Roger to take up his more customary position on the right wing. The rest of the team played where they had finished the match against the Town Hall (apart of course for Owen, who had by then already self-harmed and concussed his way off the pitch).

Given the hysterics engendered by the entrance of the men in pink, it took some time for the officials, opposing players, and the largely non partisan crowd to finally pick up on the fact that Owen was wearing 0 on his back. Simon had given his team sheet to the referee just before they had entered their respective changing rooms. Obviously the linesman's wobble had distracted the referee's attention, as had the crowd following their eventual exit from the sanctuary of their portacabin. The fact that Owen had on a pretty standard yellow goalie jersey seemed to also suggest an air of familiarity to the circumstances and helped to temporarily camouflage proceedings (this canary wasn't singing). Within ten minutes of the match commencing, however, attention suddenly shifted dramatically to him.

A speculative high ball into the Pork and Mutton penalty area was neatly and confidently caught by Owen and as he came in to land he was over-aggressively shoulder-charged by the opposing number 9 which led to his landing face down on the ground. The referee blew his whistle for a foul and reprimanded the offending forward. Owen now found himself doubly prone, both in his current position and from the attention he received from both the referee and the crowd. His mid-air acrobatics registered his number 0 shirt to all and sundry. He was just beginning to discover the weight such a number carried alongside the widespread and highly distasteful lack of zero tolerance being expressed around him.

"Who gave you permission to wear that on your back?!" the indignant referee demanded. His bad day was clearly becoming worse.

"What do you mean permission? It's a number, is it not? And has just as much a right to be there as the number 1 that my opposite, erm, umm, number is wearing, surely?" said Owen, starting to dig a hole for himself outside of work.

"Not on my watch it hasn't!" shouted main man in the pink who clearly wasn't.

"I am proud of the number I am wearing. If you only knew, it means a lot to me. If you can let me explain __" Owen stated before being cut short by Roger.

"There's no time for that now Owen, I am sure he has more important things to do like referee this match."

At this point, the cavalry or rather Simon arrived on the scene, diplomatically confronting the referee, "What's the problem here? Where in the rule-book does it stipulate that a goalie must wear number 1? If you can show me, all well and good, otherwise can we kindly get on with the game please."

With nothing more than a shake of his head, the referee blew his whistle and said "Free kick to Pork and Mutton. Let's play."

All of this heated conversation would be subsequently noted by the referee for inclusion in his post-match report alongside the less than charitable public response to what the match officials and Owen were wearing. Before the game was over he would have other complaints to add.

As the game once again progressed, abuse and ridicule were increasingly being deflected away from the match officials and noticeably directed more and more toward Owen. A small band of rival supporters shifted their position and gathered behind his goal to scoff and generally have a go at him in order to put him off his game. This ploy failed to work in the negative way intended and only served to strengthen both his resolve and that of his teammates ahead of him. Pork and Mutton FC and their goalkeeper were put under constant pressure during the first half but managed to sustain the barrage of attacks coming on and off field. It was still 0-0 when the half-time whistle finally blew. Owen was clearly going from zero to hero (although he clearly would have preferred the reverse).

Regardless of the scoreline, it had been a most eventful first half, but the interval brought little respite for Simon. Immediately after blowing his whistle the referee ran over to Simon to voice his displeasure with regard to Pork and Mutton FC's new kit. The requirement to wear the inflammable bright pink had not only alighted the crowd but also the referee and he was clearly still on a short fuse. Simon was little prepared for the new verbal onslaught that was to follow the referee's immediate touchline arrival.

"I will be letting the authorities know all about the earlier carry on. Not only that, what is all this blatant advertising on the front of your shirts? Most distasteful, I have witnessed nothing of its like before! I will hold you responsible for turning this football world upside down. We are made to wear pink, your goalie wears 0, and you have this rubbish across the front of your shirts!" the referee shouted indignantly causing Max to come over.

"Excuse me intruding, but you are talking complete nonsense. You clearly don't like disruption of any sort, even for the better. Not in my backyard, eh? Locked into tradition, pipe and slippers, no ruffling of feathers, all for a quiet life. That's you to a tee, I'm sure!" Max was returning fire with fire and when he identified himself as the new sponsor and funeral proprietor all hell started to break loose.

"So you're the culprit who is chiefly responsible for this fiasco! Corrupting the league and bringing the game and its administration into disrepute," said the referee, prodding his finger directly into Max's chest to reinforce the point.

"First of all, remove your finger. Second, I find your silly and misguided attack is just as much political as it is personal with regard to the way you see me conducting my business, the funeral sector in particular, and capitalism in general. I simply return people to their maker as best as I am able and see nothing wrong in that. I am neither trickster nor thief! I am proud of what I do and am trying to bring it out of the shadows where you want it to remain. These shirts are the future, make no mistake about it!" Max loudly accused his assailant as the temperature rose another notch.

"Poppycock!" was the ref's simple reply.

"Yeah, really! I know what you guys from Lower Lenin Street are like. It would have been different if my name was Marx rather than Max. Just go whistle!." Things were certainly heating up.

"You're no Bacall!" the ref immediately responded.

"And you're no Bogart!" said Max just as quickly.

Some of the younger players had little idea where this was all going. Before the matter could get any further out of hand Simon managed to direct the referee away toward his two linesmen situated on the halfway line sharing cut-up oranges with players drawn from both teams.

Before Simon joined his players, in order to make his planned interval team talk, he received a tap on his shoulder, and as he turned he saw Donna Duce standing before him.

"Scusi, do you mind if I make a little suggestion?" she enquired.

"Not at all, fire - sorry, I mean - ask away," correcting himself, given all that had just transpired.

"I think your team is sitting back too deep and allowing too much time to your opponents. While you have soaked up the pressure successfully until now it is unlikely to last until full-time," the triplet's mother said.

This was the first time that Simon was engaged in direct conversation with Mrs Tripolini and it was clear that she knew quite a bit about football tactics. Simon heeded her words as they were much in line with what he had been thinking, not least the need to try and reduce the stress placed on their goalie. He called the team together (minus Doug, who was presumed to be on a toilet break at this juncture) and adjusted the line-up as follows:

(0) Owen

(2) Mario   (5) Massimo   (3) Marco

(6) Salvator

(7) Roger   (8) Stuart   (4) Norman   (11) Byron

(9) Ever   (10) Jonathan

Simon believed this allowed his players to make the most of their limited attributes and skills alongside shifting the balance of the team toward a slightly more offensive stance.

This made a noticeable difference from the commencement of the second half. They dominated possession for the opening ten minutes and Byron crashed a low drive against a post from close range. You could see that Tea Pot Cafe were getting rattled and were struggling to cope with Simon's changes. Pork and Mutton got their just reward with a beast of a goal in the 66th minute by Ever. Roger played a one two with Stuart and then sent over a hard low cross which Ever reached just ahead of their keeper. The force of the ball into the near post and the glance off the head of Ever ensured it went like a bullet into the net with his hairpiece following its trajectory, but unlike the ball, being deflected by the goalkeeper to unnecessary safety around the post. This was the second game in a row that Ever's wig could be credited with being involved in goalscoring assists. Before returning it to its rightful location he ran around the pitch holding it aloft in celebration and this earned the referee's censure in a booking. Simon exchanged a knowing smile with Mrs Tripolini and a thumbs up from Max.

In the midst of all of this Simon had missed the injury sustained by Roger in crossing the ball so ferociously. He clearly wanted to come off and be substituted. The second half had been so engrossing for Simon that he hadn't paid any attention to the whereabouts of Doug since his half-time disappearance. He now had to make a decision: search for Doug and risk playing with ten men or get on the pitch as soon as possible himself. He chose the latter course and signalled to the referee that he would be coming on to replace a limping Roger.

"Where the hell was Doug?" Simon said as he got within earshot of his injured teammate, who just shrugged in response, before instructing Byron to move over to the right wing, sending Norman out to the left, and then joining Stuart in the centre of midfield.

For the next ten minutes Pork and Mutton FC continued much as before. They continued to press and were unlucky not to be rewarded with another goal when Jonathan was questionably ruled offside. Unlike the not so distant past, the team were no longer willing to be as generous and hospitable to opposing attacks. They were galvanised in their resolve to keep the lead and to try and deliver Owen a clean sheet as reward for all his first half endeavour and troubles. Lacking both sufficient fitness, and footballing guile in the unfamiliar territory of seeing out a victory, they finally succumbed in the last minute of the game. Salvator, who had been outstanding throughout the game, was late in a tackle in the penalty area, and the proceeding spot kick was dispatched into the net just past the outstretched hand of Owen. The match was drawn 1-1 and although it still felt like a victory for the four veteran players of Pork and Mutton FC it tasted more like a defeat for those newly engaged in the enterprise. This contrasting mixture of emotions was also similarly reflected in the faces of Fred, Max and Mrs Tripolini as they clapped the departing team from the sidelines.

As he walked back to the changing rooms with the other players Simon asked, "Anyone seen Doug? He's just disappeared into thin air."

No one in the group appeared to have a clue of his whereabouts until Byron eventually chipped in, "The last time I saw him he looked a little queasy and was gasping before heading off in the direction of the changing room toilets."

As they approached the facilities a sheepish looking and blushing Doug greeted them, "Sorry lads, but I got myself locked in the toilets and have just been released by The Links' groundsman." After this admission he immediately departed, heading straight off to join his father who was waiting in his shiny black Jaguar E-Type. A trophy vehicle if ever there was one, surrounded by more mundane parked cars, including one belonging no doubt to the match referee, all seemingly envious of their illustrious neighbour but wisely keeping their respectful distance.

Although Simon thought Doug's rather sudden reappearance at the end of the game just as peculiar as his earlier sudden half-time disappearance he rather casually put it down to the fact that the guy was a strange one at that. Rather than dwell on the matter further he decided to head back to the Pork and Mutton with all of the remaining players and Fred, minus the family Tripolini who were off to light some candles at the Catholic church they had already frequented earlier that day.

CHAPTER 9:
Nothing Happens

Simon and his close footballing companions were unsurprisingly even more heartened by the draw against the Chi after a few pints had been downed and exploits retold. The game in hindsight, especially after all the drinks and stories had been so easily swallowed, so greatly cheered Simon that he forget all about of the demanding work schedule ahead of him and the need to cover colleagues enjoying their annual leave entitlement. No one had intended to stay for so long, or consume as much, at Fred's pub lock-in but his calling of time on this occasion was more willingly delivered and more warmly received. Most of this new band of brothers couldn't wait for the opening game of the new season against Bulman United. Only a few weeks ago Simon, and the other stalwarts in the group, would have viewed such a fixture with much greater trepidation and foreboding than they were showing when the beer was flowing. The continued fine hot weather also played its part in positively attending to Simon's uncharacteristic sunny cheery disposition ahead of a busy week and daunting fixture.

The first part of his work week went very much as planned and there were no major unwanted surprises or nasty hidden lemmas knocking him off his stride. Simon should have known from past experience that this was too good to last and on Wednesday, after another frenetic day at the Town Hall, his return home to some well-earned peace and quiet was torpedoed by a letter from the RaBHL (North). He accidentally tread on the envelope upon entry but there was no mistaking the league administration stamp on the back of the envelope now partly disguised by the added presence of his own shoe stamp. He was not expecting any communication from them and any thoughts he had of recriminations following the friendly match with The Tea Pot Cafe had been totally obliterated by the heavy drinking session and subsequent post match analysis. He decided to open the letter immediately and quickly digest its contents rather than second guess and worry over its likely pronouncement.

RaBHL (North) Football Administration Office

66b Lower Lenin Street
(over the Co-op)
East Shields

23rd July

Mr Simon Washington
Secretary, Pork and Mutton FC
3 Freedom Square
West Shields

Dear Sir

We have just received a match report from the referee, Mr Arthur Crown, who officiated your friendly game with The Tea Pot Cafe. He has brought to our attention several matters worthy of comment and consideration which we would like to relay to you in light of our previous communication which had concluded, I would like to take the opportunity to remind you, with the hope that Pork and Mutton FC's continued future participation in The Restaurants and Business Houses League (North), Division 2, would 'not result in your creating any additional problems in our administration of an established and well-respected league or any further unsettling of our staff'. It is a mere three weeks since I last had cause to write to you, on behalf of our organisation, and I am now occasioned to do so yet again.

Whilst we do not hold you directly responsible for the welcome that our officials received and the subsequent abuse generated by their pink change of kit we would emphasise to you that this has been entirely in consequence of your decision to change your team colours and adopt a new all black strip (the restrictions on alternatives to pink imposed by the the colour choices of other teams you will be playing against is not considered by us to be completely mitigating in this regard). The referee feels that both your team and your entourage could have been more understanding and supportive of himself and the linesmen in carrying out their duties and alleviating their anxieties. We have now been subsequently informed by one of the linesman that he will no longer officiate any of your matches given that he refuses to wear any colour but black and he has returned his bright pink change strip along with a conditional letter of resignation only to be activated should he ever be required to put on that kit again. I am only mentioning this particular fact to you to make you aware of the problems generated and to encourage your having a smidgen of empathy toward the challenges match officials face.

The match referee also reported on two other matters the likes of which he had never come across before (in his twenty years of impeccable service with us). As you are doubtless aware, it is a matter of tradition that players are numbered 1-11 with goalkeepers assigned number 1. We are informed that your goalkeeper not only wears number 0 but does so with missionary zeal, according to Mr Crown. Although we appreciate that the rest of your players are suitably and appropriately numbered we consider it strange for the conventional number 1 to be discarded in favour of zero. We would like to point out the irregularity of this but have to acknowledge, alas, that the rule book appertaining to the league does not have anything explicitly or implicitly to say on the matter. Given this, whilst you are at liberty to continue usage with 0 rather than 1, we would hope you would reconsider your going against established practice. Additionally, the referee has formally complained about your team advertising the wares of your sponsor on your shirts. He found this to be both distasteful and disrespectful (for the dead and also the living left behind). He further alluded to Mr Mortimer's unfortunate and unwarranted intervention into the conversation he was having directly with you at the time and its subsequent direction and tone. This raises possible serious breaches of protocol and etiquette. According to Mr Crown, he and your sponsor Mr Mortimer, got involved in a serious verbal altercation regarding the latter's advertising on your football shirts promising 'Heaven *under* Earth' as the referee politely puts it. We have spent hours examining documents, rules and regulations to find that there is nothing sadly, in statute or in writing, to prohibit your wearing of the sponsored shirts and any particular lettered advertising placed upon them. Unfortunately we did not anticipate such a tasteless thing ever happening to cater for outlawing it. The league administration hopes, however, that this unwelcome innovation will not be something that the game will generally embrace moving forward and that shirts will remain pure and unadorned (alongside having numbers limited to 1-12). As a body we are not against change per se but remain at a loss why you have to be so different to other teams in your league and why you continue to generate so much negative fallout.

This letter is for information and reflection only and does not require any direct reply or acknowledgement. League officials have been informed of its contents and what to expect when they take charge of your league matches should you decide to continue along your current path.

Sincerely yours,

Mr Iam Wright-Pratt
Senior Administrative Official
RaBHL (North)

Simon's first response was a sigh of relief that there was nothing here which could significantly threaten Pork and Mutton FC. Yes, the league administrators may have had their nose put out of joint but such irritations were of little consequence to Simon and he wouldn't bother relaying such information to his players prior to their opening game of the season a few days hence. He decided to immediately telephone Max about the contents of the letter given he was badly mentioned in dispatches, so to speak.

"Thanks for letting me know, Simon. I agree with you 110% that the league and its correspondent are merely belly aching and making another mountain out of a molehill." For Max, it was very much water off a duck's back and showed an organisation imprisoned in a given mindset displaying an abject poverty of imagination.

"Yes, typical Lower Lenin Street written diarrhoea, not to be taken too seriously."

"That referee, Arthur Crown, is also a complete idiot. It must be the first time that half a crown is less than a full shilling! Arthur - arfa, half a - get it?"

"Good one Max, although you don't need to literally spell it out for me, we only got rid of the old money a few years ago."

"Sorry, it was a bit unnecessary, just like their letter!"

"I must admit Max, I wasn't expecting this broadside from the league administration. It's somewhat ironic, isn't it?"

"Meaning exactly?"

"Well, let me spell this one out to you! I expected nothing from them, not even regarding Owen's choice of zero, yet nothing - by stirring them up, had clearly happened!" Simon replied, with a smile that Max could only sense by the way the words were delivered.

"Touché, and it's of nil consequence!"

"They have made so much ado about nothing. Our goalie would have been simultaneously delighted and displeased by that!" said Simon, thereby both trumping and triumphantly ending the conversation, believing he had playfully gotten at least one over on Max.

CHAPTER 10:
Tackling the Minotaur

Simon and Max kept the drama of the letter to themselves in order to prevent it derailing the limited preparations for the forthcoming opening game of the season against Bulman United, a team with a tough and brutal reputation that Pork and Mutton FC had much experience of in recent seasons. The continued lack of rain would ensure that the pitches at The Links would be almost as rock hard as their opponents. Those in the know were all too well aware of the likelihood of yet another bruising encounter against a savage tackling outfit renowned for its less than charitable or chivalrous approach to the game. These cloggers would ensure that Simon's newbies would endure a bone shaking baptism of fire.

Bulman United were a side to be avoided at the best of times and had almost been thrown out of the league last season for their ungentlemanly conduct and dire disciplinary record. It was not uncommon for the St. John ambulance to be in attendance prior to being called on the understanding that they would definitely be needed and that the injuries generated would be severe rather than slight. Their stretcher would always make an appearance when Bulman did.

Simon uneasily recalled the two games they shared last season and the manner of Pork and Mutton FC's defeats - 4-0 and 5-0 - and their having been literally kicked off the park and finishing with only eight hobbling men, on both occasions, left standing on the pitch when the final whistle was blown. It was not uncommon for teams to have to postpone fixtures after facing Bulman due to the consequent lengthy injury lists that usually followed. Such games tended to resemble war zones, with casualties to match, and the adjudicating officials acting more like modern day UN peacekeepers but without the famous blue helmets.

There was one game toward the end of last season that entered RaBHL (North) Division 2 folklore involving Bulman United and The Cretan Taverna which almost resulted in the former getting thrown out of the league and did result in the latter failing to get promotion out of the division. It had been the usual bad tempered and rather tempestuous Bulman fixture but on this occasion they were losing 4-1 with twenty minutes to go. Their recognised tactic had been to literally hammer the opposition rather than the match officials but on that day it was clearly not working. In those final twenty or so minutes they found another means to save the game following an alleged accident between their captain and the referee which resulted in a whistle blower being stretchered off for the first time in league history. One of the linesman took over and had his own touchline position taken up by the only apparent neutral volunteer now running the line with Basil (his accompanying poodle). This made for a strange sight as dog walker became dog runner, holding flag in one hand and lead in the other, and he and his mutt shared matching (now flowing) perms and associated linesman responsibilities. During the long stretch(er)ed out injury break the possibly innocent Bulman United captain had been engaged in a prolonged conversation with his manager and they supposedly hatched a plot to get the game abandoned by taking out the other match officials as accidentally as he had taken out the referee. This new tactic was quietly shared with their teammates with none of the re-start match officials, including the canine, knowing they were now marked men.

The genius of this oneupmanship ploy was just like something directly taken from the manual of Alistair Sim and his *School for Scoundrels*. It was, however, just as equally difficult to successfully employ as to concoct. The main initial target had to be the former linesman now promoted to on pitch activity but he proved more agile and skilful in avoiding bodily contact than his predecessor for the first ten minutes of his reign. His demise came from a Taverna corner when the two defending centre backs took him out by making him the unsavoury filling in their sandwich. He managed to get himself up from the floor but was now so unsteady on his feet and lacked the requisite lung power to sufficiently blow on his whistle that his reprieve only finally came when the last remaining fully functioning official arrived from the touchline to mercifully take over.

With ten minutes or so left on the clock and time running out for either Bulman United or referee number three with his team of man with dog and newly deputised wandering innocent bystander out looking for her lost cat, being almost press-ganged into temporary (almost military) service. Referee one was in A and E, referee two was in recovery in the changing rooms, and referee three was on his own covering no man's land. There was no shell hole to give him adequate respite and any bombardment would most likely be directed at him as Bulman's players would never stoop so low as to attack an animal or a lady, surely? The centre backs had done a good job in making their culinary delight look more spontaneous and less blatant than it actually was so that referee three was not fully aware of what could be awaiting him. The Cretan players were more clued in to what was apparently going on and started to escort the naive referee around the park and try and place protective cover around him. Regardless of these well meaning efforts, he did not last long and his end came inadvertently, courtesy of Basil and his owner, rather than more directly from the singular tactics now being employed by Bulman United. With only five minutes remaining an argument took place between their left back and the stand-in linesman which only served to over excite his dog which in turn attracted the attention of referee three who decided to book the player concerned. The player continued with his ungentlemanly conduct, however, and decided to show his disapproval of the decision by pushing referee three who then fell backward over Basil's lead and smashed the back of his head into the forehead of the poodle's owner and both were out cold. Basil's tongue helped to revive his master first but it was clear neither could continue. Referee two was brought back from the changing room half dressed and in no fit state to continue controlling a game such as this. He did carry out two decisions upon his return, however, sending off the wayward left back, after hearing witness testimony, and then duly abandoning the game allowing Cat Woman to continue, unmolested, in her search for missing pussy.

Bulman United somehow managed to survive the scandal and in the replayed fixture managed to get a 2-2 draw which cost The Cretan Taverna dear as this ensured they missed out on promotion by one point. It was one of the more intelligent Cretan players who provided Bulman United with its most fitting nickname of 'The Minotaur' in recognition of Ovid's classification of it being both 'part man, part bull'; a vicious and savage monster from Crete with the body of a man and the head of a bull. This characterisation of the ferocious playing style of Bulman, especially its taking no prisoners, quickly took hold and most teams became apprehensive of having to play against it, just as entering the Minotaur's labyrinth of old struck fear in the ancients.

Simon, and the other members of the original gang of four, purposely kept this tale to themselves otherwise a number of cry-offs in anticipation of cry-ons would probably have resulted. Warnings were only given once the team were together in the sanctuary of the changing rooms prior to battle and the distribution of the shirts.

"Lads, the team we face today have a well-deserved reputation as a hard team with a poor disciplinary record," Simon said as calmly as he could.

"Let's not hold back, Simon. They have a roll call of misdemeanours that sound more like indictments for war crimes!" Norman confessed.

"Yes, they aren't called 'The Minotaur' for nothing!" sounded Roger, striking added fear in some.

"What is this Minotaur por favor?" asked a clueless Salvator.

A few of the younger faces dropped even more on hearing a much edited and censored version of how their opponents got their nickname. Following this, some of the new players, quite understandably, appeared less keen to receive any shirt between 0 and 2-11. Doug was delighted to be given the gift of the blank number 13 shirt, held in reserve, safely removed from the dangers of mortal combat. Simon knew that the demands of leadership in the face of the enemy meant that he could not sit out this engagement and that the substitute number 12 shirt would have to be given to someone else, but whom? He looked around the room and there were clearly some willing takers but he also had to consider team formation and his mind had already been made up over his breakfast earlier that morning. He gave out the rest of the properly numbered shirts with the team lined-up as follows:

(0) Owen

(2) Mario   (5) Massimo   (3) Marco

(6) Salvator

(7) Roger   (4) Simon   (8) Stuart   (11) Norman

(9) Ever   (10) Jonathan

It was Byron who would be 'sacrificed' against 'The Minotaur' and he was a more than willing non-starter. The team formation was that which had played so well in the second half against the Tea Pot Cafe with Roger, rather than Byron, playing outside right out on the wing.

As the teams exited the now familiar portacabin changing facilities of The Links Simon was greatly surprised by the players warming up and about to face him. Yes, they were still wearing the somewhat ironic chaste and holy all white kit of last season but many previously identifiable brutes were no longer here. It provided him with some prematch relief which he shared with his teammates.

"Lads, our opponents are not fielding some of the dirtiest players from last season, and they have quite a few new players I haven't seen before," said a slightly relieved Simon.

"That's right. I can't see Hacker Ackerman!" answered Roger.

"Nor that Welsh geezer, Badass Baddams, who gave me a right good kicking," replied a far happier Norman.

Things improved further when Simon engaged their team captain directly in what turned out to be unexpectedly jovial conversation. He too was a welcome stranger to Simon and he openly confessed that "Bulman United are currently under orders from the league administration to get their house in order and clean up their act otherwise this stay of execution won't last long. That is why I am now here, and in this role."

"You don't know how much of a relief it is to hear that."

"We had a massive clear out of players who were unwilling to accept the conditions set out in a formal letter from Lower Lenin Street."

"It's also a great relief to know we aren't the only team receiving unsavoury notifications from Iam Wright-Pratt on behalf of RaBHL (North)."

The first twenty minutes or so of the game was nowhere near as dramatic as Simon, Roger, Norman and Stuart had long feared or the remainder of Pork and Mutton FC had just been given to expect. Both sides knew that the proof of the pudding was in the eating and there was a caginess and hesitancy in early proceedings just in case their opponents were unable to change their notorious past behaviour and face the wrath of the league. This made it much more like a practice match between two sides engaged in shadow boxing rather than really getting stuck into each other. This continued throughout the rest of the first half with very few notable efforts on goal or even very few efforts at anything if truth be told. As the half-time whistle blew and the unremarkable 0-0 scoreline took an unearned and undeserved breather it was clear to Simon what had just occurred. His players had spent most of that half doing their best to avoid full-on direct contact with Bulman on the basis of past experience, or information recently received, whereas their opponents were uncharacteristically doing their best to avoid doing their worst given the dire retribution such would occasion from the league administration. It had all turned into something of an anticlimax and the game was far less bitter than the half-time oranges and far more timid than even Doug had been. It had to be the most boring goalless half ever witnessed on The Links but at least Owen was ecstatic.

Simon told the team to inject a little more passion into the match but it was as if almost everyone had fallen into a collective stupor where lethargy rather than enterprise carried the day. The game played out to its logical conclusion with neither goal being really threatened and no name entering the referee's book, so even that remained blank. At least Owen had got what he had always cherished – a clean sheet – and wasn't in the least disappointed by the failure of his teammates to score what would have been a decisive goal. Still, Simon settled for sharing the points with Bulman given that they had never tasted anything but major defeats (and heavy casualties) against them in the past, but was less than delighted with the team's overall performance and lack of endeavour.

"Today we could have got our first ever win against those guys but missed the opportunity. It was a game crying out to be won and we blew it! Correction, we had neither the desire or energy to effectively do even that. We can do so much better," Simon ruefully said, knowing full well he would have accepted a point before the game, especially as the players had also come through unscathed.

"You mean we played the match like a game of blow football but without the puff?" Stuart suggested.

"That wasn't quite the point I was trying to make. I'm off in search of missing excitement and hope to watch some paint dry," Simon sarcastically concluded.

"Why would anyone look forward to that?" quizzed Salvator.

CHAPTER 11:
Letting Off Steam

The days following the game proved just as quiet as the match itself. For Simon there was no drama at work or at home and no more letters from the league administration, thankfully, hitting his doormat. So it was all quiet on the Western Shields front with no projectiles delivered from the East. This could all be the calm before the storm rather than the just experienced reverse. The upcoming match against FC Lokomotiv BRC (British Rail Catering), a totally unionised team composed of socialist leaning chefs and waiters, kitted out appropriately in deepest all red, was a fixture Simon always looked forward to. It had nothing to do with the likelihood of beating the opposition, his side always suffered heavy defeats, but everything to do with the comaraderie that the match usually engendered. FC Lokomotiv played by the rule book and in this league, given some of the teams, that was a real blessing of sorts. Pork and Mutton FC already had a point in the bank after only one game, rather than after playing five or more, and this helped add to his cheerful disposition.

It was the Saturday night before the Sunday morning fixture and Simon was still deliberating over the team line-up, or more correctly, the midfield and attack as the defence picked itself. It was not as if there was extensive competition for places and the team was still looking threadbare, actual bodies wise. He knew they could do with a player or two especially given Doug's unreliability and failure to demonstrate, as of yet, any footballing talent - so the blank number 13 shirt was rather easy to allocate. The team's inability to create or take the opportunity to score and collect all two points from beating a surprisingly neutered Bulman remained a matter of some concern. Simon decided to stick with the two forwards but strengthen their ranks by playing Roger alongside them. He knew this would be a risky venture given that they played a back three, albeit with Salvator playing just ahead of them. Should they need extra energy and stamina in the weakened midfield he would call on his reinforced attack to drop back to help out. Simon decided to make himself substitute with the expectation of replacing Norman for the second half should there be no unforeseen injuries or glaring loss of form before then. So the starting XI would be:

(0) Owen

(2) Mario   **(5) Massimo**   **(3) Marco**

(6) Salvator

(11) Byron   **(8) Stuart**   **(4) Norman**

(7) Roger   **(9) Ever**   **(10) Jonathan**

The allocated team shirts, formation and match tactics were passed on to the players as they stood outside the closed entrance gates of East Shields Welfare Ground, the shared home of BRC. This was Pork and Mutton's first true away game of the season and entailed for most of the players a coordinated two mile trek across town. It was 10.20am and the ground was still locked. As they looked through the ornate iron gates the new members of the team were clearly impressed by the pitch, facilities and a stand.

"Wow, they have a blinking stand!" said Doug loudly as he was somewhat nervously taken aback by all the splendour.

"We have entered the big time although we are still waiting to get in!" joked Roger.

FC Lokomotiv through some alleged beneficial political stitch-up had managed to bag use of a ground more familiar with a higher level of football, at least on a Saturday anyway, when East Shields Town amassed a fan base of upwards of 300. This was a Sunday, however, and for BRC, God or the socialist alternative had 'made them high and lowly, And ordered their estate' – and what an estate it was! The groundsman arrived a few minutes later to let them in and show them to the visitors dressing room – they had a dedicated groundsman and identifiable home and away semi-professional changing facilities – the Mutton's newbies were clearly further impressed. As the team got changed into their kit and Simon was about to give them a final gee up his words were drown out by the sound of singing coming from the home dressing room nearby. Their opponents had just burst into a chorus of *The Internationale*.

"Well, that should keep Lower Lenin Street happy, and any other political masters!" shouted Roger sarcastically, trying to be heard above the din.

"If they play like they sing then we should have no problem," said Jonathan, just as the noise finally subsided.

"Many of these commie caterers happen to be commis chefs but they made a right Eton mess of that! Too many cooks and all that I suppose!" Roger loudly joked, hoping that his opponents would also benefit from his humour.

The first half passed quickly and very successfully for Pork and Mutton FC. Simon's team selection appeared truly inspired with his lads walking off at half-time holding a 2-0 lead with Ever bagging both goals. The first came after only five minutes when he slotted home a glorious through ball from Stuart that had caught FC Locomotiv BRC cold. Several easy chances followed to increase their advantage but these were carelessly squandered - Jonathan was especially profligate in front of goal, twice firing over the bar when scoring would have been far easier and letting the woodwork intervene to tap out what should have been a comfortable tap in. Relief came, however, in the 40th minute when Ever volleyed in his second of the game from ten yards out following another assist from Stuart after a free kick was floated into the penalty area. Both goals for Ever without any intervention from his coiffure.

"This is going well, although it could have been even better," Simon said to his teammates as they formed a circle.

"Their playing is even worse than their singing! These fat ladies may have sung but the game's not over yet, not by a long chalk," added Norman.

"That's right Norman, no time to be complacent. Our dominance in the first half was largely owed to the good work of you guys in midfield containing any threats and creating goalscoring opportunities," Simon emphasised.

What was clear to Simon was that the midfield needed refreshment not only from the half-time oranges but from a fresh pair of legs. The problem was that Jonathan was playing below his expected level and clearly merited replacement.

"Listen lads, I'm going alter my earlier plan. Sorry Jonathan, but I'm making the switch now, and you're sitting out the second half."

"You are the boss, I suppose," Jonathan replied somewhat grudgingly.

"I am coming on to further bolster the midfield and play in the centre alongside Stuart allowing Byron and Norman to play a little wider than before, leaving Roger and Ever up top," Simon said. This was followed by nods all round, with the exception of Jonathan and disinterest of Doug.

The second half commenced, just like the first, with Pork and Mutton dominating possession and creating and missing chances to further extend their lead. The main culprit this time was Roger who let two great opportunities go abegging in the first ten minutes following the restart. FC Lokomotiv knew they had to make changes or they would be receiving seconds that they wouldn't care to digest. With thirty minutes left to go they made a substitution that helped turn their fortunes around. They brought on a player that neither Simon or his older established players recognised, but all had immediate cause to fear, due to the simple fact that he entered the fray wearing a pristine white pair of Hummel football boots.

"Look at him, what a poser!" scoffed Roger, firmly belonging to the conservative tradition of football boots being black and nothing else. He had even found Jonathan's Stylo Matchmakers to be an abomination - but had kept this to himself.

"Not so fast Roger, it takes courage to wear those and he may have the talent to match," Norman wisely counselled.

"If he's that good surely they would have played him from the start?" whispered Simon in reply, largely to console himself rather than Norman standing close by.

The guy in the Hummels immediately showed himself to be less of an arse and more of an artist. He took up a position in the centre of midfield facing Simon and Stuart and from that moment on took control and directly ran FC Locomotiv operations but was no Fat Controller. His dominance on the park allowed BRC to push up further into Pork and Mutton's final third. These relentless forays finally paid off in the 72nd minute when a mistimed clearance from Marco was seized upon and deftly stroked home, past a stranded Owen, by means of a right white boot. It was obvious to anyone present, not least the handful of Locomotiv supporters, that an equaliser was inevitable. It came in the 80th minute during their chanting of 'Red Army, Red Army' when a left white boot came into contact with the ball twenty yards out from goal. The end of the game could not come soon enough for Simon and his team and they were grateful to hang on and collect another point when the whistle blew at 2-2. They all knew that they should have put the match well beyond doubt before the entry of the Locomotiv messiah and his crucification of them. There was no doubt about it, they had let off steam and given up a victory that they had not tasted for almost a year.

At the conclusion of the game the Pork and Mutton FC players were invited for a drink in the East Shields Town Clubhouse by the BRC captain, and all accepted apart from Doug who did another hasty disappearing act after receiving some changing room ribbing. Simon was especially keen to take up the offer as he was intrigued to discover more about the man in the white boots. The home captain was more than happy to spill the beans and solve this particular mystery.

"Your Mr Hummel is our Dr Ally Balls. I will introduce you in a minute, if you like? He moved from across the border only a few weeks ago and was introduced to us by his cousin who already played for our team. He had some experience of playing in the third tier of Scottish football for a couple of teams just North of the Border when he was a medical student. He has now taken up permanent full-time employment at All Shields General Hospital A and E - so white boots man was also white coat man," said the BRC captain quite openly.

"So he's not actually a British Rail employee then?"

"More through family association really, but he's no ringer either. This is only his second appearance for us but it is also his last. He scored a hat trick in our 3-0 opening home match win against The Cretan Taverna, a display witnessed by the scout of East Shields Town who just happened to be at the ground on other business. He was quickly offered signing on terms a few days later. FC Lokomotiv, by mutual agreement, have now terminated his contract by cancelling his registration, this came into effect immediately after today's game," replied the opposition captain.

"I knew you and East Shields Town had a close thing going on what with the ground share and all. But he will be a difficult player to replace," Simon admitted.

"To be honest, we couldn't really refuse and didn't want to stand in his way either. His new team manager requested that he start his final outing for us as substitute with any involvement restricted to no more than 30 minutes - and then only if really necessary - you guys made that happen," he concluded.

"Now it all makes perfect sense. Also, as everyone in football knows, a team with Balls is always better than a team without!" Simon said, with a smile that similarly infected his opposite number.

CHAPTER 12:
Vlad the Inhaler

The less than convincing performance against FC Lokomotiv was now only a few days old, and still fresh in the memory, as Simon and the rest of the team gathered on The Links playing fields for a hastily rearranged midweek home game against The Irish Club. Such matches were rare and only happened before the dark nights closed in. This particular one was shifted from the forthcoming Sunday to allow the Gaelic contingent to spend a weekend away in Dublin at one of their players Stag Do. It had been a lovely late summer's day and the sunshine continued to prevail as Simon did a roll call. To his surprise, the one missing player yet to arrive was not the unreliable Doug but Byron. As the game approached kick-off without any sighting of his preferred selection, Simon had no choice but to give the number 12 shirt to Doug who was just as happy to receive it as the giver was to gift it. Following the unanticipated absence of Byron the team was set up as follows:

(0) Owen

(2) Mario   (5) Massimo   (3) Marco

(6) Salvator

(7) Roger   (4) Simon   (8) Stuart   (11) Norman

(9) Ever   (10) Jonathan

This would be the same formation that ended the previous game against BRC but with a slightly different mix of players with Jonathan keeping his berth up front and Roger taking up the Byron position in midfield. Simon duly hoped that they would not need to call on any contribution from Doug, if that could in any way be avoided.

Doug Mortimer had yet to be really involved for Pork and Mutton FC so far this season. He was a bit player yet to get a walk on part with a tendency to go missing even when inactive on the sidelines. Straight from the kick-off Simon noticed he had disappeared again.

Doug's rather lukewarm engagement with his father's patronage betrayed his youth alongside a hitherto undiagnosed uneasiness. Any teenage rebellion was largely channeled into his overall appearance that nostalgia would later term a Goth of sorts. His overall demeanour, pale skin, help in dispatching the dead, uncool interest in Victoriana, and tendency to hide away alone in his bedroom with curtains drawn in protection against the light, had all given rise to his nickname, when at school, of Dracula. He had let this slip, during an unguarded moment, when in touchline conversation with an out of form Jonathan during the latter part of the recent game against BRC. The latter had then subsequently mentioned it to Roger who, in turn, publicly announced it in the dressing room, to Doug's absolute horror and embarrassment. This led to some harmless well meaning banter, a few signs of the cross, and one of the Tripolini brothers playfully dangling a crucifix in front of a now red-faced, but no less anemic, Doug.

It was clearly apparent to anyone watching or playing, hence excluding the absent Byron and the wayward Doug, that the green and white hooped shirts of the Irish Club were starting to run rings around Pork and Mutton. They were scurrying all over the park like a team possessed. The future stag party participants were playing with an urgency and a purpose as if they were in a hurry to get the game over and make for the airport to order the first of many rounds. For all their efforts they were unable to make their advantage count in the final third of the pitch and seriously threaten Pork and Mutton's goal.

As they walked off for the pitch at half-time with the scoreline still blank, Roger remarked to Simon, "The Irish Club forwards were like a jigsaw, always going to pieces in the box!" As they laughed Simon received a tap on his shoulder.

"Sorry to interrupt, Simon, but I am unable to carry on. I've taken a bad knock to my left ankle and I can't run it off," Ever said with resignation in his voice.

This was the news Simon feared. He quickly grabbed a quarter orange segment and sucked on it as he surveyed the terrain around him. Doug was still nowhere to be seen.

"Anyone know where Doug's gone?" Simon asked forlornly.

"If it's OK, Jonathan and I will head off to see if we can find him, he might be locked in the toilets again?" Roger replied.

This small search party made its way straight for the timber facilities. After first checking the changing rooms without success they then went to the toilets where they heard the sound of coughing, gasping and wheezing coming from a locked cubicle.

"Is that you Doug? It's Roger, I'm here with Jonathan."

"Yes, just give me a second," was the affirmative reply coming from within.

The unlocking of the toilet door took a little longer than promised to those waiting patiently outside. Its eventual opening revealed an even paler looking Doug.

"Are you OK? You don't look well. We've come to get you. Ever is injured and we need you on the pitch for the second half," Jonathan's words immediately turned Doug an even whiter shade of pale.

Roger caught a glimpse of something blue, rather like a cigarette lighter, badly concealed in Doug's right hand which he suspiciously held behind his back.

"Have you been secretly smoking in there while we have been working our socks off? What are you hiding?" asked Roger indignantly.

"I've never smoked. I now know you two cannot keep a secret. I am asthmatic and this is my inhaler," Doug blurted out.

"We never knew, but that explains a lot!" Jonathan added.

"Well, who could have guessed?" said Roger somewhat ashamed.

Doug's escort were both taken aback by his news just as much as he had been by theirs.

"My symptoms are often triggered by stress although my father blames this on what he calls 'my all too frequent retreats to the unhealthy confines of an unhygienic bedroom'. Dad believed my involvement with the team would help rather than worsen my condition and I agreed to give it a go so long as he didn't disclose this to anyone. I wasn't looking for any sympathy or pity - there is plenty of that in the funeral business!" a more composed Doug explained.

Well, the cat was now truly out of the bag and Roger and Jonathan would have to let Simon know before deciding whether Doug was well enough to play the second half. The returning three joined Simon in a small huddle away from the other team members. Their quiet conversation seemed to help settle Doug down even more, perhaps aided by the relief borne from no longer carrying this particular secret. Simon offered Doug the opportunity not to play if he did not feel up to it. He declined this easy way out and in an uncharacteristic display of bravery opted to take up his place on the pitch. He was posted out wide on the right wing, where it was thought he would do least damage to his own team's chances, with Roger giving up that berth to take up the vacancy left by Ever up front.

For the first 25 minutes of the second half the sun continued to brighten up the late summer sky and the action duplicated much of the first half with the one notable exception of a goal to break the deadlock. Doug was supposed to stay out on the wing but more often than not had a tendency to drift back, or inside, to aid the opposition's attacking threat. He helped play them onside on two separate occasions only for their efforts to be foiled by a great save, courtesy of Owen, followed by a Massimo clearance off the line when all appeared lost. Doubts were beginning to be expressed whether it was such a good idea to have Doug playing at all and he helped confirm such sentiment by scoring an own goal. He somehow got himself between the passing lane of two Irish Club attackers in his own penalty area and intercepted the intended through ball. With the slow setting sun in his eyes serving to draw a veil over his vision his pass back to the goalkeeper went inadvertently directly into the net. His team mates were less than overjoyed but their opponents were now fittingly cock-a-hoop.

Storm clouds were slowly gathering both meteorologically and for Doug. There were calls from some teammates to get him off and for the next 15 minutes he was, once again, a sad lonely figure now exiled on the margins receiving neither ball nor favour.

"Just hug the touchline and stay out of the way!" he was instructed by his captain.

"Things are starting to look black," Roger said to Jonathan, pointing to the heavens rather than the scoreline.

Things were were set to change for Doug. He was about to re-enter the spotlight in a more positive way just as the clouds came rolling in to register an eerie darkness. In the 85th minute he picked up a loose ball which had uncannily drifted out to where he was standing and he charged directly for the Irish goal, head typically cast down, dribbling as he went, ignoring friend and foe alike. Within a matter of seconds the ball was in the net and Doug deserved full credit for putting it there, smashing it in from 10 yards after skilfully evading the last line of defence with a neat sidestep. Everyone present was amazed and even the referee felt compelled to congratulate him, with his applause generating ire among some of the stag bound revellers. As the light continued to fade, and appropriately, in the dying minutes of the game, Doug received his first intended pass from a fellow team member, a gorgeous through ball played out to the right edge of the penalty area by Roger which he instantly dispatched into the top left hand corner of the goal. Further celebration followed, as did the final whistle. In the space of around five minutes (and one written paragraph) he had finally made himself part of Pork and Mutton FC and its limited folklore.

The narrow and very late 2-1 victory served to slowly brighten up and intoxicate the atmosphere in the changing room. It took a while in coming, but after some delay, the shock of success, somewhat begrudgingly, gradually triggered friendly banter rather than the more usual silence and despair engendered by the countless defeats of seasons gone by. Doug did not partake in the ensuing jovial exchanges but was the obvious subject of most of it; he had returned to the margins and sat in a corner having voluntarily withdrawn himself. The team clearly appreciated his contribution and now wanted to welcome him into the fold.

"Heah, Doug, what's up man? Great job out there. You ain't Dracula any more but Vlad the Inhaler!" Roger loudly suggested, with only those in the know getting it.

"Roger really! Show some sensitivity man, it's not something he'd want you to advertise. Can I suggest another instead, today Doug has finally made himself Count!" Simon responded.

"We have just unearthed a talent that had been buried for some time!" Norman chipped in, and it was this comment that finally drew a smile from its target.

"What are you guys talking about?" asked a confused Salvator unable to translate the words hidden between the lines.

CHAPTER 13:
Nobbled by Baying Munching

A fter returning home from the subsequent over-indulgent victory celebrations at the Pork and Mutton Simon received a late telephone call from Byron.

"Hi Simon, Byron here, sorry about disturbing you at this hour, but I would like to apologise for not getting to the game tonight."

"Well, we were all surprised by your no show. I know that it's not like you Byron. At least the good news is that we won and Doug made good."

"Profuse apologies once again, and I deeply regret not being there to be part of it. I'm glad that my unintended absence didn't cost the team. I would like to explain what transpired to prevent me getting to The Links. It's a bit of a long story…"

Simon listened attentively to the lengthy account relayed to him with his concentration only occasionally broken by either the sound of Byron feeding coins into the machine or the loud tapping on the external glass of the telephone box by disgruntled people impatiently waiting to use the facility.

Byron commenced his long-winded narrative by stating that as a hard-up student he had taken the opportunity to add to his grant by doing various part-time jobs. Apart from his new occasional bar work at the Pork and Mutton he also did some seasonal work for the Town Hall and the Post Office. The former involved doing electoral registration during the late Summer and the latter the Christmas post, both saw him pounding the streets of West and East Shields. Neither occupation had given rise to a serious mishap before, until now, and it was the Town Hall work which served him ill this day.

Having a couple of hours free, well in advance of kick-off, Byron decided to finish off his electoral registration quota. There were eight houses in a street nearby to where he lived who had not returned their forms. As such it was his job to call at said houses and complete the forms and get an occupier's signature otherwise they would lose their right to vote and possibly incur a hefty fine too.

Only once had someone refused to agree to this process when they slammed the door in front of Byron's face. He decided to push the form through their letterbox and as he turned away the door opened and the irate and rude occupant came rushing out loudly bawling and clasping the unwanted paper. The man then tore the form into pieces in front of a bemused Byron before stuffing it into his own mouth and eating it. At this juncture, Byron thought it wise to hasten a retreat and provide no additional paper to feed the man's disagreeable appetite. Most people were quite happy to receive his assistance in completing the forms and had not returned them due largely to procrastination or forgetfulness rather than any malice.

Byron had found that a number of old people kept their front door open so that when he knocked they would invite him in calling out from a room somewhere in the house. Sometimes the cry would come from a bedroom where, often as not, an ageing pensioner would be bed-ridden. Byron had become accustomed to all this.

He had successfully completed seven of the electoral registration forms and had only one to go. The last person on his list was recorded as a Mr Boris Gladbach. Byron failed to mention to Simon that he had mused about the name with his mind drifting to both an attractive girl in his class at the Poly with the same surname, who he hoped might live here and answer the door, and the team Borussia Mönchengladbach taking the German Bundesliga by storm. Both were pleasant thoughts as he had a growing interest in girls and a lengthier interest in football. Being somewhat so preoccupied, he knocked at the door and heard a noise he assumed to be a voice welcoming him in. The door was open and he became disappointed that it was probably not the girl but an elderly person who was requiring his services. The noise appeared to come from a room at the end of a long corridor. Byron shouted hello as he entered the inner room to find a middle aged man rising up from his bed in a somewhat confused and surprised state. In an instant Byron noticed the now suddenly baying and snarling large dog in the corner of the bedroom agitated by it's owner startled demeanour. He thought it wise to get out rather than reason with either occupant and immediately headed back from whence he came mistakenly leaving the bedroom exit door open. Byron was reasonably quick but the dog was quicker and before he could get to the front door and close it for the safety of the street the dog had gained up on him. It announced it's unwelcome arrival with it's teeth embedding themselves into his posterior. This served to satisfy the dog's sense of intrusion and Byron somehow managed to depart the scene but hardly in one piece. This was to be the second time on electoral registration duty that Byron had fed someone else's angry appetite, the man eating the form and now the dog munching at his buttocks.

Instead of heading for the match he had to to attend All Shields General Hospital A and E to receive a tetanus injection. The giant needle was finally administered, after three hours of waiting, by a familiar face - the Hummel white boots man who had previously also left his mark against Pork and Mutton FC.

"That's quite a story. No one could make all that up. What a night for all of us! By the way, how is your flesh wound? At least you showed Balls!" Simon said to lighten the mood.

"It's a bit tender presently and my mother has suggested I buy an inflatable rubber ring to sit on when at lectures. No chance of that! I won't be missing any more matches that's for certain too."

"Listen Byron, you were just unlucky and possibly the victim of mistaken identity. You thought you were facing Boris's Munching Gladbach but ended up nobbled by Baying Munching!"

CHAPTER 14:
Blitzed Bombed
bei Bierkeller

Three games unbeaten, with four points in the bag (two for the win, and a point each for the draws). This placed Pork and Mutton FC in the top half of the league table lying in fifth place. This was unfamiliar territory and these dizzy heights reached were liable to give Simon vertigo. He was aware that their success to date was built on fragile foundations. The squad was limited and inexperienced in key areas of the pitch. There were bound to be major challenges ahead that would test the team's vulnerability over a 30 game season.

The midweek match against the Irish had freed up the coming weekend which gave some of Simon's teammates extra licence to freely go out on the lash. Roger managed to talk Owen, Jonathan and Byron into joining him for a Saturday night drinking session at the German Bierkeller located in the disappearing no-man's land between East and West Shields following urban sprawl and the search for building lebensraum. The selection of said venue was largely, but not entirely, based upon the quality and lower price of drinks alongside the even lower cut dresses of the Fräuleins working there. Pork and

Mutton's forthcoming game, a week hence, would be against The Deutscher Bierkeller, and Roger, somewhat strangely, also excused the visit on the grounds of viewing it as an opportunity to carry out some much needed reconnaissance on their future opponents, given that a number of the players worked there, albeit in lederhosen. It would be a rather bizarre spying and scouting mission given he would be unlikely to glean much footballing information from the men cooking in the kitchen or the others playing in the Oompah Band. What he, and Simon (as well as Norman and Stuart) already knew is that The Deutscher Bierkeller had a very good team and that they had only narrowly missed promotion last season on goal difference to Cafe Versailles and this time around they would be demanding reparations.

The Bierkeller itself had only been established five years ago - with the team representing it of even younger vintage, welcomed into the league two years later following the rather sad demise of FC Strudel after a suspicious fire destroyed the premises of its sponsor. It was a very popular venue, enjoyed by a more permissive, relaxed and tolerant generation, in an age when any lingering wartime hostilities were fast disappearing. Byron, himself, was a good example of this. His planned attendance was not driven by any thoughts of revenge following his recent escapade with the Germans, if a dog can have a nationality. He had heard through the grapevine that Mädchen Gladbach worked there and he still harboured hopes that their paths might cross. He had also benefitted from being on a town twinning exchange to the Ruhr when he was sixteen and looked forward to re-kindling some of those happy moments alongside getting the opportunity to once again practise his O'Level German. Owen and Jonathan were going simply to enjoy the booze and firm up their emergent friendships with Roger.

As was usual in such places, especially on a crowded Saturday night, the beer was flowing fast and the noise of loud music, aided by even louder boisterous conversation, was deafening. To make any any sense of what was being said, the small group huddled closer together, just like those around them, making them look more like close comrades in arms conspiring to carry out a putsch rather than merely recent acquaintances. Byron was clearly out of his depth swimming in this sea of alcohol hoping that a lifeboat of sorts in the shape of Fräulein Gladbach would drift by to rescue him.

"Who are you looking for? Is this conversation boring you?" Jonah asked Byron.

"No, but to be honest I've heard the story of when Roger met Owen countless times already tonight."

Roger was not allowing himself to take much of Owen's repeated reminiscences in, his out on the town radar was already kicking in, allowing his mind, and more importantly, his eyes to wander. They did not have to travel very far as the wench servicing their table was becoming increasingly attractive as the empty glasses were stacking up around him. Unattached girls, whether singularly or in a group, did not attend such places, which to Roger meant that the female employees were more likely to be fairer game and rather more chased than chaste. A fox can only be caught by the hounds once, but these girls had been caught many times, or so he thought to himself.

"Guten Abend gnädiges Fräulein!" Roger said after being sufficiently primed by Byron.

"So you speak German? Wie heißt du?" she replied engagingly and with familiarity.

"Sorry? No, not really. Not at all in fact, if truth be told."

"She's asking your name Roger," Byron unnecessarily interceded.

"Don't tell him, Pike!" joked Owen taking his cue from an episode of Dad's Army.

"So Roger Pike, what can I do for you? My name is Lotte and I'm at your service."

"I wish that were true! I mean the service not my surname, which isn't Pike, and you are definitely a her not a Herr!"

"Now behave yourself, like a good English gentleman."

"Who said I was either good or a gentleman?"

Endless replenishment of alcohol served to make Roger forget another key principle of such establishments, with male employees being exceedingly over protective of their female co-workers. Lotte was happy to flirt with Roger, no doubt boosting any potential tip alongside business profits. and started developing what appeared to be a genuine liking for him during her frequent forays to the table to answer their needs and recover discarded plates and vessels. These were the days when exchanging meaningful glances, well before the advent of exchanging often meaningless mobile phone numbers, could be the start of something big. Roger was getting gradually stone(d) with his stein, increasingly intoxicated not only with the heady brew on offer but with the girl too, and he was sold.

"If I play my cards right__" blurted Roger.

"You look more like a busted flush!" Jonah said, interrupting not only Roger but an increasingly tiresome Owen who began playing the same old record from his personal jukebox.

Byron saw this as his cue to float away from the table and not only relieve his scarred buttocks from the increasingly inhospitable wooden benches but to search for the Gladbach girl who had failed to answer his earlier distress signal. Before double vision set in, and the loss of his bearings, he managed to catch a fleeting glimpse of her, some distance away, trying to look after a rowdy group of customers. Negotiating the heavy traffic on the sea lanes all around him, he unglamorously sailed into her latest port of call and announced his arrival by slipping on some misplaced German mustard that had found its way to the bottom of his shoe. This sent him flying into her, and the table she was attending to, inadvertently adding some spice to an already heated debate taking place over the bill. He thought it best to make an embarrassing retreat, turning his back on a Gladbach for the second time in a matter of days. Returning to his own table only to find Owen once again immersed in delivering the same groundhog day monologue while his other companions sought solace in pouring liquid refreshment down their throats while politely faking attention.

As the night moved toward the midnight hour, Roger's advances toward Lotte became more pronounced and noticeable due to the drink and dissipation of customers heading for the night clubs. She made little effort to repel such advances and he was getting even more of her attention than earlier. Unfortunately for Roger, others too had their eyes drawn toward him. Unbeknownst to him, a member of the Oompah Band also had affections for Lotte, which had been reciprocated on many an occasion, and they were becoming increasingly jealous of the evolving situation.

Big Karl played the large tuba and had the frame to handle not only that but anything else coming his way. He stood two metres tall in his socks before he put on either his shoes or football boots (when playing up front for the Deutscher's). There was only so long that he was willing to blow his increasing frustration into his eighteen foot long instrument. It was all about to quickly come to a head.

"It's getting late and I think we are all spent in more ways than one," said Jonah before signalling for the bill.

"Lotte, don't I get a goodnight kiss?" Roger asked as she arrived with the tally.

"You can have a little one but nothing more," before placing a friendly kiss on Roger's cheek.

"Come on, don't be shy, you can do better than that!" the recipient said as he rose awkwardly from the table to make a land grab of a cuddle.

The waitress offered little by way of resistance to either Roger's arms or his charms. Big Karl had enough and stormed from the stage at lightening speed for such a big man, approached Roger with a less cordial reckoning for the night's entertainment, and laid him out cold with a single blow to the chin.

"He's clearly Roger and out!" cried Jonathan but no one was laughing.

None of those left on the premises, in a fit state, missed any of the commotion. Fräulein Gladbach, rushed to console a tearful Lotte while Owen acted to restrain Big Karl as Jonathan and Byron did their best to revive the fallen.

"Karl, Liebchen! What have you done!" cried Lotte.

"What have I done! What about him? And you are no Hildegard of Bingen!"

The owner of the Bierkeller was not best pleased with what he too had just witnessed. He took Big Karl aside, seemingly only mildly rebuking him, and giving him his marching orders to return to his fellow musicians and keep step with them. This allowed Owen to help scrape Roger up from the floor and the two girls to finally compose themselves and offer smiles in the direction of the bruised (whether buttocks, chin, or ego). Herr Weber, said proprietor, looked little fazed by events, probably because they were not that uncommon.

"I am sincerely sorry about this. As recompense I will reduce your bill by half and also organise a taxi for your party," he said.

"It was good to see you, however, briefly," Byron told the Gladbach girl just before leaving.

"I hope to see you at the lecture on *War and Peace* timetabled for Monday," she invitingly replied.

Lotte failed to offer Roger any such future comfort and it appeared that he had already had his Lotte.

The events witnessed at the Bierkeller were agreed to remain there and not be shared with other members of the team. Simon was still just as much in the dark when the Pork and Mutton FC players gathered a week later at the Old Temperance Memorial Ground, somewhat ironically, home to Deutscher Bierkeller and located within a hand grenade's throw of that establishment. This all served to bring less than happy memories to Roger, whose thoughts quickly passed to Big Karl, whose arrival, towering over the rest of the other soon to be opponents, could not be ignored. Spirits were clearly being stirred, on a ground designed for abstinence. Simon, however, had other alcohol related problems to deal with which were also not his doing, and they came from an unanticipated source. The usually wholesome Tripolini brothers looked worse for wear..

"All three of you look as terrible as each other. Have you caught something infectious? I trust you wouldn't be here if you had!" Simon said as he greeted their arrival.

"Our condition is not infectious but it is self-inflicted," Marco replied, holding his head.

"We were at our Aunt's 60th Birthday party yesterday and we all seriously over-indulged on grappa," Mario confessed, before swallowing what looked like an aspirin.

"We hadn't drank that stuff for a while and it took us all by surprise. I wouldn't be surprised if we were still well over our limit!" Massimo added, while simultaneously shaking his head in disbelief at what they had stupidly done to themselves.

Simon could ill afford to drop any of the triplets nor could he further add to their confusion by changing the defence around immediately prior to kick-off.

His most pressing problem before leaving the house this morning was what to do about Byron, Doug and himself with regard to the team set-up against the Germans. Over his breakfast tea and toast he had mulled over the options and finally decided that Byron would keep his usual place and Doug would be substitute, especially given that it was turning into a fine clear Sunday morning, which the triplets would fail to appreciate. Simon sacrificed his own chance to play and made himself reserve given Doug's last display merited a promotion of sorts. The starting line-up was becoming a familiar one:

(0) Owen

(2) Mario   **(5) Massimo**   **(3) Marco**

(6) Salvator

(11) Byron   **(8) Stuart**   **(4) Norman**

(7) Roger   **(9) Ever**   **(10) Jonathan**

The Deutscher Bierkeller were dressed like the West German national team in their white shirts and black shorts. It was a time before replica kit became freely available but they came pretty close to the real thing. Simon thought that they looked like a pretty classy outfit and was particularly impressed by the giant number nine at the halfway line showing great skill at keepy uppy for such a big man, totally unaware that his admiration had fallen on Roger's nemesis. Simon's eyes were then cast upon the Tripolini brothers and their rather less than pristine state. How would they be able to cope on this of all days?

Things started to unravel for Pork and Mutton immediately after Big Karl officially kicked-off when Roger decided to kick-off on his own without the permission of the referee's whistle. The German had simply tapped the ball forward to his inside right and made a run out to his left for a return pass close to the vicinity of Roger who decided to take him out with a very early calling card of a bruising slide tackle.

"We'll have none of that my lad! Name?" said the referee.

"Chamberlain," answered Roger.

"What did you do that for Roger, it makes no sense?" a clueless Simon added.

The resultant Bierkeller free kick was directed into the box but posed little initial threat given Big Karl hadn't recovered quickly enough to spearhead this attack. Two of the Tripolini brothers, Massimo and Marco, inadvertently went to clear the innocuous ball and collided with each other. The ball reached the safety of the touchline but the defenders were less lucky with both looking the worse for wear following this most recent get together.

Roger's week long simmering thirst for revenge had yet to be fully satisfied and he was determined to ignore collateral damage such as this or any casualties from friendly fire. Just as Big Karl was managing to run off the knock, and barely ten minutes into the game, Roger repeated the medicine, albeit with a slightly higher dosage. His seeing red was brought to an end by the referee ordering him off the park. It was the second time in just over a week that Roger was out again.

"I don't know what this is about Roger, something's up, this is not like you. You're not a dirty player and you don't have a reputation for putting it about, not on a football pitch anyways!" Simon said.

"Just leave it for now, it's a long story," was all Roger could say in response.

Not another one! Simon thought to himself, having already been privy to Byron's lengthy tale of woe. They were down to ten men with a full eighty minutes left to play. The only good news was that the giant German was hobbling again.

Following Roger's departure things settled down for a short while as Big Karl worked off the after effects of the foul to move less gingerly. His return to match fitness was heralded in the 24th minute when he headed in from a corner, climbing well above the two, still confused, Tripolini brothers left flailing in his wake. It was clear that Big Karl was the main focal point of the German attack and he was marshalling his troops all over the field to service that end. He added a second just before half-time when he easily lost his Tripolini markers to connect with a cross sent over from the far right wing. Being dazed and hungover there were times when the Italians didn't know whose side they were on, appearing less partisan in their affiliation. Simon knew he did not have the option to replace them and that they needed patching up at the interval otherwise a heavy defeat was guaranteed.

In order to strengthen the defence for the second half, Simon asked Norman to drop back and sit alongside Salvator in front of the struggling back three, with Jonathan falling into the midfield berth he vacated. This left Ever running a lonely unforgiving furrow up front to provide an outlet of sorts until his energy gets fully sapped for Doug to then take over this burden. Such a set up was unlikely to harvest any goals but at least it might just stop the Bierkeller's potent centre forward from adding to his tally. Such hopes did not last long as he helped himself to a third and a hat-trick in the 55th minute when he tapped in from a couple of yards after the ball ricocheted off Massimo's rear to put Pork and Mutton further behind. Big Karl was running amok for the second time in a week, but on this occasion to the credit of those he represented. He added two more before the end, both headers, one a forehead bullet from another corner involving a Tripolini error and the other a near post glancing affair after cutting in from the left to meet the cross.

Doug's entry into the game had come slightly earlier than planned but he offered little in terms of respite or reward with his cutting an even lonelier silhouette against the bright cloudless sky. The German centre-forward's potent air raids had delivered a resounding victory for the Germans whilst the British (with their Australian, Italian and Brazilian allies) had seriously bombed. Much of their undoing came from earlier alcohol engendered events outside of Simon's control, Roger's getting blitzed at the Bierkeller and the Tripolini's doing the same at their Aunt's 60th birthday celebrations certainly damaged the cause. A 5-0 drubbing was not to be welcomed even though such a scoreline was not unfamiliar in seasons previous to this one and against teams such as this. They had lost here last season, just as heavily, when Big Karl had not been around or awarded his wings.

"Who is that guy?" Simon asked the opposition captain as they shook hands at the end.

"Oh, that's Big Karl Göring, and he's just got another one over on your Mr Chamberlain!"

"Another one? Your team seem a little too familiar with our Roger?"

"I think it would be better if you ask him yourself," he replied before abruptly leaving to join in his team's victory celebrations.

The silence of the changing room was broken by Simon asking Roger outright, "What's going on between you and their big fella, Göring is his name I'm told?"

Jonathan, Owen and Byron shared nothing but guilty glances between themselves. The tension in the room was rising with everyone awaiting a response from Roger.

"What a player! He certainly made sure we were göring, göring, gone!" Stuart said, being first to reply, without any encouragement from the floor.

"I don't care to hear his name thank you! We can talk about this privately later Simon, if you don't mind?" said Roger somewhat defiantly.

"Well I think all the team deserve an explanation now not later! Whatever joy we shared from beating the Irish Club has now been flattened by the German Luftwaffe!" an irritated Simon answered.

CHAPTER 15:
Unholy Orders

The fallout from the Bierkeller match was concluded with Simon receiving another less than cordial letter from Iam Wright-Pratt, Senior Administrative Official, RaBHL (North) informing him of their ongoing displeasure being further added to by their having to formally sanction Mr Roger Chamberlain - 'suspended for two games due to violent and ungentlemanly conduct unbecoming of a league player'. This was another Chamberlain, Simon thought to himself, who had retaliated somewhat belatedly against initial naked German aggression, but unlike Neville, he had not been so easily appeased. But Pork and Mutton FC had the luxury of neither guns nor butter and were now stretched to the limit player resources wise, with only twelve less than fully fit players to call on for the upcoming couple of matches, unless they could find some new recruits.

Byron got one of the art students at the Poly to customise an old poster of Lord Kitchener from the First World War calling for volunteers, but crudely replacing his Lordship's head with a football, and now newly titled 'Footballers - Pork and Mutton FC Needs You'. This was hung up on a pillar near the bar but failed to garner any takers in time for the forthcoming match against Austin's Fryers.

Terry Austin owned two large fish and chip restaurants located in East and West Shields respectively named Austin's Fryers. Trade was brisk but none of his orders were holy and sole was definitely not on the menu. The nucleus of the team he managed and patronised were the male fryers who worked in his establishments alongside those who were part of his supply chain including local fishermen and the vegetable (potato and pea) wholesalers. The team were an average performing outfit quite unlike Terry's business which was not only hugely popular but had several awards to its name. He continued to willingly financially support Austin's Fryers FC in the hope that it would emulate the success of his restaurants. He only allowed those who were primarily involved or somehow connected with his business to wear his colours, either through their wage packet or their invoice. Just like a religious order you needed to be, or become, an insider to gain entry. But good fryers were not always good footballers, and vice versa, and his direct suppliers had to be product and price sensitive ahead of their football orientation. This impacted on, and often hampered, player recruitment; being based on a lower order priority to that of his main business to which he was clearly avowed.

Austin's Fryers had been members of the league for some six years without gaining promotion or finishing in the bottom four. Like most teams, they found Pork and Mutton FC to be reliable donors of maximum points and would be expecting much of the same this time around. If Terry Austin had cast a cursory glance at the league table he would see that his team were lying in fifth place on five points (W2 D1 L1) with Pork and Mutton three places below them on four points (W1 D2 L1) albeit with a familiar southernly trajectory. His confidence and expectation would have remained somewhat unshaken.

Six years ago Terry had spent more time deliberating on his team's colours than on the financial implications of his support. After much thought he had decided on an all gold strip including tops, shorts and socks. There had been two main reasons behind this. The first reflected his boyhood support for Wolverhampton Wanderers when growing up in the Black Country before heading up North to marry the future Mrs Austin. The second related to his other great love, fish and chips, as the colours would not only serve to resemble the finish on his award winning batter but also the gold standard he wished to achieve. He also quite liked the idea, as an afterthought mind you, that others may start referring to his team (and his business acumen) as 'Terry's All Gold'.

With no extra volunteers forthcoming, Simon had to make do and mend with the already drafted. The only decision he had to make was whether to play himself or Doug and the implications of that for team formation. Simon decided to go with caution rather than valour and include himself in a four man midfield, with only two up front, to help bolster a defence now lacking in confidence. Doug would, once again, be held in reserve, but this time as a substitute:

(0) Owen

(2) Mario   **(5) Massimo**   **(3) Marco**

(6) Salvator

(7) Byron   **(4) Simon**   **(8) Stuart**   **(11) Norman**

(9) Ever   **(10) Jonathan**

Just before kick-off Roger turned up to cheer his colleagues along and joined Doug on the touchline. It was clear from his demeanour and conversation that he was disappointed in letting his colleagues down. He knew that the team could ill afford the behaviour he displayed against the Bierkeller but at least he had the courage to face the fallout and this was appreciated by Simon and the others as they acknowledged his presence in their various friendly ways.

"Good luck lads. Howay Pork and Mutton!" Roger shouted loudly in response.

"Yes, come on," was the best a timid Doug came out with.

Roger's presence on the touchline was over-shadowed by the Fryers manager's loud luminous gold tracksuit which successfully competed with the morning sun and acted as a beacon to his players.

"What's he look like, a proper Charlie! His outfit's already giving my eyes jip!" Roger announced.

"Roger, keep it down, we don't want any more trouble," Doug spluttered.

"You talking about me mate?" an approaching Terry asked.

"No, no, you misheard, sorry. Roger was talking about the referee. You look great," Doug answered trying to de-fuse the situation.

"Yes, terrific, should be on a catwalk, honestly," Roger unhelpfully added.

"Roger is it? Well Roger, you might be jolly now but you bloody won't be if you don't button it," Terry promised before the referee's whistle made him retreat.

"Ponce," whispered Roger.

The game started surprisingly brightly for Pork and Mutton FC with two glorious opportunities in the first ten minutes, both of which were squandered by the two forwards equally. Jonathan fluffing his lines after being one on one with their goalkeeper and Ever misdirecting an unchallenged header over the bar from five yards. Nothing of any subsequent significance took place before the referee blew for half-time and mercifully ended what had become a somewhat dour encounter. The oranges, too, were lacking in flavour.

As Simon called the players together for a team talk he looked across at his opponents forming a huddle with their dressed Jimmy Saville lookalike and wondered whether Terry will fix it, as he knew they would be more disappointed than he with the current scoreline.

"We're doing fine lads, keep it up! We are holding our own and I want to keep things as they are. We should be one or two up rather than nil-nil. Doug, I'll only bring you on if there's an injury or inclement weather suddenly intervenes," Simon declared.

"Right, fine, no problem," said Doug, who was now quite enjoying being with Roger on the touchline.

"I do want a little more from the four of us in midfield. We need to stamp our authority on the game and stop it drifting away. If we take ownership that will create more opportunities and goals will come. Let's go get them!" Simon shouted trying to re-energise his troops into action.

Things did not turn out as hoped, however, as Pork and Mutton FC found themselves a goal down within five minutes of the restart. An innocuous Fryers cross was deflected out for a corner and an equally aimless and harmless centre into the penalty area somehow found its way into Owen's goal courtesy of Salvator's attempted clearance lacking any compass. Simon told his players to keep their heads up and not allow themselves to get downhearted by this latest piece of bad luck. His vocal motivation had an impact and for the next twenty minutes or so they dominated possession without directly hurting the opposition. Pork and Mutton's reward finally arrived in the 75th minute when Simon found himself free in the box to hammer in a low drive from ten yards following a crafted pass by Byron. The game then once again settled down, just like the first half, with little to report with neither side having the courage to go all in.

Simon and Terry had to settle for a 1-1 draw with both parties trying to take something positive from the game. Pork and Mutton FC had managed to save a game that they would usually lose and Austin's Fryers had picked up an away point at The Links (with Terry not mentioning the fact that they shared playing here with a number of teams, including Simon's).

As he walked off the pitch Byron said to Simon and Roger that, "The team were getting quicker on the draw than Tony Hart."

On overhearing this Salvator butted in saying, "We have more draws than a chest!"

"A chest has drawers not draws," answered Roger, aiming to correct Salvator's less than perfect English.

"Yes, that is what I said we are, drawers!" the Brazilian cheerfully replied.

They all had to laugh at how he had somehow cleverly salvaged his error just as the team had done his earlier one. But there was some truth in it, five league games played and three draws. Glass half full, only one defeat; glass half empty, only one win.

CHAPTER 16:
Greeks Bearing Gifts

P ork and Mutton FC now found themselves in 9th place in the division with their next game against the team lying directly below them, The Cretan Taverna. The Greeks were clearly underperforming and were obviously still suffering from getting the stuffing, and their promotion hopes, knocked out of them by Bulman United's disgraceful conduct last season.

With only three days to go before match day Simon was still awaiting a response to the call to arms left hanging, just as he was, albeit in the Bar. He did receive some team news but it was a subtraction rather than an addition to the squad. Jonathan Cruft informed him that he had twisted his ankle coming down a stepladder while papering his hallway and would be unavailable for selection. Thanks to Jonah, it would now be Simon's turn to paper over the cracks and he may be a roll or two light.

It was Fred, or rather Doris, the cleaner at his Pub, who was about to offer the team a possible lifeline. During her weekday morning employment she had noticed the poster and had casually mentioned it to a few of her neighbours in passing and then thought nothing more of it until a stranger came knocking at her door. He had introduced himself as

Yiannis Loukanis, the son of, and apprenticed to, a local butcher in West Shields, and a friend of a son of one of her neighbours. He had heard through this grapevine that Pork and Mutton FC were recruiting and he was presenting himself to that end. Within the hour Yiannis found himself in front of Fred carrying on this conversation having been sent there immediately by Doris who'd already guessed the team were desperate by their having recourse to such a naff poster. Being a Friday evening, Fred managed to contact Simon by telephone and arrange an immediate meeting at the Pork and Mutton.

Simon listened to Yiannis outlining his footballing credentials and his reason for wanting to sign up. Needless to say, he was well taken by what was disclosed, especially previously having trials for a couple of teams at a level well above that which he was willing to now join. Yiannis was nearing the end of his apprenticeship and about to fully commit to his father's business and was more sure of himself than he had been earlier in his training; his confidence with both meat and ball had grown over the intervening period.

"I have recently kept my hand, or rather my foot, in by playing friendly matches for both The Sausage Makers Guild XI and Shields' Butchers Association," he said.

"And how did you get on in those?" enquired Simon, not really needing to be impressed any further.

"Well I have a pretty respectable eight goals return from ten such games to boot, not forgetting head!"

It would have taken a lot less than this to convince Simon of the need to include Yiannis in his squad and without further ado the team now had a new striker ready to wear their colours.

The away game against The Cretan Taverna was to take place in East Shields at the dilapidated Community Park and as the majority of Pork and Mutton FC gathered outside the changing facilities awaiting Simon's slightly later than expected arrival. They were further surprised by his turning up with a stranger (Yiannis) in tow along with the no show by the usually punctual Jonah. Simon had not wanted to pass on the bad news regarding the injury prior to the match and had much less opportunity to announce the new signing in advance of their arrival.

"Lads, meet Yiannis – he is, in a way, our new poster boy! Or I should say he answered it's call. Just in time too as Jonah is unable to play today following a minor accident at home. He sends his best wishes for today though. Yiannis, meet Pork and Mutton FC."

"I wonder where he plays? He looks half decent," said Byron to Owen quietly.

"Well he ain't no goalie that's for sure – too sensible by half!" was the reply.

The introduction of Yiannis added extra suspense to team selection and shirt distribution. Just before Simon made his judgement call Roger once again turned up to offer his support and mark the near end of his suspension.

"Great to see you. Only a week left to go. Meet Yiannis our latest recruit," said Simon.

"I'm Roger, pleased to meet you Yiannis, I haven't heard all about you."

"Likewise, I'm sure."

Although the sun was shining there was a certain definite chill in the air prematurely announcing Autumn was on its way. Simon had decided that regardless of prevailing weather conditions Doug would play. It was largely a diplomatic decision, especially following the signing of Yiannis; erstwhile commitment to the cause had to be recognised and be seen to be recognised. Simon had already explained this to Yiannis on the way to the ground and he was content enough to await his opportunity and earn his place in the team. Doug, to his credit, was both surprised and delighted to get Jonathan's usual number 10 shirt. Pork and Mutton FC would have the same formation as adopted in the previous draw with The Fryers allowing a settled way of playing during challenging times:

(0) Owen

(2) Mario **(5) Massimo** **(3) Marco**

(6) Salvator

(7) Byron **(4) Simon** **(8) Stuart** **(11) Norman**

(9) Ever **(10) Doug**

Yiannis happily received the number 12 shirt and in another crafty diplomatic man management move Simon gave Roger the blank 'number 13' shirt (the spare reserve shirt without number or essential purpose), to wear covertly (rather than covetly) under his jacket thereby adding to his feeling of being a part of, rather than apart from, the team.

Before kick-off Simon had been more than a little apprehensive about how Yiannis would be received by the others and any unsettling impact this may possibly have. He was also more than a little worried by the opposition who may take this opportunity to start turning their poor season around. Such concerns were not conveyed to the rest of the team and his players appeared in good heart.

The Cretan Taverna wore the blue and white colours of Greece, but in homage to an island often disassociated from the mainland, they did so with a twist, having quartered blue and white shirts and white shorts. These very smart strips rivalled those of Pork and Mutton and suggested a classy footballing outfit with Saville Row (or higher league) ambitions. That said, the teams were evenly matched in the early exchanges which bore testimony to their respective positions in the league. The game was quite open and played in a friendly sporting spirit, with several good chances missed or saves made, with neither party having that killer touch in front of goal.

Things changed dramatically in the 30th minute however when a badly mis-timed back pass by a Taverna defender beat his own goalkeeper and gifted Simon's team the opener. This mistake was amplified by the lengthy protestations of the their goalie loudly berating the guilty team mate who responded in equal kind to the abuse he was receiving. Something was clearly amiss here and deeper than than the original error. The referee and their own captain had to get them to calm down and an uneasy peace was restored, but only for a little while.

This most uncivil of civil wars broke out again ten minutes later when their unforgiving goalkeeper himself erred this time spilling an easy catch into the path of Doug who, somewhat taken aback and with the sun in his eyes, fired the ball over the bar towards the offending celestial obstruction. This earned the ire and revengeful rebuke of the scolded Taverna defender directed at his own goalkeeper with Doug avoiding criticism from any quarter. At this point their goalkeeper totally lost it and instead of placing the ball down for a goal kick intentionally fired it at very close range into the reproductive equipment of his teammate. This generated silence and gasps from all present. The referee had seen and heard enough and immediately booked both the missile launcher and his target, once the latter had recovered his manhood. Things once again temporarily settled down letting the game reach its intended intermission without any further incident.

The half-time interval, however, was just as eventful as what had gone on before. As Pork and Mutton FC were sucking on their orange segments a commotion erupted between the two protagonists involved in the previous ructions leading to quarrels breaking out between the entire Cretan side. The Taverna captain was trying his best to keep the now sparring partners apart while the rest of his team were disintegrating into one warring faction or another. This now attracted the attention of the referee and other match officials who rushed to attend to the disorder that was getting out of hand.

"What the hell is going on here? I have never seen the like of this before. You are wearing the same colours for goodness sake!" said the man who was supposed to be in charge.

"I am not!' said their goalie.

"You know what I mean!" the referee replied.

"There is bad blood here," their captain confessed.

"I am not having those two spilling it all over my pitch. I would be well within my rights to immediately send them both off. Either you get them to leave voluntarily or I will be forced to send them packing!"

The Cretan Taverna captain took up the referee's generous offer and somehow managed to get these prime miscreants to separately take their leave. He could hardly refuse, he might be losing two players but at least he could use his substitute, and any further rumpus here, and later from Lower Lenin Street, would be contained. They were now both a goal down and a man down, and needing to put an outfield player in goal, but his team were no longer self-imploding.

"I am sorry about all this and what happened earlier," their captain said to Simon following the peace settlement.

"I guessed something was clearly amiss between those two," Simon answered, his hunch already confirmed by Yiannis's translation of some of the dialogue previously exchanged between the warring parties.

"There is a lot more to this than meets the eye. It all blew up because the player who scored the own goal, Hatzidakis, has just broken up with his fiance who is also the cousin of the goalie, Stathakis, and there is now the very real possibility of a vendetta developing between the two families. So this may not be the end of the matter. The behaviour witnessed today is totally unacceptable and occur 'Never on a Sunday'. I truly hope that attention will now be focused entirely on the match."

"I hope so and thanks for explaining matters. By the way, can I introduce a new player of ours, this is Yiannis."

"Yassas," said Yiannis formally.

The Cretan Taverna captain was slightly taken aback to find someone from Greek extraction as part of the side he was facing. But they were clearly strangers, without shared loyalties, and Simon discovered from their brief conversation that the Greek communities in West Shields and East Shields were largely unconnected, with the those in the former associated with mainland Greece whilst those in the latter were strongly tied to Crete.

Opportunities came and went for both sides following the game's recommencement but adding to the tally proved elusive even with the disadvantages faced by the Cretans. With twenty minutes to go Simon decided to replace Doug with Yiannis, given that he was clearly struggling fitness wise and guilty of being the most profligate in front of goal. It turned out to be a decisive move. Within ten minutes of his entering the fray he managed to turn his marker on the edge of the penalty area and smash a low shot into the corner of the goal with the new stand-in goalkeeper trying his best to get near the projectile. That was enough to drain any remaining fight in the Cretan Taverna side and the match ended 2-0. Pork and Mutton FC had certainly benefitted from Greeks, or more precisely Cretans, bearing gifts, whether inadvertently or intentionally, and they were now upwardly mobile once again.

CHAPTER 17:
Who's In(n)?

With 7 points from 6 games (W2 D3 L1) Pork and Mutton FC had already amassed as many points as they had for the whole of last season and there were still another 24 games to go. They also had Roger back following his suspension and a new promising striker, Yiannis, added to the squad, so things were clearly on the up in more ways than one. Simon hoped it would not be a false dawn as he viewed the league table, serving to reinforce his newly discovered, but acutely calibrated, positivity showing the team's current standing in seventh place well away from the sixteenth bottom slot they usually frequented. It was a good thing he didn't suffer from vertigo as these were dizzy heights he hadn't experienced before. Of course, team selection had become more problematical, with fourteen players to choose from leaving two disappointed and another with the number 12 shirt. In reality, the defence picked itself (with Simon as utility backup cover), so competition for places was restricted to the midfield and attack. They remained heavily over-reliant on the fitness and form of Owen and the Tripolini brothers and Simon was still looking for more recruits, especially here.

After a pretty uneventful working week, and having received no last minute injury or fitness notifications, Simon continued to sit there pondering his team for tomorrow's home game on The Links before shifting his attention to watching *Match of the Day*. He had no benefit of scout reports on the opposition or any other available intelligence apart from reference to the current league table and past matches played between them. The morning's opponents were in ninth position with 6 points (W2 D2 L2) having scored 11 and conceded 5. This goal tally and difference was not only better than Pork and Mutton FC (goals for 7 and goals against 9) but both their defeats had been by only 1-0 and against teams vying for the two promotion spots, including The Deutscher Bierkeller. Simon was not aware of any of this or of the fact that their two victories had been 3-0 and 5-0 respectively. He would have known had he wisely kept past issues of the newspaper. The one residing on his lap only contained last week's results, the league table and tomorrow's fixtures. At least he knew that his forthcoming opponents played out a 2-2 draw against Peking Duck United who were themselves unbeaten and sitting in fourth place. Simon had carefully avoided any such press coverage of his team in the past as it never made such pleasant reading - merely serving to confirm how bad you are when you already knew! He realised, somewhat belatedly, that in future he really should keep cuttings of this page of the football section of the local newspaper as a valuable source of reference and form guide. From now on his scissors would be out.

Whatever Simon knew about tomorrow's opponents related almost entirely to the past. Until the end of last season they were known as Temple FC and based at the drinking establishment called The Temple Inn, regularly frequented by the legal profession serving the Law Courts nearby. This gave rise to their nickname The Lawyers and they used to play in a palette of sky blue shirts and dark blue shorts. For a good number of years the proprietor and club patron had been a formidable lady called Shirley who Simon had come across on the few rare occasions he needed informal legal advice from a chum of his. This always resulted in any minor recompense being immediately satisfied in liquid form at her hostelry. He remembered her as quite a matriarch, with a dominant frame and personality to match. The regular clientele would always refer to the boozer as Shirley's rather than what was painted on the pub sign swinging high outside. Temple FC had been a mid table team that always beat Pork and Mutton FC without too much trouble or sweat. Something then happened following Shirley's sudden disappearance which led to the pub coming under new management. One of the popular, and humorously contrived (Simon thought), rumours at the time was that 'Shirley had ceased being Temple by simply doing a moonlight flit to sail away on the good ship lollipop'.

All Simon really knew was that new owners had just recently taken over and then immediately changed the name of the pub to The Shirley and the team's colours to claret and sky blue striped shirts and matching blue shorts. From this season they were to be known as Shirley Inn FC, and being much the same side as before the rebranding, they were just as likely to dish out the same punishment to Pork and Mutton FC as previously. Not being in need of any legal instruction for some time, Simon had not recently frequented The Temple Inn, Shirley's, or even The Shirley, so knew nothing more, and had simply presumed the new name was in homage to the recently departed even if she left under an alleged cloud.

But there was so much more to all of this than Simon or most people knew. Rather late in life, at the age of 48, Shirley had befriended a merchant seaman called Captain January who was about to retire overseas and wanted a companion and future intended. She had to move quickly to take up his offer and after initially deciding to turn him down had a sudden change of heart and quickly caught an airplane to be with him. Contrary to circulating gossip, she tended to all her debts and outgoings before her hasty departure so the only cloud she left under came after takeoff before climbing to the required flying altitude.

The new proprietors were both willing and able to move quickly; wanting to reunite with their son, who had made the move to West Shields much earlier, lodging with his maternal grandmother during some difficult teenage years. Joyce and Joe Hallsome hailed from a place called Shirley within the Borough of Croydon, South London. Their naming of the pub, The Shirley, was in recognition of the area they left behind rather than in honour of the previous recipient of the license. Of course, the coincidence was not lost on them, especially having been known unofficially as Shirley's, and the new name allowed some continuity with the old. The football team remained virtually unchanged apart from a new name and new kit just in time for the start of the new season. Shirley Inn FC wore the colours of Crystal Palace, who Joe supported from boyhood, and he was a hands-on patron directly co-managing the team alongside his playing captain, and son, Justin, with promotion now firmly in their sights.

As the credits rolled at the end of *Match of the Day* Simon concluded that he was no nearer his final team selection and that he would have to sleep on it. By the time he had removed himself from his slumber and was peering into the bathroom mirror removing his weekend build-up of facial hair he decided to make a further cut and remove his name from the team sheet to give Roger a game in his stead. On the way to The Links he also decided that Yiannis would get a full match, taking up the berth usually frequented by Jonathan, who was returning from his decorating mishap, possibly prematurely, so Simon thought only giving him the number 12 shirt. So Doug would be joining Simon in watching the game from the sidelines, which he now minded more than he had ever done before. Whilst this allowed for the continuation of a settled formation, with only a minor tweak in some of its components, Simon was now confronted with a first world problem he had never had before - the luxury of having and keeping players happy who are left out of the starting XI:

(0) Owen

(2) Mario   (5) Massimo   (3) Marco

(6) Salvator

(7) Roger   (11) Byron   (8) Stuart   (4) Norman

(9) Ever   (10) Yiannis

Prior to kick-off and predating Donald Rumsfeld by some three decades, Simon had more than an inkling that 'there are known knowns; there are things we know we know. We also know there are known unknowns; that is to say we know there are some things we do not know. But there are also unknown unknowns - the ones we don't know we don't know.' The latter were the most problematical ones and just as likely to catch Pork and Mutton FC out as any future US Secretary of Defense or aspiring football manager. Simon did not know of his opponents enhanced playing quality, of their newly found managerial dynamism, and freshly installed captain who could play a bit.

What had not changed in their reincarnation as Shirley Inn FC was that their nickname as The Lawyers continued, with their association with the legal profession remaining firmly established both at the bar and on the pitch. The team managed to unite a group of disparate individuals, who were more used to fractious jousting with each other, and thereby make a strong case for both prosecution and defence. Somewhat ironically, the defence lawyers played in attack and the prosecution lawyers played at the back, with the non-legals sitting on the fence in midfield, including Justin. Whoever coined the old proverb 'attack is the best form of defence' must of had Shirley Inn FC perceptively in mind!

From the first give and go Pork and Mutton FC realised they had a match on their hands when one of the non-legals made a heavy illegal challenge that left something of an impression on Norman's left calf without registering an entry into the ref's book.

"Come on ref, that was blatant! Take his name!" Simon shouted from the touchline where he usually wasn't so animated.

"Free Kick, Pork and Mutton FC. Get up and get on with it," was the ref's response.

"That's right. Stop whinging, don't you know this is a man's game!" the relieved offender cried.

For the next fifteen minutes the game took a prickly and nasty turn with minor playing infringements warranting increasingly aggressive tit for tat responses that failed to elicit any response from the senior match official. The referee needed to re-establish his authority before chaos and casualty ensued. Somewhat fortuitously, a second punishment that failed to fit the crime helped matters on this occasion. Ever accidentally collided with a Shirley FC defender and was unjustly given a booking after the referee was hoodwinked by the ensuing amateur dramatics. The sight of the referee's book alongside use of his pencil calmed things down for a while and a semblance of order was restored.

Normal unruly service was resumed again shortly after and lasted until the first goal was scored in the 38th minute.

Against the run of any sort of play, Yiannis managed to collect a loose ball and evade a couple of frantic tackles before being cynically taken down by the last defender in the penalty box. It was a clear penalty and even this referee could see it. As he blew his whistle and pointed to the spot the question was whether the perpetrator would be sent off. After a rather weak opening statement in mitigation of the foul by the offender the referee signalled his summing up by sending the guilty party off the field. It was a case of just desserts (although a double whammy in keeping with the times) and most of Shirley Inn FC respected the official's application and upholding of the law. Ever Reddy stepped up and put a weakly driven penalty away, benefitting greatly from their goalie misreading his brief and diving in the opposite direction. The 1-0 lead went as quickly as it arrived, however, when The Lawyers scored immediately from the re-start. Before the advantage could even be tasted, Justin Hallsome, with the ball escorting his feet, waltzed his way into the penalty area and vented his spleen by unleashing a ferocious shot into the net. They may be a man down but Shirley Inn FC were no longer a goal down. This is how things remained until the half-time whistle brought much needed respite.

The oranges and rest helped settle things down after the restart with both sides now suddenly more interested in playing football than seeking disproportionate revenge for little niggles. Both captains, and the match officials, were happy for this improved turn of events and the game flowed banishing the earlier staccato. The first beneficiaries were Pork and Mutton FC who put together what some would mistakenly call a training ground move (rather than a genuine fluke) to score from a free kick that somehow totally confused and paralysed The Lawyers defence. The funny thing is that the goalscorer, Byron, was just as perplexed, as a ball clearly meant for a cleverly freed up Yiannis somehow ended up, via the referee's torso, at his feet for an easy tap in. This 60th minute lead, unlike the earlier one, lasted a little longer but was finally relinquished in the 70th minute when the Shirley Inn FC substitute (who had only been on a couple of minutes) volleyed home a pinpoint cross from his captain. It was now 2-2 with the game neatly balanced largely due to Pork and Mutton FC having the extra man. This body count advantage did not last long.

Ever was clearly exhausted and Simon decided to replace him with the possibly match unfit Jonathan (following his step ladder accident) on the grounds that it couldn't do any harm. What he failed to realise was that it may do no good either, and after playing an innocuous cross field pass the substitute, and his captain, both recognised that his ankle was still not up to it and he had to ingloriously leave the field three minutes after coming on to it. With ten minutes left to play and numbers even the match was poised on a knife-edge. It was finally settled when the best player on the park (or rather, The Links) headed home a corner in the last minute, 3-2 to Shirley Inn FC.

Simon knew it had been a close match and that he had made some key mistakes, not least in his team selection, in trusting a player's confirmation of their fitness, alongside lacking the requisite football intelligence on his match day opponents. He vowed to redress these in future and his thought turned to next week's paper with his team dropping down the pecking order. He imagined the game being reported on by a major national daily with its back page headline reading 'Just Hallsome!' - a less than good source of nutrition or well-being for Pork and Mutton FC.

CHAPTER 18:
The Goldwasser Boys

"You are right, no doubt about it, the Poles are a gallant and resilient people," Roger answered the ancient looking barman as he was handed a cheap pint in The White Eagle while waiting for his mate Jan to show.

"We had to be, and we've done a lot for this country of yours too. But when they don't need you any more they just spit you out. Do you know, they didn't invite me or any other fighting Poles to march in the victory parade at the Cenotaph in 1946 even though we all did our bit?"

"No I didn't to be honest. Why not?"

"Scared of upsetting that bugger Stalin. Not the first betrayal, or the last."

Although it wasn't the most salubrious watering hole in East Shields it was certainly one of the more interesting. It proudly displayed the scars of its recent history, unlike its closest watering hole, The White Elephant, a mile or so distant but many lifetimes away. As he surveyed the large function room cum bar he could not fail to notice history captured in black and white on the walls helping to take one's eyes away from the fading grandeur all around. The wallpaper had seen better days, as had most of the seated occupants, and the very country they still felt some allegiance to. Many had settled here after the war as displaced persons in need of both work and escape from past and present European terrors. By and large, they came, they saw, they integrated – as best they could. These were not the discarded heroic pilots of 303 Squadron but men brought to help fight the new peacetime economic Battle of Britain, fought not for the freedom of the skies but the extraction of the black gold from within the underbelly of the earth. Working in the coal mines had given them a status and a stake in the wider community and they had recently joined in a display of solidarity and muscle at the national level.

Roger glanced across at a group playing dominoes close by. He heard the coin land in the tobacco tin in the centre of the table as one of the men knocked, unable to rid himself of one of his rectangular burden and forced to offer the agreed round relief in compensation. All the players bore the scars and marks of their craft, the unplanned and unwanted tattoos made abstract by the coal dust laying transparent beneath unprotected skin. There was much to observe here, even though it was not unfamiliar to him, his having been here many times before and now being treat very much as a regular without sharing any of the traits of his fellow drinkers.

He was getting restless, awaiting the arrival of his increasingly late friend, and closely approached some of the photographs that had earlier attracted his attention. The people captured in the frames were unknown to him with their likely whereabouts even more so. Most had been taken several decades before, and rather strangely, few featured working men like those reflected by the light back onto the glass through which Roger was staring. No flat caps were on parade here. Military men were present and correct and they were joined by neatly dressed and coiffured intelligentsia. They now shared the same walls just as they had almost certainly shared the same fate. Before his surroundings seduced him in empathetic nostalgia, Jan arrived apologising profusely for his clear lack of punctuality.

Jan Kowalczyk was a longstanding friend of Roger going back to their schooldays. He had the usual second generation mixed loyalties and issues, even more so being Polish-Ukrainian, but he was considered to be a true friend. Up until five years ago they had played for the same football teams through childhood to manhood until the demands of Jan's work intervened. His father had ensured his avoidance of the coal mines but not the shipyards. Their friendship continued in the bars and clubs, rather than on the pitches, of West and East Shields. Marriage too, then got in the way, with Roger fulfilling his duties as best man followed, with a respectable delay, as godfather to the Kowalczyk's first arrival. Tonight's get together was the new normal, meeting every couple of mid weeks at The White Eagle with the full blessing of Mrs K, where men, whether married or single faced few temptations to wander. Roger felt no qualms in being here even though Pork and Mutton FC were scheduled to play this Polish club on The Links in a few days time. His visit had nothing to do with gleaning intelligence for Simon, no such mission had even been contemplated, with his captain remaining totally unaware of any of his winger's specific nocturnal manoeuvres; whilst Jan had some limited interest in, and knowledge of, Roger's forthcoming opponents, his main focus now was on home and work.

They were not here to discuss football but life in general alongside playing a game or two of darts. That was the plan, and it was usually followed, but tonight's intended programme failed to materialise. Within five minutes of Jan's arrival a group of raucous young men suddenly came careering through the double doors of the main function room diverting their path away from the bar and heading directly toward where the two friends were sitting. They were being shepherded there by a rather merry, short and stocky figure who was cordially met by a rising Jan just in time for them to exchange both a handshake then a bear hug.

"This is my cousin, Anton Topolnicka" Jan informed Roger, before introducing his friend to the slightly inebriated.

"It's a pleasure and honour to finally meet you Roger. I know my cousin thinks most highly of you," said Anton, before his party left just as quickly as they came to descend en masse to the bar like a small flock of pigeons swooping down on newly thrown crumbs.

Within minutes Anton returned alone accompanied by a tray containing three empty small glasses and a full bottle of clear liquid with what appeared to be gold flakes lying like sunken treasure on the bottom.

"Today is my birthday and you must drink with me!" he proudly exclaimed, picking up the bottle and giving it a good shake transforming it into a gold snowball of sorts. Just as quickly as the glasses were filled they were emptied, then refilled, then emptied again.

"What is this stuff?" asked Roger, in an agreeable tone, somewhat belatedly.

"This is Goldwasser from Gdansk," answered Anton, "and the three of us will finish the bottle together."

"But Anton, you know my wife won't be happy if I come home half cut and I have work tomorrow too!" pleaded Jan.

"Don't be ridiculous Jan, we are Poles and we are family."

Argument was futile as the alcohol was working its magic and the gold was being readily deposited into the human vaults. Roger thought it strange that his path and Anton's hadn't crossed before given the length and depth of his friendship with Jan. The explanation, however, was simple. Anton had been working in a coal mine in Nottingham until a recent transfer to the pit in East Shields four months ago. He was a regular at The White Eagle - but only at weekends, his birthday excepting. They discussed work and life with no mention of football. At the close of the bottle they exchanged goodbyes and the wayward vodka provider returned to the group at the bar welcoming him back like a long lost relative. Darts were no longer on the agenda, as consumption had been exceeded, and both Jan and Roger had a united preference to set their increasingly muddled sights on home.

As they merrily escorted each other part of the way home they both mildly regretted their weak resistance to Anton's insistence and how easily they had wandered away from their usual gender fluid of beer. Jan was familiar with what they had enjoyed, and was less affected by it, but he was still more worse for wear than usual and his wife's radar would warn her of this when his footsteps came within range. It was too late to worry about that now he conceded to himself. Unlike Jan, Roger had no one at home waiting for him and few immediate cares to worry about apart from sharing concerns about work in the morning. To help take his mind off what awaited him at home, Jan suddenly shifted the topic of conversation.

"On another matter, I understand that your team is playing The White Eagle on Sunday."

"Yes, that's right, but I'm surprised you know about it, or are even mentioning it, given it's football!"

Football talk had usually been off limits following Jan's decision to stop playing so the vodka had unexpectedly loosened his tongue, Roger thought to himself, and he was more than a little staggered (matching the unsteadiness of his walking) by the fact that Jan knew of the upcoming game.

"How did you know?" Roger repeated, somewhat intrigued.

"You can blame the Gents, I suppose," Jan answered cryptically.

"Which Gents? Do you mean Anton and his group?"

"No, silly. I popped into the Eagle's toilet before meeting you and on my route back to the bar I happened to glance at the noticeboard informing members of the match."

At this point their conversation was halted when two buses, their respective conveyances home, came round the corner at the same time and they had to make a run for the bus stop. Just before Jan immediately boarded his, he turned and shouted, "By the way, you will see Anton again on Sunday, he plays for The White Eagle!"

We were now a few weeks into Autumn and the long hot Summer had become little more than a memory being suddenly replaced by unheralded chills and damp. The weather would start to make a greater impression on future matches as playing surfaces like The Links took a pounding from more than just studs and trainers. Players too had to adjust to the changing conditions. In light of all of this, Simon once again pondered over team selection being especially mindful of the nature of the defeat they had just experienced which had sent them down the league table with Pork and Mutton FC and Shirley Inn FC now trading places (ninth and seventh respectively). This provided for a neat sandwich with The White Eagle as the filling, on equal points, but a superior goal difference to their next opponents.

As the players gathered, in their what today would be considered as their home dressing room, Simon made some last minute decisions prior to dishing the shirts out. Being a dull and wet Sunday morning he had decided to play Doug out on the left in place of Norman and also include himself instead of Byron, who would be substitute. The blank 'number 13' reserve shirt was given to Norman, and would only see the light of day if someone pulled up prior to kick-off. Jonathan would be shirtless and sidelined until he could prove his ankle had totally recovered its strength. But the formation itself, however, remained a pretty stable one:

(0) Owen

(2) Mario   (5) Massimo   (3) Marco

(6) Salvator

(7) Roger   (4) Simon   (8) Stuart   (11) Doug

(9) Ever   (10) Yiannis

That said, Simon did want to have some flexibility in its deployment during the match. He wanted Roger and Doug to sit a little further back on the wings and help cover the centre of midfield when the team came under pressure allowing him to drop back and aid Salvator sitting in front of the back three. He also asked Ever to take up his vacant spot in midfield if the team found itself pinned back with Yiannis alone up front as the outlet for any relief balls. Simon recognised that this would involve a special challenge and responsibility for Doug, the natural loner, whose only real evidence to date of being a team player was when in the employ and vicinity of his father. His limited playing time had largely involved solo activity or self-exiled inactivity. The hope was that his increased bonding with the team might carry him through and it was worth a shot. If things were going well and the team were dominating possession Simon wanted Roger and Doug to utilise the wings and push forward to support the front two and add to the attack. That in a nutshell was today's Pork and Mutton FC game plan. Being somewhat straightforward, thankfully, it was quite easy to digest, even for a rather anxious Doug, and a hungover Roger.

As the players left the sanctuary of the changing facilities they were greeted by the first of many heavy showers. This did little to lighten Roger's mood but rather strengthened his desire to be elsewhere, regardless of missing the opportunity to renew an acquaintance. Running onto the pitch for the warm-up he looked across at the opposition doing the same and saw, as expected, given his informant, the short and stocky figure of Topolnicka preparing for battle in the red shirt and white shorts worn by the Polish XI. At that moment their eyes were drawn, somewhat inextricably, together and a friendly acknowledgement silently conveyed by an exchange of nods already made weary by Saturday night excesses. The match would turn out to be a rather epic affair, and just like their earlier midweek encounter, not fully follow the script.

The referee's whistle announcing kick-off was greeted with another sudden heaven blessed soaking that helped dampen the players spirits on the field and further dishearten those washed-up and sidelined on the touchlines. The Links provided no refuge to nature's calling apart for dogs enjoying the convenience of their daily release. The match may have started glum but it did not take long for it to lighten up.

After only five minutes a pass from Simon intended for Stuart skidded out to Doug camped on the half-way line and in his confusion of being in the no-man's land of Simon's game plan decided to take the ball and run. With the dark clouds overhead escorting his solo drive forward he ignored both friend and foe and charged directly for The White Eagle goal. He waltzed past desperate sliding tackles, without need of a partner, and finished his dance with a swivel then a glide, stabbing the ball home just before being flattened by the incoming enraged goalkeeper. Doug had given them an early lead but was clearly the worse for wear as he lay winded and dazed face down on the turf. The referee thought that conceding a goal was punishment enough for the sixteen stone missile who now sportingly picked up the scorer as if he were a sack of potatoes rather than a casualty. This provided little relief to a somewhat groggy and breathless Doug, now found prematurely and unapologetically replanted on the grass. Insult was added to his injury when the sun briefly burst through the clouds to applaud his suffering. With the stuffing now clearly knocked out of him it was unlikely that he could carry on for much longer. For the next ten minutes all the pressure came from their opponents and all followed Simon's game plan including a struggling Doug. This did not prevent The White Eagle coming close on a couple of occasions, being foiled by the woodwork and a great save from Owen.

Simon's decision to sub an ailing Doug was made for him in the 20th minute of the game when a heavy tackle from Topolnicka robbed him of the ball and any ability to continue. Fortunately, for the team, little use was made of this gain in possession from the Polish ball winner after a teammate wasted the chance he was given and fired over the bar from close range. Byron now entered the fray just in time to support a midfield clearly under the cosh. Roger and Anton's paths had rarely directly crossed during the match with both covering different parts of an increasingly congested midfield. What was becoming clear, however, was that Topolnicka could certainly play and was their main conduit between defence and attack. Over the course of the next twenty five minutes he managed to legally and professionally pick the pockets of his opponents on three separate occasions, the last resulting in an equaliser in the 39th minute. This time it was the hardworking Stuart who was taken by surprise and had his possession exorcised without recourse to any religious intervention. This provided the opportunity for Anton to supply his centre forward with a glorious through ball that he dispatched with great aplomb into the roof of the net in penitence for his earlier sinning. This was and was not daylight robbery; the 1-1 half-time scoreline being richly deserved by the visitors and less so by the hosts.

Topolnicka was clearly the water carrier for the Polish side being the hard working provider of most of their goalscoring opportunities alongside breaking down most of the threats they faced. His influence and midfield authority continued throughout most of the second half with Pork and Mutton FC largely camped in their own half fighting hard to gain and then keep possession. Even with the heavy cloud bursts the pitch held up well and was not yet in the position to turn itself into a quagmire given the recent overly long hot summer. The ball came off the surface quick and fast and gained extra impetus from the prevailing weather conditions. An intended pass from Marco to Byron skidded and overshot its target giving a throw-in to The White Eagle. At this point the opposition made a 68th minute substitution and the new arrival came onto the pitch then immediately off it again to take the throw-in. No one was marking Anton as he silently drifted into the inner edge of the penalty area to receive the long throw-in from 'Hokey Cokey'. The defence and supporting midfield all stood transfixed as the recipient brought the ball under his control before playing the ball tamely to their expectant centre forward to smash wildly past a slowly defrosting Owen. From that moment on the game looked well and truly lost.

Or that is how it seemed were it not for the craft and graft of Yiannis seemingly forlorn up front. Apart from collecting the occasional long ball from his over-stretched teammates, to relieve the relentless assaults on their Monte Cassino, most of his success had come from skilfully slowing the game down by holding onto the ball as long as possible and taking it on a journey to the more obscure areas of the pitch. This often served to frustrate the opposition whose usual recourse was to give away a free kick, corner or throw-in. As the game progressed such activity became more common.

"Heah, come on ref! Young Yiannis here is drawing more fouls than a graphite artist illustrating poultry!" was Norman's over clever remark from the touchline.

Whilst Pork and Mutton largely failed to take any advantage from Yiannis's sacrificial endeavours, being largely risk adverse in the current circumstances whilst their opponents continued being increasingly bold, it did provide their out of condition players with a necessary, and increasingly regular, breather. Reward came, in the last minute of the game, when another seemingly innocuous challenge resulted in a free kick just inside the opposition's half. This was quickly taken by Yiannis who had little choice but to play it back to his nearest offensive teammate Roger who was clearly running on empty to join him in enemy territory. An immediate return pass caught the slowly retreating Polish defence cold and Yiannis now had his first clear route to goal. Apart from their goalie, no one stood in his way, not even Topolnicka. Using his final reserves of energy he easily rounded their slow moving elephant of a goalkeeper to deftly send the ball into an empty and welcoming goal.

This would be another game with honours even but with a clear moral victory for the Poles, who played the better game. As the players walked off the pitch Anton headed straight for a breathless Roger.

"Well played Roger, your team certainly showed a fighting, never say die, spirit. It is certainly something we Poles can identify with!"

"Thanks," was the best that Roger could offer in reply along with a silent nod and a friendly but limp handshake. The game, a boozy night before, and his age, had all caught up with him, unlike Anton who had a far healthier disposition.

Simon congratulated the opposing team captain on their display and sportsmanship and said that Topolnicka was the best player on the park by a country mile. He replied in the affirmative and continued by confessing, "Here at The White Eagle we are most fortunate in having such a player in our ranks. I am sure you won't know this but because of the first half of his surname, Topol, allied to his ball winning and playing skills, Anton is known, for obvious reasons, most affectionately by us as Fiddler on the Hoof!"

CHAPTER 19:
Playing Neverland

The last game had been a hard drawn one and taken a great deal out of all the players at Simon's disposal. That said, he knew the next game was likely to be just as hard against College Caterers FC, from Shields College Training Restaurant, with its endless stream of late teenage apprentices filling its ranks. These students never got any older as they were replaced every six months or so by a new, ever so slightly younger, fresh crop with energy to match. The odd rare sprinkling of mortal lecturers might reduce this imbalance, but not by much. As Norman told Simon the last time the teams met, "It's like playing Peter Pan United but without Tinkerbell!"

On his way to the away ground on Grosvenor Road Simon had little need to ponder, having decided days ago what his team selection and set up would be. If all players showed up, and he had been given no reason to think otherwise, then he would include anyone under the age of twenty from the beginning, regardless of form or ability. So Salvator, Byron, Doug, and Yiannis were all in from the start. If one then went through the rest of the age profile in ascending order (but also recognising their playing attributes) it would suggest the following starting XI:

(0) Owen

(2) Mario   **(5) Massimo**   **(3) Marco**

(6) Salvator

(7) Byron   **(4) Simon**   **(8) Stuart**   **(11) Doug**

(9) Ever   **(10) Yiannis**

This would leave Roger, Jonathan and Norman vying for the number 12 jersey. To be honest, Owen was slightly older than Roger (by two months) but a goalkeeper was essential. The use of these simple metrics also hid the fact that Simon did not even know Ever or Jonathan's exact ages but merely presumed a difference and remained unwilling to risk the latter after the farce a fortnight ago. Norman was older than Roger, and that was common knowledge among the oldies, making Simon's decision easier to justify. So Roger would be substitute and available to fill either attacking flank better than Norman could anyway. Simon was fully aware that the average age of his opponents was always around 18, rising or falling by the number of catering lecturers taking part. He knew for certain that age was not on his team's side, as it was glaringly obvious, but had no knowledge of the exact disadvantage (simple maths and birth dates would have disclosed a squad average age of 24.86 with a team selected average age of 23.45). Had Simon known Ever's true age and picked Roger instead then the average would have been further reduced by more than half a year.

As the team changed into their kit a couple of the sidelined older players were not happy – Jonathan and Norman would be sitting out their second game in a row and neither took it well. Stopping players from playing, especially towards the close of their careers when the clock was ticking, never went down well. Simon promised that both would be included in next week's starting line-up in order to placate them and prevent these grumblings from undermining team unity.

Age was not the only consideration going into this game. Weight and motivation were also factors coming into play. Pork and Mutton FC did carry excess baggage on the park but not as much as previous seasons given their recent more youthful recruitment. It was the older players, and the drinkers, who could benefit from shedding some pounds - unfortunately they tended to be the same people. Simon, himself, was hardly a role model for the others and too many takeaways were starting to make a big impression. "Strange how takeaways defy mathematical logic to invariably add rather than subtract," he once confessed to Fred in an unguarded moment. This was a key factor in his not mentioning this aspect of his thought process. His team mates were neither jockeys nor boxers so not subjected to formal recorded weigh-ins but he surmised that on average they were upwards of eight pounds heavier, even with the likes of Jonathan and Norman sitting this one out. Of course, such weight advantage should help in the tackling and holding-off aspects of the game but clearly hinder the sprinting and stamina components.

"Lads, we need to go out there and win. Picking up just one point out of the last four is no longer good enough and we've dropped just below mid table. You're better than that! You fought hard to get a draw last week and I want you to fight even harder to get a win today!" Simon declared before fixing his focus on the rather unique and distinct challenges and motivations of their opponents. There were some specific things he didn't know, or given adequate thought to, and some general things he did, and had.

You did not need to be a total genius or College insider to recognise that whilst the lecturers may have some interest in league promotion the majority of students did not as they would not be around a season hence to enjoy the full fruits of their labours. The catering staff had enough on their plates to try and enhance the flavouring of a stodgy curriculum without requesting additional sacrifices. Doubtless, if asked, most of these students would reply, like Groucho Marx's quip on lacking concern for future generations, 'what have they [tomorrow's intake] ever done for me?' If they had been music students we could say that they were by and large primarily interested in a movement rather than an entire composition; or in footballing parlance, a given game took precedence over a long drawn out fixture list (which they would never be able to individually complete anyway, had they been so inclined). It was perfectly understandable that such students, given their dedication to all things food, should draw close similarities between playing a soccer match and having a meal in that any enjoyment belonged to the immediacy of its consumption.

None of this was part of Simon's pitch to his teammates, as it had not been picked up on his radar, even though it would have significantly added to it. He reflected instead on the opposition's inconsistent results (a couple of big wins and six even heavier losses), their inexperience and indiscipline, and frequent player turnover.

"Today's opponents currently sit three places below us with two points less and a goal difference of -16. Yes, they have often given us a drubbing in the past but we also had an occasional win even though we weren't that great. We are a different team now and clearly better than them. The league table shows they are there for the taking!"

Simon did have second thoughts about mentioning such defeats but only did so to highlight the opposition's inconsistency and to use them as a further barometer test of how far his team has progressed. He and the other three veterans all knew that consistency in itself meant little and they would have benefitted from a little more inconsistency in past seasons rather than being so consistently bad themselves. Their own variable results this season served to confirm this. Simon only wanted the good consistency not the bad.

One thing he and the others had noticed from previous encounters, which he relayed to the group, was that the Caterers XI always performed better if they had at least two lecturers in their team controlling, steadying and driving the youngsters along. They also knew that the caterers benefit, like all teams, from having a more settled side rather than all the seemingly random chopping and slicing due to teenage unreliability and irresponsibility. The latter could not be verified of course, as Pork and Mutton FC had neither the means nor the inclination to carry out such detailed reconnoitring. As Simon came running out onto the pitch, with his team following closely behind, he carefully looked across at the team opposite in yellow and blue stripes and clearly saw that there was only one lecturer wearing playing gear. This widely shared observation was perceived as a good omen bolstering team confidence even before a ball was kicked since, as everyone knows, you were unlikely to win anything with nothing but kids.

For the first ten minutes or so both sides gave as good as they got. If anything, the catering students plus one (their lecturer) slightly edged it, playing a close passing game that especially tested the early energies of Pork and Mutton's midfield, now in better shape to face the challenge (with its average age of 23). Doug and Byron were about the same age as their opponents and carried the same poundage which would help as the game progressed in the forgiving chill of that early Autumn morning.

The first breakthrough came in the 14th minute when an innocuous tackle by Stuart on the edge of the penalty area, was adjudged differently by the referee, resulting in a booking and a direct free kick. The lecturer, with his authority still currently intact, placed the ball down on the deemed spot and waved several eager students away. He then took off his round spectacles, which had been firmly tied to his head, and in what seemed like slow motion, cooly blowed the surrounding cold air in their direction. After gracefully rubbing them with the front end of his shirt he placed them back where they belonged. His little ritual concluded, he then sent the ball over the impatient wall, and the ball feeling suitably blessed and reflecting the languid pace of its master, floated into the top corner of the net. For whatever reason, Owen had been transfixed on his line, reduced to the role of a mere spectator. The goal celebration was rather over-cooked and only ended when the flotilla of students caught up with, then anchored, their leading wayward vessel.

This first blow served to enhance the respect afforded the bespectacled marksman and the students followed his commands. For the next twenty minutes the game was played at a frantic pace with Simon and his teammates fortunate to maintain the current disparity. They were hemmed back with little opportunity for forward advancement. Their crossbar and both goalposts had been called into active service and Owen was no longer hypnotised by man nor ball. He had made three fine saves that more than cancelled out his earlier napping. With so many missed opportunities to add to their tally, but expecting more to come, the catering students were becoming rather over-confident, verging on the cocky. Their lecturer did his best to restore some respect for the opposition and reminded his immature players that no game was ever won and over after only 35 minutes. Simon knew that if they could hold out until half-time that they would have a good chance to turn things around if either the catering students heads started to drop or their incarcerated indiscipline finally escaped. Things were to turn out even better than that though when Pork and Mutton FC received an earlier right of reply just before the interval. Instead of making a simple clearance one of the catering defenders thought they could easily dribble their way out of the penalty area past Ever, but he was wise and alert to their insanity. He gained lawful possession from the negligent landlord and fired the ball past a disbelieving, and soon to be aggrieved, goalkeeper. After retrieving the ball, now nestled comfortably in the back of his own net, he threw it at the miscreant along with a number of loud expletives that bore testimony to the rapid contagion of madness spreading throughout their team. The referee's whistle provided the opportunity for much needed solace but Simon and his teammates knew that the catering lecturer would henceforth have his hands full maintaining order and morale.

It was a very noisy, orange refreshed, break with what looked like a kangaroo court taking place within direct earshot of Simon and his players. Although there appeared many witnesses for the prosecution intent on giving the careless centre half his marching orders (and substitution) the lecturer prevailed in his defence. This caused further offence to their goalkeeper who decided to up sticks, rather than protect them; he left the pitch, tossing his gloves behind him, and headed straight for the changing rooms but not before taking his top off and throwing it into the first tree he passed. To prevent further mutiny the bespectacled one remained with the group and finally settled them down just before the restart. He went and picked up the abandoned gloves lying forlorn on the grass, asked the substitute to come on and traded his spot on the park for their now ill-fitting tracksuit top. He would have to wear this in lieu of the discarded goalkeeping jersey, now living the high life, neatly camouflaged in the overhanging branches. Such was the price that this Captain Bligh had to pay to quell the simmering mutiny.

The players of Pork and Mutton FC were not too surprised by what had gone on, after all goalkeepers were a little mad, and they had Owen after all. But there is nothing like facing a goalkeeper in spectacles to raise the confidence of any team - the cherry on the top would be the addition of rain, as no one had yet invented optical wipers, and goalkeeping gloves would be of little use to aid perception. What was clear right from the restart, however, was that he was less proficient in his new role than in his previous. Mr Cool had gone from Steve McQueen to Ted Heath and his team would surely follow. He dropped a few easy catches that added an unnecessary nervousness to the ranks and his early positioning left a lot to be desired. The student feedback he received was less than positive and they were loathe to kick the ball back to him if it could at all be avoided.

In the 53rd minute a moment of indecision by their right back over whether to play the ball forward or back led to Yiannis robbing him of it and playing a simple pass to Ever for his second goal of the game. There were now more heads dropping than during the French Revolution but the lecturer was no Robespierre and the only reign of terror being experienced was the catering students fear whenever the ball headed in his direction. The whole balance and structure of the game had changed. Students were running around like headless chickens using up what limited reserves of energy they had to keep or regain possession without co-ordinating any attacks of note. Simon and his teammates knew that the opposition would soon be running on empty and any remaining discipline would evaporate once they conceded another.

Goal number three duly arrived in the 66th minute. A poor shot from Doug fortuitously came off their right back's shin to go out for a corner. Stuart sent over a high ball that the lecturer somehow managed to catch, to everyone's surprise, but being somewhat restricted by his borrowed tight-fitting torso cover, he was unable to throw the ball with either the strength or direction intended. It was as if he were in a straitjacket better suited for the lunacy witnessed earlier. The ball followed a gently arced trajectory to land at the feet of a grateful Yiannis, standing a few feet away from the now marooned goalkeeper, who returned the ball from whence it came but well past the hapless provider into the goal. Only a few weak insults were hurled by the students as their lecturer retrieved the ball and they now appeared resigned to their fate.

At this point Simon decided to substitute Ever who had been noticeably flagging. The arrival of Roger not only served to re-energise the attack but also unknowingly brought down the team's average age to 22.9 years and poundage reduction by an average of a few ounces. More goals would surely come, even without rain assistance, Simon thought to himself. But there was no raining of goals either. Two minutes into his entry Roger struck a beautiful drive towards goal which was pushed, at full stretch, around the post. It was an excellent save that not only restored some confidence in the opposition's goalie but freed much of his right sleeve from the rest of his borrowed garment. That particular armpit's liberation served his team well allowing the man in specs to play a blinder for the remaining twenty minutes or so of the game. One more goal did get added to Pork and Mutton FC's tally, a penalty in the 87th minute following a deliberate hand ball, neatly dispatched into the top right corner by Roger despite the best efforts of their goalkeeper, who almost got a hand to it, splitting the material under his left armpit in the process. It was men against boys plus man (in glasses).

When the final whistle blew Simon went up to the catering college lecturer to shake him by the hand and congratulate him on his performance. There was no exchange of shirts, they were too valuable a commodity, but Simon would not have wanted what was left of a third-hand tracksuit top anyway, had it been one's to give. Its temporary owner was happy to ease himself out of what remained of its lockdown. As he gathered it into his arms its rightful owner approached, "Sorry about this Peter", the lecturer said, "but I will get my wife Wendy to mend it before the next game."

CHAPTER 20:
The Fortunate Cookie

With ten points already banked Pork and Mutton FC had already well surpassed the points total of last season but had twenty-one more matches yet to play. This already provided some justification for not throwing the towel in. Although Simon had yet to establish a team of recognised winners they were no longer viewed as a bunch of perennial losers.

The next game was a home fixture on The Links against Peking Duck United, formerly known as The Peking Duck, a Chinese restaurant and takeaway, first established seven years ago in a less than salubrious area of East Shields. In truth, East Shields was the poor relation to West Shields and was anything but picture postcard. It's heart betrayed its heavy industrial past and run down housing and commercial stock. The prosperity and growing stature of its neighbour was starting to have noticeable positive spillover effects on its margins as the two districts increasingly morphed but the centre of East Shields remained largely impoverished and increasingly jealous of the pressing Western influences on its borders. Centralising more local government activity in West Shields Town Hall had not gone down well and gave rise to growing suspicion and widespread resentment which Simon was all too well aware of. Mr Wu, the proprietor of The Peking Duck, was well known as a key figure in the establishment of a Chinese community enclave with his restaurant business alongside his joint-ownership of an Oriental Supermarket acting as magnets. Football had, in a way, been very kind to Mr Wu following his arrival here as part of the the 1960s diaspora from the New Territories, and his financially supporting a team in the League was largely in recognition of that. Like many others who followed the same route he found work in the catering industry, working his way up from washing dishes to the taking of orders. His initial employment and entry into the country was only possible with the support of already well-established family ties in the UK. His rise to local prominence was a consequence of the utmost good fortune which led to many of his fellow countrymen being in awe of him. Within a couple of years of his graduation to waiter he won a substantial amount of money in a regional spot the ball competition by placing an X exactly where the missing ball was located. This provided the initial deposit for his restaurant in East Shields which would provide him with a generous standard of living and a front of house role requiring neither pencil nor paper. He was viewed as a success in all the quarters that then mattered to him and life was good. Things were about to get even better, however. Four years ago he won a huge sum on the football pools and the manner of his winning, rather than the amount, led to his being known, and revered, by Chinese near and far as The Fortunate Cookie.

Now Mr Wu, somewhat unusually, was not much of a gambler and never considered himself as particularly lucky. He had won spot the ball on only his fifth attempt at that competition then stopped believing lightening doesn't strike twice. A few years later he tried the football pools on occasion without any payback, which did not surprise him, given the likely odds against. He only decided to have another, and possibly final go, in consequence of accidentally treading on a dropped fortune cookie in his restaurant late one Monday evening. He picked up the slip of paper which had been contained within and it read 'Swim in life's rich pool'. He thought little of this at the time and placed its message, for some unknowable reason, inside his inner jacket pocket rather than a bin nearby. On his way to opening his restaurant next morning, in advance of the popular lunchtime special, a seagull kindly made a deposit on his shoulder. For some, this would be seen as a sign of future good luck and riches, but for Mr Wu it was just inconvenient crap. He would now have to slightly amend his travel arrangements and head directly for the dry cleaners owned by his business friend Mr Huang. Everyone there expressed how fortunate he was to receive this blessing from on high, to which he just nodded in reply, whilst also thinking that only dry cleaners were the true beneficiaries of such aerial bombardments. Anyway, if one stood under a flock of birds for long enough one's chances of becoming their particular private convenience would surely be suitably enhanced, and you do not see many people pursuing that strategy, he thought to himself. Before passing his jacket to Mr Huang's assistant he checked the pockets only to find the already forgotten message from the day before. After revealing its contents, and its finding, everyone surrounding him expressed how doubly fortunate he was going to be. Mr Wu knew there was no point in trying to dissuade them of their beliefs and that it would be futile his trying to convince them that finding a discarded fortune cookie in a Chinese restaurant was hardly unusual.

That Tuesday's lunchtime business was busy, as he had anticipated, and he and his staff had little time to think let alone take a breath. After closing up for the two hour interregnum before the evening opening, he headed back to the dry cleaners for his jacket in the expectation of its having received the promised express personal service of the proprietor. The property next door to his destination were having their upstairs windows cleaned and Mr Wu, without thinking, avoided walking under the ladder and neatly side-stepped his way into Mr Huang's, who had witnessed his movement. He was not slow to point out that his friend still upheld this particular superstition. This made Mr Wu think and he continued thinking all the way home. Maybe there was something behind all of this superstitious nonsense after all. When he got home no one was there, as his wife and daughter were away visiting relatives in London. He put on the radio just in time to catch the end of the local news. The first about a lonely elderly lady who had learned to swim at the age of seventy-six and how this had transformed her life. This was followed by an interview with the manager of East Shields Town discussing his team's chances in the upcoming weekend game against Ashindon Rovers.

All of these outlined events formed a connect in the mind of Mr Wu that led him to fill in his football pools coupon for the matches taking place on Saturday. He had forgotten that the football season was just about to start again. The only special date pencilled in on his calendar, for Monday the 10th of August, was that of the return of his wife and daughter early next week. It was only now that he realised something significant to him, and probably others of an oriental disposition, that Saturday was the 8th of August, as he filled in his columns of predicted eight score draws. Eight, eight, eight – these numbers carried a meaning and a superstition that had long since been cast away at the back of his mind, the promise of great fortune and prosperity. He completed his coupon and placed it in the envelope along with the postal order and felt unusually confident that his multitude of X's would deliver like his previous singular X had done (but suitably multiplied).

This story, and what happened subsequently, became public knowledge not only in East and West Shields, but further afield. The national and local newspapers all contained slight variations of the tale, alongside photos of a beaming Mr Wu holding a cheque for a small fortune, with the manner of his winning, as well as the amount, receiving equal billing. For someone who was not really a gambler or superstitious his stock rose with those who were. His winnings also opened doors previously closed or at least ajar to him enabling his joint purchase of the Chinese supermarket, his purchase of a fine new home in West Shields, and continued support for good causes in East Shields. The local newspapers, unlike the nationals, continued to cover Mr Wu's upwardly mobile rise and community-orientated philanthropy. The most recent editions highlighted his purchase, then opening, of a restaurant in West Shields, newly refurbished as Peking Duck number 2.

Simon, and some of his teammates, were aware of most of this given the widespread ongoing coverage of Mr Wu's activities in both the East Shields Gazette and the West Shields Chronicle. He also knew that the team they were facing today was on the up and reflected the ambitions of their patron. The Peking Duck's membership of the league followed shortly after the now famous 24 points jackpot pools win. It came about three years ago following an expansion of the the division from 14 teams to 16. No one, to date, has admitted the true reasons behind this enlargement but many different rumours circulated at the time which reflected badly on the football authorities in East Shields after they accepted two late applications from their own patch, The Peking Duck and Smithfields nightclub, and rejected outright three timely applications from teams based in West Shields. Mr Wu's newly acquired status as local feted neighbourhood treasure did much to smooth and smother any simmering controversy but accusations of Eastern bias never really went away. Still, his team had done reasonably well, finishing 12th, 10th, and then 8th last season, showing consistent progress throughout, and adding some justification to their initial inclusion. This season they were doing even better, greatly benefitting from a wider pool of players following their now being two establishments rather than one, and subsequent name change to Peking Duck United (somewhat ungrudgingly allowed by the league's administration). They were currently sitting second in the league, still unbeaten after nine games with six wins and three draws alongside a very healthy goal difference. They looked likely favourites to gain promotion along with The Deutscher Bierkeller sitting one place and one point above them.

It was a cold early October morning that greeted the players as they ran out to face each other on the less than hallowed turf of The Links playing fields. Peking Duck United were kitted out in the same gear they had worn when they hadn't been so united. Dressed as before in their all red strip with gold trimmings and a not to be missed large gold X emblazoned across their chests. These shirts, and the shorts and socks that matched them, were designed to capture much of Mr Wu's backstory. The red so beloved by the Chinese and endowed with lucky meanings associated with happiness, joy, success, good fortune, beauty, fire, and vitality; taking centre stage at festivals and weddings and the principal component of the national flag. The gold standing for wealth and riches and given added particular significance by the X reflecting Mr Wu's appreciation of this symbol for being the means to his attaining prosperity.

As promised, Simon now included the previous two 'outcasts' Jonathan and Norman in his starting XI, along with Roger, who had been on the bench against the catering students. This meant that he was changing a winning team and that three other players would have to make way to maintain harmony.

"Lads, the changes I am making today will all be in midfield. The defence and attack remain as before. Roger, you are a straight swop for Byron, who will get the number 12 shirt. Norman will replace Doug and Jonathan will take up my position."

"So I'm not playing upfront then but playing out of position?" asked Jonathan somewhat disgruntled.

"Yes, for the benefit of the team," Simon answered.

So Pork and Mutton FC lined up as follows:

(0) Owen

(2) Mario   (5) Massimo   (3) Marco

(6) Salvator

(7) Roger   (4) Jonathan   (8) Stuart   (11) Norman

(9) Ever   (10) Yiannis

For the first twenty minutes or so nothing of note happened as the two sides gently sparred in the area around the halfway line. There was little to separate the teams apart from the referee's occasional intervention and the kit each side wore. The impasse was suddenly broken after 27 minutes when The Peking Duck right winger broke out from all the midfield congestion and glided past Salvator, then Marco, then Owen, to successfully land the ball into the now empty gaping airstrip of a goal. It was elegant in its execution and served to suddenly brighten up a drab game adding some life to the proceedings. It was as if a firecracker had just exploded and the teams were abruptly woken up. From that moment on it became a high intensity game expanding its domain across the whole pitch with the referee doing his utmost to keep up with the increasingly relentless pace. Pork and Mutton FC managed to create as many goalscoring opportunities as their opponents and missed just as many. Further chances came and went until a Chinese takeaway in the 42nd minute resulted in The Peking Duck adding another goal to their tally. Jonathan was clearly less than comfortable in his new midfield role and was guilty of trying to dribble his way out of his own penalty area when he was caught out and robbed of possession. The delighted recipient had a clear line of sight of goal that he easily digested to make it 2-0. Half-time could not come quickly enough for Simon's players as they were certainly in need of a rest and regroup. It duly arrived before any further damage was done.

It had been a while since Owen had enjoyed keeping a clean sheet and he let the others know that he was unhappy about the number and nature of the goals being conceded, "Can I remind you all of how hard I fought for the number on the back of this shirt - well it's failing to match up with reality!"

"Take it easy Owen, stop your belly aching! We all know you live your life in customs control, always having nothing to declare!" Jonathan shouted.

"Listen Jonathan, I don't take kindly to your contrived humour and your just costing us a goal was far more laughable!"

"None of this is helping. We all respect Owen's missionary zeal. I don't need to remind some of you that our goals against count at the same stage last season was almost three times as bad as this," Simon said.

"That's right, we have never had a season as good as this," Roger added.

"Owen, I promise you, we will be good for nothing again quite soon," Simon assured him.

This appeared to do the trick of not only calming his goalie down but injecting some much needed belief back into the rest of the team too. Simon also decided to make a tactical change and instructed Jonathan to play up front alongside Yiannis while subbing Ever with Byron to re-energise the midfield. The second half commenced just like the first had done, with little progression too far away from the centre circle, but with both sides now obviously aware that the next goal would most likely determine the final outcome of the game. Byron's addition to the midfield helped bolster the containment of the opposition following this tense restart although the same could not be easily said about Jonathan advancing the goal threat. The midfield chess game (or Xiangqi) continued throughout most of this half with few openings of any note. The Chinese defensive wall was difficult to reach, let alone break down. Yiannis managed one speculative long range shot that came crashing off the top of the bar and safely out of play in the 70th minute which had followed on directly from a great save and long throw out from Owen. The 'tipping point' goal finally arrived in the 80th minute to confirm, rather than alter, the course of the match. Peking Duck were awarded a rather dubious penalty after a harmless, if rather clumsy, tackle by Salvator was adjudged to be just within, rather than just without, the box. He wasn't even booked for this so-called infringement leading to an un-choreographed raising of eye brows then a dropping of heads. To add insult to injury a poorly taken penalty was pushed onto the post by Owen only to return back to the penalty taker for him to finally finish the job, 3-0, and that is how the game remained. They had clearly been beaten by the better side, even if their opponents had been slightly flattered by the scoreline. Simon and his teammates were now in no doubt that Peking Duck United had to be recognised as serious candidates for promotion. Once again, Mr Wu was doing something right, Simon thought to himself, and was a most fortunate cookie.

CHAPTER 21:
Sunday Roast (with all the trimmings)

Some defeats are harder to take than others and the last match was not one of those. They had lost on home turf after being fairly beaten by a better team. They were now somewhat becalmed in mid table with a good chance to get the wind into their sails again in the forthcoming fixture against Smithfields, who currently found themselves firmly rooted at the bottom of the division, a position Pork and Mutton FC had usually monopolised. Simon's side would have to make the trip to East Shields in order to collect the points required to propel them along the road to redemption.

You could not say that Smithfields had seen better days. The team itself was of recent vintage, the same as last week's opposition, but unlike Mr Wu's XI, during their three season stint they had hardly covered themselves in glory to justify their somewhat shady initial inclusion. They were one of the few sides that Pork and Mutton FC had the audacity to occasionally beat but in winning that battle they never won the war and Smithfields had always, rather annoyingly for Simon and his veterans, finished just above them at the end of the season. This was always only by one or two points which made it even more galling. This added some extra edge to the forthcoming match which Simon saw as a further kind of litmus test for his side.

The nightclub that carried the Smithfields name always had a reputation as a bit of a dive where the drinks were expensive and the clientele cheap. If you wanted to view the world from the gutter this was the place to come. Located on the seafront next to the amusement park it provided more seedy entertainment of its own. No one remembers the origin of the name but it was appropriate given its reputation as the local weekend 'meet' market for the easy trading of human flesh. Punters with any taste and sense would only visit it once, and only by accident, but it still remained the coming of age venue of choice, which said a great deal about the paucity of the nearby competition. For some strange reason the RaBHL (North) Football Administration had always held its annual awards ceremony at Smithfields rather than the plushier venues available in West Shields and many believe this had something to do with the team's less than transparent entry into the league. Whatever freebies and quid pro quo's had taken place, there seemed to be some hidden association connecting the interests of the nightclub and the Lower Lenin Street office nearby.

These speculations surrounding Smithfields were put to one side as Simon pondered over team selection. Jonathan's poor form following his DIY injury remained a major cause for concern and he and Ever were not getting any younger. Added to this was the fact that both Jonathan and Norman were making noises regarding their lack of playing time which was starting to unsettle others. Neither had scored a goal this season yet, while Ever already had five to his name, followed by Yiannis and Doug on three apiece. Simon knew that deeds not words had to determine the match day line-up and he would pick his best eleven regardless of sentiment or reaction.

Given the limited resources at his disposal some of the players were untouchable - namely all the defence, including Salvator - even though they now had eighteen goals in their against column. He had some interchangeable flexibility in midfield, not only with himself as the versatile utility player, but with Roger and Byron on the right and Norman and Doug on the left. Stuart was the team's engine room, being the mainstay and key fixture of central midfield. Yiannis and Ever had already established some sort of effective partnership up front but the latter was unlikely to last a full ninety minutes so a fully fit Jonathan could probably be best utilised as a super sub. These were the parameters with which Simon was working and now served to guide his deliberations which he openly expressed to the team prior to kick-off and shirt distribution. To his surprise this helped to fully clear any prevailing bad air over past team selections with those registering previous grumblings now recognising the competition for, and need to earn, playing time. After all Simon had already demonstrated the need to put the team first when he had dropped himself on more than one occasion, including the last match. As he told his assembled players, aided by Abraham Lincoln, "I can pick every one of you some of the time, pick some of you all of the time, but I cannot pick all of you all of the time."

Following team buy-in and agreement for form to trump opinion, Simon relayed the line-up to face Smithfields, just as the wind and rain also arrived to make announcements of their own:

(0) Owen

(2) Mario   (5) Massimo   (3) Marco

(6) Salvator

(7) Byron   (4) Simon   (8) Stuart   (11) Doug

(9) Ever   (10) Yiannis

This was not only the same starting eleven that had beaten the catering students two weeks ago but the one best suited to today's opposition and prevailing weather conditions. Unlike then, however, Jonathan rather than Roger was given the number 12 shirt to give him the opportunity later in the game to hopefully play the super sub role. Both Roger and Norman accepted their sitting out of this game following their minimal impact on the last and they respectively recognised the superior claims of Byron and Doug, especially the latter's goal contributions in overcast conditions.

From the get-go Pork and Mutton had the upper hand and most of the opposition looked heavily worn by the bacchanalian delights of the night before. It would be wrong to say that Smithfields were disinterested, as they had turned up for the match, but they appeared rather less than inclined to fully engage. All the 50:50 balls were ending up being 80:20 in Simon's side's favour suggesting that the game was clearly there to be won. The biggest threat to their success was the state of the pitch which had more sand on it than grass and rarely produced a decent true bounce. It was more welcoming to bucket and spade than boot and ball and undermining of any skill or artistry. The wind and the rain did not help and were given full licence to do their worst on this unsheltered neglected wasteland that must have seen better days.

Doug was the only noticeable player to delight in the prevailing gloom, and in the 18th minute he went on one of his solo runs finished by his confidently stroking the ball past their diving goalie, to share this pleasure with his teammates. This served to lighten the mood of Pork and Mutton FC and boost morale just at the time when the weather was most likely to dampen the spirits; with the unrelenting wind blowing the now torrential rain directly into their faces. Within ten minutes Doug had added a second, receiving a low through ball from Stuart that somehow kindly skidded its way to him, on what was left of the grass, and eagerly smashed low into the net. The yin and yang was clearly there to be seen, with Smithfields looking increasingly bedraggled whilst Pork and Mutton appeared somewhat cleansed.

The outcome of the game was starting to have an inevitability about it, not least because the opposition failed to use the prevailing wind to their full advantage. They were largely reduced to playing a long ball game that either ended up in the hands of Owen or passing their forwards by and going out of play. This was the age before the fixation on possession stats but anyone foolish enough to be watching in this weather would realise Pork and Mutton FC were totally dominating the game. They had more possession than the Devil and goal number three duly arrived in the 40th minute courtesy of a penalty following a handball. Ever neatly despatched the ball home even though he had what looked like a drowned large rodent on his head rather than a hairpiece. That is the way things remained into the half-time break without any break in the weather. It was also pretty clear that there would be little respite for Smithfields in the second half.

As expected, the scoreline became 4-0 immediately after the restart, but in a rather unexpected way. A heavy back pass went out for a Pork and Mutton corner. Byron sent over a high cross which their goalkeeper completely misjudged and the ball was blown directly into the goal; weather, accident or design we will never know, but Byron was fully credited with it although the wind should have been given the assist. That goal now put the team's goal difference back into positive territory for the first time since the third game of the season, a point only recognised at the time by Simon. The game and the weather both settled down for a time with neither side making any further headway. By the 70th minute Ever was clearly running on empty and it was time to bring on Jonathan to try and re-energise the team. This seemed to dislodge the newly established equilibrium and Yiannis spurned a glorious opportunity to add to the lead following super sub's entry into the increasingly phoney fray. The return of the rain on 80 minutes heralded a great mazy run by Doug that was only brought to an untimely and abrupt end by an illegal challenge just outside the penalty area. Jonathan collected and kept the ball, ignoring all other more legitimate claims, before placing it on the designated spot. Taking advantage of a poorly constructed Smithfields wall he found a gap to drive the ball home, leaving the goalie barking profanities at his lack of protection. It was his first league goal of the season and his celebration was embarrassingly overdone given the scoreline and that it wasn't the Cup Final at Wembley. To be fair to him, it also probably marked his public expression of relief in ridding himself of any pent-up frustration. Another goal was added just before the final whistle to make the score 6-0. It came following a one-two between Yiannis and Byron that was neatly driven home by the former prodigal making amends for his earlier miss.

The result, and the manner of the team's victory, had clearly been a renewed statement of intent. All the team had done what Simon had asked of them.

"Well done lads! The opposition weren't great but you can only beat what's in front of you, and we certainly did that, along with the weather! We gave Owen his clean sheet and got our goal difference back into positive territory again."

The defence had not been seriously challenged but had certainly played their part in containing any threats from the opposition. The midfield and forward line had undeniably made the greatest contribution and fully justified Simon's match selection. Doug and Byron had goals and assists to their name and all the forward line (including super sub Jonathan) had found the back of the net. Given previous history with Smithfields, Simon found this game one to savour. He was looking forward to his Sunday roast (with all the trimmings) although it would feel like second helpings given that he had just enjoyed his first!

CHAPTER 22:
Trunk Calls

Victory against Smithfields resulted in Pork and Mutton FC climbing up to seventh in the table with a very satisfactory return of twelve points from eleven games (W4 D4 L3). What was especially pleasing to Simon, and doubtless most of the others, was the emergence of a real team alongside its core members. In seasons gone by a bad side had largely picked itself, providing not only limited competition from within as well as without. There was now a clear reversal of fortune giving some payback for the effort expended and the renewal of vows to further commit. The sheer enjoyment of playing, of actively participating, was starting to make its way back into their game, although by different channels, for the individual players concerned. Those now on the sidelines, paradoxically perhaps, felt this even more so, as they waited patiently for their chance to feed their passion rather than simply walk away and seek rations elsewhere. Simon would never allow them to feel marginalised or on the periphery but presented them as giving up of the greatest sacrifice for the good of the group. A strong bond was growing throughout the squad and it needed to be nurtured.

The upcoming game would be a difficult one against another East Shields team, The White Elephant, who were another team pushing for promotion and currently placed fourth in the league. Pork and Mutton FC would have the home advantage of The Links but that hardly counted for much as they had only won once there so far this season after five attempts. Simon knew that this pub team had always been a tough nut to crack and his side's record against them was an unenviable one with defeat after defeat. You did not need to suffer memory loss to fail to recall any past successes, there hadn't been any. This particular elephant would never forget its previous easy triumphs and would be confident of plucking more low hanging fruit.

The White Elephant Public House was surrounded by a regiment of uniform terraced houses daily spewing out miners to the colliery nearby. There was a time, not so long ago, when the returning weary minstrels, with blackened faces, were welcomed back home to their tin baths but now, following the National Coal Board's introduction of workplace showers, they arrived cleansed of any subterranean sins. Most of the redundant metal vessels now permanently hung out to dry on wall nails in backyards. When not at work or in their allotments, these elite members of the working class would be the scrubbed-up clientele frequenting the pub's premises in search of light relief from heavy toil. They were all regulars, returning like homing pigeons when they had money to spare. Both their pockets and their hearts were usually lightened by the visit with beer and dominoes swiftly removing said burdens. Few unattached women were in attendance in front of bar although all the men behaved like perfect gentlemen whenever they presented themselves. This was a man's world and it was cherished for being so; a refuge and temporary exit from the cares waiting impatiently outside. It had once been known, rather more grandly, as the Seaton Hotel, even providing a silver service in the formal dining rooms upstairs. The change of name happened so long ago that none of the subsisting could recall its origins but agreed it now had a better fit given that its current proprietor had spent the last four years trying to dispose of it without any takers. Just like the coal mine down the road it was becoming a veritable money pit with escalating upkeep costs but without the luxury of support from the public purse.

Neither Simon, nor any of the players of Pork and Mutton FC, including its more likely suspects, admitted to having ever been within a hundred yards of the White Elephant let alone crossing its less than hallowed threshold. It was always known as a very territorial boozer with a catchment area to match, being a very local Local. It was not on anyone's pub crawl list, long considered unwelcoming of a fleeting visit during a beverage fuelled journey. Both geography and social distancing ensured that the regulars remained regular and irregulars most irregular. It had a monopoly on much of the loose change within a mile's radius of its beer taps and expended limited energy in getting new customers while treating its loyal customers as kidnapped passengers. They were not taken for too much of a ride, however, as drink prices were kept at a level far lower than they needed to be.

The football team was drawn from the community it served and was largely composed of coal miners with a little sprinkling of male bar staff for good measure. They played in an all white kit, which rumour has it, pays homage, somewhat surprisingly, to the exotic of Real Madrid rather than the workmanship of Leeds United. Whatever the truth of the matter, they were always well turned out. The formal spotless white linen bedecking the dining tables of the old Seaton Hotel may have been long gone but they somehow lived on in the strips the miners now wore. These were their holy Sunday robes to be tarnished only above ground.

There was a strong friendly rivalry between The White Elephant and The White Eagle with most of the players bonded by the camaraderie of the colliery. It was a derby of sorts determined largely by occupation rather than geography alone. That said, the make up of the two sides was very different. While many of the Polish miners were regulars at both establishments, and keenly assimilated at many levels, they would only ever consider representing the team most connected to their place of birth. This was just as true of darts as of football so while a few non-Poles played for The White Eagle no Poles played for The White Elephant. This was all well understood and accepted with good grace without any hint of animosity. You may find an occasional Robson, Charlton or Armstrong in The Eagle side but you would never find any surname ending in a ski or czyk in The Elephant XI. While the odd Border Reiver descendant may be invited to trespass, and did so, those of Polish extraction did not.

Loyalties aside, Pork and Mutton's next opponents, unlike the Holy Roman Empire at the Battle of Vienna, were doing fine without Polish help, having just strung together five victories on the trot. Simon knew this would be another serious challenge for his team and provide additional evidence of their standing against the better teams in the league. They had already suffered defeats against the other league front runners - Deutscher Bierkeller, Peking Duck, and Shirley Inn; all sides now placed just above The White Elephant. Given the result from the last game Simon had little need to ponder over his team selection. His limited footballing wisdom suggested little need for any tinkering and to go for an unchanged XI without worrying too much about the same players sitting it out for two games in a row. They had a formation that was now gaining noticeable traction with personnel that could play that system. But this was the calm before the storm and things were about to unravel and upset his plans.

As Simon was about to enjoy his late Saturday brunch he received a telephone call.

"Hello, Simon? It's Salvator here, I'm calling from London."

"You're what! Why?"

"Because of my father back in Brazil and my need to be at a christening here tomorrow."

"I can hear you, but I haven't a clue what you are talking about!"

Salvator eventually explained how he had just arrived in London, at the sudden behest of his father back home, to represent the Samba household at a christening of the first grandchild of his parents best friend marooned back in Rio. He did not know that his attendance was the product of a small dinner party held at his parents home only days before, following a seemingly innocuous off the cuff suggestion by his father, aided and accepted by a few caipirinhas and more than a little wine. Mr Samba Senior did not view this errand for his son as an inconvenience, but rather as an obligation, and any cursory examination of a world atlas would show just how small a country like Britain is compared to Brazil making such travel largely insignificant.

Simon's meal was now spoilt by what had happened at someone else's a quarter of the world away. He digested the news, and his brunch, as best he could and spent the rest of the immediate afternoon cogitating. Should he take up Salvator's slot or should he play two midfielders closely in front of the back three? If he did the latter then Norman could play alongside him but what would that mean for the formation laying ahead of them? These thoughts were interrupted by another ringing of his telephone.

"Hello? Ever here, I'm calling from Edinburgh."

"Not you too!"

"What do you mean, who else is up here?"

"Nothing, sorry, it's a long story. How can I help you?"

"I'm sorry to say I can't play tomorrow. My wife has suddenly whisked me away on a surprise weekend break celebrating the anniversary of our first date together – which I'd completely forgotten all about. Who the hell remembers that anyway! Apologies again, but there's no way I'll be back in time for tomorrow's game."

As Simon put the receiver down he prayed for no more calls today wanting the next trunk call to be when The White Elephant arrive to play at The Links tomorrow. The resumption of silence allowed Simon to realise that his hands were now largely tied; with two men down and Jonathan as super sub it meant that he had to make best use of the remaining eleven. This now confirmed his decision to play alongside Norman as deep cover for the defence and Roger replacing Ever up front but dropping back into midfield should the team ever find itself under the cosh:

(0) Owen

(2) Mario   **(5) Massimo**   **(3) Marco**

(6) Simon   **(4) Norman**

(7) Byron   **(8) Stuart**   **(11) Doug**

(9) Roger   **(10) Yiannis**

Thankfully there were no more surprises for Simon and he was able to distribute the shirts to what remained of his troop with the number 13 (blank) top left safely back at base, absent with leave. Everyone, apart from Doug, appeared in good spirits, doubtless cheered by the Indian Summer of a morning that had greeted their arrival. The banter was upbeat and confidence was being carried over courtesy of last week rather than being undermined by the minor tribulations of this. Jonathan predictably, and somewhat understandably, was none too pleased at being sidelined once again especially given Ever's absence. To date he was less super sub and more sub optimal but he had at least just ended his goal drought.

You could tell that The White Elephant were also up for the game. Their players looked fresh, keen and with fit young bodies clearly able to cope with the demands placed upon them. Heavy drinking and heavy work had yet to make their mark and betray their calling. They were like a pack of whippets awaiting release and at the sound of the referee's whistle they were off, but in a choreographed well-drilled way, quickly cutting through Pork and Mutton's midfield, and its new defensive cover, only to be thwarted by Owen's goalkeeping heroics. How he succeeded in getting his left glove to the low driven shot no one knows, but he did. The subsequent corner was somehow scrambled away but these opening minutes confirmed Simon's prior belief that this would be a difficult morning, just like all their previous encounters against this side. For the next fifteen minutes most of the activity took place in Pork and Mutton's half but they resisted all pressure to yield. Roger played his part by dropping back into a retreating midfield and Yiannis made an occasional run to hold the ball and provide a breather for his teammates protecting their goal. Owen's view of the game, up until now, was that of a relentless tide of white shirts coming toward him like surf coming in from the ocean but he somehow managed to continue to ride the waves.

Simon was pleased that everyone was doing what was expected of them, and even more, but he knew they could not remain penned in their own territory absorbing attack after attack without conceding sooner rather than later. As the game progressed the fitness levels of his side were being increasingly tested and the half-time break could not come quickly enough.

When the referee blew his whistle for the sanctuary of the oranges it was, Norman said, "Like The Relief of Mafeking all over again but unfortunately, on this occasion, their opponents were hardly bores!"

Whilst they heartily enjoyed their quarters with a sense of triumph for 'going-in' at 0-0 they were in danger of group thinking that their work was already done. Simon did his best to dissuade them of this and to prepare them for the renewed onslaught to come. All of the team were looking worse for wear and any one of them would have welcomed being substituted. Jonathan would have to enter the fray, but when, and for whom? Players running on empty were increasingly likely to pick up injuries or develop cramp so the timing and particular use of their sole substitute was a priceless resource that could change a game. This was a final gambling chip that would have to be bet wisely.

Following the game's restart Pork and Mutton FC were more careful in keeping hold of possession and spent less time chasing either their opponents or the ball. For these first few minutes The White Elephant just sat back and took their foot off the gas allowing Simon's side to almost grab a shock opener. A neat collection of short passes and midfield exchanges allowed Yiannis sight of goal and he hit a low drive from twenty yards which just whizzed past the outside of the post. This had the consequence of waking the opposition up from their mini slumber and they started to aggressively press for the ball higher up in Pork and Mutton's half. In the 65th minute Norman almost lost possession in his own penalty area and had to concede a rather cheap corner with the resulting set piece proving rather costly. A delightful curved centre was met by the forehead of Elephant's number nine who found both space and time at the back post to finally make the breakthrough they deserved.

Simon now feared that this could open the floodgates as resistance and resolve was beginning to break. He decided that now was the time to try and re-energise his team before despondency took over. Jonathan was called into action and came on in place of Doug who was clearly struggling with both his breathing and coping with the opposition's marauding right back. This led to some further reorganisation as Doug headed off in search of his inhaler. Jonathan took up Roger's position who in turn swapped wings with Byron allowing the latter to finally arrive at the berth vacated by Doug. A game of musical chairs - albeit without the music or the chairs - orchestrated under the guidance of Simon.

This helped to stabilise things for a short while but the team remained largely hemmed in and unable to advance beyond the halfway line. They became increasingly reliant on speculative long balls aimed only for Jonathan as Yiannis had little running left in him with the rest of that precious commodity being devoted to his propping up an ailing midfield. On 75 minutes Norman had given all that he could give and an earlier knock on the leg now made its presence better known. He was barely able to make it to the touchline, tumbling over it like some exhausted marathon runner, his exit clearly signalling that he, and possibly they, were done in. Perhaps Simon had played his final card too early? They were now a man, as well as a goal, down but they were not yet out (although some may also have wished to throw in the towel). Stuart dropped back, deeper and deeper, in order to help Simon and the defence but plugging this gap merely served to open others. Tired legs and players playing out of position created spaces which The White Elephant was able to exploit and a second goal inevitably followed in the 83rd minute. A series of well worked passes easily unlocked what remained of the defence allowing their centre forward to make it a brace. Miraculously this scoreline was not added to before the referee's whistle thanks to interventions by post and crossbar serving to deny Elephant's number 9 getting a deserved hat-trick and preventing any further damage to Pork and Mutton's goal difference. All of the team had run themselves into the ground and, much like Norman, were worthy of being wrapped in foil blankets as they collapsed on the pitch (if they had been popularised then). No one needed a fat lady singing to know that they were finished unlike the opposition who were still in need of a chorus or two.

"We must be mad Simon," Roger said, quietly gasping.

"We can take that as a given. But what are you specifically driving at?"

"Well, for some strange reason, we have just put in quite a shift for the miners!"

The match provided another reality check. They had played the top four teams and lost each match, failing to score in three of those games, with only two goals to their credit and thirteen goals against. Given that they had not lost any of the other eight league games played, (W4 D4) scoring nineteen and conceding only seven, there was a clear gulf between Pork and Mutton FC and the teams chasing promotion. They were now a mid table side and in the pack of also rans. But this was clearly progress over past seasons, The events of the last few days were testament that when it came to seriously challenging for honours the squad was overly thin on the ground but slightly overweight on the park, somewhat patchy on top and paunchy in the midriff.

CHAPTER 23:
CORE, Blimey!

The latest defeat dropped the team down to ninth in the league and occasioned some walking wounded at the end of the game resulting in Simon's closer monitoring of all of the squad over the forthcoming week. Salvator and Ever returned North and South from their respective capital jaunts uninjured from carrying out said family obligations. Both felt some responsibility for the defeat that they missed, but may still have had a hand in, and their unsolicited apologies were well received by teammates. Doug assured Simon that he was no longer suffering from breathlessness and that he had made no immediate further demands of his inhaler. Norman's feedback was not as promising and the knock he received had not yet been fully shaken off. Almost everyone else was present and correct, or so they said. Jonathan had confessed, but only in passing, that the twenty-five minutes he had played chasing long ball after long ball had taken a lot out of him. Simon himself had woken up with very stiff legs on Monday morning and was walking very gingerly throughout the early part of the week. This was something he failed to mention during his telephone conversations and he avoided visiting The Tripolini

Deli until he no longer walked like a cowboy about to get into a gunfight.

The upcoming match was an an 'away' fixture on The Links against the Consortium of Restaurant Emporia (CORE). A rather grand title, Simon thought to himself, for a large food court with a variety of small eating outlets located in a converted former department store on Ocean Drive. It benefitted from a large footfall near both West Shields town centre and the seafront bisecting these two busy destinations. The team that represented it was a veritable United Nations catering to both domestic and foreign tastes, but missing a U Thant to hold things together on the pitch. Their playing style, if they had one that could be identified, was a rainbow cocktail of confusions where the individual components didn't readily mix. The food of the world came together to play the football of the world, but most unfortunately, all on one plate. Sometimes, depending on the players of the day, they would record a success, other times, a failure. They were one of the most inconsistent teams in the league and always had been. Their match day performances were often viewed as random events so unlike God, they did play dice. They could just as easily be solid as rotten. CORE was consistently inconsistent, individual results wise, but always managed to finish in 13th or 14th position and so somehow find a stable resting place above their forthcoming opponents after everything came out in the wash. Simon consoled himself by believing this was unlikely to be the outcome at the end of this season however.

Pork and Mutton FC were still on a general upward trajectory of sorts and CORE were currently five places below them with the expected mixed bag of results and a miserly haul of six points out of a maximum of twenty-four (W2 D2 L8). It was certainly a game there for the winning depending just as much on which CORE players turned up to face them, and how they played together, as on Simon's own team selection.

Norman would be rested to allow his injury to heal. Both Salvator and Ever would return to the starting XI, that much was decided even before Simon had finished off his light Sunday morning breakfast of tea and toast. By the time he put on his coat and collected the team kit bag containing the shirts the only other decision he made was to make no more decisions until he got to the ground and saw his players in the flesh. Just as he closed the door behind him the telephone rang and before he could retrieve his key and get back in it stopped. Time was pressing so he decided to head straight to the ground fully expecting all of the squad to be doing the same. When he got there most had already arrived ahead of him, the only missing bodies were the Tripolini triplets and Jonathan. Norman had managed to make his way to the ground in advance of everyone else even with his slightly noticeable limp. He wasn't expecting to play but only lived ten minutes away and wanted to cheer the side on. He had even brought along a folding chair with him fully expecting to literally sit this one out. As kick-off time approached Simon was getting concerned about the four missing bodies and whether the missed telephone call had anything to do with it. Had mobiles been invented then he would have had his answer but alas communication lines remained tenuous at best. He would have to wait and hope. With five minutes left to go and an increasingly impatient referee he had little choice but to go with what he had. He decided to hold Norman in reserve as last resort just in case the others arrived during the game. This left nine players of sorts facing an expected complement of eleven who knows whats. The team needed something akin to major heart surgery regarding its immediate reorganisation and Simon, let alone Christiaan Barnard, was unlikely to be fully up to the task. So the hastily constructed line-up was composed of the following:

(0) Owen

(4) Simon   (6) Salvator   (3) Byron

(7) Roger   (8) Stuart   (11) Doug

(9) Ever   (10) Yiannis

All of the remaining four shirts, numbers 2, 5, 12 and blank (aka 13), were given to Norman with instructions to simply look after them until the others arrive. With Halloween only days away it was as if the team had been tricked rather than treated.

Simon counted the opposition as they came running out on the pitch in their green shirts and red shorts, all ten of them plus a goalkeeper, accompanied by a track-suited group heading for the touchlines. They had arrived in force to meet his depleted troops. A knowing sympathetic glance from the referee to Simon after the coin toss said it all. They lost that, as his heads call landed tails, and another greater loss was widely expected ninety minutes or so down the line. Their lack of personnel generated an over-confidence and carelessness in the opposition that almost resulted in a goal in the opening minutes. Stuart intercepted a lazy pass meant for their inside right and got the ball out to Doug who played a beautiful through ball to Yiannis that he hit first time just wide of the target. CORE were more careful and respectful after that early warning, no longer underestimating the under-strength side facing them. For the next ten minutes or so they tried to threaten Pork and Mutton's goal but the cobbled together defence easily held them at bay. At the moment, the disparity of numbers was not working too much against them. Optimism grew further when a long ball from Roger somehow found its way to an isolated Ever who turned back the years by deftly turning the teenage centre half marking him only to hit the upright. Up till now the best chances had fallen to them. What was becoming clear to Simon and the others was that CORE was a collection of individuals rather than a team, with just as many bad players as good, and either unwilling or unable to understand each other (being seemingly divided by footballing culture as much as by language). Their manager tried his best from the touchline but whatever he communicated was lost in translation on the park. The task for Simon and the rest of his team was to swiftly identify their opponents strengths and weaknesses so as to contain the former and exploit the latter.

The next fifteen minutes of the match was a getting to know each other affair with all the delicacies of a first date. Of course, there was also a certain fragility in that relationship which showed itself with the embarrassment of a goal in the 30th minute after one of CORE's standout players hoodwinked Doug, leaving him for dead, before charging his way past Byron then smashing the ball in the net. As a rather displeased Owen emptied the goal of its litter one of the missing arrived. It was one man and his dog.

"Where the hell have you been and why bring the dog?" Norman asked.

"Where have I been? You must be joking. I came at the usual time but no one was here so I assumed the match was off. I then went home and tried to call Simon without success so I decided to exercise the dog and passed by here."

"You idiot. Don't you know the clocks went back last night! You came too early then too late. You need to rush home and get your kit."

"Sorry, right. Why are you sitting in a chair and not playing?"

"I'm still injured and I came to offer my support with the support of this folding chair. Anyway, we have no time for all this now. Leave the dog with me, take this top and change at home - we need you directly back here."

Jonathan passed the dog's lead to Norman in exchange for his usual number 12 shirt - thereby promoting him to dog sitter. Soon they would have ten players on the park after one of the cavalry arrived, albeit originally on dogback.

Jonathan made his entry in the 35th minute and by the 40th minute he had equalised. The dog did not share in his new teammates, or Jonah's, delight being disappointed by his owner's rejection and missing out, only temporarily it hoped, on its extended walkies. Up until that moment the number 12 had done little apart from apologising for being both late and early, only enquiring about the absent Tripolini defence after finally realising they weren't there. Having been brought up to speed, Jonathan continued his momentum into the opponents penalty area and got his boot to a hopeful through ball from Yiannis, who had just retreated into the midfield to accommodate the new arrival up front.This was just the timely boost they, and especially he, needed. Apart from the occasional dog whining there was little else to shout about before the referee's whistle, followed by a bark, brought the game to its scheduled stop.

It was difficult to decide, as both sides took to their oranges and rest, who was happier with the current 1-1 scoreline. There were clear positives and negatives to be drawn. Pork and Mutton FC had just equalised and were playing without a full complement alongside missing their entire back three. Simon felt that with his usual XI, and given today's fielded opposition, they would be coasting this game. CORE on the other hand would view their performance as an improvement of sorts, following in the wake of three heavy defeats, given they were holding a team five places above them (with double their points tally). Of course, some of this gloss was removed by the opposition being reduced in number and the team's failure to hold onto a lead (unlike Norman) until half-time. There were reasons to be cheerful for both sides although CORE would probably have been more inclined to settle for a draw at this stage than Pork and Mutton.

A goal within five minutes of the restart showed that things were far from settled however. A sloppy back pass from Doug left Byron somewhat exposed and the stand-in left back was unable to recover his ground before the ball was intercepted by one of the better players of CORE who calmly rounded Owen to make it 2-1 and game on again. It was getting pretty clear to Simon where the goal threats were coming from and how best to counter them. Pork and Mutton's frailties were on the left of midfield and defence (Doug and Byron) exactly where CORE's best players directly faced them.

Simon now made some immediate adjustments to the team formation swapping positions between himself and Byron, and Roger with Doug, alongside getting Stuart to play slightly deeper and wider on the left to further support containment of CORE's best players. For the next ten minutes or so this helped shore up things, especially with Yiannis getting more firmly established with the amended midfield trio. From then on the balance of the game started shifting in Pork and Mutton FC's favour as they gained greater possession allowing them to test the opposition's rather wobbly back four. Ever was back to giving their young inexperienced centre back a pretty torrid time and he ended up gaining a penalty after the teenager carelessly mistook his leg for the ball receiving a booking in the process. Being as spritely as Ever could sometimes be, he immediately picked himself up, checked his wig, and his run up, before sending their goalie the wrong way and the ball the right. Back to square one and even-stevens after 63 minutes.

It was at this point that Simon had to finally give up on the Tripolini triplets turning up. They surely wouldn't have made the same mistake as Jonathan and something else must clearly be amiss and the unanswered telephone call may have been Jonathan or had something to do with their unexpected absence. He signalled to Norman that it was time for him to make an entrance, but without his throne as he wasn't Cleopatra or even Joseph L. Mankiewicz in his director's chair, and it would be just as lavish as the movie to keep him on the sidelines for too long. It was worth the risk to now even the numbers up, albeit with the addition of one dodgy leg. The dog committed a cardinal or ordinal sin of sorts by only allowing Norman to take the numberless shirt from the pile that now made up its temporary bed rather than the numbers 2 and 5 which remained. This was one conquest Norman could not make. He tethered said animal to one of the folding chair legs before spiking it deeply into the more friendly yielding turf. As the substitute cum reserve cum late official starter had his studs checked by the linesman before coming on his seemingly comfortable tailed companion immediately decided to swap the once precious shirts for something more alluring and became an armchair football fan.

Maybe the dog was a secret canine pundit as it had just taken its seat when things were about to get rather tasty. After a short period of intense pressure Pork and Mutton FC took the lead in the 68th minute following a corner expertly delivered onto the head of Ever by Byron. The young man who had just been literally man marking him had lost his own and the scorer's bearings. CORE's manager had seen enough and he directed his lost boy to the touchline to be replaced by a smaller but older player. The 3-2 scoreline lasted barely two minutes when their newly arrived substitute managed to easily dispossess Norman of the ball on the halfway line and send a high ball towards the penalty area for their centre forward to chase down until he got entangled with Salvator leading to both falling at the final hurdle. The referee awarded a soft penalty which allowed their first goalscorer to add another to his tally. This was becoming a topsy-turvy encounter by the minute. Chances then came and went for both sides with fatigue playing an increasingly important role in what was unfolding before the dog's, and everyone else's eyes. Yiannis was starting to menace the opposition defence after being instructed by Simon to join the attack and this gamble finally managed a return when he grabbed a close range goal following a fortunate rebound off their goalkeeper. It was now 4-3 with only five minutes left of normal time and surely they could hold this advantage. Well, almost not, when with only two minutes left on the clock Norman somehow managed to get himself between the ball and the goal to miraculously clear just ahead of the opposition's potential hat trick hero and the goal line. If the dog had hands even it would have applauded but at least the tail wagged. The result was finally confirmed when a labouring Jonathan broke free of a very tired defensive pack and sent the ball into the back of the CORE net with the last kick of the game. What a game, not to be missed, 5-3, and the dog joined the celebrations jumping down from its chair and barking appreciation at its owner.

It had been a very close shave for the team and defeat would have been more than cutting. Jonathan had finally arrived in more senses than one but the Tripolini mystery continued into the changing rooms and beyond. Later that afternoon Simon received a telephone call from Massimo which provided the solution.

"Hi Simon, sorry about earlier today and our no show but I did ring you a couple of times to let you know without getting through."

"I did hear the phone ring when I was just leaving home for the match. What happened?"

"Well, I am phoning on behalf of all the family, but especially my mother, to sincerely apologise for our absence but it was unavoidable. We received sad news from Italy very early this morning that a close uncle of my mother had just died. She had felt that it would be disrespectful for us to play football today and insisted that we attend mass and light candles for the dearly departed instead."

"You did the right thing. Your mother needed your support today much more than we did."

"I hope our loss didn't result in yours?"

"No, we eventually managed to win, but it's a long story better left to another day. I think we have all experienced a Sunday we will never forget. Give my deepest condolences to your mother and brothers. I will pop in and see them during the week."

CHAPTER 24:
Crazy Horses

Victory in the last game had been a very close affair. Players edging toward the periphery were now back in the fold after having shown themselves up to the call. This did as much for team bonding and morale as the two points that now only marginally raised them one spot to eighth. Simon's home telephone thankfully remained silent, following Massimo's contact, for the rest of the coming week apart from a wrong number on Friday night that prematurely set Simon's inner alarm bells ringing. After putting the receiver down, and with the approaching weekend now upon him, he rested a little easier in the hope that he would have a full squad of fourteen to draw upon.

Sunday's match was once again at The Links but unlike the last this was officially down as a home match. The particular playing pitch might be different but the ground would be the same and the level of fan base support likely to be little different (even with or without Jonathan's dog). This time the opponents were The Four Mile Inn, a former old coaching inn, once located in a then rural approach to East Shields and that distance from its old centre. Almost two centuries later and the Inn is no longer as isolated being now surrounded by, and serving, a salubrious suburb of West Shields. In the past people had merely passed temporarily through its doors on route to elsewhere, now its clientele were wealthy residents living permanently nearby, with most having finally settled for what they had always been looking for. This sense of contentment also pervaded the football team who always ended up somewhere in mid table with little restlessness to move beyond those confines. Promotion would only disturb the tranquility being enjoyed by all and very likely upset any apple cart. Further ambition was viewed as dangerous and everyone associated with the club had found a sort of equilibrium and inner calm. This was football clothed in yoga. There was a time when coaches used to come and go here, but no longer. Even the current football coach had been in situ for ten years and expectations were that he would remain for another ten or more. Likewise, the players, once signed, never felt inclined to join another club. The owner of the inn was just as undemanding and had been for a long time. When this outsider first came he wanted to change the name to The Coach and Horses believing its old title was rather meaningless, merely serving to mark a distance no longer of travelling interest to anyone, without recognising that his clientele viewed it as a more than acceptable modern marker of social distance from East Shields. They quickly changed his mind and the Four Mile Inn continued being their Shangri-La.

For much of this season to date Pork and Mutton FC and The Four Mile Inn had been playing leap frog with each other in the standings. The latest results had seen the two teams swap places once again, with Simon's side just ahead. The fact that this appeared to matter little to the opposition took away some of Simon's satisfaction as he had yet to achieve their inner spiritual peace. He was desperate to remain above them in the league as he and his team were motivated by a newly discovered ambition and the drive to regain respect. Unlike their opponents, Pork and Mutton had enough of flatlining, and like Oliver Twist were asking for more but knew it wouldn't easily be served up.

Their chances of winning today had improved now that all of the squad were punctually congregated together in The Links changing facilities prior to kick-off. Jonathan had turned up first, along with his dog. He had decided that it had brought both him and the team good luck last time and would do so again. After all, hadn't he also first come across his teammates when out walking the pooch? True, the dog had yet to write up its review of the last game, but appeared just as happy as its owner to be there.

"You can leave that mutt outside, it's not coming in the changing room." Simon insisted, having a full house already.

"Thank goodness for that," said a more than relieved Norman.

Although the dog's exile prevented its direct involvement in shirt distribution, Norman still missed out, getting none of the allocation. Simon went with what he still considered his strongest side given the prevailing dry and bright weather conditions so Norman and Doug would sit this one out (minus the former's folding chair) and Jonathan got the increasingly familiar number 12 shirt:

(0) Owen

(2) Mario   **(5) Massimo**   **(3) Marco**

(6) Salvator

(7) Roger   **(4) Simon**   **(8) Stuart**   **(11) Byron**

(9) Ever   **(10) Yiannis**

The selected XI, plus Jonathan now joined by his dog again, came running out together giving the false impression to anyone watching, including the opposition dressed in red and white tops and red shorts, and the match officials in their customary pink, that the animal was the team mascot. Both the referee and Four Mile's captain stated as much to Simon at the coin toss which he immediately corrected. This was no dog of his.

It was good to have the triplets back again, Simon thought to himself, as the referee blew his whistle. Both the game and Jonathan's dog quickly settled down into a gentle lull with little really happening for the first twenty minutes of game time. Neither goal was mildly offended, let alone seriously threatened, and there were few tackles let alone bookings. There was scant call for either the referee's pencil or of his really being there during this period of phoney war and the preservation of widespread good karma. The opposition appeared less keen to break this apparent truce, with their coach showing no desire to drive his horses any harder from the sidelines. Simon was much less pleased and started to take matters into his own hands by pressing forward with the ball whenever he could. Hostilities were officially declared on 30 minutes when, to everyone's surprise including his own, Simon fired off a speculative rocket into the roof of Four Mile's net from well outside the penalty area. This should have turned the match into more of a contest but Four Mile just turned the other cheek and seemingly invited Pork and Mutton FC to add to their lead. A shot from Yiannis clipped the top of the crossbar in the 38th minute, Ever missed an easy opportunity after the defence left their back door open two minutes later, and the red carpet was laid out for Roger just before half-time but he seemingly tripped over it. He, and the others, did manage to successfully stay on their feet and bag most of the oranges at the break however. Simon knew that missing these easy chances might come back to haunt them but kept such thoughts to himself as he tried to gee up his players.

"Listen lads, so we missed some great opportunities to extend our lead, but all that's in the past now. If we keep playing like we did in the last ten minutes or so we will not only get others but take them. Let's keep the pressure on."

Such generosities do not stay on the banqueting table for long and Simon could just about hear Four Mile's coach politely advocating their removal to the still contented huddle surrounding him. There was no sign of any panic in the very relaxed opposition.

The resumption of the game followed the same pattern as the start of the first half rather than its near ending. This was another period of strictly limited excitement with both goalkeepers less than gainfully employed for long periods of time. The horses of Four Mile hadn't yet bolted but the stable door was now firmly closed to Pork and Mutton FC. It was just as Simon had feared, and they may yet rue their earlier profligacy in front of goal, but at least they were maintaining their advantage during the ongoing stalemate. But things were about to get worse. A rather innocuous tackle, by an over apologetic defender, resulted in Ever having to finally limp off after 65 minutes.

"I'm going on, Norman would you mind looking after my dog?"

"No way! I never really was a dog lover anyway, and your dog just confirmed that last time. I'm here to play football rather than do your dog sit! Ask Doug, I'm sure he's more inclined."

Doug was happy to take voluntary charge of canine duties after the dog appeared more agreeable to this proposal than the previous. Things would not turn out as planned and it would become a *Dog Day Afternoon* months in advance of the cinematic version's release.

The opposition started to press more after the dog handover. The still mild-mannered coach succeeded in getting his players to up their tempo from a trot to a gracious canter while being hindered in passing on his instruction by the noisy restless mutt nearby.

"Would you mind awfully if I kindly asked you to keep your mascot quiet?"

"Sorry, I will try, but it seems to have a mind of its own. But it's not my dog nor the team's mascot, it belongs to our number 12 over there," Doug replied, pointing.

"Yeah, he's a right pain - the dog I mean," answered Norman.

Four Mile started started to press higher upfield and create chances of their own which led to no immediate direct return apart from increasing the sense of panic in Pork and Mutton's ranks. Yiannis and Jonathan provided important relief outlets as the team came under mounting intense pressure. A long ball out of defence, from an increasingly harassed Mario, somehow found its way to a closely marked Jonathan just inside the opposition's half. He managed to control the ball and beat his nearest man but with few options ahead of him lost possession from his blindside after deliberating far too long. He was over eager in trying to regain the ball and got the man instead. The referee's whistle blew and he came running over with book and pencil in hand, not planning to take an order or expecting any disorder. While Jonathan was cautioned the dog became less so, easily escaping Doug's inept handling, to make its way directly onto the pitch. Before the referee had fully noted Jonathan's name the unhappy pooch made a mark of its own not far removed from where the official kept his other, more precious, pencil. He may have been wearing pink but was no longer in the pink and joined his attacker in going barking mad. He made his way to Doug on the sidelines.

"I'm booking you for failing to control your dog. Go and get it off my pitch! It's a pain in the butt!"

"I know what you mean," said Byron on overhearing the ref's remark.

"But it's not my dog, it belongs to our number 12, the player you were booking, Jonathan Cruft," confessed Doug.

"Well I will sort him out! Just get the dog first. You let him go so your booking stands!"

The referee waited on the touchline until Jonathan passed the dog back to a now less than willing Doug. The dog showed his unhappiness by baring his teeth to the assembled, none of whom were dentists. Doug made his way back dragging the unwilling dog with him.

"I am also booking the dog. Name?"

"I hope you're not asking the dog!" said Norman.

"I'm not blinking Dr Dolittle! I was asking him," looking directly at Doug.

"No idea, never asked," Doug answered apologetically.

"We don't know either, but you must be crazy, it's an animal for goodness sake!" Ever replied on behalf of himself and Norman.

"I have booked plenty of animals before, granted two legs rather than four, but it no longer makes any difference to me! Don't call me crazy again or you both will enter my book too!"

"But we haven't done anything and there's no way I'm getting booked because of that mutt, whatever he's called," Norman said wanting to play no part in the dog's defence.

After returning back onto the pitch and a safe distance away from the dog, with as yet no name, the referee called Jonathan and Simon over.

"I understand that is your dog. I am booking it for ungentlemanly conduct. Name?"

"That's mad! You must be joking, surely?" a disbelieving Simon interrupted.

"I am neither insane nor a comedian. I will ask again, name?" looking away from Simon and directly into the face of Jonathan.

"I have already given you my name!"

"I will ask you again for the final time!"

"And if I don't?"

"Then I will hold the entire team to be in contempt."

"Just wait a minute, you cannot be serious? None of this makes any sense," said Simon.

"I'm warning you, best refrain from questioning everything I happen to say otherwise it's the book for you too my lad."

"Leave it Simon! I will give my dog's name but only under protest. He's called Eusebio. Do you add my surname to that?"

"Don't try to be funny with me! Calling your dog Eusebio, you are taking the proverbial! I am sending you off for insubordination. This will all be going in my match report."

"This has become a complete dog's breakfast," Simon whispered to Roger and Salvator after taking himself well away from from the referee's earshot.

"You're not kidding. The ref's the biggest basket case since Moses," Roger quietly replied.

"I hear what you both are saying but I don't understand what breakfast or Moses has to do with any of this?" said Salvator, totally clueless.

They were down to ten men again for the second week running but with no one to call on and fifteen minutes left to play. Jonathan grabbed the dog from a now relieved Doug and made his way directly home after collecting the rest of his things from the changing room.

Holding on to the lead proved just as difficult for Pork and Mutton FC as it had been for Doug especially as the opposition coach was now able to softly command his team to giddy-up into a steady gallop. For the remaining minutes his side suddenly became the Light Brigade and continued charging forward at the increasingly overwhelmed defence who gave away corner after corner following the relentless Four Mile onslaught. They got just reward in the 88th minute when corner kick number twelve met both a part glove of Owen and full skull of their own centre forward to land where greater force determined, into the centre of the goal. The equaliser once again returned the missing yin and yang back to the game. At least calm had been restored after the storm and the 1-1 scoreline kept Simon's side above the opposition in the league table. He had wanted more but any further advantage had been lost, in horse racing parlance, by a head.

CHAPTER 25:
Back in the Doghouse

Simon knew that once the referee's report had landed on Iam Wright-Pratt's desk in East Shields it would attract his full ire and a letter would surely follow in its wake and spoil any breakfast it so interrupted. Even thinking about Lower Lenin Street's likely response made him more than a little queasy as he believed, not without some justification, that they had it in for the club. The league administrators would lose little sleep over getting rid of Pork and Mutton FC if they could find a believable excuse to do so. It didn't have to be terribly reasonable or valid, Simon thought, just persuasive enough to carry the day when the committee's attendance was appropriately loaded. He was convinced that they had a prospective team from East Shields just waiting quietly in the wings for that day to finally dawn. They needed to show the league that they were now a footballing force to be reckoned with alongside being as squeaky clean as possible. They were making great strides in the former but large waves in the latter thereby serving to diminish any progress made.

It did not take long for the expected letter to duly arrive post-haste from 'Condiments HQ'. It was obvious from the spicy tone that Pork and Mutton FC were blamed for getting the league officials hot under the collar and in a bit of a pickle. They were in unfamiliar territory of being in a jam of sorts, trying to preserve their own authority whilst also conserving the referee's reputation. Simon carefully dissected the letter's contents several times over and found a few surprises in its predictable sermonising. It started with the status of a decree, then an admonishment, reducing to a slap on the wrist, after each re-reading. It had been a difficult letter to write rather than read, he concluded. The league administration had to do something but in the full knowledge that they would be firing blanks dressed up as full ammunition. It was only the bang that would register and not the desired hit. Simon looked at the letter again while tucking into what was becoming a hearty and edifying breakfast.

RaBHL (North) Football Administration Office

66b Lower Lenin Street
(over the Co-op)
East Shields

5th November
Mr Simon Washington
Secretary, Pork and Mutton FC
3 Freedom Square
West Shields

Dear Sir

It is with consternation that I find myself in the position of having to formally write to you, yet again, regarding events involving your football team. I had hoped, alas, that this would not be the case and that Pork and

Mutton FC would no longer generate this degree of controversy and bring our administration of the game into disrepute. That I am forced to write to you again suggests otherwise.

I am perplexed, after reading the referee's submitted match report of your most recent game (two days ago against The Four Mile Inn). This is already the second time this season that we have had the occasion to send off a player representing your team. I request that you demand that your players conduct themselves properly at all times and I hold you and themselves fully accountable for any behaviour deemed unbecoming. Mr Bone (the officiating referee) also booked Eusebio (the offending dog) for its rather savage response to his decision-making. While upholding the punishment afforded to Mr Jonathan Cruft and his subsequent two match ban I do not concur with the cautioning of animals of whatever species. The league administration takes full responsibility for the competency of the referees who officiate our fixtures. That said, I do believe Mr Bone has extenuating circumstances which partly excuses the strange decision he made. Although his behaviour clearly warrants further investigation, he was clearly suffering from shock after nearly losing assets which only he and his wife should enjoy. Regardless of that, you obviously cannot book a dog for ungentlemanly conduct and hence Eusebio's caution is quashed. Please inform Mr Cruft of my decision and strongly advise him to never bring his dog along to another game that is under our jurisdiction. His suspension remains valid, however, given that he is responsible for the dog at all times. Can I also suggest he consider having his dog muzzled when out among the public.

Mr Douglas Mortimer's booking also stands as he had a hand, or I should say failed to have a strong enough hand, in the distasteful proceedings by allowing the dog to trespass onto the pitch in the first place.

I did telephone the coach of The Four Mile Inn to get his perspective of what occurred and he felt that events had been blown out of all proportion without succeeding in spoiling an otherwise sporting and competitive match. His sympathies somewhat bizarrely were with the dog and its owner. I trust that this is not a case of West Shields uniting together against the administration here in East Shields but a fair and true assessment from the sidelines.

I look forward to a time when I do not have good cause to write to you as frequently as present.

Sincerely yours,

Mr Iam Wright-Pratt
Senior Administrative Official
RaBHL (North)

Simon put the letter down and placed his empty teacup and accompanying saucer on top of it fearing its contents were now deemed so slight that they would defy gravity and gently waft away. He was not to know, somewhat ironically on this occasion, that all the letters emanating from Lower Lenin Street were in Baskerville font. For the next few days he enjoyed recounting the details of its contents to all those associated with Pork and Mutton FC and anyone else who would care to listen. Only Byron and Norman continued believing that the dog got off lightly.

CHAPTER 26:
Grounded, Hounded
and Sounded

There was little doubt that the latest communique from Mr Wright-Pratt had served to cheer Simon and most of his teammates up and the rest of the working week passed gleefully by. With no cry-offs he looked forward to tomorrow's league game against The Tea Pot Cafe. They had met in a pre-season friendly, when Simon was just getting his reformulated side together, sharing the spoils in a 1-1 draw. As he sat down early Saturday evening with his local paper to read the usual page devoted to the league he was shocked to read the headline 'Give A Dog A Bone'. The football journalist, Toby Sure, had somehow managed to source the finer details relating to last Sunday's events and been given extra column inches by his editor to provide full and frank disclosure. It was clear that he was relishing his opportunity to shine as a wordsmith rather than having to face his usual constraints with little space to move far beyond listing the results and league placings. The referee was one target and the dog's owner the other, best captured by the reporter's tagline of 'dog makes a show of Crufts', intentionally adding the s for effect. He was less scathing of the dog probably because his readers were most likely animal lovers.

There was a photograph of a dog that looked like Eusebio alongside another photograph of the world famous Portuguese (cum Mozambique) striker Eusebio da Silva Ferreira of Benfica, recent recipient of his second European Golden Boot. The article made great play of the fact that the Ballon d'Or winner, who had made nearly 500 appearances for club and country, had never been booked whereas his namesake had only two appearances to its name and had just received a caution from Mr Bone following its move on his vitals. Although the piece added that this booking had been subsequently quashed it highlighted the fact that the dog had also been given its own order of the boot and grounded by the administration from making any further league appearances. Included was a very guarded statement from Iam Wright-Pratt confirming the referee's temporary suspension until further notice that also half-heartedly denied the reporter's suggestion that the official was being, somewhat ironically, hounded out by the league administration due to his latest embarrassment.

Simon would have much further preferred his team being talked about for footballing reasons but at least his side were not being lampooned, unlike poor Mr Bone. The dog had captured the headlines rather than Pork and Mutton's improved performances. The season would reach its half way point tomorrow and Simon was desperate to mark it with a win to consolidate their place in the top half of the table and provide more evidence of their rate of progress. The Tea Pot Cafe had managed to salvage a draw from the jaws of defeat in their last encounter thanks to a last minute penalty and several missed Pork and Mutton opportunities to extend their 1-0 lead. The closeness of that game had shown Simon, quite early on, that his side could compete successfully against those who had previously humbled them. His confidence grew even more when he looked at the league table, now getting minor billing after the Eusebio story, and saw his side having a two point and three place advantage over their next opponents.

The match was back at The Links again but officially deemed as an away fixture being just as much home to today's opponents. As he waited for the others to arrive Simon noticed a slightly larger than normal crowd gathering around their designated pitch hoping that it had less to do with the newspaper report of yesterday and more to do with the amount of support the Cafe usually generates. Once everyone presented themselves for duty – with the exception of Jonathan, given his suspension and wise decision to keep both his, and the dog's, head down – Simon decided to go with the same playing XI that had started last week's match against Four Mile. The only remaining issue was who would get the number 12 shirt and, less importantly, the blank. After checking the mildness of the weather outside again he decided to give the substitute berth to Norman whilst simultaneously promising Doug a place in the team for next week's home game at The Links against Bulman United regardless of the weather or today's result. The side lined up as follows:

(0) Owen

(2) Mario   **(5) Massimo**   **(3) Marco**

(6) Salvator

(7) Roger   **(4) Simon**   **(8) Stuart**   **(11) Byron**

(9) Ever   **(10) Yiannis**

The Chi wore their usual all green strip and the match officials pink, but without generating the level of ridicule that was occasioned on first airing the last time these two sides met. The majority of the twenty or so spectators showed themselves to be behind the home team, as Simon had earlier concluded, but also no longer so against Owen or his number 0 jersey. A couple of the fans did turn up to see the dog but left after he failed to make a showing. Simon was sure that some may have been undercover league administrators making sure their advice had been heeded or more newspaper reporters looking for another story. Perhaps Wright-Pratt had been there, with or without disguise, as Simon had never actually met him, or even Toby Sure for that matter. They always attended the annual awards ceremony an event barred to the likes of Pork and Mutton FC.

The first half belonged to Simon's side, especially Yiannis, with the opposition finding it difficult to cope with him. He got his name on the score sheet in the 15th minute when he received a well-timed through ball from Byron to beat the offside trap and stroke the ball deftly home. Ten minutes later and the score should have been doubled after a mis-timed tackle on Yiannis in the penalty area resulted in its failing to be converted by Ever. This was a bit like history repeating itself, Simon feared, with missed opportunity following missed opportunity. His fretting was brought to an end in the 37th minute when Yiannis connected his left boot to a speculative cross from Roger that any one of the two centre halves should have easily cleared. The team went into the half-time break with a two goal lead and a defence that hardly needed to break sweat. Owen had yet to be tested, quite unlike their pre-season encounter.

The orange quarters tasted sweeter than usual although the whistle signalling the arrival of the interval hadn't been welcomed in its customary way. It was one of those halves that could have gone on for ever, especially after the second goal went in.

"Keep it up lads, don't relent, I want you to carry that rhythm through into the second half. The game is only half won and we must not surrender all we have worked for in the previous forty-five," Simon said.

He had little to worry about as the game fortunately panned out much as before. There was little to cheer the home crowd though and Owen had the time to politely converse with an optimistically expectant group gathered behind his goal. While the words were with him the deeds were further upfield. Ever hit the bar in the 60th minute and Roger had a cheeky lob cleared off the line five minutes later. Another goal must surely come and help anoint the team's improved standing. It, and the richly deserved Yiannis hat-trick, duly arrived on 69 minutes courtesy of a penalty, awarded following a deemed intentional hand ball. Ever sportingly gave the ball to his fellow attacker which he gratefully dispatched without any intervention from the opposition goalie. With around fifteen minutes remaining and the game clearly won Simon decided to make a change. His goalscoring hero had clearly run himself into the ground and merited a well-earned rest. Norman came on and took up Byron's position on the left allowing him to join Ever up front. Further forays into the opposition's half took place but without reward and both sides appeared content with the 3-0 scoreline remaining unchanged for the rest of the duration. Simon did glance across at Yiannis several times during this period of the endgame and noticed him to be in what appeared a lengthy dialogue with a man he didn't recognise taking place far removed from the touchline and Doug.

At the end of the game all of the players made their way to the changing facilities apart from Yiannis.

"Where's our hat-trick hero?" Stuart asked.

"I saw him talking to some geezer outside. He must be still out there nattering away," Roger answered.

"You guys get changed and head off. I'll hang around and wait for Yiannis and make sure everything's OK," Simon said, worried that something may be up.

The players made their usual farewells leaving their captain alone in the changing room awaiting his most recent recruit's return. Five minutes later Yiannis finally arrived, surprised to find Simon still there.

"I didn't expect anyone to be here, I hope you weren't waiting on my account? If you were, I'm sorry for keeping you."

"Is everything alright? It's just that I noticed you engrossed in a prolonged conversation with that stranger."

"It was nothing really," Yiannis said blushing.

"You can tell me it's none of my business if you like, but who was he, and what did he want?"

Simon's questions were met with silence for a few seconds until Yiannis plucked up the courage to reply as he had not been intending to have this particular conversation so quickly after concluding the other. He began by first clearing his throat of any obstacles that could get in the way of his confession.

"It's not something bad, at least for me anyway, and I haven't done anything wrong, I think? I do have some news for you which I wanted to chew over and digest first before discussing it. Never mind, better sooner than later I suppose."

"I hope I'm not pushing you or putting you in an awkward position by asking?"

"No, you have a right to know, it's just the timing. I have just been approached by East Shields Town. That stranger was their scout and he was sounding me out about whether I would be willing to have a trial with them. The funny thing is, he was only there because of the recent publicity generated by Jonah's dog!"

More blessed fallout, Simon thought to himself.

CHAPTER 27:
Breaking Bad

It was now halfway point in the season and Simon and his players had just finished with a win that placed them in sixth position in the division - now all confirmed in print by the latest edition of his usual Saturday newspaper. Although they were a world away from the leading pack, and any chance of promotion, they were also even further removed from the wooden spoon position that they often tended to make their own. He knew that there was a large dose of truth in the old adage that the league table never lies but remained cautious enough to realise that it can also flatter to deceive at this stage in the season. A lot of people would be very surprised by their current position, viewing it as little more than a flash in the pan, an aberration before the inevitable fall. Simon spent longer than usual taking in the statistics basking on his lap and felt entitled to draw extended satisfaction from it:

RaBHL (North) Division 2

	P	W	D	L	F	A	Pts
Deutscher Bierkeller	15	13	1	1	50	6	27
Peking Duck United	15	11	4	0	42	5	26
Shirley Inn FC	15	10	3	2	35	10	23
The White Elephant	15	11	1	3	34	14	23
Austin's Fryers	15	8	4	3	27	16	20
Pork and Mutton FC	15	6	5	4	30	24	17
Bulman United	15	5	7	3	21	17	17
The Four Mile Inn	15	6	3	6	23	22	15
FC Lokomotiv	15	5	5	5	17	21	15
The White Eagle	15	4	6	5	20	32	14
The Tea Pot Cafe	15	4	5	6	15	27	13
The Irish Club	15	2	4	9	18	29	8
The Cretan Taverna	15	2	2	11	12	32	6
CORE	15	2	2	11	14	42	6
College Caterers FC	15	2	2	11	10	40	6
Smithfields	15	0	4	11	9	40	4

The team had already banked as many points this season as they had amassed over the previous two full seasons taken together and it made heady reading so it was sensible that he remained seated in his most comfortable armchair.

Had he, and the three other original members making up their gang of four, known before the start of the season that the team would be residing where they are now they never would have even considered turning off its ventilator. Hindsight may be a wonderful thing, but foresight can be even better, and no one saw this coming. Simon was thankful that they had not carried out the coup de grâce that few would have blamed them doing, and some even welcomed. He may well be getting ahead of himself, but it was no longer apocalypse now. They had, he earnestly hoped, finally broken bad as he continued to slowly savour this public statistical recognition of their feat.

They already had thirty goals registered in their goals for column, more than double the return when compared to the same point last year; with Yiannis and Ever having bagged eight goals apiece, followed by Doug on five, Jonathan on three, Byron and Simon with two each, Roger one, and an own goal. This made them the fifth highest scoring team in the league currently but still far removed from the half century of goals netted by The Deutscher Bierkeller, twenty-nine of those credited to their bustling centre forward Karl Göring, who was way ahead in the league's goalscoring charts. Simon pondered why no one was chasing big Karl's signature, given his outstanding record, rather than his own player Yiannis. The defence had conceded twenty-four goals and eight teams had conceded less (all five teams above them and the three directly below). The two teams residing in the promotion spots, The Deutscher Bierkeller and Peking Duck United, had been the most uncharitable in leaking only six and five goals respectively. Simon's side, like many others, had failed to score against either of those downright miserly defences. He knew that Owen would be less than satisfied with only keeping four clean sheets so far this season but their goalie did not know that they had only managed to prevent the opposition from scoring once during the whole of the previous campaign (conceding ninety-seven goals in the process with fifty-two of those coming in the first fifteen games). So even here there were clear reasons to be cheerful.

Regardless of Owen Bigalow's curious take on zero, Simon was convinced that there are no goalless draws in life and its many challenges. You can allow failure to beat you or you can positively respond to it. Losing and winning are aspects of the same thing, of participating and engaging, of not giving up or doing nothing. No one wants an empty life consisting of nothing but endless blanks, not even their goalie, Simon philosophised to himself. One needed to recognise the victories in every defeat and the defeats in any victory to move forward in the most profitable way. Victories need defeats to keep up our guard just as defeats need victories to inject us with hope. Both he and the rest of his team were becoming more aware of all this and how its articulation played out. Not only events, but more particularly your responses to them, determine outcomes; both the results and the enrichment process in achieving them.

CHAPTER 28:
Being Adam's
Keen and Able

S imon's enjoyment of this newly minted edition of Saturday's sports section was cut short by a loud banging on his front door. He was so taken aback by the ferocity of his usually tame lion head brass door knocker making such a sustained and savage noise that he dropped his newspaper from where it pleasantly rested even before jumping out of his armchair. He wasn't expecting anyone at this or any hour today and had planned to turn his attention to tomorrow's return fixture against Bulman United after attending to the tea dishes piling up in his sink. He already knew it would be another tough match, now further confirmed in black and white, with both teams currently evenly matched on seventeen points and only separated by goal difference.

He now rushed to answer the nuisance call located at his threshold. In his haste to get there, propelled by both the sustained loudness of the knocking and worried by the confident authority betrayed by its impatience, Simon failed to announce his own response. He suddenly, and just as forcefully, yanked the door open only to find the caller, still attached to it by means of the knocker, unavoidably following the newly established direction of travel. They now collided in the hall which had seen better and more welcoming entrances than this. It was difficult to express the usual pleasantries of a first time meeting given these circumstances and both men attended to disentangling themselves before normal service could be resumed. They had both served to startle each other and now they needed to recompose themselves. Before any real progress could take place on that score the unexpected visitor apologised for the nature of his impromptu arrival and simultaneously handed Simon his newly disengaged knocker back along with his other calling card. These were both somewhat graciously received by the host, who now cordially invited the somewhat familiar looking stranger in while closing the front door, minus said brassware - which was placed on the hall table to be fixed back later.

Simon glanced at the business card, as he directed its owner into the living room, and saw that it belonged to a Mr Adam Robson, Chief Scout, East Shields Town Football Club. He now realised why his guest looked familiar, he had seen him with Yiannis at the last match.

"Now that we both have our bearings, can I once again apologise for my more than abrupt arrival at your home. I got your address from Iam Wright-Pratt. I know that I could just as easily have telephoned, since Yiannis gave me your number, and that may have been more convenient, but I prefer to discuss such matters directly, in person, face to face. This has always been my preferred way of working, so I hope you don't mind."

"I understand, and Yiannis and I had a brief conversation after you watched him at our game last week. Please follow me into the parlour where we can talk more comfortably."

The journey to their seats gave Simon a little extra time to better observe his visitor and only now did he realise that he had watched the scout play for the very club which he now represented fifteen or more so years ago just before his long career ended. The intervening years had been rather less than kind to Mr Robson, his face had certainly aged more than it should and the smell of his breath suggested alcohol may have contributed. He not only behaved, but also looked, decidedly old school. He had on a rather drab, and equally dated, black suit with one side jacket pocket containing a notebook gently protruding from within its clutches neatly balanced on the opposite by a hip flask of sorts. On the plus side he still had a full head of black hair, brylcreemed and neatly parted, had not replaced muscle with too much fat, and stood upright without any sign of a stoop. If he had looked down he would have realised his shoes hadn't seen any polish for weeks, Simon further reflected.

The scout was not here in search of a shoeshine boy alas but rather one of Pork and Mutton FC's most important players.

"I am here to let you know that Yiannis turned up for his trial with us two days ago and we were so impressed by him that we want to sign him up. I know he is both very keen to join us and more than able to make the transition. I trust you will concur that his football development would be greatly enhanced by playing for East Shields Town rather than a pub team, albeit an improving one, in the lowest tier. That said, we are greatly impressed by his sense and expression of loyalty to Pork and Mutton FC and his being committed to honouring his current obligations with you. This puts us both in a bit of a bind since he will only join us if you release him and he will regret, and even possibly resent, missing this opportunity if you do not."

This errant to 3 Freedom Square was clearly in the best interest of both Yiannis and Town while at the expense of Simon's side. Pork and Mutton FC could rightly insist on keeping the player and Mr Robson knew it. Simon had listened carefully to the scout's words. Should he give up the prodigy in their midst? Being keen and able made Yiannis more than a rightful son of Adam, Simon thought to himself, wondering why he was drawing yet more religious parallels.

"I will be just as honest with you as you have been with me. I would never knowingly stop Yiannis, or any of my other players, from doing what I believed was in their best interests. I completely agree that while such loyalty as this should be admired we both recognise it can also be misplaced. I have no desire whatsoever to hold Yiannis back but, and I am sure you fully understand, I am also duly obliged to consider my own team's interests too. I am not trying to negotiate or play hardball here either. We do appear to be in yet another entanglement that we both wish to agreeably resolve! It just needs a little wisdom of Solomon."

Over a cup of tea, followed by a swig or two from the chief scout's hip flask, they quickly concurred over their future course of action. Yiannis could continue playing for Pork and Mutton FC until the onset of their long winter break, four games hence, while also training with East Shields. Before the two month recess kicked in (designed to save the pitches, if not the players, from too much seasonal damage) Mr Robson would be most willing to help Simon, if necessary, find a suitable replacement by drawing on his extensive local contact list. This was unashamedly verified by his taking out the notebook and flicking open random pages directly under Simon's nose. Now all the ballast from his side jacket pockets were on the table. Finally with something of an amateur magician's flourish he retrieved, from his inner pocket, a season ticket for all of Town's remaining home fixtures and offered it to his host as a thank you rather than a bribe. Simon accepted it in the spirit it was offered and their business for the time being was happily concluded.

As the team gathered in The Links changing room Simon managed to take Yiannis to one side.

"I want a quiet word. Just to let you know, I had a conversation with Mr Robson yesterday about how best to resolve your future."

"Yes, I know. He called around at my house immediately after being at yours. I really appreciate all that you both have done and I am really happy with the outcome."

The young lad was given his normal number 10 shirt just before Simon informed the rest of the side, with a tinge of regret alongside a large dollop of delight, that this was the first time that a player from the club had been wanted by anyone let alone East Shields Town. Spontaneous applause rang out from all those present as an embarrassed Yiannis sought refuge by pulling his shirt over his head.

Jonathan was the only one missing from this celebration as he was still serving the last of his suspension. Doug had been promised a place in the starting line-up the previous week and duly received the number 11 shirt previously worn by Byron (who would now be sitting this game out as Norman was once again given the substitute slot). The rest of the team largely picked itself, not least in the light of their last result. Simon had briefly toyed with the idea of dropping himself instead of Byron, but given today's opponents, having the slightly more defensively balanced option made better strategic sense, at least at the outset:

(0) Owen

(2) Mario   **(5) Massimo**   **(3) Marco**

(6) Salvator

(7) Roger   **(4) Simon**   **(8) Stuart**   **(11) Doug**

(9) Ever   **(10) Yiannis**

215

As the team escaped the confines of their cramped changing room there was none of the trepidation displayed prior to the previous encounter against Bulman. This was now a side that had discovered its self-belief without any sign of hubris. They ran onto their designated pitch with the confidence of a team happy in their own skin and with a sense of entitlement that they belonged there. This was most true of the stalwarts who were especially enjoying the disappearance of ridicule that had always been present in recent seasons past. It was noticeable how, as their performances and results greatly improved, the demeaning comments from the opposition and the touchline got increasingly less. For Simon, and some of the other veterans, caution still remained close at hand, not least regarding the team that faced them today.

Just like Pork and Mutton FC, Bulman United were playing a brand of football not usually associated with them. They too were trying to leave a tarnished reputation far behind, based less on ineptitude and more on pure thuggery. They had once taken man marking quite literally but now replaced it with playing the ball rather than the man. Such was the extent of their household cleansing, with all previous serial violent offenders sent packing (although not without a fight), that they would now be sitting on top of the fair play league - had such existed at the time.

The omens pointed to a clean, fair and competitive match between two upwardly mobile teams focused on the football. The prevailing weather conditions, however, were less than obliging and not so set to fair. A cold wind took advantage of The Links open spaces to announce its arrival prior to kick-off and was escorted by a light drizzle that turned into a sustained heavy downpour that greeted an early Pork and Mutton corner in the 5th minute. This led to nothing apart from the opposition goalie displaying great handling by easily plucking Roger's rather wild, yet tame, cross from the darkening skyline. For the next fifteen minutes or so the referee saw more service than either forward line, having to intervene on several occasions due to an unforgiving pitch that made the ball skid and players slide uncontrollably. The man in the middle did not book anyone, realising that they were fouls generated without malicious intent.

"No one here is Esther Williams, so take care, its *Dangerous When Wet!*" the ref shouted, thereby immediately, and rather inadvertently, showing both his age and his being a bit of a film buff.

Only one player was in their element and not allowing their prematch spirits to be dampened - Doug was beginning to relish his increasing involvement in what was starting to become, through no fault of the other participants, another bit of a lacklustre affair reminiscent of the last time they met. On that occasion Doug had been given the blank (aka number 13) shirt as reserve, meaning spectator status only, and it was the height of summer. He was now making his presence felt after two dangerous solo forays deep into enemy territory in the 22nd and 28th minute respectively that generated no real reward apart from another wasted corner collected nonchalantly by the Bulman goalkeeper and a free kick that Ever blasted high into orbit without any sign of re-entry. Somewhat unfortunately, another ball was procured, so this dull and damp affair could continue where it left off.

With half-time slowly approaching the pitch was getting cut up better than the orange segments being prepared on the sidelines by Byron. The ground was quickly becoming little better than a quagmire and adding significantly to both teams laundry bills. Bulman United were once again becoming a very dirty team but only requiring a box of Daz, rather than the rule book, to be thrown at them. At the conclusion of this game their strips would need to get back to being just as 'whiter than white' as their disciplinary record had become.

As the teams took an undeserved interval break neither side had the match or their laundry yet in the bag. Unlike some Scandinavian porno movie, the players would have to wait to get their kit off until the final take, but hopefully the second half would turn out better than the first. Although neither side had earned it, the rain did mercifully relent to allow the intake of the butchered vitamin C.

As soon as the referee blew to restart the match the rain took it as a signal to continue its cascade; it too had only taken a little breather. Simon had taken a knock near the end of the first half and planned to run it off in the early part of the second. He didn't mention it in his half-time deliberations.

"Lads, we need to take a few more risks, and gamble a little more, by pushing a few more bodies upfield to support Doug's runs. We also have to improve the supply lines to the front two because Ever and Yiannis are having to come deep in order to get involved in the play."

It didn't take long for Simon's instruction to start making an impact, just as the earlier tackle was beginning to do on him, when a fast counter attack in the 53rd minute resulted in Yiannis hitting a twenty yard sizzler that thundered off a post and found sanctuary in the bushes nearby. Before the ball was retrieved Simon signalled to Norman to prepare for his earlier than planned entrance into the game.

"Stuart I'm going off. You take over my position, and the captaincy. I'll tell Norman to play inside, on the left of midfield, and you make sure he gets to feed Doug out on the touchline as much as possible." It was clear to Simon that Pork and Mutton's number 11 had a hearty appetite and was hungry for more given he was dining at his most perfect table.

The fifteen or so minutes following Simon's premature departure from the field of play were marked by sustained Bulman United pressure. Owen and his teammates were mightily relieved to see an easy chance spurned by an opposition forward's mistimed and misplaced strike at goal. This was quickly followed by a seemingly late tackle, in his own penalty area, by Massimo that could just as easily have resulted in a spot kick rather than being played on by a generous and forgiving referee. The match had suddenly become alive with both sides clearly going for it - the gentle sparring with its overly polite gameplay was clearly over. A change to the scoreline occurred in the 71st minute and it was Pork and Mutton FC who benefitted from the breakthrough. Norman won possession of the ball deep in his own half and carried it a full twenty yards before finding Doug out on the wing who did the rest by going on another dazzling solo run that ended with both man and ball in the back of the Bulman net. While the substitute had been the provider of the celebratory joy that followed it was clear, on this occasion, that Max Mortimer's son had concluded this undertaking, possibly putting the result of the game to peaceful rest.

Much would still depend on the continued heroics taking place in defence. The team were holding onto the lead by their finger tips. Pork and Mutton's goalie just managed to reach a dipping shot that he turned over the crossbar. This was quickly followed by his somehow getting his outstretched left hand glove to a volley that then kindly ricocheted off the nearby post for another corner. The clock was ticking and play was becoming more frantic as if one had just set off a fire alarm and there was only one exit in the direction of Owen's goal. With three minutes remaining Salvator became the first player to enter the referee's book for blatantly pulling down Bulman's marauding number 10 just outside the penalty area and leaving telltale scratch marks on his thigh. The resulting free kick beat the wall, and Owen, but not the crossbar, before continuing its merry way behind the goal then striking another piece of woodwork, the trunk of a tree. It was clear that Simon and his side were now riding their luck and it was becoming a question of whether it, or time, would run out first. In the last minute of the game everyone thought they were given their answer when Bulman United were deservedly awarded a penalty following their 20th corner of the match. Owen had misjudged the incoming cross and found himself stranded well off his line where the ball was then despatched off the head of the opposition centre forward. A goal looked certain with a welcoming net awaiting the ball's arrival. Out of nowhere Salvator again allowed his fingernails to illegally intervene and protect their 1-0 advantage. The referee blew for handball and had little choice but to send the Brazilian off. Yet another suspension but first the suspense. If the penalty was converted there could be no complaints. Bulman's thwarted centre forward stepped up to take the kick but slipped in his run up and the very tip of his right boot gently stubbed the embarrassed ball into Owen's safe keeping. Salvator's sacrifice had somehow been worth it result wise, but along with the rain, only served to further dampen the manner of the winning.

CHAPTER 29:
Feeding Leviathan

That most fortunate victory kept Pork and Mutton FC in touch with the top five and also provided additional clearance with those directly below them. Simon, doubtless, just like the others, was delighted to spend the rest of Sunday on dry land, in clothes that were no longer heavy in water content. As he looked out of his living room window, to the North Sea far in the distance, he had more than a little sympathy with any ancient mariner cast out there today. The weather only got worse as the day progressed and the whole team had fortuitously skedaddled The Links portacabin for the sanctuary of their respective homes in advance of the next deluge. The rain refused to go away and continued to overstay its welcome until finally departing in midweek to be replaced by a bout of high pressure that saved their next fixture from being postponed. The scheduled home return fixture against FC Lokomotiv BRC (British Rail Catering) had been in the balance due to the pounding that The Links had been receiving from the heavens and the soles opening it up. The all clear only arrived late on Friday afternoon.

Apart from the uncertainty over the game much of the week played out as expected. Simon received formal acknowledgement from Mr Iam Wright-Pratt of Salvator Samba's two match suspension alongside unnecessary notification of Jonathan Cruft being available for selection again (neither of these came as a surprise, even the football administrator's stale, supercilious, earnest and less than endearing writing style was found to be just as predictable). Work at the Town Hall carried on much as before, with his in-tray and out-tray taking turns in rising and falling but never quite emptying. Things always got busier in the run-up to Christmas but Simon was quite thankful for the slightly increased workload that appeared to help make a slow and depressingly drab earlier part of the week pass faster. There was one surprise that did catch him out and it came in the form of a telephone call on Saturday afternoon just as he was about to leave the house to utilise what remained of his gifted season ticket.

Simon picked up the handset with more than a little trepidation, as he was becoming familiar with bad news awaiting him at the end of the line, and his concern increased when the caller identified himself.

"Simon, ciao, it's Massimo here."

"Please, tell me everything is alright?"

"All good, don't worry, me and my brothers are fine, fighting fit and looking forward to the game."

"Thank goodness, my heart rate has just returned to normal! So why were you trying to scare the living daylights out of me?"

"Haha, molto bene - you English! I hope to bring you good news not bad. It is something of a long story but please hear me out."

Massimo then recounted what happened earlier that morning. A lumbering giant of a man, heading upwards of six foot six, crash-landed, rather than drifted, into the Tripolini deli with a large bucket in each hand, the jangling contents of which announced themselves with his every movement. He was collecting for charity and had just come from the High Street in search of sustenance for his toils ahead. After adding a few extra coins to the load Massimo showed the stranger to a table where he could rest and silence his buckets for a little while. The man perched himself as best he could on one of the dining chairs which not only let out a groan following his arrival but appeared to markedly diminish in size. As Massimo took his order, for coffee, two rounds of sandwiches, and a large slice of cake, he could not fail to notice the enormous pair of boots protruding from underneath the table. They must be size 18 at the very least and you couldn't pick them up off the shelf even if you could lift them. He wasn't expecting Charlie Cairoli, or any other clown, to visit his establishment on this or any other day. The old woman who lived in a shoe, along with her children, would have been delighted to have this amount of real estate.

After finishing all that was placed before him he politely called Massimo over and ordered another slice of cake along with a refill of his coffee mug. On the return of this latest request he then engaged his provider in conversation about the two scarves hanging so prominently, that had so attracted Simon a few months earlier. Only a *Reader's Digest* version of the story was offered up before discussion shifted to football in general then somehow landing on the Tripolini brothers involvement in Pork and Mutton FC. The latter appeared to spark greater interest for the stranger than much of the preceding. He told Massimo that apart from his more recent charity work - which now took up large swathes of his leisure time - he did little else of any note apart from collecting his dole. After three years of unemployment this was his way of doing something meaningful in his life. He had come to realise that pounding the streets with Faith and Hope (the nicknames he had given to each of his buckets now prominently, but somewhat crudely, painted on their respective outsides) in search of missing Charity was just as demanding on flesh as on shoe leather, if not more so. He was looking for other ways to improve his fitness and was wondering whether football in general, and Pork and Mutton FC in particular, was the answer; also confessing that it would give him another reason to leave the house. Massimo saw no reason to dissuade the upright stranger and had suggested he come along to tomorrow's game and have a chat with Simon. That is where the deli conversation abruptly ended as a rush of punters came in search of tables including that of the now ready to vacate colossus. He and his buckets quickly took flight after settling the bill but without leaving his name. Massimo then added one other piece of information - that this modern day Goliath had a recognisable Scottish accent.

"I hope you don't mind my inviting him to the game tomorrow and your having a chat with him? Beggars are not choosers, I think you know what I mean."

"Not at all, and I do. I'm just delighted you didn't give him my home address as I have just fixed my knocker!"

"Sorry? You have lost me. What's this knocker thing you're on about?"

"It's another lengthy story, but one that isn't worth repeating. I agree that we can ill afford to turn down any prospective player interest at present. Obviously we are still very much in the dark with regard to the stranger's playing credentials let alone his identity."

"True. We will shine a light on him tomorrow. One thing's for certain though."

"What's that?"

" He doesn't need me bigging him up! Ciao Simon."

The match between East Shields Town and Whitley Spartans had little to commend it apart from a great solo goal from someone very familiar to Simon, Dr Ally Balls of said white Hummel boots fame, and the half-time homemade pie, which was delicious. The latter brought back fond memories of his mother's cooking while the former reminded him of the damage the medic inflicted, without any redress to the BMA, the last time they met FC Locomotive. Simon did take some comfort in the fact that even a top team like the Spartans couldn't stop Balls from scoring. As he made his way from the ground he caught a brief glimpse of a large figure someway in the distance with a bucket in each hand about to disappear down one of the many side streets leading away from the stadium. Could this possibly be their potential mysterious recruit, Simon thought to himself, fully expecting a full reveal tomorrow.

The home turf of The Links also had little to commend it with the scars of the previous week still showing themselves as proudly as any facial cuts from a German fencing duel. Perhaps the players from British Rail Catering will struggle on a surface such as this, Simon hoped, with little faith, and even less intended charity. Team adjustments would have to be made more in light of Salvator's suspension rather than Jonathan's return. With three wins and one draw in the last four games minor tweaks rather than major changes recommended themselves. Simon kept the number 6 shirt normally worn by the Brazilian for himself and gave the number 4 shirt to Norman and asked him to swap midfield positions with Stuart. Byron was selected ahead of Doug only on the basis that it was a fine morning with no hint of inclement weather. He would be sitting this one out, albeit standing on the touchline, as the number 12 shirt was passed to Jonathan who was back accompanied by his usual minor grumblings, but thankfully without Eusebio. So the team lined-up as follows:

(0) Owen

(2) Mario   (5) Massimo   (3) Marco

(6) Simon

(7) Roger   (8) Stuart   (4) Norman   (11) Byron

(9) Ever   (10) Yiannis

Just before kick-off Simon ran to the touchline to have a few words with his substitute and reserve.

"Oh, I nearly forgot to mention, can I ask the two of you to keep your eyes open for a huge guy, with or without buckets, who will be turning up at some point during the game."

"Who is he?" Doug queried.

"Have we gone up in the world and hired a magic sponge man?" was Jonathan's attempt at gleaning more information.

"Look, no sarky comments! He's almost as much a mystery to me as to you. He's very, very big, I understand and has a noticeable Scottish accent. There, you now know almost all that I do. Just be welcoming when he shows."

Simon left the two of them on the sidelines now wondering as much as he but somewhat even more curious given he hadn't fully explained the buckets.

"Well he can't be a winger, given his size," Doug consoled himself, while simultaneously getting Jonah agitated.

"It's alright for you young blokes, but I hope he's not more competition for me! I'm getting fed up always hanging around being Mr Super Sub waiting for things to happen. It's no fun at this age and the weather won't be improving any time soon."

"And what's all this with the buckets? That's completely weird."

"Doug have you not just heard yourself? You never fail to surprise me!"

It turned out to be a disappointing first half for Simon and his team. Neither the prospective new recruit nor Pork and Mutton FC had bothered to turn up against a side four places below them but playing like they were four places above. Half-time couldn't come quickly enough and they were fortunate to reach it with only a 2-0 deficit. An early FC Lokomotiv goal, after only four minutes, had served to unsettle the defence when a speculative long through ball caught both Simon and Marco cold allowing the incoming right winger to almost effortlessly strike the ball home from ten yards. The opposition did its utmost to prevent the onset of calm or the return of any order by laying siege to an increasingly beleaguered penalty area given only limited respite by reinforcements drawn from midfield. This left the two forwards of Pork and Mutton isolated and largely withdrawn until they too were pulled back deeper by the play in order to offer safety outlets rather than goal threats. Few teams could sit back and take this amount of sustained pressure without conceding and Simon's side were not one of those. The opposition rattled the crossbar, then the post, followed by Mario committing an unnecessary foul just outside the box, that earned him a booking and them a direct free kick that was turned to temporary safety by the right glove of Owen. They added to their tally in the 39th minute when a sharply incisive one-two opened up the defence just as deftly as a surgeon's knife.

Simon knew that defeat was guaranteed if the team failed to shift the territorial struggle further upfield alongside gaining a far greater share of possession. Although his options were few he knew containment was not one of them. The best course of action was to go on the offensive and bolster the attack without being over reckless elsewhere.

"Whatever we're doing isn't working. We need our midfield and attack to push, stretch and widen the area of play so that we can create and exploit any space ahead of us. This will require more running with and without the ball, especially by the forward line."

The plan almost had an immediate positive rate of return when their first attack, following the restart, resulted in a corner which was narrowly headed wide by Ever. The effort did have an announcement effect on the opposition making them realise that control of the game may not totally be in their own hands. This attempt on goal also restored some confidence in Pork and Mutton FC and their ability to escape the confines of their own penalty area. For the next twenty minutes or so they finally made a match of it, now giving just as much as they got. The reversal in footballing fortunes, as compared to the first half, was clear and rewarded on 65 minutes with a reduction in their deficit. The goal came courtesy of Yiannis, getting in behind the defence and hitting home a through ball from Byron. Ever limped off on 70 minutes to be replaced by Jonathan, who was unlucky ten minutes later to have a shot cleared off the line. This was the substitute's first, and last, contribution to the game as a heavy tackle led to his being helped off the pitch. The scoreline was threatened once or twice by the opposition after that, but remained unchanged at 1-2 until the whistle finally blew. It was their first defeat in five matches, but at least they had given it a go, unlike Massimo's mysterious customer. With two possible injuries and an ongoing suspension they were certainly in need, if not of him, of Mr Robson's contact list.

CHAPTER 30:
O(h) Hec(k)

The defeat to FC Lokomotiv BRC was to prove far more costly than even Simon expected as he and his players trundled off to The Links dilapidated changing facilities. The game's aftermath was to cast a long shadow over much of the following week and shade into their next match against the Irish Club.

Pork and Mutton FC's playing resources had never been plentiful and most of the time stretched but now they were on the rack. Simon held little hope that either Ever or Jonathan would be fully fit for the upcoming game. He could not call on the services of Salvator given that the player had one more game of his suspension to run. They would be losing Yiannis to East Shields Town after the next two fixtures and their possible 'big' new signing had yet to show let alone make his presence felt. By early Wednesday evening things had not really improved, although some matters had been settled. Incoming telephone calls from both his injured forwards confirmed their status as having moved from in doubt to unavailable. As the two oldest players in his squad, Jonathan and Ever had shown that their powers of recovery were not what they had been in their prime, knocks were longer lasting and stamina more easily drained. Several outgoing calls to the scout who had nabbed their most promising player were not answered and Simon had also received little joy on the other recruitment front when Massimo called to say that their giant must have simply climbed back up the beanstalk and disappeared just as effectively as Lord Lucan a few weeks earlier.

That was the state of play as Simon took his heavy overcoat off the hallway stand and headed out into the cold of the night to go and watch the rescheduled East Shields Town home fixture against Oldcastle Athletic. He had been inclined to give the game a miss but was largely motivated to go by the vain hope of seeing either Mr Robson or catching another glimpse of bucket man. Any thoughts of actually enjoying the match hadn't even entered his head as he slammed the door behind him - at least the door knocker held fast. Some seconds later his home telephone rang but he was too far gone to hear it.

The dark gloom served to sympathise with Simon's prevailing spirits, although the occasional lamplight failed to brighten them, as he made his way to the ground with little to observe on route. As he walked up the appropriately dark, almost pitch black, lane leading up to the entrance turnstile he could hear the discordant sound of jangling buckets nearby. He raced around the corner and crashed into a huge pillar of a man holding a bucket in each hand. Only one of them was left standing and as Simon picked himself up from the floor his eyes rose slowly upwards. He identified the man immediately by the telltale wording painted on each of the buckets.

"Sorry about that. I was hoping to bump into you but not quite like that!" before paying homage to each appendage with silver coins from his trouser pocket.

"Why would you be looking for me?"

"Well, I think you're the man I'm looking for. Your size, the buckets and your Scottish accent suggest you must be."

"Listen mate, I don't know what you're after and I ain't done nothing wrong, just collecting that's all."

"So am I, in a way. I heard about your visit to the Tripolini Deli and the discussion you had there. I'm with Pork and Mutton FC, my name is Simon Washington, and was hoping you're still interested given your no show on Sunday?"

"So you ken all about that do you," putting his buckets down just as much to rest his weary arms as to ease the conversation.

"Most of it. Massimo from the deli filled me in. I don't know your name or what happened regarding the other day?"

"My full name is Hector Lyall but you can call me Big Hec as others do. And yes, I'm still very much interested as it happens. I was intending to come by but ended up having to accompany an elderly neighbour to A and E after they had a sudden fall at home. By the time this was sorted both the match and my lunch were long passed. I was planning to return to the Deli later this week to explain."

"Well, I'll be honest with you, we are desperately short of bodies at the moment. Given this, I hope you do not think me being too forward in asking you to sign up now?" before pulling out from his inside overcoat pocket the signing-on form still, somewhat fortuitously, residing there from Sunday.

"Well Simon, I wasn't expecting all this tonight! But I cannae see there's much to really lose," before immediately adorning said paperwork with his barely legible scrawl.

"The match on Sunday is against The Irish Club on The Links. Be there for 10.30am and bring your boots as you'll definitely get some playing time."

During these few sudden and unexpected moments together neither party had raised the important matter of the new recruit's preferred playing position or his actual footballing credentials. It was as if the entire focus had been on the urgency of making both the offer and the commit with anything else seen as a luxury threatening to burst that bubble. Simon never even questioned whether size 18 football boots even existed or whether Big Hec even owned a pair (assuming they were available).

As Simon passed through the turnstiles into the ground he assured himself that his journey there had already been worth it. If he could now manage to locate Mr Robson then so much the better. He spent little time during the drab and goalless first half observing the game played out in front of him. His attention was drawn away from the field and around the stand and terraces. He had yet to spot his target when the referee blew his whistle and allowed the players to take a less than deserved breather. Simon only realised Dr Ally Balls absence when no white boots came trundling off the pitch which helped explain East Shields poor performance against a team in relegation trouble. As bodies circulated all about him in search of half-time sustenance or a stretching of legs he decided to stay put until the traffic subsided and only now immersed himself in his match day programme. Simon duly noted that the doctor hadn't even made substitute and speculated that the player was most likely out with an injury possibly requiring the physician to heal himself. Momentarily lost in the superficial depths of the few pages of footballing trivia before him, a familiar voice calling his name swiftly allowed his return to reality's shallows. It was none other than Mr Robson himself.

"Evening Simon, I thought you would be here. I did try and return your call earlier but you were out, in all likelihood on your way to the game. Obviously I had a good idea where you'd be sitting. I had the advantage in spotting you first, just like a good scout should! I'm afraid I don't have an instant remedy, player recruitment wise currently, but trust that some of my contacts will bear fruit over the coming weeks."

"If you could try please, that would be greatly appreciated, as we have become in desperate need."

Simon was in far better spirits when he returned home than when he had left even though he had just witnessed a game that would have warmed few hearts apart from Owen's. He was cheered by the fact that the evening had not been completely goalless, at least as far as he concerned, he had another player to call on alongside the promise of more to follow. For some strange reason his bedtime hot chocolate tasted a little sweeter than it had the night before even though he had no more than his customary two sugars.

The match against the Irish Club couldn't come around slowly enough to enable the walking wounded to miraculously recover. As Simon greeted what remained of his squad Hector was the last to arrive awkwardly squeezing his giant frame within the restricting confines of the changing room door. His entrance was clumsy and slapstick, more Chaplin than Astaire, drawing a large intake of breath from his unfamiliar audience, not least from Doug. Leaving this communal inhaling aside, the first thing that somehow entered Doug's mind was how do you arrange the burial for a guy like this? Thereby serving to further shock him into thinking he might be a chip off the old block after all. Their latest recruit looked nothing like a footballer, seemingly confirmed by the largest pair of rugby boots that you have ever seen dangling around his neck. This footwear clearly had seen better days, brown battered leather atop wooden studs, with laces tired by their endless tying. Still, they were in no position to be choosy and any body is better for business than no body, as Max Mortimer would surely say.

Given today's missing bodies and the twelve available, Simon selected a formation least unsettling for the players at his disposal. Roger moved into the forward line where he had played on occasion and Byron once again switched wings allowing Doug to take up his vacated berth and the position he was most comfortable playing. Simon continued his standing in for Salvator with Norman playing the midfield role he was accustomed to. This left Big Hec as substitute - with Simon fully expecting his debut appearance at some point in the game but not knowing when or where:

(0) Owen

(2) Mario   (5) Massimo   (3) Marco

(6) Simon

(7) Byron   (8) Stuart   (4) Norman   (11) Doug

(9) Roger   (10) Yiannis

Things didn't start too well considering that the team had yet to leave their changing room. As Simon passed Big Hec the number 12 shirt he had to immediately take it back as it was just far too small for him - there was just no way that his head or neck would get through its opening nor would the rest of it be able to contain his massive torso. It was the door fiasco all over again although he had managed to eventually get his body through that. This was something else that Simon had failed to seriously consider. The shorts and socks that Simon had brought along in his kitbag were equally redundant. Fortunately for him, and the rest of the team, Hector was able to reveal a black tee shirt but with the name of the rock band *Black Sabbath* emblazoned across the front hidden under his blue tracksuit top. This would have to suffice for now and it was fitting in more ways than one.

Prior to kick-off Simon discovered that the presence of Lyall the Scot helped strike far greater fear in the opposition than that recently endured by his teammates. During the warm-up Hector had attracted an inordinate number of concerned Irish Club glances when doing stretches on his own well removed from any kickabout frolicking. Their captain looked mightily relieved when the colossus left the field prior to the coin toss. They too must have been wondering when, and in what capacity, he would be utilised against them with each player probably just hoping that they would not end up directly matched against him.

It was a bright crisp late Autumn morning but the team in hoops were less than radiant with their focus from the off being sidelined by the sidelines. The substitute was perhaps even more menacing from the touchline than on the pitch, like some chained up animal waiting to be unleashed. He kept himself busy by retrieving any ball that went out of play but rather than kicking the ball back he always picked it up and threw it. This fact was barely noticed in the heat of match day combat, only Simon had picked up on it and then kicked any subsequent thoughts on the matter into touch, as his full attention returned to events on the pitch. The first twenty minutes or so had proved to be a rather cagey affair with both sides trying to gauge each other. The game generated few fouls or clear cut chances. Both sides were wary to get too involved in making strong tackles or even playing football as a contact sport. Pork and Mutton FC may understandably have been rather reticent in their full engagement given ongoing injuries and their threadbare resources while The Irish Club possibly remained overly reserved so as not to inadvertently hasten Big Hec's early entrance onto the pitch following any harming of their opponents. As the first half progressed toward its later stages this polite state of affairs started to disintegrate somewhat and the breakdown in diplomacy was occasioned by the need for the opposition to chop down Byron as he collected a loose ball and raced toward goal. He fell to the ground like a sack of potatoes landing face down just outside the penalty area ending up with white lime newly deposited across his forehead like a plimsoll line. Roger took the free kick and only managed to blast the ball into the defensive wall temporarily taking out one of the human bricks in return. Normal football service now resumed. In the 37th minute Owen not only managed to turn a shot around the post but ably collected the incoming cross from the ensuing corner. A few minutes later Byron accidentally collided with the opposition goalkeeper when chasing down a through ball from Roger. It was easy to see who came off the worst for wear with Byron badly limping following this momentary encounter. He tried to run it off in the brief time remaining before half-time but without any noticeable success. As the whistle blew to greet the break neither side had managed to find the net although threat levels had now been duly raised. It was clear to Byron and his captain that he would be unable to continue and that the substitution would need to be made. The when had now been answered although not the where.

"Hector you need to come on for Byron in the second half. What's your best position?" his captain belatedly asked after taking him to one side.

"I don't know, or if I really have one? I haven't given it much thought to be honest."

"Neither did I, given all the haste and desperation. But you must have some idea surely?"

"Not really. I've never been all that bothered about the playing. I did rugby at school, since football wasn't on the curriculum, and only really attend East Shields Town home games to collect for charity. I rarely watch the matches and much prefer the delights from the nearby catering vans."

"You're kidding I hope? That helps explain the rugby boots and your constantly throwing the ball back," said Simon, trying hard to contain this latest piece of devastating news.

"'Oh no, I only bought the boots two days ago at the local charity shop and presumed they would do for football, they were not only a bargain but also miraculously my size. How lucky is that!"

"Yes, lucky for some!" Simon replied, valiantly trying to hold back any hint of sarcasm.

He would ask Roger to drop back into midfield and get Hector to go up front alongside Yiannis, hoping that is where he would do least damage. Simon trusted this would cause just as much consternation for the opposition as it had for him. But his problems were far from over. As the oranges were being finished off, and Big Hec readied himself by taking off his tracksuit top, the ref came running over to the two of them.

"If he's coming on then where's his official kit?"

"Sorry ref, he can't get the team shirt over his head let alone on his body! He's only just signed up. He'll be better dressed next time, I promise you. Unfortunately he has to wear his tracksuit bottoms as he has no team shorts or socks that fit either!"

"I trust you know this is all quite irregular! Not to mention the boots being barely within the laws of the game."

"Yes, I fully appreciate all that, and it won't happen again. Is there anything else we can do to help with Hector's playing gear?"

"I will allow it this time. Luckily he is identifiable and distinct from the opposition. I'm hardly being picky but any chance of getting a number put on the back of his tee shirt?"

"I will ask Norman. He often carries a piece of chalk around with him."

"I wasn't expecting to be a blackboard today as well! It had better wash out as I'm not spoiling my top for anyone."

The Irish Club were in a temporary state of disarray as they tried to decide how to, and who would, deal with the man mountain wearing the *Black Sabbath* tee shirt with a white number 12 now chalked on its back. The same could be said for his own teammates with Big Hec displaying little knowledge of the offside rule bringing every one of their attacks to a premature halt. Simon quickly tried to explain the fundamentals of the rule to him but then decided just to tell him to stay ten yards behind Yiannis. This seemed to work and he was proving himself to be useful as a barrier which opponents found difficult to circumnavigate. His nuisance value did help to bear some fruit in the 57th minute following a corner won, and then taken, by Roger. Big Hec tried to head the cross that came floating in but found gravity unforgiving. His failed takeoff not only managed to take out two defenders, both crashing into him, but even more importantly, so distracted the goalkeeper thereby allowing the ball to reach an unmarked Yiannis who gratefully accepted the gift. A smiling Hector emerged from the heap to celebrate with the jubilant goalscorer. He had, at last, used his frame to good effect and the goal was allowed to stand even though the opposition claimed he had impeded play by just being present on the pitch.

This incident added some much needed spice to the game and tackles were starting to fly in from all angles. The referee did manage to settle the game down after handing out a couple of bookings, one to Hector for a late challenge and another to an Irish Club defender, who took it upon themselves to foolishly but bravely retaliate. The opposition were starting to press for an equaliser and were unlucky to see a long range effort deflect off the crossbar to safety with Owen taken unawares. Pork and Mutton were having to drop back ever deeper to try and contain the growing threat. Their lead was surrendered in the 79th minute when a period of sustained pressure was only stopped by Mario conceding a dangerous free kick just outside his own penalty area. Big Hec, who had been drifting back more and more towards his own goal as his stamina quickly drained, formed a one man wall that successfully blocked the resulting direct effort to score but conceded a corner in the process as the ball flew distantly skyward off his shoulder. This turned out out to be little more than a minor reprieve. From the ensuing corner two earthly bodies collided as the ball bobbled apologetically into the net. Owen knew much less about what happened than Big Hec did but both went to claim a ball that was destined for neither. The latter had proved to be just as much a nuisance in his own penalty area as in the opposition's and had inadvertently taken out his own goalkeeper and simultaneously deflected the ball over the line. It was now 1-1, with ten minutes or so left, and a somewhat groggy, if not concussed, keeper.

It was clear to Simon, even in advance of the referee's instruction, that his regular number 0 was out of the game and he gently helped him to the touchline with the assistance of his latest recruit. Big Hec apologised profusely as they escorted the walking wounded off the pitch and added a request to take over goalkeeping duties. While Owen could make little sense of this, or of most things presently, Simon saw it as a noble gesture by someone wanting to make amends and had the added benefit of allowing him to avoid going in goal himself. Hector's size and rugby background could also possibly work in their favour. By the time they returned to the field of play he already had on his blue tracksuit top and politely rejected Owen's large gloves for being too small.

The last remaining minutes proved to be a baptism of fire for the substitute between the sticks. Simon's decision was less than universally welcomed by either side. Teammates worried about the loss of Owen and whether the replacement was up to the job, rather than being a man down, while the opposition wondered if they could get man or ball past the obstruction before them, rather than how best to utilise their man advantage. As it turned out, any ongoing concerns only persisted with the Irish Club, as a fighting rearguard action by Pork and Mutton FC, with everyone playing their part, kept the scoreline at 1-1. Hector merited being mentioned in dispatches for not only making a point blank save on 85 minutes but also a penalty save in the final minute after a reckless tackle by Massimo earned the offender a booking. As both sides headed off toward their respective changing rooms they had a better sense of Big Hec's worth and Owen was now, remarkably for a goalkeeper, fully compos mentis.

CHAPTER 31:
Germany Calling,
Germany Calling

Taking just one point from the last two games had done little for Pork and Mutton's league standing. They now dropped a place to seventh as FC Lokomotiv leapfrogged over them on goal difference, after winning three on the bounce, and two of the chasing pack were only one point away. The next fixture was the return match against the current league leaders, Deutscher Bierkeller, on The Links. Given the pasting they had received from their opponents earlier in the season, Simon had little confidence things were likely to improve soon. Salvator had served his suspension and should be available for selection but doubts still remained over both Ever and Jonathan's fitness. It was early Saturday evening and neither had telephoned Simon to tender bad news so he assumed the best. One thing that was certain was this would be the last game in team colours for Yiannis before his dizzy elevation to East Shields Town. Hopefully the side would give him a good send off although that would be a challenge, especially if Big Karl made a reappearance against them. History has always shown that any sort of rematch against the Germans is never easy.

The game would not only mark a watershed moment for Yiannis but would be the team's last match before the start of the league's annual winter break lasting until the beginning of February. These scheduled weeks of inactivity would hopefully provide much needed time to strengthen the side and fill the gaping void left by the young striker's departure. Simon was still awaiting the promised potential player leads from Mr Robson and hoped that these would be forthcoming over the ensuing weeks, still believing the scout to be a man of his word as well as his drink. Just before Simon had the opportunity to turn his thoughts away from all of this toward tomorrow's game the telephone rang and he picked up the receiver with some trepidation.

"Hello, is that Simon? Adam Robson here. I'm making a long distance call from Hamburg, so I'll have to make it brief. On my flight here was an ex player of mine, now working as an air steward, who is interested in getting back to play regular football but at a lower, less demanding level. He hasn't played for the past two years due to these new work demands increasingly interfering with his match day availability on Saturdays and Wednesdays. The good news is that with your matches scheduled for a Sunday these pose no problem for him. There is the added benefit of his being an experienced forward, hence an ideal replacement for Yiannis."

"This sounds great, and I fully appreciate the call and trust it's not inconveniencing you. I am sure you have more important and urgent things to attend to out there in Germany."

"I do, for sure, being out here mainly for business and a little pleasure. But I do like striking while the iron's hot. The player I am talking to you about is standing right next to me. He was serving me drinks on the plane on the way here and we're still in the airport. He would like to introduce himself, his name is William Joyce."

"Hello Simon, Will here. Mr Robson has told me all about Pork and Mutton FC. I am returning on the same plane to Oldcastle Airport later tonight as part of my cabin crew duties. He was most insistent for us to meet sooner rather than later. He's a man who always delivers on his promises."

"Hi Will, we have a game tomorrow, 11am kick-off, at The Links against the league leaders. Why don't you come along around forty minutes before so we can have a chat then meet the lads? It would be great to have you on board, please excuse the pun, but I couldn't resist."

"Don't worry I get plenty of those with this job, and worse! Even Mr Robson confessed, after a few drinks, that he didn't know I was still a high flier! I look forward to meeting you tomorrow."

Simon heard the line go dead at the other end before putting the receiver down with a lighter heart than he had answered it while thinking of the coincidences leading up to this moment. He was used to things being up in the air but rarely solutions!

Simon met Will as arranged, twenty minutes before the other players usually arrived, and was most impressed by the latter's playing credentials and his expressed positive interest, although he couldn't help noticing that the new boy had also drowned himself in Brut 33. There was little doubt that he was good enough for Pork and Mutton FC but were they good enough for him? Simon just hoped that the real team would show up today and pass their audition. Fortunately for him, everyone was present and correct and eager to please. Will received a warm welcome although Jonathan was hardly delighted by this sudden arrival but wisely kept it to himself.

Team selection, drawing from all of the players on their books, was now viewed as a luxury Simon had long missed. He knew that today's opponents would give no quarter and his team had every reason to fear the goalscoring talents of tuba playing Göring who always blew hot, never cold. With all this in mind Simon opted for a familiar, tried and tested. line-up, albeit for the last time given Yiannis's imminent departure:

(0) Owen

(2) Mario   **(5) Massimo**   **(3) Marco**

(6) Salvator

(7) Roger   **(4) Simon**   **(8) Stuart**   **(11) Byron**

(9) Ever   **(10) Yiannis**

The real challenge was who would be given the substitute berth. Big Hec had yet to show his true worth aside from possible cover for Owen in goal so was quickly discounted by Simon on those grounds, although in truth he appeared to be more than happy just belonging to the group and the camaraderie it engendered. So it was really between Norman, Jonathan and Doug. Arguments could just as easily be advanced for any of them but Jonathan got the nod ahead of the others given that he was being fashioned as the team's super sub alongside the fact that both his rivals had played the week before. With no warm-up mishaps prior to kick-off these four went to join Will on the touchline with Doug wearing the now redundant blank reserve (number 13) shirt underneath his tracksuit top but feeling better because of it nonetheless.

"Simon, look! Guess who's missing from the Germans? Can you not see? That big palooka Göring isn't over there! He's nowhere to be seen and I have counted all their players," Roger said with glee and possibly a tinge of disappointment.

"You're ahead of me here, he's a difficult person to miss and I did, just hope they do too! So we are not facing our nemesis today and they are lacking the league's leading goalscorer. How strange, something must have happened? Things have certainly taken another turn for the better," Simon confessed.

He was intrigued by this absence and approached his opposite number before the coin toss to try and discover more. The Deutscher Bierkeller captain told him that he had received an unexpected telephone call from their centre forward a couple of days ago .

"Karl called me from Berlin and told me he was there with Lotte on honeymoon after just tying the knot. Neither of the newly married were good at keeping secrets so it must have been done on impulse and in secret."

"Wow, so we both didn't see this coming!"

"That's right. Only last week I shared another celebratory after match stein with him, and nothing seemed amiss or untoward. He has told me they will be back in ten days or so, until then we just have to make do with the loss of our talisman."

The referee stopped any further fraternisation when he pulled out the coin for the toss. The German called heads but it landed tails, giving him his second loss of the day and they hadn't even kicked-off.

The first half quickly passed with both teams giving as good as they got. Tackles were hard but fair and goalscoring opportunities were few and far between. Players were given little time to dwell on the ball and space was at a premium. Going into the interval break at 0-0 against the current league leaders, who had dropped only four points in eighteen games, was an achievement in itself. Simon and the others knew the game was far from over but the oranges had rarely tasted sweeter.

"Roger, just to let you know, Göring is in Germany enjoying his honeymoon with his wife Lotte."

"Lucky bleeder! So he's out there doing the business and still scoring while his team are not!"

Will appeared to be getting on well with his new comrades on the touchline and was well pleased by what he had witnessed on the pitch. He wasn't yet in the position of giving Simon and his teammates any advice, although he had seen some things that could be improved on, diplomatically holding his counsel for now. Simon demanded more of the same from his side for the second half. He knew that Jonathan would need to enter the fray at some point given the tempo of the game, not least because Ever was struggling to run off a knock to the ankle he had received ten minutes before the break.

The substitution took place earlier than planned after their out of sorts forward felt the full impact of another badly timed tackle just outside the opposition's penalty area. Simon called Yiannis over to take the free kick and told him to have a pop at goal. He duly obliged, his dipping effort flew over the wall only to be greeted by the crossbar before entering the safe keeping of the gloved resident standing below. That was the closest Pork and Mutton FC had got to seriously threatening the scoreline and it had taken them all of 55 minutes to do so. The Bierkeller fared little better, clearly missing their aerial ace Göring, who was busy on another kind of more active service with Lotte in Berlin. They did not look like a side that had been banging in the goals at a rate of over three per game.

Neither Simon nor his teammates could afford to be complacent, however, and they received a reminder of the opposition's potency when Big Karl's stand-in had a header cleared off the line by Marco following a corner in the 68th minute. This marked the start of a period of sustained pressure on Owen's goal that finally resulted in a less than deserved lead for the Deutscher being registered in the 80th minute. The goal came courtesy of Helmut, their team captain, who managed to volley home from ten yards after being left unmarked at the far post following yet another corner. Simon's less than secretive informant was no 'Deep Throat' although he had remained in the shadows for most of the game. He had taken them all by surprise by moving stealthily upfield towards the end of the match remaining as undetected as an U-boat stalking its prey. Although there was little fear that the floodgates (rather than the watergates) would open, as in their earlier encounter, it was an especially bad time to concede a goal.

In seasons past, Pork and Mutton FC would more than happily settle for going down 1-0 against any club sitting on top of the league. This side was now different and Simon and his teammates were unwilling to casually throw in the towel and concede such a hard fought game even against opponents of this stature. They wanted more than the mere tokenism of a moral victory which would do little for their points total and not give Yiannis the send off they felt he deserved. Simon demanded one more effort from his players and told them to get further upfield. He also got Roger to join the forward line and recruited Salvator into the heart of the midfield. This was a risky venture, but needs must, and they wanted to carry the fight to the enemy. Even Will Joyce appeared admiring of this decision and continued his encouraging cheering from the touchlines. In the 88th minute proof of God's existence, for Simon anyway, duly arrived. With time running out, Sunday's on-field prayers were finally answered, and Pork and Mutton drew level thanks to a speculative effort from Yiannis on the edge of the penalty area. The match ended 1-1 and this was appropriately, in more ways than one, his departing shot. A farewell reception was held at the pub after the game at which all the team attended, including Big Hec and a newly signed up Will. Many more shots were enjoyed at the bar than had taken place on the pitch although Yiannis himself skilfully avoided the alcohol ahead of Monday night training with his new club East Shields Town.

CHAPTER 32:
This is the Winter
of Our Content

It had been a glorious summer and now the winter wasn't bad either. There was no big freeze like just over a decade earlier when almost everything ground to a halt. The season's hibernation did allow time for Simon and some of the others to dwell on their achievements to date. With 21 points already banked they had consolidated their position just above mid table (W7 D7 L5) and for the first time ever, in their less than illustrious past, had entered the New Year with a goal difference still in the black with 34 goals scored and only 28 goals conceded. Yes, they had now lost their main goalscoring ace to East Shields (Yiannis had eleven goals to his credit before his adieu) but others, most notably Ever and Doug, had shown themselves somewhat adept in front of goal and there was the promise of bedding Will into their ranks. While great strides had clearly been made there was a great deal of self-satisfaction to be gleaned from both the catching of one's breath and the prolonged period of reflection engendered by the league's pause.

Not that Simon and the team simply rested on their laurels to miraculously awake refreshed and primed when everything resumed at the beginning of February. The opportunity was never missed, weather and availability permitting, to hold informal training sessions at West Park. These Sunday morning exertions often entailed seven-a-side games on the five-a-side grass pitch but sometimes involved utilising the nearby all-weather hockey pitch if the former facility was not free, usually because some kids had got there first.

Big Hec would invariably end up in one of the goals, although on a rare occasion he did get the opportunity to play outfield but only if Simon or one of the others felt charitable and swapped positions with him. This did not really help to develop his footballing skills beyond the penalty area but everyone, including himself, felt it was all a bit late for that. After all it was the company rather than the ball that he craved. In light of all of this the group felt that he deserved to be more than just Owen's stand in.

"Big Hec, we don't want you or those buckets to go to waste on our match days. Jonah once suggested, largely in jest and before we really got to know you, that you could be our magic sponge man. I think in hindsight he was right. What do you think?" Simon asked.

"I am happy to do anything that increases contact with my teammates, as this certainly does! Not forgetting, it has the added bonus of my buckets getting both a regular workout and a bath every Sunday."

"In that case, Jonah would you mind doing the honours please, and present Big Hec with the team sponges that I just happen to have brought along with me in the team kitbag,"

"Happy to oblige Simon, but should he not kneel as I award him the official title of The Order of the Sponges? Better still how about filling his buckets with water and christen him in his new role?"

"No need for any of that Jonathan!" Simon answered, giving the sponges unceremoniously to Big Hec himself.

The sessions did allow their most recent signing, Will Joyce, to form a lively upfront partnership with Ever Reddy, so that Yiannis's departure to better things appeared not to be as great a loss as initially feared. Mr Robson had clearly, if rather fortuitously, turned up trumps here not only for Simon but also East Shields Town, with Yiannis quickly carving out a name for himself in their reserves. While no further significant exchanges took place between the Pork and Mutton FC captain, cum secretary, cum interim manager, and the chief scout it was clear from their ongoing, albeit infrequent, discussions that the latter still felt indebted to the former and even provided a couple of new leather footballs in lieu, delivered dangling in a string bag. During the winter recess Simon continued to show himself to be just as much a utility player off the pitch as on and was always of a superior rank than a general dogsbody. Even the frosty relationship with the league administration appeared to be thawing given that recent letters were no longer less than cordial or suggestive of special treatment.

On their final Sunday morning session before the season's restart, with a full roster turning up and no sign of early pitch invaders, Simon decided they should play a formal game of seven-a-side with his acting as referee. This would better allow him to observe his players up close and personal ahead of next week's league fixture. Unlike previous sessions this one now took on a greater air of seriousness. Simon decided to play two halves of 30 minutes each with a ten minute break. He opted to form the two teams as follows:

Owen

Mario   Massimo   Marco

Stuart

Ever   Will

o

Doug   Jonathan

Byron

Norman   Salvator   Roger

Hector

He viewed the first seven as definite starters for the forthcoming game against Austin's Fryers. The only real competition related to the unfilled midfield positions - which excluded Salvator's virtually guaranteed deep-laying defensive role - with five in contention (excluding super sub striker Jonathan and replacement keeper cum sponge man Big Hec).

Scoring was never that easy at the best of times but the five a side goals were difficult to breech when draped in the frames of Big Hec and Owen. The definites justified their naming and deservedly got to the break holding a 2-0 lead courtesy of a brace from Will with assists from Ever. The emergent striking partnership was working well and could have scored more were it not for the earnest defending of Salvator alongside the countless blocking of Big Hec. The possibles struggled to threaten Owen's goal and Roger was less than comfortable in playing a defensive role. Simon decided to shift the team around for the second half and allowed Roger to join Byron and put Doug into the defence with Jonathan on his own up front. This appeared to generate a greater fluidity in both attack and defence and the change was rewarded with a goal ten minutes into the re-start. A swift counter-attack provided the extra man for Roger to smash the ball home from close range. Five minutes later Jonathan went close when he hit the bar trying to chip over the diving goalkeeper. The match was settled when Will repaid the previous favours of Ever and set him up for an easy goal just before the end. The definites had won, as expected, but the possibles had put up a better than expected showing and Doug had surprised everyone by his versatility and defending. While there had been no storm clouds or rain he had greatly exceeded expectations although he still managed to get soaked after colliding into one of Big Hec's buckets now containing sponge and water left close to the touchline.

CHAPTER 33:
Going for Gold

Simon had some important decisions to make going into the game against Austin's Fryers. The opposition had consolidated their fifth placed position since the season's half way point by widening their points gap and standing over Pork and Mutton FC. Their last four games before the winter break had registered six points (W2 D2) and they were now on equal points (twenty-six) with The White Elephant, albeit with a slightly inferior goal difference. Simon's side had picked up four points in comparison (W1 D2 L1) and allowed Bulman United to leap-frog over them in the league. Although this was technically an away fixture for the team it would be taking place on the familiar territory of The Links given that both clubs made use of these facilities for their home games. While neither side could claim territorial advantage - playing on no one man's land if you will - Simon knew that this game could prove pivotal for their season and help stall the opposition's ascent.

He had a full and fit squad to choose from and was also hopeful of catching his opponents cold and off guard following the lull in league proceedings. In their previous encounter they had shared the points in a 1-1 draw that had been a rather tame and cagey affair quietly marked by a rare Simon goal. On that occasion Pork and Mutton adopted a cautious approach against a team and track-suited manager dressed in all gold. Simon remained unsure whether to follow the same conservative strategy and get something out of the game or be more cavalier and risk losing it. He had a restless Saturday night mulling over this and the best team selection capable of achieving victory so that fortune really does favour, rather than punishes, the brave.

The cold light of day and the frosty morning that accompanied it did little to finally settle Simon's remaining doubts. Tea and toast did help and the upbeat music coming out of the radio improved his mood somewhat. He looked at his late night line-up scribblings and stared at the blank piece of paper awaiting his ink. Without any further hesitation or any more crossing outs his pen and mind were rested on completion of the following:

(0) Owen

(2) Mario   (5) Massimo   (3) Marco

(6) Salvator

(7) Roger   (4) Byron   (8) Stuart   (11) Doug

(9) Ever   (10) Will

This was a bold step, having a more fluid and attacking midfield than the one which faced the Fryers previously. As a form of extra insurance Simon decided to include himself as substitute to buttress the defence if such need arose. Should all the team be present and correct prior to kick-off this would leave Jonathan, Norman, and Big Hec, (plus buckets) remaining on the sidelines, with only the plastic having any chance of legitimately entering the fray.

The rested pitches at The Links were in good condition for early February, doubtless aided by Winter being especially kind, although the surface was hard and unyielding to studs underfoot. The three exiled to its outer margins were not too displeased given this and even Simon was relieved to be sitting this one out for the time being. It wasn't the best day to take a tumble or be whacked by ball or foot in one's nether regions. That said, the climate wasn't too friendly to standing around either, and stamping of feet and blowing of hands quickly spread like a benign contagion among the spectators regardless of their affiliation. Big Hec had been the sensible one not only bringing along his goalkeeper gloves but also a flask of tea. But before taking a sip he was interrupted.

"That won't put hairs on your chest big fella!" shouted Terry Austin as he came over to exchange unpleasantries.

"Don't you worry, I have more than my fair share already," Big Hec replied as the protagonist drew closer.

"Stop stirring Terry, I'm sure Hector's tea is just fine as it is!" Simon added.

"No need to be so snappy lads. I was only going to offer bucket man a sip of brandy from my hip flask, that's all."

It was now even more obvious that he had come more fully prepared for what the weather might throw at him. Not only was the Fryers boss wearing a large quilted overcoat hiding much of his trademark tracksuit, buried like treasure beneath, but also had an Ushanka Russian fur cap atop his head, with ear covering straps fastened around his chin. If this was the Cold War then he was clearly winning.

"I'm happy with my tea and magic sponges thanks. I don't need anything else, medicinal or otherwise."

"That brandy of yours must be powerful stuff" quipped Norman.

"Meaning?"

"Well it's blinking obvious mate, you're sprouting hair all over your head!" Norman joked, causing Terry to hastily retreat while the remainder heartily laughed.

Things on the pitch were yet to be so easily settled. Unlike their previous meeting, the two teams were clearly up for it and having a go from the onset. There was a fair amount of stiffening of sinnews and summoning up of blood not only in response to the freezing temperature but also because both sides clearly attached extra significance to winning the match. They not only had each other in their sights but also the teams directly above them. A defeat for either would leave them out in the cold for longer than the scheduled ninety minutes being played.

No one was hanging about and Owen was immediately called into action when the opposing centre forward tried to catch him unawares with a speculative long range effort from the centre circle after a simple return pass from his inside forward straight from the kick-off. The ball did not keep in the goalie's safe keeping for long but was released faster than any pass the parcel to Mario on the right who just as quickly passed it on to Roger running in space ahead of him. Progress was then halted by a crunching late tackle from behind, heralding both a free kick and a booking for the player callously and unceremoniously bringing Roger to the floor. Big Hec was on the scene in the blink of an eye, doubtless taking warmth from Roger's predicament, with his buckets, freezing cold water and sponges, now adding to the player's obvious discomfort more than the initial challenge had done. Or so his now audible cries suggested. The winger was seriously motivated to instantly recover and joined the referee in sending the unwelcomed medical attention back from whence it came. Byron floated in the resulting free kick which Will headed narrowly wide past a despairing goalkeeper. They had failed to draw first blood, unlike their opponents, who had left such a mark on Roger's left calf.

The Fryers got their own early opportunity to score in the 12th minute when Marco was forced to concede a corner after a loose back pass from Doug. A beautifully curved cross found the head of one of their advancing centre halves who had given Ever the slip and it was only the lightening fast reflexes of Owen that saved the day. The scoreline remained unchanged at the cost of another corner which was far less skilfully despatched than the first, with the wayward ball not even entering the field of play. From that moment on most of the attacking threat came from Pork and Mutton FC courtesy largely of the emerging partnership between Ever and Will. The latter was showing himself to be more than an able replacement for Yiannis and almost as potent as the aftershave wafting from his chin. He hit the woodwork on 28 minutes following a neat one two with Doug that almost worked to unlock a staunch and resolute defence. A few minutes later Ever had a neat lob cleared off the line. The breakthrough came five minutes before half-time when their new boy opened his account for the team. A great run from Doug out on the left wing saw him skip past two of their players, and keeping his head while others lost their footing, he hit a sublime through ball that Will gratefully received to neatly slot into its new home in the corner of the net. This was the last meaningful action before the break when every orange would imitate a frozen Jubbly.

The 1-0 lead was hard earned and well deserved but the match was far from won or lost. Terry Austin knew as much as he called his players together into a close knit huddle for their interval team talk.

"Come on you Fryers, you can beat this lot. We know all about scraps and what to do when the chips are down! We have battered better things than this!"

Simon could tell from their outward demeanour the opposition were neither down nor out. They were clearly fired up when they lined up for the restart and ready to show their true mettle. While their shirts were pure gold their spirit was now being cast molten. From the restart they pressed and harried for every ball and it became increasingly draining to hold them at bay. Simon could clearly see, as the game continued to unfold, that his teammates were not all as fit as their opponents. Before he could add a much needed injection of energy to an ailing midfield the Fryers drew level. It was a well-crafted equaliser that owed just as much to their getting extra players forward as to Pork and Mutton's failure to get some of their own players back. This 57th minute reward for flooding players into the attack should have been better anticipated and better picked up. The problem was that a number of players were struggling and that it wasn't an easy fix to stop the tide turning. Roger had bravely battled on after his early abuse but Doug had drifted back out to the margins rather than provide the defensive cover he had displayed in last week's training game. Stuart was the only one consistently coming back to support the defence with Byron trying, but obviously struggling, to keep up with the play after being clattered into five minutes earlier.

The time for any further indecision had now passed and Simon came on to replace Byron who welcomed the attention of Big Hec as his escort off the pitch. The fresh pair of legs would support Roger on the right side of the park and Stuart in protecting the defence.

"Doug you need to pull your finger out and help the lads more. You're on the pitch to participate not observe! I would have taken you off if Byron hadn't been injured. We need you, so stop hiding!"

Ever was pulled back from the forward line leaving Will as the only remaining constant outlet in enemy territory. This 'Maginot Line' strategy was now being employed on a needs must basis in order to contain and constrain any opposition advance. It worked for a reasonable period of time with everyone following the new script as best they could while energy levels continued being sapped. It is said that all battle plans work until first contact with the foe and this was especially true of this encounter, Roger after all could vouch for that. To Terry Austin's delight the Fryers took the lead they had been threatening to gain in the 78th minute. The goal came following a lengthy series of prolonged attacks that hardly caught Pork and Mutton unawares given their frequency. Their undoing came from a lightening exchange of passes that allowed an opposition forward to get in from behind and nonchalantly tap the ball home.

The writing had been on the wall for some time and it was now neatly and fully embossed. Just as both sides seemed resigned, whether happily or unhappily, to their fate destiny intervened with one final twist. Six minutes from the end and with Fryers right winger bearing down on goal Doug robbed him of the ball and sent a long ball speculatively upfield. It somehow found its way to Will, or most likely he found his way to it, evading one tackle after another before being intentionally taken out just before his entry into the Fryers penalty area. The offending player was the same one who had left an earlier calling card on Roger and now he was ordered off the pitch by the referee. Little advantage was gleaned from the resultant free kick but having an extra man seemed to reinvigorate Pork and Mutton and raise their spirits. The opposition started to sit back more and allowed Simon's side to come onto them. With the game almost concluded and the referee looking at his watch Simon found Roger free out on the wing and he sent over a hopeful cross that somehow found the head of Ever and then the back of the net. The whistle blew immediately afterward and the scorer celebrated without dislodging his hairpiece on this occasion as any insulation was greatly prized on a day like this. He had gone six games without a goal so his somewhat restrained joy was counterbalanced by Mr Austin's losing his own piece of fur, throwing his hat to the floor in disbelief at the last gasp equaliser. Honours even yet again, but with more luck than judgement on their side this time, Pork and Mutton FC showed they could draw anything apart, that is, from a crowd.

CHAPTER 34:
Drat Ma

The upcoming match against The Cretan Taverna was something Simon was looking forward to with relish. Pork and Mutton FC had registered an away victory against them earlier in the season after the Greek side had largely defeated itself and subsequent episodes of self-harming continued to haunt them for some time. They appeared to be a team on the slide picking up few points along the way but conceding plenty in return. They had gone from a promotion chasing team the season before to mere cannon fodder now. They were in need of some sort of divine intervention; even occasional help from the demigod Minos would do rather than frequently paying sacrifice to the other minus of their goal difference. What Simon did not know was that matters had recently been forcefully resolved by the just-in-time marriage union of Hatzidakis (their left back) to the heavily pregnant cousin of Stathakis (their goalie). This should now serve to end any ongoing bad blood hostilities from within their pacified camps. By the gods, or at least by Zeus, they were all in need of finally sorting themselves out.

This was a time when the impact of women on football was usually off the pitch rather than on it. At the highest levels they could ruin or make a player's career without themselves kicking a ball. Engaging with the three B's - booze, betting and birds - were widely viewed as familiar habits rather than serious addictions that helped sustain local economies and the national press. Women rarely took centre stage unless as trophies on the arm of some errant wayward footballer. This was all pre-WAG, with most females being effective and silent partners supporting from the wings; ably prompting their sons, husbands and boyfriends to glory or at least sustainable careers. It was even far more mundane, but no less important, at the lower levels too, as Pork and Mutton FC's unfolding season had already witnessed and would do so again.

Just as Simon was contemplating his line-up for tomorrow's game he received a tea-time telephone call from Byron.

"I'm sorry to say I will have to rule myself out for tomorrow. My mother insists that I need to fully recover from the after effects of last week's blows before I make myself available to play again."

"If you, and more importantly your mother, are totally sure?"

"I even missed two days of my college course following her prognosis of my condition and she then wrapped me up in cotton wool for a few more days after that. In a way I am more mummified than King Tut at present! That said, I have to pay more than just lip service to 'mum knows best'."

"I fully understand Byron. One never gets in the way of a mother and her offspring. I appreciate your letting me know and take it easy."

Even before he could digest the implications of Byron's absence his telephone rang again but this time it was a voice that Simon did not immediately recognise but found seductively inviting. She introduced herself as Nancy Cruft, Jonathan's wife, who he had only fleetingly met at the barbecue at their home before the football season began.

"I'm phoning on behalf of my husband. He has got a serious bout of the flu occasioned by his rash eleventh hour decision to take it upon himself to unblock his mother's drains. I told him not to go. I just don't understand why he couldn't just get her to call Dyno-Rod out directly instead. It was bitterly cold and extremely late when he dashed out of the house on Thursday evening and he didn't get back home for ages."

Obviously his mother, rather than his wife, had been more persuasive and this was the result, or so Nancy implied. He had managed to eventually clear the blockage but only in exchange for another, a clogged up nose that would not be so availing of his brushes. After putting down the receiver Simon become apprehensive as he was superstitious enough to not only believe that things usually come in threes but also that they may not be necessarily good – such as already having two strikes and awaiting the inevitable third. It wasn't only in baseball that you could strike out and Simon's fears were realised a couple of hours later. He had more than half expected it.

"Apologies for calling at this late hour, Simon, it's Owen here. I'm afraid to say I cannot play tomorrow. I went to my mother's for lunch today and ended up humping some really heavy furniture around for her and I've sprained my right wrist. Stupid I know, but you know what mothers are like and I was on my tod, as my lazy good for nothing brother didn't show, but she wanted it done there and then."

"Not another man down. This is the third call today and I have already lost Byron and Jonah for tomorrow. In a way, you are all out on mother's orders! Forgive me, I should ask, how is the wrist?"

"It's all now bandaged up but will need a couple of days to heal. Unfortunately I'm unable to pick anything up at the moment so I've already abandoned my plans to hit the nightclubs with Roger tonight!"

Somewhat ironically, Simon was relieved by this third call, as he believed that must be the end of the evening's disturbances. About half an hour later the phone did ring again, taking Simon aback and causing him to spill the hot cup of tea until recently residing on his lap. This time it was his mother calling him to inform him that his sister had just given birth to a baby girl and he was now an uncle. Another one out, but joyously so. Both were doing fine, Simon much less so, given his attainment of unclehood almost cost him his manhood.

For the rest of the night the telephone thankfully remained silent with only its owner being needlessly restless after digesting his news and cogitating its impact. Now three men down and counting, he just had to hope the remainder would all show. As he waited nervously at The Links, having arrived well in advance of anyone else, and just behind the early birds catching the worms, he continued pondering over his line-up even though his mind had largely already been made up by circumstance. Today Hector was a shoo-in for the goalkeeper's jersey. It would not be Owen's number 0 shirt however as even this would struggle to contain his replacement. The big man needed to bring his tracksuit top along with himself this morning - there was no doubt in Simon's mind that buckets would form part of his attire. As that box was ticked and the rest of the available players duly arrived Doug was given the number 12 shirt partly on the basis of his last display but also because Simon wanted to give Norman a full game. He had not been directly involved in the last two matches but had remained loyal in his commitment and had been in the side that secured the 2-0 victory over The Cretan Taverna last September. Given a full eleven plus one the line-up had really picked itself given the interruptions of the night before and was still capable of delivering the victory Simon expected:

(1??) Hector

(2) Mario   **(5) Massimo**   **(3) Marco**

(6) Salvator

(7) Roger   **(4) Simon**   **(8) Stuart**   **(11) Norman**

(9) Ever   **(10) Will**

The big unknown was Big Hec and how he would fare in goal, but doubts over his ability in that department only explains the first question mark after his number. The additional question mark arose over the colour of the tracksuit top he was wearing in lieu of a goalkeeper's jersey. Before the game commenced the referee called Simon and Big Hec over during the warm-up and was not happy that the blue tracksuit top clashed with the blue and white quarters worn by the opposition. The matter was only partly resolved by borrowing a brown bib from another team's substitute standing on the touchline of a match about to take place adjacent to this. It was then fully resolved with the help of the match officials. The bib's neck opening had to be enlarged and its side bands cut with scissors gleaned from the referee's manicure set. Both he and his fellow linesmen donated their spare boot laces to hold down the released bib sides from flapping in the absence of any string. Someone had suggested using some of the loose goal netting when they were thinking up a bib fastening solution but that was clearly against league administration regulations and and would be viewed as wanton vandalism by the council. Big Hec's torso now looked like some badly wrapped up parcel and Simon could only hope this post would safely deliver - it was now out of his hands and in those of another - bucket man himself. Big Hec had far more confidence than his captain, largely owing to his placing his trusty buckets behind him in the back of his goal with Faith on his right and Hope to his left.

After all this early fuss had died down Simon could not fail to notice that The Cretan Taverna players appeared to be in good heart and strong resolve, with no sign of past bickering, or one of its prime instigator's, the left back Hatzidakis. The other, their goalkeeper Stathakis, was back there between the sticks but with his temperament under apparent control and smiling along with his teammates as they popped shots at him from all angles. This was all far more reminiscent of the old Cretan promotion chasing team before their undoing by Bulman United last season, Simon worryingly thought to himself, aware that there is always touchdown at the end of any slide where bottom hits ground and you bounce back up. The steeper the slide the greater the momentum. A pre coin toss up conversation with the opposition captain served to enlighten Simon further and he was informed about the recent wedding truce bringing about inner harmony and peace. Their missing defender was at the hospital where his new wife had just become a new mother to their first child, a boy. "Back of the net," said their captain exuberantly. Needless to say, Simon lost the coin toss and much of his earlier optimism besides.

The early exchanges were fair and friendly with neither side claiming any clear advantage of possession or any meaningful shots on target. This was not unlike their earlier encounter except that Pork and Mutton FC missed the previous input of Hatzidakis more than The Cretan Taverna did in breaking the deadlock. His replacement was proving more than capable in his stead and was ably marshalling Ever and Roger as they made occasional forays into his territory. Goals would be a lot harder to come by today than the Cretan goals against column had suggested. Both midfields were holding their own and neither defence came under any sustained pressure. Both goalkeepers had yet to have their mettle seriously tested and half-time was already rapidly approaching. The closest anyone got to almost threatening the netting, apart from the earlier Big Hec hullabaloo, came courtesy of Will who broke free from his marker and cracked a rasping shot whistling just past the post in the 44th minute. That was the only sound of fury emanating from a restrained first period.

As Pork and Mutton FC tucked into their oranges some of the Cretan players were enjoying cigars passed out by Stathakis in honour of the new arrival. A large bottle of ouzo was also doing the rounds with no opposition player unwilling to kiss its lip. The Greek civil war was most clearly over. For Simon this was just as surreal in its way as September's half-time had been, but completely its opposite, and just as unrestrained in its way.

The infusion of spirit during the break injected even more life into the opposition without their also suffering any noticeable loss of puff. They came close to scoring on two separate occasions within five minutes of the restart. The first crashed against the crossbar and the second struck Big Hec on his shoulder before heading skyward for a corner which he subsequently reclaimed. Things then settled down again for ten minutes or so as Simon and his teammates played themselves back into the game. Stuart and Will were getting increasingly involved in the match and the latter earned a corner after a neat one two between them resulted in a shot being deflected out to safety by a Taverna defender. Roger floated in a cross that Ever headed just wide of the target. With only a third of the game left it remained surprisingly goalless but Simon's side were pressing increasingly upfield more than before.

Things were set to dramatically change in the 70th minute when a lobbed through pass caught the Pork and Mutton defence out and left the Cretan centre forward free to race unchallenged for the ball. Sweeper keepers were yet to be born, apart from those at the zoo cleaning up after elephants, so that their giant goalie, as was customary textbook practice, simply held his ground rather than advance to try to clear the threat. The attacker easily collected the ball and speedily bore down towards Big Hec's penalty area. Only at this moment did his remaining, but rather substantial, barrier to goal instinctively come charging out towards him, narrowing the angle with every stride, but leaving himself open to being chipped. You could forgive the Cretan player for somewhat bottling it when faced with the laced colossus seemingly heading on a collusion course directly for him. Instead of a courageous chip and taking any resultant impact on the chin, or elsewhere, he decided to change course at the last minute and go around his advancing nemesis. Grievous bodily contact failed to be avoided, however, and it was less a meeting of minds and more a gathering of bones, with the goalie ending up on top of this assembly. As the referee blew his whistle it was clear that the prostrate Cretan wouldn't be puffing on another cigar for a while. It was a penalty but deemed careless rather than malicious so undeserving of any additional punishment. What was clear is that their injured player wasn't up to taking it, yet alone carrying on. He was carried off the pitch by his accidental assassin who was about to face yet another penalty just as he had done a few games ago against the Irish Club at the beginning of December.

The Cretan substitute looked a bit worse for wear as he came on the pitch after using his sideline inactivity to finish both his cigar and what was left of the ouzo. It was a surprise to everyone when he headed straight upfield and placed the ball on what he thought was the penalty spot and readied himself as best he could to take it. It was at this point that both the referee and his captain decided to intervene. The former, not seeing double, placed the ball in its true position while the other gently persuaded his teammate to give someone else the opportunity to score. With few willing takers the captain took direct responsibility himself and fired in a low drive that

Big Hec managed to get a hand to and turn onto the post before being cleared out of harm's way by Marco. This was the goalie's second penalty save in his very limited playing time with Pork and Mutton FC and further justified Simon's keeping faith with him.

Nothing much else happened to rival the excitement of all that until the 80th minute when a goal was finally scored to enter both the goals for column of Pork and Mutton FC and the goals against column of The Cretan Taverna. Salvator had easily won the ball off the opposition substitute in his own half before sending a long ball down the left to Norman then ably finding Will who deftly turned his marker before banging the ball home. It was a rare moment of pure class that was justly rewarded. In the remaining minutes they nearly added to their lead with Ever going close yet again but the game appeared destined for 1-0 especially after the Cretan captain hit the crossbar at the death. The defeated took their loss well and both during and after the match there were none of the recriminations witnessed previously. Simon was left only to ponder whether this notable sea change in behaviour owed more to the direct absence of Hatzidakis or, which now seemed increasingly more likely, to the harmony engendered by his recent marriage and the arrival of his newly born son.

CHAPTER 35:
Shirley Not

The narrow, and somewhat fortunate, victory achieved in the last match was especially significant for two main reasons. It was impossible to find any one who had been involved with Pork and Mutton FC who could recall doing the double over any opposition, never mind not conceding in the process. It also showed Simon and his teammates that they had an able goalkeeping replacement should future need arise in Big Hec. The club were still lacking in having other specialist defence options, unlike the healthy competition in both midfield and upfront. That said, it would be difficult to justify mucking about with the Tripolini brothers as they very much came as a self-contained package and Salvator had more than earned his place in the side.

Even a goldfish could easily remember the countless times that most teams had done the double against Simon's side in the past. They had avoided it so far this season but the upcoming away match against Shirley Inn FC posed a major threat to their continuing this unheard of feat. The opposition were one of four teams battling for the two promotion spots and were currently in second place having just leapfrogged over an increasingly undercooking Peking Duck; their haul of 33

points from 21 games was nine more than Pork and Mutton
had bagged to date. The two mile journey to their playing
pitch was around the same distance as The Links but now
seemed more onerous, in Simon's mind anyway.

His work week prior to the game had proved somewhat
uneventful and served to match an equally quiet social calendar.
There was no pre-match reconnaissance to The Shirley to
glean additional insights and gossip, or to any other watering
hole for that matter. For seven days life had been just as dull
as the weather with no surprises, pleasant or otherwise. His
telephone had remained mercifully silent. Simon's expectation
of a full squad to choose from was not disappointed as he
waited for the last of his teammates to show before handing
out the shirts. No one was too shocked with the starting XI,
although Norman was silently aggrieved at losing his regained
spot to Doug, and Jonathan was a little more vocal after missing
out on what he considered was his number 12 shirt to Simon:

(0) Owen

(2) Mario   (5) Massimo   (3) Marco

(6) Salvator

(7) Roger   (4) Byron   (8) Stuart   (11) Doug

(9) Ever   (10) Will

This was much the same line-up that had lost, albeit with
only a minute to go, to this opposition the last time they met.
The only differences now were the inclusion of Doug instead
of Norman, Will replacing the departed Yiannis, and Simon
commandeering (so Jonathan thought) his own super sub
role. As Simon joined an increasingly disgruntled Jonathan,

quietly miffed Norman, and a more than happy Hector on the sidelines he noticed his nemesis Justin Hallsome lining up for the opposition with father, Joe Hallsome, ready to send out team instructions nearby. This was expected to be a difficult match for Pork and Mutton FC and so it turned out, in more ways than one.

From the off Shirley Inn FC were buzzing and within three minutes caught their opponents napping. They intercepted a misguided pass from Doug allowing their inside right to race upfield and lay off a simple through ball for their captain to smash into the net. It hadn't taken Justin, or his team, long to get back to where they had previously left off.

"Well this is a great start isn't it! Just pathetic! That kid's only playing because of his dad!" shouted an agitated Jonah.

"Maybe if I'd been playing instead?" said Norman, offering some tepid approval.

This was hardly a full-scale mutiny, but did get noticed by Simon, but not by Big Hec, who was just happily tucking into a Bounty. In their previous encounter Shirley Inn FC had come back from going behind twice before scoring the very late winner and Simon was already wondering whether his side had the same fighting spirit. He didn't have long to wait to find out. Will was clearly starting to make a nuisance of himself and received unwelcome, but possibly well-warranted, attention in return. This drew a number of free kicks and a booking as well as a feeling of deja vu for a number of the players taking part. It also kept Jonathan quiet for a bit. While little additional benefit was gleaned from these passages of play the team did settle down and pose a few problems for their opponents

Things unravelled a bit in the 25th minute when Salvator inadvertently returned a favour previously given to Will and conceded not only a free kick but a booking for his effort. In the eyes of the referee, at that moment, he looked more Argentinian than Brazilian. Salvator was clearly upset by the damage caused by his careless rather than callous challenge and apologised profusely to his victim as he helped him up from the floor. He would have been even more distraught had he known of the referee's optics and most surely would have suggested the customary glasses for someone misdiagnosing not only his intent but also, and even worse, his nationality. This incident was nothing less than the prelude to worse things to come. The resulting direct free kick was turned over the crossbar following a tremendous left-handed save by Owen. The follow-up corner was cleared but only to the outside fringe of the penalty area where it was hammered back towards goal past a despairing and helpless goalie. They may be tied on bookings but they were now 2-0 down.

"Lads, this is rubbish! What the hell are you doing? This line-up isn't working and only a fool would expect it to!" Jonah's fresh comments were clearly meant as much for Simon as his teammates on the pitch. He hadn't paused to think that if he had been substitute it was unlikely he would, as yet, have impacted on matters or even remembered that the last time these teams met he had let his colleagues down by only lasting a few minutes.

"Jonah, I think your comments are no longer helping," Norman quietly advised causing Big Hec to register a feint snicker just as he was about to bite into a Marathon.

"I don't know what's got into you today or what game you're playing? We don't need an in-house heckler or arguments off or on the pitch, thank you. So kindly just button it please." Simon politely asked.

"Why should I? Who do you think you are anyway?"

"I know who I am Jonathan, I think you've forgotten where you are, can we have a modicum of decorum please?"

"What's this modicum of decorum business?" Big Hec asked, seeking genuine clarification that was mistakenly seen by Jonah as a supporting act of insubordination.

"It's rubbish, that's what it is. Like those lot there! You're as clueless as Big Hec!" Jonah shouted to chastise his colleagues as they returned, already somewhat crestfallen, to the centre circle for the restart.

"I don't think you should be kicking off again before your teammates do?" joked Norman trying to defuse the situation.

"That's almost as funny as the bunch of jokers out there!" answered Jonah whose behaviour was now attracting the attention of the linesman nearby.

"Would you kindly stop your nonsense or do I have to flag the ref over?"

This seemed to work for a while and Jonathan wasn't looking for more publicity in the papers anytime soon. One did not need to be within his earshot to know that Shirley Inn FC were the better team and had greatly improved since the last meeting between them. Simon was loathe to take any one off or put himself on while his less than super ex sub was present. His team were not playing as badly as some thought nor was there an obvious candidate letting the team down, at least on the park itself. Simon also felt that his place was on the touchline where he was better able to try and control matters should they deteriorate any further. Things stabilised before half-time and Will had a goal chalked off for being caught well offside meriting a grin and sarcastic applause from their off field agent provocateur. The forward did get a goal back shortly after, however, deftly heading in a Roger delivered corner to the far post in the 43rd minute. Everyone associated with Pork and Mutton FC were delighted with the fightback apart from Jonathan who rapidly transitioned into Mr Subdued. The scorer's goal celebration was rather intentionally over done and then singularly directed with raised fingers rather than hands. This elicited an immediate response from its target who had to be gently but forcibly restrained from entering the field of play by Big Hec. This kerfuffle was only temporarily ended with the referee warning the misbehaving parties over their behaviour.

The referee's whistle for half-time brought more verbal shelling and little rest allowing Jonathan the opportunity to get up closer and more personal. He headed straight for Will discharging a barrage of abuse before pushing him to the ground. At that instant Roger picked up one of Big Hec's buckets, containing water and sponges, emptying all of its contents directly over the leading protagonist's head. This may of helped him cool down and absorb his situation before storming off in a rage. At least Jonathan was now gone and the team could concentrate on the rest of the match.

Much of the second half was a bit of an anti-climax to all this - that was until the police arrived in the 80th minute or thereabouts. Before then Justin Hallsome had got another goal to restore The Shirley's two goal advantage, which would surely have delighted the recently departed as much as the goal scorer himself. There was little chance of coming back from this Simon quietly thought to himself from the now eerily silent touchline. Jonathan may be gone but he wasn't making himself forgotten as the boys in blue arrived to consult with the players in black and officials in pink. His final act of disturbance had been to make allegations of intentional physical attack against his person by Roger. This served to delay the conclusion of the game, adding assault to injury time, and may have threatened its abandonment altogether had not the referee and the many other witnesses not intervened to give their full accounts of said proceedings and where blame truly lay. Roger avoided being carted off in handcuffs, Will refused to press charges of his own, and the match allowed to finish 3-1 to The Shirley - had Jonathan been present he would probably have been disappointed, relieved, and pleased respectively by these outcomes.

"I'm sure it will be a lot easier for the team to come back from this than it will be for Jonah," Roger announced to the group.

"Until he apologises to the group it will be Jonathan from now on," added Simon.

"Its Mr Cruft for me, he's already over familiar, and I've known him far less than you guys," Will said, receiving a surprising thumbs up from Owen.

CHAPTER 36:
Polish Tango

Defeat was one thing but fallout was another. Simon wasn't looking forward to getting another 'charming' letter from Mr Iam Wright-Pratt. Nor was he relishing making contact with Jonathan over all that had passed. Roger had shared anxieties, would the police take matters any further and/or would the League's governing body interpret his actions as another example of his displaying violent and ungentlemanly conduct on the pitch? The next few days passed slowly for the two of them. Simon decided he would not rush to make first contact with his possibly former teammate until news arrived from Lower Lenin Street. Roger decided, after a day or two of uncharacteristic fretting, that it would be business as usual until he heard otherwise. By the Wednesday all was still silent, the captain neither receiving nor giving communication and his right winger preparing for his regular bi-monthly visit to The White Eagle and drinks with Jan. What neither Simon or Roger knew at this stage is that the referee had decided not to file an incriminating report on the events of last Sunday. They were also unaware that the police had called in Jonathan and cautioned him for wasting police time. So no news was actually good news on this occasion, had they both only known.

As Roger entered his East Shields watering hole destination he was pleased to see his old friend Jan already standing there having a drink at the bar with some of the Polish Club's veteran clients. As he presented himself the ex-military old-timers did the distinctive Polish salute almost in unison that took him aback, although pleasantly so. One of the group almost dropped the records held under his non-saluting arm in the process but quickly recovered their capture.

"I've seen you guys do that quite a few times in greeting each other here but I wasn't expecting to be so honoured. I know it's something to do with your military past and quite unlike the salute we Brits use. Forgive my ignorance but why do you raise only two fingers to your temple in this form of address?" Roger asked.

"Well, one finger represents homeland and the other honour," answered the agile old man holding the records.

For a second this inadvertently returned Roger's mind to the events of Sunday and he concluded that Jonathan's disgraceful behaviour had let Pork and Mutton FC down by offering a different metaphorical two finger gesture to that which had been offered here. None of this, or his brush with the law, would be a topic for discussion tonight.

"Can I also ask about this pile of records you so gallantly saved from their doom a few seconds ago?"

"Ah, well spotted. These are my collection of Polish tango music. Interwar tunes reminiscent of a more innocent time, before the totalitarians came. The unwelcome hordes invading first from the West and then from the East, entombing the living behind rubble, brick and wire for more than three decades. I brought them along tonight because my friends here were in need of listening to them again. You observed I nearly dropped them. Well friend, I have saved them many times before!" their saviour replied in a nostalgic and sad tone.

After a further round of sociable drinks, Roger and Jan went off to play a game or two of darts, leaving the rest of the bar group enthusiastically organising the playlist. Neither thought any more of it as they took respective turns at the oche until their concentration was broken by the music loudly filling the air. This proved to be something of a distraction especially as many of the club regulars were singing along as if transported to another time and place. One too, couldn't help to be moved, by the music's reception, so arrows and their escorts returned to the bar to rejoin the ensemble. What surprised Roger, caught up in the moment alongside the others, was that he enjoyed what he heard although he couldn't understand the Polish lyrics being sung. Yes it may be old fashioned stuff, the sort his mother and father would have danced to, but it was pretty good nonetheless. He looked at the playlist but to no advantage as it had been written in a language undecipherable not only to him but written in a hand whose composition proved equally challenging to Jan.

"I see that you are both struggling to read my handwriting, these modern boys! The last song you heard was 'The Last Sunday' sung by Mieczyslaw Fogg and the next one coming up is 'It was Your Mistake' by Janusz Poplawski, to be followed by Fogg's rendition of 'I'm Waiting For You'," its author explained.

On hearing this Roger was taken aback.

"Are you OK Roger?" Jan asked.

"Oh, sorry, I was just taking it all in."

Blooming heck what a coincidence! Is what he was really privately thinking to himself. Last Sunday's game, the alleged assault, his awaiting news on the consequences - it was like it had all been pre-ordained and captured in the shaky scribble, on yellowing paper, set out before him. Towards the end of the evening one song in particular stood out for Roger, along with most of the crowd, who requested its playing several times.

"What is that number they all seem to love?"

"It's not a number, it's more than that, it's a classic! The song is called 'Play Fiddler, Play' with vocals by Adam Aston," answered the record provider.

I hope this is not a premonition for Sunday, Roger thought to himself, made aware by Simon of the nickname given to Jan's cousin Anton, in advance of their scheduled reacquaintance.

Meanwhile, and elsewhere, Simon was more than a little miffed that Jonathan had yet to make any contact. He certainly wasn't going to blink first, especially as he was still awaiting news regarding possible league retribution. By Saturday morning he hadn't heard anything from either party and now at least felt somewhat reassured that the usually diligent, if rather overbearing, league administrators were unlikely to raise a stink. This realisation did not motivate him to call Jonathan but rather, contrarily, stiffened his resolve against doing so. His teammate had been in the wrong and owed all of Pork and Mutton FC a massive apology. One of the oldest players had displayed the least wisdom on the day. It takes two to tango but Simon had no intention of engaging with this partner. He would wait and see if Jonathan turns up tomorrow - even if he did, he would not be selected, Simon convinced himself - he had no intention to reward bad behaviour.

Jonathan was a no show the following morning as the team gathered in East Shields Park for the away return match. His absence appeared to bring with it much relief for all concerned and any remnants of last week's unsettling finally dissipated. After sitting out the previous match, Simon decided that both Norman and he should return to bolster the midfield and try to counter the threat posed by The White Eagle's best player, Anton Topolnicka, who had starred in the 2-2 draw earlier in the season. Since then the Polish side, surprisingly and somewhat inexplicably, had displayed inconsistent form and mixed results to be left languishing in the lower depths of the division. A serious injury to their midfield general had hardly helped matters, sidelining Anton for a prolonged absence of eight games equally split either side of the season's winter break, but other talented players had failed to deliver – they were more than a one man band, as their centre forward had shown in the previous encounter. 'Fiddler on the Hoof' was back to full fitness and his teammates were back on song stringing together a three match unbeaten run making Simon fully expectant of a challenging match. Byron was given the substitute berth and joined Doug and Big Hec on the touchline as Pork and Mutton FC lined-up as follows:

(0) Owen

(2) Mario   (5) Massimo   (3) Marco

(6) Salvator

(7) Roger   (4) Simon   (8) Stuart   (11) Norman

(9) Ever   (10) Will

The game did not disappoint and proved to be a lively affair, especially in the battle to control midfield. Pork and Mutton FC were successful, in the early exchanges, in containing the midfield menace, having learned their lesson previously. They took the lead in the 20th minute when Will got on the end of a speculative Norman cross to volley the ball home. This was his third goal in as many games and he was starting to show the form Mr Robson had talked about. White Eagle had not expected a quality opponent like this and from that moment focused greater attention on him. As a mark of some subsequent respect they made sure that at least two defenders were in very close proximity for the remainder of the rest of the half. While Will had his liberty curtailed Ever was gaining greater freedom. He wasted a good opportunity in the 33rd minute heading wide at the near post after being left unmarked following a Roger corner. A few minutes later a long clearance from Salvator immediately turned defence into attack by finding Ever in acres of space. The forward raced towards goal, skipping past a newly arrived defender endeavouring to obstruct his progress, before unleashing a shot that clattered the crossbar to safety. The Polish side came just as close three minutes later when their centre forward headed against the woodwork following a Topolnicka free kick. Simon's side had just edged it so far but the game was more evenly balanced than the advantage held, and opportunities spurned, may have suggested. They were exceedingly fortunate to get to half-time without conceding, coming under sustained relentless pressure following Anton's taking back control of midfield. Those final pre-orange minutes witnessed a goal line clearance by Mario and a marvellous one-handed save by Owen.

Simon knew that the first ten minutes or so of the re-start could be pivotal to the outcome of the match. He hoped, but did not expect, that the scheduled pause in proceedings may work to their benefit, coming just as it did when his opponents were getting into their stride. On this occasion hope trumped expectation as The White Eagle struggled to find the gear and rhythm displayed just before the break. It was Pork and Mutton FC who came closest to altering the current scoreline when a long range shot by Roger was parried away by the goalkeeper into the path of Ever who was unable to adjust his feet in time and spurned the 58th minute opportunity. This warning, acted as a shot across the bow rather than just a tame shot wide, and served to galvanise the opposition's resolve to get back into the game. From that moment on they took the initiative with Anton acting as the main catalyst. Simon and Norman tried as best they could to contain the man who was now, once again, pulling the strings - but it was proving increasingly difficult to do. He had found his second wind while they were losing their first. Norman was clearly flagging the most and Simon was seriously contemplating his substitution. Even before Byron came on and replaced him after 70 minutes The White Eagle had come extremely close on two separate occasions to drawing level. It was largely thanks to the goalkeeping prowess of Owen and the steadfastness of an upright that things remained as they did.

Simon knew that Byron was more of an offensive option than a defensive one and they were more in need of the latter. This led him to now question whether he should rather have named Doug as substitute given his surprising display of defensive acumen during their winter break training. Faced with what he had, Simon asked Roger to come inside to help him try and marshall Anton, and instructed Ever to drop back a bit to further aid the midfield's emptying right flank. Byron was charged with linking attacking play on the left and supporting Will so preventing his being increasingly isolated up front. These tactical adjustments worked for ten minutes or so to suppress any threats and even gave rise to a goal scoring opportunity uncharacteristically squandered by Will following a mazy dribble by Byron. Just as Simon began thinking things might be going to plan they started to unravel. He was no strategic Napoleon, and like all generals in the field, he came to realise that humans were not easily controllable pieces on a chess board patiently awaiting external input. The final ten minutes were all White Eagle. They made changes of their own, bringing on a fresh midfielder that allowed Anton to push further upfield and support their attack more directly. Pork and Mutton's central midfield was being pushed deeper and deeper and this way and that. The flanks and forward line were no longer in the game and the side lost any semblance of group cohesiveness. Giving instruction does not mean taking instruction, especially on the pitch in the heat and uncertainty of battle, brought on by what the nineteenth century Prussian military genius von Clausewitz is said to have attributed to 'the fog of war'.

When the equaliser duly arrived on 88 minutes it was neither undeserved nor surprising but still very fortunate. Just before then another wooden obstruction had come to Owen's assistance to deflect the ball away for a corner after ricocheting off Marco's left kneecap. As the resultant corner was floated in Owen lost sight of the ball and only succeeded in fisting the fresh air. Thankfully, Massimo beat their centre forward to the ball and headed clear from the melee of bodies surrounding the goalie. This reprieve was short-lived, however, as the ball somewhat magnetically found itself arriving at the feet of Anton, duly stationed yards outside the penalty area, who sent it straight back, through a forest of legs and most probably inadvertently, but not innocuously, deflected off one of the referee's, into the welcoming net just as Owen achieved touchdown. Another draw to add to that of their previous meeting and their ninth of the campaign.

"I don't know what it is Simon, but we manage to draw more often than even Billy the Kid," said Salvator.

"That may well be true, but one thing's for certain, it's helping to really improve your English!"

CHAPTER 37:
A Different Class

There was a sense of deja vu prior to the forthcoming return match against the students and staff of Shields College. Just as before their previous encounter, at the end of September, Pork and Mutton FC had only taken one point from the previous two games, losing and drawing against the very two same teams both then and now. Simon knew they could also do with a little more history repeating against College Caterers FC, a team they beat handsomely away, and was optimistic about this student reunion on their home turf of The Links. It was viewed as a timely fixture well set to re-energise their stalling league campaign and stop their slide down the league table. They had dropped down to seventh position, not only providing the opportunity for Bulman United to overtake them, but allowing a chasing pack of two other teams - FC Lokomotiv and Four Mile Inn - to remain close behind. A win against these 'neverlanders' was deemed essential. The opposition were one of the teams vying for the wooden spoon, an award that Pork and Mutton FC were not unfamiliar with themselves. Being caterers at least they would find some use for it. Not that the lecturers were that keen, and avoiding its possession stirred them more than the spoon ever could.

Even before Simon got to pondering over the significant age and weight differentials between the likely respective line-ups his usual Saturday morning housekeeping routine was interrupted with an unexpected telephone call from the Cruft household. Once again, it was the wife not the husband making the call, and just as before, Simon found her dulcet tones mysteriously alluring.

"Simon, sorry to trouble you, it's Nancy Cruft here. I don't know why I'm telling you this but I've thrown Jonathan out after catching him red-handed dallying with some fancy piece a couple of weeks ago and I'm concerned that I haven't heard from him since. I was was wondering whether you knew of his whereabouts?"

"I have absolutely no idea I'm afraid. To be just as honest with you, your husband has been somewhat of a pain for the team recently and we haven't seen him. I am as clueless as you regarding his current living arrangements. All I can further tell you is that he didn't turn up for last week's game and is unlikely to show tomorrow, or any time soon for that matter." Simon carefully avoiding detailing Jonathan's unseemly role in the episode against Shirley Inn.

"Oh, I see. At least we both now have a better idea of what he is like! Could I kindly ask, If you, or any of your teammates should see him or have any further information, would you let me know please? His dog, Eusebio, is the only one here pinning away for his master."

"Of course, happy to help in any way, if I can."

At least Jonathan's rather fraught behaviour made a little more sense now, Simon thought, but he resisted worrying Nancy about the police incident and the fact that the local constabulary may have more of an idea where her husband is now residing.

There were no more unwanted disturbances to Simon's regular Saturday routine. His afternoon proved to be more

enjoyable as he watched East Shields Town handsomely beat
Lynemush Colliers 4-0, witnessing Yiannis's first ever goal for
his new side after coming on as substitute. At the end of the
match he was invited by Mr Robson to join the chairman and
the players at the bar for celebratory drinks. He even managed
to have a brief private chat with Yiannis, who was nursing a
soft drink, but in fine fettle. At least this was one former player
who was noticeably happily settled in his new home.

In terms of form, Pork and Mutton FC would be fully
expected to prevail over tomorrow's opposition. Simon decided
to play both Byron and Doug out on the wings with Roger
as substitute. Norman would be sitting this one out after last
week's exertions with Big Hec once again manning his buckets
rather than the goalposts. The captain felt that it was wise to
go with this blend of youth and experience, of age and weight
reduction, and increased pace and attacking threat out wide:

(0) Owen

(2) Mario   (5) Massimo   (3) Marco

(6) Salvator

(7) Byron   (4) Simon   (8) Stuart   (11) Doug

(9) Ever   (10) Will

While no matches are easy this one should be easier than
most, so Simon thought, nestled in the cosy sanctuary of his
living room, with his feet comforted in his fur-lined slippers
and his hands gently caressing a hot mug of cocoa. There
was no way he could be aware that he would't be facing the
usual crop of students and staff otherwise his ease would have
been shattered with that realisation. There would be a larger

contingent of college lecturers in the side tomorrow, and not all of them involved with catering, although some had the potential to cook up a storm. Likewise, the usual company of students would be missing and their stand-ins mainly drawn from a mixed bag of apprentice butchers and trainee physiotherapists united only by a joint interest in manipulating muscle and flesh. All the players Pork and Mutton FC had faced last time would be missing this, as the entire group were away on a hospitality and culinary themed weekend field trip with their bespectacled lecturer once again acting as minder. Tomorrow's surprises would reveal themselves in good time but before then *Match of the Day* was about to capture Simon's full attention.

As Pork and Mutton FC came running out onto The Links on an unseasonably mild early March morning they now found themselves sharing a pitch with a group of strangers enthusiastically warming up at the other end. Simon's initial thought was that these were another group of lost boys who had mistakenly confused themselves with where they were supposed to be playing that day. The Links, with its several adjacent pitches, had a habit of causing visitor uncertainty - but not on this occasion - and it was the home team that was left totally bemused. That was until the opposition's stand-in captain confirmed they had more than squatters rights. Simon should have known better from the outset because the yellow and blue stripes facing them had always been the Caterers colours, although never as ill fitting on some of their players as now. There appeared to be at least five mature lecturers, three of whom had somehow managed to defy the odds and shoehorn their bodies into the playing attire provided. This marked them out as people who obviously took a strong interest in food and somehow further justified their right of abode. Although Simon took some comfort in this, he was more concerned about the two remaining slimmer models who looked pretty useful and more than proficient with the ball. He did not know these were ringers brought in from the Physical Education Faculty or that all of the students were there on playing rather than catering merit. History showed that there had always been something of a positive correlation between a rising number of lecturers and the result going in their favour, so things did not bode well, Simon concluded. Had he known the rest then he would of been even more pessimistic, clearly College Caterers FC, or their surrogates, were not planning to throw in the towel any time soon.

Things did not go well for Pork and Mutton FC from the get off and go. One of the well-kitted out lecturers easily waltzed through the heart of the midfield immediately following kick-off and fired off a quick shot that caught Owen but not the crossbar unawares. The ball was thence safely redirected to a nettle patch located well away from goal. At least the home keeper had adequate protection on this occasion, unlike just prior, to retrieve the ball courtesy of his gloves. For the next fifteen minutes it was just like Rorke's Drift except wave after wave of attack was repulsed by men dressed in black. Massimo headed a ball off the line and a last ditch tackle from Salvator in the penalty area prevented the Caterers from getting their just desserts. As the match progressed the opposition continued to press for a lead that was not so forthcoming, causing frustration to slowly start creeping into their play. Although Simon and his team had to continue their rearguard action for most of the first half Will started to come into the game more. At first he was the main outlet for any pressure relieving ball deep out of their own half and he had little ambition other than hold the ball to slow the game down and allow others to take a breather.

As the interval break became more imminent, and the Caterers were increasingly bereft of ideas, gaps started to appear in their defence and Will started to exploit the opportunities these provided. In the 34th minute he got on the end of yet another speculative clearance but now found himself with more space to manoeuvre than before. Up until then he had been very closely marked by two of the lecturers kitted out more like the incredible hulk than footballers and roughly prevented from directing any real threat on goal. With his captors now inexplicably awol and being free of these man-handlers he had almost a clear run on goal with only one remaining student defender in his way. The apprentice butcher, well used in practising separating limbs, took it upon himself to treat Will as another piece of meat. This resulted in a booking and a free kick just outside the penalty area. Both Will and his assassin were lucky to remain on the pitch, albeit for different reasons. The injured party took the direct free kick himself and watched as the trainee physiotherapist goalkeeper contorted his own body and deflected the ball to safety. The follow-up corner was easily dealt with by one of the Marvel(less) characters charged with containing Will's forays upfield. If this was a warning then it went largely unheeded. On 40 minutes Stuart won a loose ball in the centre circle and played it out left to Doug who raced down the wing and past the flailing leg of a trainee physiotherapist before slotting a through ball to Will who was racing into the penalty area. Just as his left foot was about to connect with the ball he had both feet intentionally, and somewhat cynically, removed by the same aspiring butcher as before, who had come back for seconds. The referee immediately blew for the penalty and then sent the guilty party packing. With the usual penalty taker (Roger) not being on the pitch and Will not yet in a fit state to take it Simon handed the ball to Ever. Although he had been largely engaged in defensive duties for most of the morning he gladly accepted the opportunity to go on the offensive and briskly despatched the ball into the top right corner of the net. Even with a thousand physiotherapy sessions there was no way that the goalie could have reached it. The opposition's heads did not drop, even though they could consider themselves unlucky to be behind in terms of the score if not so in bodies on the pitch, and they were unlucky not to equalise just before the referee blew for half-time.

After the ritual of orange segments, and immediately prior to the commencement of the game, the College Caterers substituted the third hulk-like lecturer playing in midfield with a younger, taller and lithe replacement. He looked lively and he was, getting his team back level within two minutes of coming on, gracefully stroking home from fifteen yards out. The defence had been caught cold from the restart. Simon knew they had the extra man but did they have the extra manpower to now hold this team, and this super sub, in check? It was apparent that Will was still suffering from the earlier abuse and after ten minutes of trying to run it off signalled his need to finally exit the game. Simon told Roger to join Ever up front in the hope that fresh legs might help them regain the advantage. This new striking partnership swapped positions as Will's replacement was singularly right-footed whilst Ever was more proficiently two-footed. This change shifted the balance of the game in favour of Pork and Mutton FC and they came close on two occasions in the 60th and 63rd minutes with Roger shooting wide from ten yards and Stuart rattling the crossbar.

Somewhat against the run of play, the Caterers grabbed the lead in the 70th minute when their super sub finally managed to give Salvator the slip and played a one two with a slim lecturer before deftly flicking the ball home. Simon and his side continued to press as the opposition started to sit back and conserve their waning energy levels. This now handed the home team the initiative alongside the momentum. They were duly rewarded with an equaliser from an unlikely source. For whatever reason, only known to himself, Massimo decided to charge forward and join the attack at a corner. It was floated over by Roger, who was aiming for the head of Ever, but missed by everyone apart from the rarely marauding centre-back who marked his arrival by heading home. This was uncharted territory for him but he had found a way to level the game in the 81st minute. Panic was now added to tiredness as the opposition desperately tried to hold out for a point. Defensive sloppiness resulted in their conceding a goal four minutes from the end. A lazy and flyweight back pass from one of the heavyweight defenders was intercepted by Roger who neatly then lobbed the ball over the advancing keeper. College Caterers FC were clearly on the ropes and about to hit the canvas but the final whistle intervened just as Ever was about to round the goalkeeper and make the score even more flattering.

Pork and Mutton FC needed this win more than they fully deserved it, with the 3-2 scoreline failing to tell the full story. Having an extra man for 50 minutes or so certainly helped just as losing Will probably hindered. His availability for the next match was already in doubt as he limped back to the changing facilities escorted by Simon. The captain not only pondered this loss, but how he had mistakenly thought his opponents had initially lost their way before his team nearly lost theirs.

CHAPTER 38:
Ex's Mark His Spot

Five months can be a long time in football and even longer in life. Pork and Mutton FC's next opponents were Peking Duck United who appeared to be imploding both on and off the pitch. Mr Wu's monopoly of good fortune, and his avoidance of bad, appeared to be deserting him, or so the local papers seemed to suggest. In his case it was increasingly appearing as if football was imitating life. Whatever problems their owner had at home or in his business appeared to be reflected on the pitch. They were on such a downward trajectory that promotion had gone from being almost certain to very unlikely. They had picked up only 2 points since the winter recess and were now laying only a couple of places above Pork and Mutton. Something somewhere was clearly amiss.

Although Simon, or any of his teammates for that matter, knew little of the true ins and outs, they had all gleaned enough from the widespread journalistic coverage to know that the Wu dynasty was losing its mystique and magic. Rumours of Chinese underworld connections had circulated just before Christmas. It was alleged that Mr Wu had offered to buy out his supermarket business partner and when this was turned down resorted to the employment of muscle to seal the deal. A high profile court case was now pending challenging the transaction as having taken place under duress. Costly legal counsels were now awaiting the physical recovery of the maimed business partner recuperating under the auspices of the witness protection programme.

Less well known was that other legal charges had also been mounting up for Mr Wu, with his having to meet expensive financial settlements out of court. Unbeknown to Mrs Wu her husband had been having a rather close relationship with one of his young female employees. This had started following Mrs Wu's increasingly frequent, but wholly innocent, visits with her daughter to family in London. It became imperative for the health of his marriage that his girlfriend seek medical assistance, less for concern about his anticipating implementation of the Chinese one child policy and more about keeping things more easily under wraps from his wife. While he had no plans to play happy two families his girlfriend was less inclined to lose the fruits of their clandestine labours. This was one form of expansion that Mr Wu had no interest in. The offer of adequate financial compensation seemed to do the trick although it also terminated the intimate relationship. The now ex girlfriend started to take liberties at work, turning up late or not at all, but still expecting to be paid for her previous troubles. Mr Wu decided to avoid recourse to the muscle that had already landed him in hot water and terminated her employment, hoping that a generous secret cash payment would make her disappear. But she came back for more and threatened to disclose all to his wife. He refused to be blackmailed any further and she not only told his wife but also threatened to go to an employment tribunal. The latter was easier to fix than the former and far less draining on his dwindling resources. On hearing her news, the wife headed to London with their daughter, this time for good, and immediately sued for divorce making use of the newly implemented Divorce Reform Act. All his ex's had been crossed and now they all crossed him.

So much prevailing bad blood surrounding Mr Wu did little to help Peking Duck United's cause. Just like their owner they had entered the doldrums and felt no longer cherished. Simon knew his side had a good opportunity to avenge the heavy home defeat experienced the last time the two teams met. Pork and Mutton FC were now merely joining the growing queue of people wanting to get their own back, either directly or indirectly, against the Wu dynasty.

As the team gathered in the away dressing room there were a number of immediate selection and formation issues Simon had to address.

"OK Lads, as you can see, Salvator isn't here and won't be coming unfortunately. He called me yesterday to say, I'm sure I understood him properly between the pauses, that he was displaying symptoms of food poisoning after his first, and definitely last, Friday night curry."

"So he'll be doing running of another sort then, out of necessity rather than choice!" said Roger grinning.

"Don't forget Roger, looking back, we have all been there before," Norman confessed.

"To continue, if I may, Will is still carrying his injury so cannot play a full game. We discussed this the other day, and it hasn't improved much since, but he is happy to be substitute and come on if necessary. I do think we need to have some fire power held in reserve so I am giving him the number 12 shirt. Sorry Big Hec but you will be missing out again."

"No problem, I'm not missing anything, I have my buckets and you guys."

"Appreciate that. The next thing to discuss, given all this, relates to how the team will set-up and who will play where today. Norman and I will play just ahead of the back-three and share Salvator's usual defensive duties while also bolstering the midfield. This will allow Roger and Doug to utilise the wings and Byron to join Ever up front."

Simon intentionally failed to mention that for the briefest of moments, immediately following Salvator's unexpected withdrawal, that he missed Jonathan's possible input, before regaining his senses knowing full well that his line-up would be even more destabilised by the miscreant's inclusion than it already was:

(0) Owen

(2) Mario   (5) Massimo   (3) Marco

(4) Simon   (6) Norman

(7) Roger   (8) Stuart   (11) Doug

(9) Ever   (10) Byron

As Pork and Mutton FC prepared for kick-off Simon and his teammates couldn't fail to notice that their opponents appeared bereft of players. There were only nine on the pitch and none on the sidelines. Their captain confirmed with the referee that they were awaiting the possible arrival of, at most, only one more player but this was the likely complement that they would have to be going with. Clearly some had already left a sinking ship although the tenth man duly climbed back on board just before the commencement whistle was blown. This all served as a timely reminder for Simon that other teams could be even more threadbare than his. As he looked around at the opposition still sporting their old kit, but with the X's emblazoned across their chests now taking on a more negative meaning, he could not help but notice that a number of the players who had caused them grief last time were no longer present on the park.

After a few minutes into the match it became obvious that Peking Duck United were not the team of old. Being a man down obviously did not help them but from the off their passing play was disjointed and they looked increasingly unsure of themselves. Byron benefitted from early confusion between two of their defenders to intercept a throw out from their goalie and return the ball from whence it came but lobbing it deftly out of reach into a welcoming net. Pork and Mutton FC had scored after only 10 minutes although for Byron it was a long time coming, being his first goal since mid October, some thirteen games ago. This particular drought may have been over but only time would tell whether there was a deluge to follow. The opposition did not immediately cave-in, however, and were galvanised into action by their captain's resolve to make a fight of it. He injected a calm and purpose into their play which almost led to an equaliser eight minutes later but the threat was snuffed out by a brilliant stretching sliding tackle by Norman in his own penalty area. This intervention, just before their centre forward was about to pull the trigger, saved a likely goal but came at a cost as he would have to carry the after effect into the rest of the game. For the next twenty minutes or so each side gave as good as they got but neither team managed to get a shot on target or cause the goalkeepers to break sweat. This stalemate was almost broken again just before the interval when Roger played a sublime through ball to Ever who then beat his marker and hit a rasping shot that rattled the crossbar before exiting stage right into safety. This was the last but one meaningful effort of the first half with the final one being Norman valiantly struggling on until the oranges arrival meant he could hobble no longer.

Now that Norman was clearly out of commission the team would have to draw on another of their walking wounded, Will, to enter the fray. Simon addressed his huddle of players.

"I didn't want to make the change so early. But you can all see how things are. It's really up to you Will and I don't mind if you want to come on a little later as they are still a man down anyway?"

"No, I'm happy to give it a go and see how the injury holds up. Let's try to make our advantage count sooner rather than later."

"Great! Byron I want you to drop into the centre of midfield alongside Stuart, allowing Will to take up his usual position up front. l will sit in front of the back three on my own, playing Salvator's role. Given what we are facing today, it provides us with a more familiar and appropriate set-up to finish the job we started."

They now had a half man advantage, technically speaking, rather than the full one they had commenced with. At least Will was well experienced in conserving his energy and avoiding making wasteful forward runs with little payback. Ever would have to be the workhorse up front. They also had the added advantage of still being a goal up.

The second half started off as a rather tense affair with each side unwilling to be the first to slip up or give ground. There was a fair amount of holding back and an unwillingness to take risks. For those opening fifteen minutes spectators would have seen more adventure in a children's playground than here. The question was, who would be bold and seize the initiative first? Peking Duck United could not afford to put off the inevitable, however, and decided to go for first mover advantage. Motivated by their captain they started to press forward and take the game to their opponents. For the next twenty minutes they laid siege on the Pork and Mutton goal but were unable to break through. Mario cleared a shot heading toward goal and Owen, keen as ever to get a clean sheet, made two first class saves. The woodwork had also helped on one occasion. A great deal of energy had been spent on trying to get and prevent an equaliser. Peking Duck were going for broke, not unlike their mentor Mr Wu, but it had not paid off. A number of their players had little more to give and withdrew increasingly into their own half allowing Simon's side to take back territorial advantage. Will had been patiently biding his time and dwindling strength awaiting the right moment to strike. On 83 minutes he chased down a misplaced pass from Doug and beat a defender before playing the ball back to Ever to tap home. On that he decided to retire from the game, more comfortable that the match, at 2-0, was finally won than he was with the injury he was still carrying. That was the final notable moment of the game and both sides had given their all even if their respective opposite directions of travel would continue, at least for now, anyway.

CHAPTER 39:
Norman's Wisdom

Their latest win gave them two victories on the trot for March, the last time that was achieved was last November and that had only been the second time in their inglorious history. None of the veteran players had been present on the first successful 'winning run' but Fred always alluded to it, from behind his bar, when given the opportunity, as he had been playing in the side at that time. Now the team had matched, then surpassed, in the sense of doing it twice in a given season, that achievement - which now made Fred unsurprisingly mute on that specific chosen subject. He was no mastermind but tonight he would play the role of Magnus Magnusson and be the quiz master as the Pork and Mutton hosted its first midweek trivia night.

Simon was in attendance and awaiting the arrival of other members of the team who had promised to attend. He thought better than to mention to Fred that the team had every opportunity to set a new record of consecutive wins by beating Smithfields in their forthcoming home fixture - after all, they had hammered them last time and should be able to tenderise them again. Better to remain in Fred's good books than antagonise him given that a £10 prize was at stake for the winning team.

As the place was rapidly filling up Simon decided to bag a table in a corner where his team's answers would not be overheard, optimistically assuming that they would have answers to submit, especially in light of the fact that neither of the college kids, Byron nor Salvator could make it. He was soon joined by Roger, better known for his drinking than his knowledge. Will would probably of helped more but he was somewhere over Germany pushing his trolley and using it as a zimmer frame of sorts as his leg injury slowly improved. The other walking wounded from Sunday, Norman, was expected to turn up along with Stuart and they duly arrived together with only a few minutes to spare. The leg injury had yet to repair itself as he made a noticeably slow and gingerly entrance alongside his escort. Pork and Mutton FC's defence had all declined the invitation to take part. Owen was booked out at a nearby social club and two of the triplets were less than keen with the other unwilling to be separated. With Doug preferring being entombed within the confines of his bedroom that only left Big Hec or Ever, one of whom was now busy with his buckets collecting outside East Shields Town, a match Simon decided to forego for this, while the other attended to celebrating his wedding anniversary. So it would be the original four against the world again. They could have done with an extra body as Fred allowed quiz teams of up to five to take part but they were just as well used to being understaffed anyway.

As the bar settled down in anticipation of the start the first issue for all the teams present was what they would call themselves. This had to be written on the top of their blank answer sheet.

"That's easy, I can answer this one without thinking or consulting," Simon said before writing THE GANG OF FOUR in unmistakably clear lettering and the rest nodded in agreement.

"I think we are ahead already," Roger quipped as the other teams noisily and energetically debated their appropriate monikers.

Any feeling of superiority was short lived as Jonathan Cruft made a surprising entrance into the bar. Without any acknowledgement of his former teammates he joined a table of three seated nearby, becoming the third man in that ring. As soon as Roger caught sight of his former protagonist he started to make a move out of his chair.

"Now Roger, down boy! We, and especially you, need to avoid any further trouble on his account." Simon's words managed to restrain him.

'Listen, there are other ways to get our own back. Winning this quiz would be a great start and put his nose out of joint," Stuart added.

"That's right, it's now about more than just the prize money at stake, it's become personal. You can better vent your spleen that way Roger," Norman said, calming things further.

This was neither a gunfight nor the OK Corral but it came close in tension and eyeballing to Tombstone. Norman and Stuart had always been the quiet and private ones in the group, if they were to be assassins they would be the silent ones. Stuart spent all of his working day on his own as a plumber in his business. Norman worked at one of the senior schools in West Shields, the somewhat inappropriately named Brightborne Secondary Modern, where he taught History and Art. Although Stuart could be known for literally throwing a spanner in the works he was not planning to do so on this occasion. Likewise Norman was willing to temporarily airbrush history with regard to any past grievances. They remained focused on the quiz while Simon had to spend some of his time smoothing ruffled feathers. It was daggers rather than bullets that were being regularly exchanged between Roger and Jonathan as the quiz master carried on regardless and raced through his questions.

Rather surprisingly, the usual categories of questions and the interval passed by without incident. This was partly owing to Simon chaperoning Roger to the bar and loo and to Jonathan becoming increasingly more interested in another newly arrived woman added to his group than constantly making eyes at Roger. Sport, TV and Film, and Geography had propelled Simon and his quiz partners into third position just one point behind the joint leaders the Kung Fu Kings and Jonathan's Vicars and Tarts. The closing Potpourri and Music rounds allowed the Gang of Four to floor their martial arts rivals and join the religious luvvies in a final question decider that served to supercharge any remaining animosity between Roger and Jonathan. While neither had contributed greatly to their respective team scores of 43/50 they did not want to let their quiz mates down in this sudden death showdown. Norman had provided the majority of his team's correct answers and all of their hopes were now largely pinned on him. Simon couldn't bear the thought of losing and how it would rankle while also quite possibly provoking Roger into more direct action. Success would offer far sweeter revenge than any form of fisticuffs, although the other members of Jonathan's team would still be innocents caught in the crossfire.

Fred outlined the procedure of determining the winners before the room went respectively solemnly quiet. The first team to press the nonexistent buzzer (raising their hand) and provide the correct answer to his question, without conferring, would win and an incorrect answer would hand the prize to the opposition. This format did not suit Roger's strategy of guessing, especially given his proficiency in being wrong, so he planned to keep mum.

"In what year did Tonga become independent of the UK?"

"Tonka is American, and makes toy trucks, it isn't a country!" immediately shouted an inebriate holding tight to the bar, not only serving to break the tense silence but drawing even more laughter as he fell over after belatedly raising both arms.

"I would like to remind the audience to stay out of it please. To the drunk on the floor, I was referring to the country with a G and not the toy truck manufacturer with a K, and you should gindly ko home," generating another burst of laughter that helped clear the air.

Both team's now looked at each other in a different, yet not dissimilar, way than before waiting for the first one to blink. Norman slowly raised his hand.

"1970 I believe, and on the 4th of June, to be more exact."

Attention now shifted back to Fred.

"That's correct, well done Norman and the Gang of Four, tonight's winners!"

"Just hold your horses Fred, not so quick! Surely he's wrong. I remember as a child watching the coronation of Queen Elizabeth in 1953 on TV and the Queen of Tonga was present so it must have been independent by then as you couldn't have two queens surely?" said Jonathan interrupting what he saw as premature celebrations.

At this point Fred became a little unsure of himself and even more so as the audience started to become a little restless. Then Norman again raised his hand.

"Yes, no doubt about it, Tonga did have a queen at the coronation, Salote Tupou III, but it was a British Protectorate and not formally a colony so the answer I gave is 'the truth and nothing but the truth'." On this occasion, unfortunately, he had neither God, nor what later would be called Google, to so help him.

If there had been a jury it would have remained split; a significant number of those present found his added detailed explanation highly persuasive, while others unfairly interpreted his response somewhat bizarrely as the intellectual arrogance of a clever clogs (given it was a quiz after all). Jonathan was less than happy with Norman's attempt to further justify the answer he had previously given. Sensing some of the simmering discontent within the room he started to play up to that part of the audience sharing both his misgivings and increasing disrespect for Norman. He ridiculed his rival, referring to him coldly as Mr Clarke, rather than the Norman of older happier times, aiming to undermine the validity of his answer by now undermining his person.

"Can I also add that I find the behaviour of the quiz master to be somewhat improper and hardly impartial given his longstanding close personal relationship to the members composing the Gang of Four. Just look at how he reacted to their so called winning!"

"Listen mate, you've already gone too far tonight! It will take a bigger and better bloke than you to challenge my authority in my own boozer. Testing my patience is one thing but testing my honesty is something else. So I strongly advise you to watch what you're saying!"

"So you don't like it when other people raise questions!" Jonathan answered unwilling to give ground and causing more audience unrest.

"Order, order! I will not have aspersions cast against myself or anyone here. To that end I will bring into play the Peacock Protocol".

Fred was searching for a diplomatic solution, to avoid being airlifted out of his own pub. All became silent as he directed what he perceived as potential rioters to a small elderly chap in a darkened corner at the end of the bar. The man Fred now introduced was sat atop a bar stool still sheltering under his flat cap and who began nervously stoking up his his pipe in response.

"This is Mr Peacock, senior statesman of this here parish, who, as many of you regulars know, has provided decades of valuable advice from his throne in the corner, with a fine record of amicable conflict resolution which puts the United

Nations to shame", enthusiastically gushed Fred, continuing his eulogy by concluding that, "Mr Peacock will decide the outcome of the quiz".

He was equivalent to the future role of VAR in football, waiting almost half a century further down the line. This was a truly rare occasion where Pork and Mutton may have been one step ahead of the game. At this the pensioner sprung into life, folding his annotated section of the newspaper containing tomorrow's race card before placing it shakily in his jacket pocket, then just as nimbly landing on terra firma removed from the celestial plane where the pub landlord had just recently placed him.

The silence became almost deafening as the room filled with an air of gravitas. The gentle placement of his smoking pipe on the bar counter sounded more like a thunderclap, and that was even before his judgement.

"I must confess my ignorance over the correct answer to the deciding question and I am in no position to come down on one side or the other. That said, however, I am mindful that the prize has to be awarded tonight and that whoever wins has to be seen by all those present as rightful victors."

This pronouncement seemed to do the trick, with no one daring to say anything in response, and all waiting and willing for him to continue. Mr Peacock, knowing full well the likely response, asked the two competing teams if they would be willing to share the prize, but given the degree of resentment between the key protagonists and the sense of injustice felt by each that they had won, this offer was declined with neither side willing to back down (although the two females in Jonathan's party weren't totally against the idea).

"Given the lack of agreement on sharing the prize, I suggest that it would be best to conclude what has become something of a duel, with one final question, to which I certainly know the answer."

Neither of the competing parties were in a position to back out now and be seen as chicken. They agreed to the peace terms alongside using the same procedure as outlined by Fred for the previous 'decider'.

"Right, if I can have all your attention. Here is the deciding question. Name the boat on which Chay Blyth, not long since, circumnavigated the globe 'the wrong way'?"

Just before he could get his arm up in time, Norman lost out to Jonathan, who obtained the right to answer first. For some strange reason, even unbeknown to himself, he blurted out "Blithe Spirit" rather than the correct answer which both Mr Peacock and Mr (Norman) Clarke knew was British Steel. Cruft had once again shot himself, and his teammates, in the foot. His answer had been more careless than carefree, but just like the comic play written by Noël Coward it did occasion the onset of laughter albeit alongside some derision. Of course, Norman knew the answer was redundant to proceedings, just as the state-owned company which lent its name to Chay's ketch would later find itself. The £10 prize was duly awarded without any demur whatsoever, not least because Jonathan and his group had already made a quick getaway minus the loot. This was the first time that Simon and any of his teammates had won any competition playing together. It was not only the first but also the last time that Fred would organise and compere a quiz night. Mr Peacock would continue to offer his esteemed services at the end of the bar.

After all the excitement and underlying tension of the quiz night the home fixture against Smithfields was always likely to be an anticlimax. As the team met in their usual changing facility it was clear from Norman's entrance that his earlier injury would prevent him from repeating his most valuable player rating of midweek. Still, now that Salvator was back and Will declared himself fit, they were were less in need of his grey cells. Simon decided to name himself as substitute and join Norman and Big Hec on the touchline. The rest of the team lined-up as follows:

(0) Owen

(2) Mario (5) Massimo (3) Marco

(6) Salvator

(7) Roger (4) Byron (8) Stuart (11) Doug

(9) Ever (10) Will

Frank and Max had also unexpectedly turned up and were there to greet the team as they came running out. Neither wanted to miss this little piece of history in the making. Simon noticed during the warm-up that Smithfields looked less hungover than usual and that there were a number of new faces in their ranks. Given they were still mired at the bottom of the league, a position Pork and Mutton's substitute was well acquainted with, this didn't strike him as ominously as it normally would. Simon took some heart in the fact that two of their regular players were finishing off a bottle of beer apiece before lobbing them past their cowering goalkeeper, with the net as their dustbin. This was viewed as a good omen indicating that Smithfields had yet to vanquish some of their bad habits as well as having someone between the sticks who appeared to have less bottle than the two already conceded in his goal.

Within five minutes of the start Pork and Mutton FC thought they had taken an early lead but the referee chalked Will's effort offside. The ball, somewhat appropriately now, joined the other empties in the back of the net. For the next fifteen minutes or so Smithfields battled hard to ensure nothing else was deposited there. They even had an effort of their own which Owen had palmed away to safety. He was not called into any further action for the rest of the first half, however, as his teammates mounted attack after attack. Their efforts were rewarded in the 23rd minute when Ever got his hairpiece to connect with a Byron cross flying in from the right wing. This lead was justly extended when Ever added to his, and the team's tally, courtesy of a penalty after 36 minutes. This was a result of one of the opposition's previous beer drinkers possibly seeing double as his attempted clearance inside his own penalty area completely missed the bouncing ball he should have been aiming at rather than the pair in Doug's private possession. Mortimer had truly taken one for the team and it was a heavy personal price to pay but at least he showed he had some balls. He also continued to manly play on, probably just as much for his father's benefit as his own, as well as to avoid any further interference with his private parts from the attention of sponge man Big Hec. Relief, both for him and the opposition, arrived ten minutes later when half-time came.

With his father in attendance, Doug was keen to stay on the pitch for the second half and Simon was happy not to rob him of the opportunity. There was little need to make any forced changes and the game looked very much under their control. No one was counting their chickens but the previously unheard of three wins on the trot was certainly within their grasp. The pub landlord and the team sponsor certainly thought so and neither felt that their attendance had been in vain. Simon could not fail to notice that the players morale had been boosted by patrons past and present being there offering further support. Everyone was delighted when Doug found the back of the net in the 67th minute after a neat one two with Will. After all, it's not everyday that you can still manage to score after taking such a whack. That goal confirmed that the match was very much over bar the shouting, which would joyously arrive at the end of ninety minutes. Owen continued to be just as untroubled in goal as he had been for most of the first half although he did make use of his free time early on in the second half by removing the empties from his goal as he wanted nothing past him. Ever signalled to come off in the 80th minute not because he was injured but because he unselfishly wanted Simon on the pitch to be part of this memorable moment alongside the other on-field veterans. Byron moved up front and Simon took up the newly vacated berth in midfield. It was somewhat fitting, the cherry on the cake, when Simon got his name on the scoresheet in the 85th minute when he hit a speculative shot from outside the box that went through a crowd of players, past an unsighted goalie, directly into the goal. 4-0 was how the match ended allowing the celebrations to begin.

Max was most relieved his son's crown jewels were still intact and returned from his car with 4 bottles of chilled champagne and real glass flutes to mark the occasion with a touch of class. Then Frank invited everyone back to The Pork and Mutton for seconds.

CHAPTER 40:
More Than Another
Miner Setback

The celebrations that followed victory over bottom team Smithfields were certainly overdone but fully justified, at least that's how it was drunkenly viewed. One of the party had mentioned, "It may be only one small insignificant step for football but it was a giant leap for Pork and Mutton FC," but Simon could not remember who, only what was said. Three wins on the bounce was a new club record so what wasn't to like. It also elevated the team into fourth place in the league passing Peking Duck United on their way there. They had now played 26 matches and gleaned 31 points (W11 D9 L6) scoring 48 and conceding 36. Never before had they had such respectable statistics at this time in the season. These were heady days indeed.

Their next opponents were a different kettle of fish, however. Although placed directly above the celebrants there was a sufficient points gap and more than enough footballing prowess for The White Elephant to have little fear or need to look nervously over their shoulder. The match was at the Colliery Ground where they were undefeated this season.

Although they looked like lords of their manor they didn't have things all their own way as they ground shared with other tenants engaged in the ignoble arts of pigeon and whippet racing. Although this was all accepted as normal activity it was seen by snobbish others as park for the coarse, forgetting that miners were in need of pastimes to fill any spare daylight hours, however fanciful or worthy of wager. Simon was fully aware that his side had been outclassed by this opposition when beaten at The Links and knew that Pork and Mutton FC had to show them due respect in the forthcoming encounter. Previous history suggested that their winning streak was about to run its own course on a ground fertilised by bird and canine deposits but proving sterile for visiting teams.

The good news was that Simon had a full set of players to choose from unlike the last time they met when neither Salvator nor Ever were available due to family obligations. Norman had fully recovered from his last injury and Will was able to waltz down the aisle unassisted by his airline trolley. Of course, Jonathan's involvement with the team appeared long gone but was he was a difficult man to erase completely. Simon did receive two telephone calls at his home during the week but neither brought news that served to disturb him. The first was from Mrs Cruft who had somehow caught wind of her husband's participation at the quiz night alongside his dalliance with one of his female quiz associates. Simon wished he had such intelligence networks - at least in footballing rather than matrimonial matters.

"I was wondering, as you were there that evening and experienced all his shenanigans, if you have anything more to add to the account I've been given? Or know the group or even the woman he was with? Or any update on knowledge of his whereabouts?"

"Nothing of note I'm afraid. You seem to have a full account of the evening's events already. Neither I nor the team knows where Jonathan is or anything about the company he now keeps."

"Ah, well. at least you've seen the type of man he is - a complete serial loser."

"I'm very familiar with that sort, or at least I was, but only on a football pitch!"

"There's me thinking you're a man of the world! Once again I must apologise for disturbing you out of the blue."

"No problem, you can call me anytime."

A few days later his telephone rang again, this time Mr Robson, the East Shields Town chief scout was on the line and he had another suitable recruit for Pork and Mutton FC. Simon was informed that Oliver Robson, the seventeen year old nephew of said scout, was looking for a team to join after coming up to stay with his uncle while his parents went off on an around the world cruise.

"I must be candid with you, the lad does have some limited footballing pedigree, and isn't a complete mongrel, but is noticeably short of the standard set by Yiannis. Given your situation, he's certainly worth a go."

"Well, if your nephew's interested there can be no harm in his meeting up for a chat. If you could ask him to come along to our match at the Colliery Ground on Sunday. The more bodies the better, especially as we are at the business end of the season with only four games to go."

As the Pork and Mutton players congregated together in the confines of their rather small and shabby changing room - made even more restrictive by the presence of Big Hec and his buckets - Simon had the luxury of a full roster to choose from. He and the other veteran players knew from experience that it would be a difficult ground to get anything from. With fortune by their side, and playing at their utmost best, they might get a sniff at a draw. But history had never been so forgiving and every visit here had resulted not only in defeat but usually a hammering. The winning streak was most definitely unlikely to continue, only a mad man would think otherwise. So Simon would need to send out his best XI to entertain that level of lunacy. The only way Big Hec would get on the park today was with his buckets but, as always, he didn't mind. Doug was also given leave to join him on the touchline, although he was a little less happy about doing so. It had not been an easy decision to give Norman the nod for substitute but he offered a little more insurance in a game like this:

(0) Owen

(2) Mario   (5) Massimo   (3) Marco

(6) Salvator

(7) Roger   (4) Simon   (8) Stuart   (11) Byron

(9) Ever   (10) Will

As they came running out Simon looked around for a teenager bearing his uncle's detailed description but only saw a group of much older, almost identical, men enjoying their woodbines and wearing the sort of flat caps that any self respecting youth wouldn't be seen dead in. Granted the recently released film *The Sting* might help revive the headgear outside coal mining and horse racing communities, but it also helped if you looked like Robert Redford in the poster.

Any strangers watching the game today were clearly behind The White Elephant and fully expectant of victory. The only exception to this were the match officials - who Simon did not recognise apart, of course, from their pink change kit - who he trusted were not so partial as those now offering up friendly abuse from the sidelines. The referee and linesmen should be prepared for this by now, Simon thought to himself, and he pondered whether the vocal comments being directed at the officials would help or hinder his team's chances. They might, on the one hand, take umbrage indirectly against The White Elephant team because of their supporters behaviour but may, on the other, resent Pork and Mutton FC because they are the reason why they have to wear pink and face such reaction in the first place. Would the men with the whistle and flags be more inclined to mistreat the symptom or the cause? Simon was taken slightly aback when the unfamiliar referee asked him in an over friendly manner, just before the coin toss, to point out Will while adding that he already knew Roger, his reputation having already preceded him.

The team were given every reason to further worry when the referee awarded the home team a dubious penalty with only three minutes on the clock. Mario was adjudged to have committed an intentional foul in the penalty area when he made what his teammates believed to be a timely and legitimate challenge for the ball. He was most surprised by the blowing of the whistle and insult was further added to injury when his name was entered into the official's book. All this immediately helped to get the limited crowd on the side of the men in pink as well as those in all white. The penalty was flamboyantly despatched when Owen was sent the wrong way by the player wearing number 9. In past seasons such a turn of events would have allowed the floodgates to open, but not this. Simon's team were now more resolute than that. For the next twenty minutes or so they held the opposition (now including the match officials) at bay and even spurned a great goal scoring opportunity when Ever volleyed a shot over the bar. Will did get the ball into the back of the net after 33 minutes but 'the equaliser' was disallowed by the referee for allegedly being offside. This came as a surprise, to both the linesman (who failed to raise his flag) and the opposition (by the usual raising of arms) with neither making any appeals in favour of this so-called technical rule infraction.

"You're kidding me ref, I'm not off, surely?" Will said, ever so politely, his aftershave helping to reinforce his point.

"I decide, not you! I am booking you for dissent."

Roger was greatly angered by the referee's latest verdict, not least because he was the one who had played the delicious through ball for Will's chalked off goal. He literally talked himself into trouble, having his name added for questioning the referee's understanding of impartiality.

"I definitely think I've seen this ref somewhere before, probably in a nightmare, but his face is very familiar," Roger whispered as he passed Simon.

Pork and Mutton FC were starting to feel that the whole world was against them. This was confirmed on 40 minutes when a speculative long range shot from outside the penalty area, that was destined to go well wide of its target, suddenly got deflected off the referee's posterior and past a firmly grounded Owen into the corner of the net. They went into half-time two goals down when they could just as easily been two goals up. At least they would get an equal share of the oranges, hopefully.

Unfortunately there were no oranges as someone from the host club had mistakenly provided grapefruits instead. Not only was the first half a disaster not of their own making but the refreshments were too. The match up to now would be bitterly remembered for poor refereeing interventions alongside an interval that was equally tart. Simon resisted bringing on Norman at this juncture as he was just as confused as anyone else as to why they were behind in the game. Mr Robson's nephew was still a no show, although he would be a little easier to spot now as most home support had retreated to their nearby pigeon lofts. This appeared to please the match officials most of all; well, wouldn't you just fancy that, Simon thought to himself. He knew that little mileage would be gained by protesting to the league administration about the quality of their provision on this occasion. It would most likely be viewed as sour grapes by Iam Wright-Pratt and his ilk, although Simon would have been delighted for them to share the bad taste in the mouth that he and his teammates were experiencing. They also had to remain disciplined on the park as they could ill afford any more bookings even though the referee appeared, for some strange reason, keen to get more Pork and Mutton entries into his book.

For the first ten minutes of the second half there was no addition to either the score or the bookings count. Someone did arrive with their whippet to increase current crowd attendance by 40% (including the dog as part of the gate) but it clearly wasn't Oliver unless he had aged, wore jam jar glasses, and walked with a limp. Simon had plenty of time to make such observations as the game had become rather pedestrian. His players were carefully avoiding too much physical contact with the opposition who themselves were embarrassed by the noticeable help they were receiving. In the 60th minute Owen was booked for time wasting after allegedly taking too long to retrieve the ball from a nettle patch. Big Hec became an entry after 70 minutes even though he wasn't on the pitch at the time. A White Elephant player had crashed into his buckets even though they were well away from the touchline and clearly visible.

"I am booking you for recklessly endangering an opposition player and interfering with play."

"Come off it ref that's complete nonsense. The big lad's done now't wrong and my lad's no worse for wear, a little damp that's all," said the opposition captain.

"Name. I'm booking you too!"

Simon was of the opinion that this booking was a form of friendly fire to help try and cover the referee's tracks, to fraudulently balance the books somewhat. The referee brought out his book one more time before the end of the game with the intent of recording another goal for The White Elephant. A delayed long through ball from their captain to their now clearly offside centre forward was flagged by the linesman but waved on by the man in the middle (who was hardly that, being rather askew). As the attacker ran through with only Owen to beat his captain shouted to him to stop and pick up the ball. At that moment the whistle blew and a disgruntled referee booked The Elephant centre forward for intentional handball. He also had strong words for the opposition captain and would have sent him off had not the flagging linesman intervened to calm matters. The remaining minutes of the game were a bit of a joke with neither side now knowing what the rules of the game were anymore.

At the end of the match Simon made sure he shook hands with their captain and their centre forward, both of whom remained true to the spirit of the game. The 2-0 defeat was the same scoreline as the last time that they played but the circumstances were very different. Some matches you lose and don't quite know why, although Simon had little doubt here. On the first occasion they had been outplayed, but not on this, with defeat courtesy of the package in pink. As he walked off the pitch he asked one of the linesmen he was passing who the referee was, "Oh, that's Richard Cruft", was his reply.

CHAPTER 41:
Spotted Dick

The manner of the defeat, rather than the loss itself, still rankled with Simon. It was made much worse by the mention of the Cruft surname, even though it might just be mere coincidence. Still, one Cruft had already been bad enough and now another had made a right show of themselves. Although Simon did not intend to push this new grievance with the league administration, and was minded to diplomatically let sleeping dogs lie given their five bookings, he was keen to know whether all of this was the result of chance rather than design, and possibly even vendetta. Granted, the team had been expected to lose, although not in this particular way, but they remained in fourth position. Of course, the gap between them and those above them had widened further but it was debatable whether it was ever bridgeable given the limited number of games remaining. What was more worrying was the chasing pack now snapping at their heels, with a couple of teams only one point away. The Four Mile Inn were one of those and their opponents in the penultimate game of the season. Simon now knew that Pork and Mutton FC would be spending what remained of their season in pantomime mode - always looking behind - without the need for audience prompts. While no

European places were clearly at stake, pride was, and the team had recently rediscovered this.

Some may wonder why Simon did not question the referee's lineage at the end of the match but he was given no opportunity as the official had beat a hasty exit. Such inquiry is usually left to the crowd during a game, especially when things aren't normally going their way, decision wise. The only way he'd get a satisfactory and immediate answer was to call Mrs Cruft. But the immediate would have to wait as it took him over an hour of rifling through drawers to locate her number which he had casually written on the back of a settled electricity bill envelope. This rare administration slip up could be excused by the fact that he expected no reason would arise to call her and, anyway, she had developed the occasional habit of phoning him for updates regarding anything to do with her husband. Although it was an early Sunday evening, and the game had ended only a few hours earlier, his curiosity got the better of him. The telephone at her end rang for what seemed like an eternity, with Simon in two minds to put his receiver down, but just then her sultry voice answered, sounding welcoming of his call although, unbeknown to him, it had hurriedly summoned her dripping out of the bath.

"Hello Nancy, I trust I'm not disturbing you at this hour? I hope you can possibly help me. Earlier today the team had a run-in with the referee who was less than even-handed. I understand his name was Richard Cruft, is he related to Jonathan at all?"

"I've already heard about all that. I'm on my way out shortly and need to get ready. Why don't we continue the rest of this sensitive, and possibly lengthy, conversation face to face when I'm less pushed for time? I don't want to sound in any way forward but we could meet at The Four Mile Inn on Tuesday at 7pm?"

"Eh, OK? I will see you then."

Pork and Mutton FC were scheduled to play there two weeks hence yet Simon, his mind racing ahead and reading too much into things, was possibly playing away there in two days time.

The evening before the scheduled tête-à-tête Simon received a telephone call from Adam Robson apologising for his nephew's failure to show. The lad had been knocked off his bike on the way to the ground and although he sustained non life threatening injuries he would be out of commission for the rest of the season. The scout added that Oliver always seemed to end up in one fine mess or another not of his own making. Simon was relieved that his almost new recruit was alright after the mishap, but truth be told, didn't miss what he didn't have. He had felt that it was more a case of him doing the scout a favour rather than the other way around. Somewhat strangely, he was even more relieved that it wasn't Mrs Cruft calling to cancel tomorrow's arrangement.

Simon arrived twenty minutes early for their scheduled rendezvous and found the Inn and its resident clientele to be a cut above those found at Pork and Mutton. He was not here on a football reconnaissance mission, however, although he did recognise one or two of their players serving behind the bar and they acknowledged him in return. Given Jonathan's true nature, Simon now thought it may have been wiser to have turned up incognito, or met somewhere else, or even not at all. They probably would have difficulty recognising each other even without a disguise but the die had been cast. He had only met Nancy once, at the barbecue at the Cruft home following the pre-season friendly against the Council. His nerves starting kicking in at the butterflies in his stomach. It had been some time since he had been out with another woman following the break-up of his longstanding relationship with Susan almost two footballing seasons ago.

He had less need to worry, however, as Nancy recognised him straight away. He would have had greater difficulty in identifying her as she was dressed up to the nines and more beautiful than he remembered. This only served to make their meeting even more public. Reintroductions and a couple of gin and tonics later, they got down to the more immediate business in hand, for her Jonathan Cruft, for him Richard Cruft. He had to give the floor to her first. She was clearly in need of a shoulder to cry on although Simon's handkerchief served a similar purpose.

"I still have some feelings for him you know, but it's definitely over. I cannot turn my emotions on and then off just like a tap but I am up to here with his serial wanderings and my forgiveness has run dry. I want to move on."

"Oh, well yes, I do understand."

"I now know of my husband's whereabouts and he wants to return home but I'm unwilling to have him back. There's just no future in it. You should be pleased."

"Why do you say that?"

"I have no reason to disturb you with those telephone calls of mine."

"I don't mind them at all."

"Oh? Really? Too kind. What can I do for you?"

"What can you tell me about Richard Cruft," Simon simply said, pushing other more pleasant thoughts to the back of his mind for now.

"He is my husband's brother and shares the worst of his DNA. He is trying to act as Jonathan's go-between on matters matrimonial and I just can't stand the blighter. I keep chasing him away. The two brothers quarrelled after the fallout from the Eusebio affair gained traction in the local media and the subsequent damage it did to Richard's standing in the league administration."

"How was one to anticipate any of that?"

"No matter. His hoped for promotion up the ranks did not materialise and for a while he took umbrage with his brother until he accepted that Mr Bone, the match day referee I seem to recall only because they called him something different entirely, was totally at fault."

Somewhat ironically, this all took place against the team in whose bar they are now sitting and finishing off drink number three with only 30 minutes on the clock. Once these Brothers Grim eventually reconciled it allowed unfriendly and unwelcome relations to be restored elsewhere. Not only proving troublesome for both Nancy and Simon but others now part of their food chain as well.

"When I heard about Richard's antics on Sunday I wasn't that surprised. I am sure his actions were not only motivated out of regards for his brother but also perhaps, somewhat bizarrely or maybe perversely - I'm not sure which, as a kind of revenge against good refereeing which the league administration had been blind to when failing to reward his previous conduct."

"The way you tell it Nancy there's a hell of a lot going on here and only God knows what the pair of them were thinking. That said, you seem to know a lot more than me and I can't get my head around how you knew about Sunday's events so quickly?"

"Let's not get into all that now. What I can say is that Richard knew of his brother's harbouring issues with the team, especially Will and Roger."

"Really? Why those two?"

Gin and tonic number four was hitting the back of their throats on 40 minutes. Before they were finished Simon not only learned that Jonathan felt Will had usurped his place in the team but also believed Roger was somehow chasing Nancy, his wife, and was guilty, yet again, of poring cold water on proceedings. The latter allegation was flimsily based on Roger paying her far too much attention while her husband attended to the needs of the barbecue. This fantasy, of his own making, was further strengthened by the night out he spent with Roger, Owen and Byron at the Bierkeller and what came to pass there. He must have initially gone there, Nancy now concluded, not to develop budding friendships but to study his new imaginary enemy up close and personal. The bucket wetting assault, which she also knew about, had merely sealed the deal for Jonathan and confirmed his suspicions that Roger was the barrier preventing his getting back with her. He was also seen as the one acting as the snitch to his wife whether at the quiz or elsewhere. She then added that nothing had ever been going on between her and Roger although it had proved impossible to convince Jonathan otherwise.

"Since throwing him out, and resisting all attempts for his return, my brother-in-law has been a right pain, acting as unwanted emissary, spy, and amateur detective, all on my husband's behalf. I wouldn't even be that surprised if Richard followed me here! I don't care anyway, Jonathan can have some of his own medicine dressed up in reality."

"So he's even more of a whistleblower than I even gave him credit for!"

Simon wasn't letting on that he was now far more nervous than just before she arrived. She was dressed to kill and he could be the target caught in the line of sight. He looked around the room and at least once or twice thought he had spotted the errand referee cum private dick but wasn't quite sure.

This was all becoming a bit surreal for Simon. He couldn't make out whether he was in some second rate B movie film noir with Mrs Cruft as his female nemesis rather than ally. He liked the idea of the femme but not the fatale; that was Max Mortimer's serious business and Simon only wore the shirt to play in. As some latter day Alan Ladd he didn't know if he was the decoy or the bait in the game with her husband. Not that the distinction would matter if Jonathan set his focus on him. He was certainly no jack the lad, finding himself in unfamiliar country and out of his depth. If she was stringing him along then it had been working up to now. Maybe he too was now imagining things, just like Jonathan. He kept these thoughts to himself as Nancy had more than enough crazy in her life at the moment and he also may have called it wrong. Only a mad man would come between Mr and Mrs Cruft at the moment. His mental exercises were interrupted by her suddenly making a quick but very ladylike exit. She did not mention to Simon that she too had just caught a glimpse of Richard in her compact so her work here was done. They may have drawn four drinks all but he had lost this game and it was the referee calling time once again.

It would be true to say that Simon spent much of the next week looking over his shoulder even though the game against The Four Mile Inn was over a week away. First they had to face The Consortium (CORE) who were almost as threatening to their ambitions, and a possible thorn in any side, just as their future namesakes were to be a few light years from now in the George Lucas *Star Wars* franchise. They could be brought crashing down to earth, or any other planet for that matter, by this consistently inconsistent team. They had just managed to beat them 5-3 last time with a scoreline that flattered to deceive given that the eventful match only got decided in Pork and Mutton's favour courtesy of two goals in the last five minutes. With the Restaurant Emporia, on any given day, you sometimes didn't quite know what you'd be getting, a bit like the food they offered.

The return match at The Links started well, even before a ball was kicked, as on this occasion, unlike their previous meeting together, the defence turned up for duty. The Tripolini brothers arrived first having already attended early Easter Sunday mass with their mother. With no other cry-offs Simon had the luxury of a full complement to choose from and he wanted to make room for both Norman and Doug to get a full runout. With that and next week's game in mind, he decided to rest himself and make Roger substitute, but only to be used if really necessary. Byron would return out on the right to accommodate Doug on the left while Stuart would do likewise with Norman in the centre of midfield. It would be wrong to say that Simon had thought long and hard about today's line-up as most of his attention this week had understandably been directed elsewhere. Maybe unconsciously he wanted Roger by his side just in case something bad happened, consciously he planned to gently grill him on what may or may not be appropriately termed 'The Cruft Affair'. They watched together on the sidelines as their teammates took up their playing positions:

(0) Owen

(2) Mario   **(5) Massimo**   **(3) Marco**

(6) Salvator

(7) Byron   **(8) Stuart**   **(4) Norman**   **(11) Doug**

(9) Ever   **(10) Will**

Simon looked closely at the referee running toward the centre circle and was relieved to recognise him as someone who was known to adjudicate fairly. There was still a cold Winter chill in the air even though Spring had recently sprung and daffodils were in evidence here and there; not dissimilar to periscopes poking up from under the ground looking for their next victim or so Simon thought, things clearly getting to him.

For the first half hour there was little excitement for flora or fauna to observe. The opposition were the usual mixed bag but with a couple of extra superior players added compared to last time and they gave as little as they got. The only real activity was on the touchline where Simon was pursuing his diplomatic mission with Roger, helped rather than hindered by the calm of the game. The former didn't want to give too much delicate information away and the latter had very little to offer because he had no beans to spill. Roger was totally clueless about everything that Simon revealed to him. His only crime regarding this matter was one of ignorance, to which Simon had also previously been guilty, but every court in the land would have to acquit apart from that found in Jonathan's (and by infection, Richard's) mind.

While the touchline conversation gleaned little the players on the park were having better luck in discovering each others secrets. Fortunately Pork and Mutton FC were the first to test their findings when Doug outpaced the left back charged with man marking him and reached a long ball from Marco that most would have given up on. He then cut inside and sent over a cross that Will neatly volleyed home to give them a 36 minute lead. This lasted less than two minutes when the opposition managed to equalise from a corner after Ever was slow in getting back to mark the advancing centre half who was allowed to head home unimpeded. The action was coming thick and fast now with everyone speeding up as if they could fast forward their way to the end of the first half. Attempting to make amends in advance of the referee's whistle Ever hit a long range shot that hit the underside of the bar before landing, with only inches to spare, behind the goal line. That was the full extent of the margin separating the teams going into the break.

The second half started much like how the first half finished, pretty frenetically, with attack followed by counter-attack. Although most of these were broken down by two strong defences unwilling to submit, quarter would have to be given at some point. The first meaningful breach took place in the 67th minute when Doug played a neat one two with Norman, turned the defender nearest him, and fired a low drive past the keeper but against the far post. Ever managed to get on the end of the rebound only to have his effort cleared off the line by the same opposition centre half who had netted earlier, thereby demonstrating he was just as good in stopping as in grabbing a goal, albeit both at Pork and Mutton FC's number 9's expense. A goal then would probably have secured all the points rather than prolonging squeaky bum time. CORE had a goal disallowed on 73 minutes for offside and missed what looked like an open goal three minutes later. As the clock was counting down more opportunities presented themselves with both sides now clearly tiring and the pitch opening up. Roger entered the fray immediately after this latest let off, replacing a flagging Norman, who had done well on his return to the starting XI. This new injection of energy in midfield powered his way though to score within five minutes of coming on. Picking up a loose ball just north of the centre circle he charged down the middle of the pitch, ignoring the viable options serving to draw opponents away to his left and right, before letting fly from twenty yards. Before the keeper could react the ball had already left him behind. It was 3-1 with only ten minutes of normal time left. This was not the last time that the scoreline would be altered, however. The opposition managed to grab another goal back three minutes later when their centre forward volleyed home a cross from the right wing. They then continued to press for an equaliser but none was forthcoming, being largely denied by Owen's late heroics in goal.

This hard won 3-2 victory would help cover their back from the attention of The Four Mile Inn for another week longer, regardless of how their forthcoming opponents had fared today. The same could not be said with regard to any of the Cruft clan and any possible renewed fallout courtesy of Tuesday night's little rendezvous.

CHAPTER 42:
Better Never Than Late

After an eventful couple of weeks Simon had hoped things would settle down somewhat in the few days remaining before his second outing to The Four Mile Inn and wanted on this forthcoming occasion to play rather than be played. His hopes were dashed early on in the week when a neighbour knocked on his door with a letter that had been mistakenly posted into their letterbox by the postman. They apologised for the delay in getting it to him but they had just returned from a long weekend away. Simon immediately recognised the envelope as it bore all the hallmarks of a missive from 66b Lower Lenin Street. He had assumed no news was good news with regard to not hearing from the league administration regarding their handful of bookings courtesy of Richard Cruft. He should have known better but did not expect that bad news was stewing for four days on another doormat only yards away.

As he opened the letter he began to wish that he had gone on the offensive and complained immediately after the officiating of that match and gathered supporting evidence from The White Elephant. Now he and his team were on the back foot and surely in hot water again with the league administration. As he read the letter he was not dispossessed of his latest opinion. Mr Iam Wright-Pratt, as sanctimonious as ever, had been notified of Pork and Mutton FC's five bookings in one match and saw this as yet another example of their indiscipline. He stressed that any repeat of such behaviour would lead him and his colleagues to consider applying a points deduction penalty. Simon realised that his side had little room to manoeuvre and would now have to be seen to be on their best behaviour, even though they really hadn't actually done anything untoward. He could go back to The White Elephant for help in implicating Richard Cruft in the refereeing fiasco but would they be willing to be embroiled in this given they were still engaged in a promotion battle? They were unlikely to want to further stir the pot, certainly at the present time. It was all more than a bit late, Simon ruefully concluded to himself, they had missed that particular boat and would get little in terms of redress. Far better to focus on the two remaining games of the season and the points at stake. They needed to play well while simultaneously behaving like choir boys. Some challenge that, he mused, still thinking they needed to get some kind of revenge against that private dick with a whistle.

The rest of the week passed quietly by without any other disturbances to Simon's usual routine. His home telephone had been unusually silent. He sat down with the local rag, armed with a cuppa loaded with PG Tips, early on Saturday evening to check the previous week's results and league standings. He found the particular sports page that confirmed Pork and Mutton's expected current position as fourth, still one point ahead of The Four Mile Inn and Peking Duck United, but with the others having a slightly superior goal difference. Any of the three teams laying well away above them were still in the hunt for the two promotion slots but only two were really in contention for the crown. It was all pretty close with little room for error whether in the first tier of three or the following. The table would have looked far different, and pleased Simon more, had The Four Mile Inn not scored two goals in the last five minutes to see off FC Lokomotiv and win 2-1. He also saw that Peking Duck United had managed to turn a two goal deficit around in the last ten minutes of their game against The Irish Club to steal a 3-2 victory from the jaws of defeat. Just like the letter from the league administration, events such as these would have been better had they never occurred rather than arriving so late in the day to further complicate matters. Pork and Mutton FC could just as easily have been three points ahead of both their rivals rather than just the one, with Simon too easily forgetting just how close their last match was:

RaBHL (North) Division 2

	P	W	D	L	F	A	Pts
Deutscher Bierkeller	28	22	5	1	89	18	49
Shirley Inn FC	28	21	5	2	73	27	47
The White Elephant	28	20	5	3	70	31	45
Pork and Mutton FC	28	12	9	7	51	40	33
The Four Mile Inn	28	12	8	8	48	35	32
Peking Duck United	28	13	6	9	45	33	32
Austin's Fryers	28	9	11	8	42	28	29
Bulman United	28	11	8	9	38	35	29
FC Lokomotiv	28	10	8	10	32	40	28
The White Eagle	28	9	7	12	34	43	25
The Tea Pot Cafe	28	7	8	13	35	48	22
The Irish Club	28	4	12	12	32	52	20
The Cretan Taverna	28	5	10	13	24	45	20
College Caterers FC	28	4	7	17	26	62	15
CORE	28	3	7	18	25	65	13
Smithfields	28	2	4	22	17	79	8

It was all pretty close except for the team at the bottom, Smithfields, already guaranteed 16th position, a berth Simon was most familiar with, rather than the rarefied atmosphere his team were now enjoying. The upcoming match against The Four Mile Inn was their cup final in a way, being probably the most important match in Pork and Mutton FC's inglorious history. Victory would go a long way to help them hold on to 4th place given that they had, on paper at least, a far easier final game at home against The Tea Pot Cafe who they had beaten earlier in the season. If it were in his power Simon would happily settle for a draw against tomorrow's opponents now. They shared the spoils when they last met and he even managed to bag himself a goal. He would willingly forego getting on the score sheet if his team could avoid defeat. Although his recent trip to The Four Mile Inn, albeit to hopefully play a kind of footsy with Nancy, had drawn a blank for both parties, he wouldn't mind the same result again - an outcome he knew Owen would certainly be delighted with. Simon was far less worried by the threat posed by Peking Duck United who had a more difficult run in. They had a tough fixture tomorrow at Shirley Inn before finishing their season with a home match against The Four Mile Inn. The fact that these two rivals meet head to head on matchday 30 had to be advantageous for Pork and Mutton FC, or so Simon believed, as any slip up tomorrow may not be totally fatal to the cause.

It was a pretty wet and miserable Sunday morning as the players of Pork and Mutton FC congregated within the visitor changing facilities. The bad weather had not deterred any of Simon's side from making an appearance even though there were some more likely than others to be destined to be sitting out the game. Everyone realised that they were at the business end of the season and vocal support from the touchline also played its part. Simon had fretted over his starting eleven yesterday but the prevailing conditions outside helped make his mind up. He brought Roger in to replace Byron and himself in to replace Norman. He had seriously contemplated switching Byron to the opposite flank but decided that Doug was more dangerous in a deluge, besides having Byron's versatility available on the bench to be readily called upon could provide some added insurance as the match unfolded. To be honest Norman was quite happy to be reprieved from today's physical exertions, and had wisely anticipated such, coming fully protected against the elements dressed in a heavy parka with a thick turtle neck sweater underneath. This compared favourably with Big Hec in the fashion stakes, dressed as he was in a rather flimsy and tight-fitting cagoule albeit with a roll neck sweater making itself visible underneath. Byron had his tracksuit and the number 12 shirt to keep him warm and full use of the large golf umbrella, that Ever had wisely brought along, to help ward off the worst of the rain. The starting XI lined-up as follows to face not only the opposition but also the elements:

(0) Owen

(2) Mario   (5) Massimo   (3) Marco

(6) Salvator

(7) Roger   (4) Simon   (8) Stuart   (11) Doug

(9) Ever   (10) Will

The players and officials were welcomed with a torrential downpour that lasted for the first fifteen minutes of the match. Tactical plans largely go out of the window when you can't even see out of the window, were you so fortunate as to be dry and warm indoors. Big Hec emptied one of his now overflowing buckets and placed it on his head so completing his style faux pas. It was difficult to read whether it was Hope or Faith. Under these conditions he was not alone in pursuing needs must and those on the pitch did likewise. Play was messy as the players adapted as best they could and it was not the time to take avoidable risks. Even Doug found the prevailing conditions not totally to his liking losing control of a fortunate through ball from Stuart that he inadvertently transported out of play with the defence caught momentarily on the skids. The touchline rather than the goalkeepers were the first port of call for both defences and one would have to wait patiently for the opening salvo to arrive.

The first shot at goal whizzed narrowly wide of Owen's left-hand post on 25 minutes shortly after the skies had stopped their crying. This marked the commencement of Four Mile Inn's siege of his goal. Two minutes later Marco deflected a shot away to safety at the expense of a corner. The resulting inswinger was punched clear by Owen when normally he would have attempted catching the ball. On 32 minutes Pork and Mutton's crossbar was badly bruised by a rasping effort from outside the box. The one way traffic continued, alongside the return of the rain, with few opportunities to relieve the pressure by looking for outlets upfield as both Will and Ever were increasingly having to track back. Just like at The Alamo, they could only hold out for so long. After another close call on 36 minutes the opposition got the lead they deserved five minutes before the break. Salvator badly mistimed a sliding tackle marginally inside the penalty area that cost him a booking and presented a great opportunity for The Four Mile Inn to finally get their noses in front from the spot kick. Their centre forward hit the ball to Owen's right which then came off his glove and onto the post before returning back to the fortunate number 9 who gratefully despatched it into the welcoming net. The surprising thing was that this lead did not get extended, or even maintained, before the onset of half-time. Pork and Mutton FC equalised in the 44th minute courtesy of a swift counterattack by Doug who intercepted a wayward ball, as the team were once again hemmed inside their own half, then dribbled skilfully this time, sailing past two opponents, before finding a racing Will who calmly slid the ball into the right corner of the goal well away from the outstretched arms of the advancing goalkeeper. This should make the oranges taste that little bit sweeter.

Which they did, as did life, when only two minutes into the restart, with the clouds and the Four Mile Inn both in full retreat, Stuart hit a speculative shot from thirty yards which took everybody, including their goalkeeper by surprise. It was unstoppable and flew into the top left hand corner like a guided missile. The scorer was as taken aback as anyone and did not know how to celebrate given that he had just registered his first goal of the season and probably for many a year, certainly Simon could not recall witnessing such an act from this source before. The rest of his teammates appeared just as shocked in having taken the lead in a match their opponents had clearly dominated. The embarrassed joy experienced was to be of a temporary nature as the situation now galvanised the team in red and white stripes to quickly eradicate their blushes. They may share the colours of Santa Claus but they weren't there to give out presents and once again encamped themselves in Pork and Mutton territory much as Santa Anna did to put down the Texas rebellion. It was as if the Four Mile Inn were sounding their own version of The Deguello and planning to take no prisoners. They managed to get the ball in the back of the net three minutes later but the goal was chalked off by the somewhat dubious raising of a linesman's flag for offside. This was only a momentary reprieve, however, further elongated by a clash of heads between Ever and his marker that resulted in them both coming off. This proved to be somewhat more awkward for Simon's number 9 than his opponent thanks to Big Hec's over enthusiastic medical attention with a wet sponge that made a complete show of totally dislodging the centre forward's wig allowing it to dive, head after rather than head first, into the one remaining serviceable bucket.

"Hector, for goodness sake man take it easy, now look what you've done!" shouted a less than happy Ever.

"Sorry, but how was I to know it was so flimsy?"

"It looks like some forlorn floating drowned rat," Norman rather unhelpfully added as the hairpiece now lived in Hope.

This all added a bruised ego to Ever's sore head. Byron was brought on as a straight like for like replacement upfront, unlike the opposition, with their substitute coming on to reinforce the front line. This made it patently obvious, if it wasn't already, that The Four Mile Inn wanted nothing less than victory.

After this latest hair-raising incident the alarm bells began to sound again. For the next ten minutes the current scoreline remained miraculously unaltered although divine intervention may have played its part. First the referee inadvertently helped by deflecting a shot away from goal that seemed destined for the back of the net with Owen grounded. This was followed by a post making its presence felt before a last ditch tackle by Salvator saved a fragment of the day. When the equaliser came on 66 minutes no one could rightfully complain. The substitute for The Four Mile Inn was making more of an impact up front than Byron, who like the man he replaced, was being forced into more defensive duties. It was the former who finished off a flowing passing movement that left the Pork and Mutton defence mesmerised. It was one touch football at its finest, reducing their opponents to little more than motionless kitted-out mannequins. It was largely thanks to the goalkeeping heroics of Owen, and his finest hour between the sticks (around twenty minutes actually), that Simon's side held on until the onset of injury time brought about their undoing. When it looked like they had somehow done enough the opposition scored in what was the final kick of the match.

With the clock ticking down Marco booted the ball out for a throw-in in the hope that the game would be over before it was retrieved. Unfortunately the ball didn't go the intended distance as it collided with one of Big Hec's buckets returning to the nearest opponent who took a quick long throw that caught the defence, but not his centre forward, cold. He raced towards goal and calmly slotted the ball home to make it 3-2 just as the referee was placing the whistle to his lips and about to blow for full-time. It was a rather cruel way to not only end the game but to allow The Four Mile Inn to leapfrog over Pork and Mutton FC in the league table. Simon and the rest of the team's hopes of finishing fourth were, if not in tatters, now heavily dependent on others.

CHAPTER 43:
Scorer, Scorer, Scorer

Although the climax of the season was close at hand, and they had certainly exceeded expectations, their latest defeat had only served to dampen spirits. At least Ever was easily patched-up once his hairpiece had dried out, although it took longer for his dignity to recover. They would be going into the final game with a full complement of players, or so Simon believed, having received no telephone calls during the week informing him of any cry-offs. The other good news was that he already definitely knew, even before going through his usual Saturday tea-time ritual of checking last week's results and the league table, that his team were holding on to fifth position having been informed through the grapevine that Peking Duck had lost at Shirley Inn by 2-0. If Pork and Mutton could defeat The Tea Pot Cafe and Peking Duck did likewise against The Four Mile Inn they would regain fourth place. Although it meant little to many in the great scheme of things, with no prizes forthcoming, it meant a great deal to Simon and his three other long-standing and long-suffering teammates. The Four Mile Inn and Peking Duck were equally committed to not relinquishing the fight, and the latter would need a big win against the former to pull ahead. Simon now realised, from consulting the local sports page laying across his lap, that sixth place was the worst ranking his side could achieve following Austin's Fryers sharing the points with Bulman United, meaning neither could catch them regardless of how their final games played out. The Deutscher Bierkeller were now almost guaranteed to be crowned champions after their latest victory, given their vast goal difference and two points advantage over nearest and only rival, Shirley Inn, who were also promoted alongside them to Division 1 after The White Elephant could only draw away against FC Lokomotiv. The Germans may as well have received the trophy right now given that their final outing was against bottom team Smithfields.

Most things appeared clear-cut, or at least the parameters set, as Simon decided to settle down for the night and watch the TV premiere of the blockbuster war movie *Tora, Tora, Tora* detailing the infamous Japanese surprise lightening attack on Pearl Harbour. He tended to avoid watching the usual diet of war movies constantly doing the rounds but had heard this one devotes considerable time to the Japanese perspective. Two and a half hours later the film was finally over although US formal involvement in that war had just begun. He decided to forego watching *Match of the Day*, although this had been a Saturday night staple, and head upstairs given tiredness had set in. Dropping off would have been much easier had he not badly stubbed his big right toe before clambering into bed. It was sore, then sorer, only forgotten when he became a snorer.

Having failed to close the curtains the night before, Simon was awakened by the sunlight streaming through his bedroom bay window. It was a lovely mid April morning, worthy of gracing the end of any football season. Without thinking he jumped out of bed only to be instantly reminded of the injury sustained prior to entry. His toe nail was now black, the skin around it extremely bruised and tender, and it was badly swollen, standing out like a big sore toe rather than a thumb.

Even putting on a sock proved to be a painful challenge let alone progressing to a shoe. It only now dawned on him that he would have to omit himself from the starting XI. Things could only get better, or so he thought, as he tucked into his cereal. He had an extra round of buttered toast, topped off with strawberry jam, in part recompense for his disappointment. Being an invalid would not stop him enjoying the after match party at Pork and Mutton laid on by Max Mortimer to celebrate the successful season's end, regardless of today's result. Max had also generously offered to attend the Peking Duck versus Four Mile Inn game to report back on exactly where his patronage had been placed in the league's final standings.

As Simon walked gingerly to the hallway to collect his coat and the team kitbag he happened to notice a neatly folded piece of paper laying on the edge of the doormat. It was a very brief note written in short sentences and large capital letters that read more like a telegram:

CANNOT PLAY TODAY. CATCHING EARLY TRAIN. RETURN UNKNOWN. APOLOGIES. GIVE BEST TO LADS. OWEN.

It must have been left early this morning and raised more questions than answers. What was Owen running away from or racing toward? It did little to lighten Simon's mood. They were already two men down and he hadn't left the house yet.

By the time Simon slowly made his way to The Links his mood was lifted by the warming rays of the sun and relief in that all his remaining pool of players were already there awaiting his arrival. His lateness had suggested that something was amiss and his hobbling towards them only served to confirm this. He relayed his other bad news regarding Owen's absence, which received a more positive response from his willing goalkeeping stand-in Big Hec than it did from his other teammates, who was overtly delighted to have the opportunity to elevate his contribution beyond those customarily contained within his buckets. Norman, as expected, was given, and gladly received, the number 4 jersey and asked to swap over central midfield positions with Stuart. Somewhat less happy was Doug who was given the number 12 jersey losing out to Byron. The blank (aka number 13) jersey along with Owen's number 0 had not made the journey as Simon had already unpacked such troubles from his old kitbag. Big Hec would be wearing his blue tracksuit top again but without the need for bib and laces as today's opponents, The Tea Pot Cafe, wore their customary all green. As the team lined up for their final game of the season without their regular man between the sticks, but with Big Hec's two buckets safeguarding the goal, they still exuded confidence and a belief that they could get the job done on the field and get all two points. There was no longer any question mark against Hector's goalkeeping ability only against his wearing a tracksuit top in lieu of a proper and identifiable keeper's jersey. At least Norman still had possession of his chalk to write the number on 1 on Big Hec's back:

(1?) Hector

(2) Mario   **(5) Massimo**   **(3) Marco**

(6) Salvator

(7) Roger   **(8) Stuart**   **(4) Norman**   **(11) Byron**

(9) Ever   **(10) Will**

Pork and Mutton FC could not have hoped for a better start and were a goal up after only 5 minutes. A somewhat innocuous foul on the half-way line allowed Roger to quickly float in a hopeful free-kick into the penalty area that Ever managed to flick on for Will to head home before the defence had fully settled itself. The lead was extended on 12 minutes when Byron was blatantly fouled in the penalty area and Ever drove home the resulting spot kick. Stuart tried to add to the tally in the 20th minute by trying his luck, as in the previous week, only for his effort to head wildly skyward. The team, just like his effort, were clearly on the up. The Tea Pot Cafe were still off the boil when they allowed Byron to dribble through from the wing into the heart of the defence and gently lob over the advancing goalkeeper on 28 minutes. Pork and Mutton FC were scoring goals almost at will and even Simon was surprised by how easily they were breaking through the defence to quickly sink the opposition. Granted it was not a rerun of Pearl Harbour and they were not the Japanese; clearly recognisable by the fact that their attacks were hardly suicidal kamikaze and it was their opponents who were guilty of committing a form of self-harming harakiri.

Although the boys in green had little at stake that was no excuse for their playing in a way to match the colour of their strips rather than the experience contained in their ranks. Their captain managed to generate the missing passion in his side and they began a noticeable pushback in the last fifteen minutes of the first half. They almost got a goal back on 33 minutes when a long range drive on his Faith hand side was pushed to safety by Big Hec for a corner. Hope almost came into play when the Tea Pot centre forward beat Massimo to a through ball on 38 minutes and stroked the ball past the goalie's left hand side only for the ball to ricochet to safety off the post rather than meeting the aforementioned bucket. Just before the break Mario almost scored an own goal when he hit a misplaced back pass that went just narrowly wide but there was to be no charity here.

Simon saw little need to make a change for the second half although Doug was obviously keen to enter the fray. The team enjoyed sharing their last oranges of the season and were all looking forward to the planned celebrations at Pork and Mutton following conclusion of the game. They had so far certainly done all they could in keeping up their side of bargain result wise. Things were going so well that Simon had even forgotten the pain that his right toe had been giving him. Big Hec had also been rather forgetful having left his buckets in his first half goal and not relocating them before the second half whistle blew.

The goalkeeper became rather unsettled when he belatedly realised this and wondered how best to get his charmed buckets back. To his surprise they did little for the opposition and Pork and Mutton went 4-0 up on 48 minutes when he hoofed a long ball up into the penalty area that somehow landed at the feet of Will who smashed the ball home raising Hope into the air. This now made Big Hec have second thoughts about where best his buckets served the team and before he made his mind up the referee had already recommenced the game. Simon's side started the second half much as they started the first. Will grabbed his hat trick on 57 minutes when Roger played a one-two with Ever before flicking the ball across the goal for Will to head the ball past the despairing arms of the goalkeeper before calmly resting in Faith. On retrieving the ball the opposition goalie threw the bucket clear of his goal and now did likewise with the other. Both were now lost in the undergrowth behind his goal. This served to unsettle Big Hec again, although he had not given up on retrieving Faith and Hope, but the referee's whistle once again intervened. In the 66th minute The Tea Pot Cafe got a goal back when a rather tame shot from their centre forward slipped through the hands of Big Hec and trickled slowly across the line. This merely reinforced the goalie's belief that he needed the buckets covering his back. He raced out of his goal but before he reached the half-way line the game had restarted and he had to run back again. Fortunately for him or rather his frame of mind, Pork and Mutton kept possession of the ball in the opposition half for the next ten minutes, coming close on two occasions but the crossbar and post kept the score at 5-1. On 78 minutes Simon replaced a tiring Will with Doug just before Roger was about to take a corner. Big Hec was getting impatient and saw this as another opportunity to try and retrieve his buckets by racing quickly upfield. This was in the days before a goalie ever thought about charging out of their penalty area to join the attack in a desperate last gasp effort to score.

"Where on earth are you going?" Massimo asked as the giant goalie thundered past him.

"I need my buckets, that's all!"

"Watch where you're going!" an annoyed Salvator shouted as Big Hec easily knocked him aside like a skittle.

"What the hell are you doing up here? Get back!" was the surprised response coming from Ever.

As the ball was floated in Big Hec wasn't hanging about but heading straight for the undergrowth and his buckets. Everyone was astonished but since he wasn't interfering with play it continued. In the confusion their goalkeeper safely collected the ball and immediately gambled by speculatively launching it downfield way over the heads of the Pork and Mutton defenders into an empty net. Just at that moment a smiling, but clearly unaware, Big Hec came out of the undergrowth with Faith and Hope safely in his hands. None of his teammates were sharing in his happiness on this occasion.

Having his buckets back in situ meant everything to Big Hec regardless of what the others thought. His confidence was back and although the score remained at 5-2 he made four important saves in the last ten minutes that may otherwise have changed the outcome. Three of these saves had been made on his weaker left hand side where he usually kept Hope. When the referee blew to end the game and he went to collect his buckets he realised that his buckets had been inadvertently placed in haste on the wrong sides and it was Faith that lay behind his left hand. From the touchline Simon could only conclude that goalkeepers are a breed apart and one crazy was enough never mind two. Even after what was witnessed today, he and his outfield teammates were yet to fully realise how mad these glove men could really be.

CHAPTER 44:
Being Number 1

This was the first occasion that Pork and Mutton FC had a celebration to mark the end of a season. There previously had been little point as there had been nothing worthy to commemorate; who wants to reflect on endless failure results wise. Friendships had been formed, and others broken, and you could live out your fantasies until reality set in, which it always did, as soon as the referee blew his whistle. No garlands were given for frequently carrying the weight of Division 2 on your shoulders. A few got something of value in the struggle and the striving to carry on regardless - like the four veterans who were present at the Pub to experience the novelty of such an event. All the others in attendance were newbies possibly part of a different emerging future club narrative. Recruitment had allowed the journey to continue when all seemed lost. It had hardly been systematic, largely dependent on connections or chance, but fortune had haphazardly favoured the brave. Which is all just as well given they were desperate for anyone able to lace up a pair of boots or underwrite the expedition, as Max Mortimer had done.

The whole current squad (minus Mr 0) were gathered in the private function room with drinks in hand awaiting Max's return from the Peking Duck United versus The Four Mile Inn match. The result of that game would determine whether the team finished fourth or fifth as today's victory over The Tea Pot Cafe meant only The Four Mile Inn could supplant them if they avoided defeat. They all wanted fourth slot, even though it came without any European or even local domestic perks. Simon thought back to the time when four wasn't such a cherished number and only he, Roger, Stuart and Norman stood between the club's survival and its termination. Four no longer signalled death but rebirth and fourth place would far exceed their wildest dreams. If anyone had suggested as much at the time they would have been classified as deranged. They were used to the gutter and looking up at the stars thinking they were out of reach but today they were just that little bit closer. After a slight delay, Fred and Max made an entrance together, which Simon found more than fitting, being Christmas Past and Christmas Present (as well as hopefully Christmas Future) with regard to club financing. They were followed into the room by two surprise guests – Yiannis and Mr Robson.

The party got off to the best of starts when Max made his first announcement.

"It gives me great pleasure to report that Pork and Mutton FC have regained fourth position in the league as Peking Duck United managed to beat The Four Mile Inn 4-3 with their winner coming two minutes from time."

A round of applause then rang out before he continued by explaining his late arrival was owing to the match being temporarily suspended by the need to replace the referee with one of the other official linesman during the course of the game. The designated referee had stopped the game after only fifteen minutes, with The Four Mile Inn already leading 2-0 following two dodgy penalties, to apparently rush off in the direction of the toilets. He did not return after ten minutes and one of the linesmen then took it on himself to go and find him while everyone else just stood around somewhat bemused and twiddling their feet rather than their thumbs - goalkeepers excluded. The errant linesman then returned to inform those present that the errant referee was somewhat indisposed and that he would be taking over. Max then explained that he had managed to bag the now vacant linesman duties for the rest of the game.

"I must confess that I was just as impartial to the proceedings from my new position on the touchline as I was when the laxatives in my pocket had somehow uncannily found their way into the referee's thermostat of tea that he enjoyed prior to kick-off!"

"You did what Max!" exclaimed Fred.

"Needs must my boy. I forgot to mention the referee's name, a certain Mr Richard Cruft. If I'm not mistaken, some of you have come across him before!"

Needless to say, this brought the house down. What goes around comes around, Simon thought to himself, which was beyond biological dispute in this particular case.

Champagne followed the merriment, and there was plenty of both. Yiannis enjoyed catching up with his ex teammates although he had also left them far behind. Mr Robson was then introduced as the guest of honour by Max, who surprised all those (bar one) present, to reveal that he had asked him to present some special player awards. At this point Max raised his hand and a drinks trolley laden with trophies and other paraphernalia was wheeled in.

The first presentation was for top goalscorer. Max was extremely proud when his son Doug came up first, coming fourth on 7 goals, growing just as much in confidence as the team over the past year. Will then followed with 9 goals, an embarrassed Yiannis came next having netted 11. Ever adjusted his hairpiece before coming forward to get the largest footballer figurine marking his notable 15 goal contribution to the team's 58 total. He had scored about the same number of goals as the whole of Pork and Mutton FC usually scored in seasons gone by.

There were also awards for the defence who had only conceded 45 goals when three figures were the previous norm. Owen's 7 clean sheets earned him a new set of goalkeeper gloves which was accepted (given his unexplained absence) by Big Hec, who also received a gold bucket with Charity inscribed on the side, and since it began at home contained within it an extremely large green goalkeeper jersey with the number 1 on the back, all of which he was clearly delighted with as tears left his eyes. The Tripolini brothers were each given a new apron with their names and designated positions of Left (Marco), Centre (Massimo), and Right (Mario) embroided in blue, black, and red. While they didn't need the instruction they were most thankful for it. Salvator was given an Oxford English Dictionary and some underpants (cleverly referred to in the presentation, rather humorously, as draws), the latter term serving to confuse him further. Byron was presented with a book of poems by his namesake and another on the history of Preston North End. Then came the team stalwarts. Stuart was presented with a soft toy likeness of Tango, Esso's 'put a tiger in the tank', to help keep the midfield dynamo's engine running and a compass, so he could better get his bearings of where the goal was. Norman graciously accepted the shooting stick presented to him, not to aid him in finally scoring a goal, it was wittingly remarked, but to provide a little more comfort and not so dog friendly support out on the touchline. Roger was given a year's membership of Smithfields night club and a beer stein to remind him, as if he needed it, of the Deutscher Bierkeller. Simon received the largest applause for those receiving awards when he was called forth in the last presentation of the day. But all the joviality was interrupted when an unannounced and unwelcome gatecrasher burst into the room, with a familiar dog in tow, just as the club captain rose out of his chair.

It had been an afternoon of revelations and this was probably going to be the biggest to date. For the first time since quiz night Jonathan Cruft made his presence known to his former teammates - he was now standing there directly before them.

"Where is he? I'm looking for that worthless piece of muck, Bigalow!"

"Calm down Jonathan, as you can see he's not here and none of us know where he is," Simon said quietly trying to calm things down.

"That's right and you're not welcome here, it's a private function and you're trespassing, so get out!" Fred shouted.

"I'll go when I'm ready and not before. I've just collected the dog from my mother's and he came with a note left by my wife. She informed me in writing that she was leaving me and Shields for good__"

"So blinking what, that's got nothing to do with anybody here," Roger interrupted.

"That's what you think. She's not gone alone, Bigalow is accompanying her! Someone here must know where they're heading! It's more than ironic, that number 0 nutter has shown no respect for the gold O on my wife's finger!"

"Maybe you are guilty of doing the same thing Jonathan?" Simon said.

After the commotion was finally removed, being gently and successfully shown the door, the room took some time to recompose itself. There was a widespread air of disbelief. Owen? Who saw that happening?

"Would you credit it. That Owen's a dark horse. At long last he's happy being someone's numero uno!" Roger quipped, breaking the ice and raising a laugh.

"We all know the goalkeeper is the final man so Owen was the last person you would have expected to be Nancy's boy," Simon retorted.

Every player had been given something to remember the season by apart from Simon. The proceedings now returned to him. Max had been perceptive in his selections to date, helped no doubt by Fred, and Simon was at a loss what to expect. He was presented with a solid silver box engraved with the words 'Pork and Mutton FC' followed by 'Lost Property' written on its lid. Mr Robson opened the box and was keen to show that it contained nothing before explaining its meaning.

"It's largely thanks to Simon here that everyone associated with Pork and Mutton FC has regained something they had not only previously lost but also still longed for. That is why the box is now empty, whatever was missing has been reclaimed. He has shown himself to be safest keeper of them all".

Simon had a lump in his throat as he received his prize and gave his acceptance speech.

"I must admit that I wasn't expecting any of this or the extremely kind words. I would like to thank you all for what you have given me and taught me. At long last, we have had a season in the sun rather than the shadows and no one can blame us in wanting another one. That said, if I have one hope it is, regardless of how long you have been associated with this club, that you realise just playing and engaging are enough of a reward."

Printed in Great Britain
by Amazon

18949862R00207